The Quest
of the Thirteen

The Quest
of the Thirteen

John DeFilippis

Crossroad Press

The Quest of the Thirteen
John DeFilippis

1. Title   2. Author   3. Fiction

ISBN 13: 978-1-937530-01-3

This novel is dedicated to my dear mother and father, my brother Jimmy, my nephews Matthew and Mark, and all my family and friends who have supported me throughout my life as I pursued my dreams. Now that I have finally accomplished my goal of becoming a published author, I hope that I can inspire all those who struggle in overcoming obstacles as they strive to make their dreams come true. It is never too late to be what you might have been, for failure is only postponed success as long as courage "coaches" ambition. The habit of persistence is the habit of victory.

Prologue

Life in the Kingdom of Mavinor had long been lived by the precepts of a set of holy documents known as The Scrolls. The Scrolls provided a set of rules and principles setting forth how the people of Mavinor should live their lives and had been written a long time in the past by men believed to be inspired by a deity known as The Author.

In these latter times, the people of Mavinor have begun to turn away from the precepts contained in The Scrolls. When they were attacked by the army of the neighboring kingdom of Xamnon, every copy of The Scrolls was destroyed. The content lived on in the minds only of those who had taken pains to learn it. This knowledge was passed down from one generation to the next, but over time, fewer and fewer remembered. The effort to rewrite them continues, but the task is incomplete in the time of the reign of King Onestus... a time when the king finds that he needs their guidance more than ever.

Part I

Chapter One

The sun rose slowly over the mountains in the east, its rays of light trickling down onto the surface of the sea directly south of Mavinor. They crawled across the sand of the shoreline and angled up the walls of Mavinor's majestic palace, sending light glittering along the mica-chipped surface of the stone. From a distance, the city appeared to rise from the sand and shadows like a mirage, shimmering in the heat of the new day.

From where Onestus lay, however, the warmth seemed a thousand miles away. He rested on a pile of pillows that somehow failed to prevent the aching in his bones; he was tucked in beneath a pile of soft furs and blankets that failed equally against the chill of the early morning air. He stared out the window, dreading the moment when he'd have to slide his legs over the side of the bed, entrust himself to servants, and dress for the day.

Onestus was a tall man, broad of shoulder and thick boned. His hair, once a magnificent dark mane, had mostly turned to gray. His eyes, still sharp and filled with life, were the focus of a weakened visage. They diverted attention from his failing body to his active mind and aided him with the illusion of health he sought to weave.

The aches were worse in the morning. By noon, he'd be able to stand upright and walk without a limp. Careful planning had removed much of the activity from his day, and his closest guards and attendants, the only others who were aware of his condition, were loyal and vigilant.

Despite all of this, Onestus knew that it was only a matter of time before the truth would have to be revealed. He was old, he was tired, and now he was ill. He would not be king of Mavinor forever, and without a new king—without the right king—the city might fall.

The door to his chamber opened, and a slender young man entered. He wore a simple dark tunic without adornment. His hair, the same gold as the sunlight, glimmered richly. Onestus caught his eye, and the boy smiled.

"Good morning, sire," the boy said. He held a tray of fresh fruit and bread, and he carried it to the table beside Onestus' bed. "I've brought your breakfast."

"Good morning Talmik," Onestus said. "I'm not really hungry."

"And yet you must eat," Talmik replied. "Today is important. Have you forgotten that you are scheduled to meet with the scribes? There are rumors of a breakthrough in the translation."

"There are always rumors," Onestus muttered. "They spread rumors so I won't question them incessantly on their progress."

Talmik stood silently and waited. Onestus sighed and pushed back the covers, bracing himself for the cool air. He was almost disappointed when he found that the sun, just creeping over the sill of his great window, had warmed the air considerably. The chill never came, and a few moments later he was seated by that window, sipping hot tea, eating breakfast, and watching the city below come to life.

In the distance he saw two groups of soldiers drilling, some facing off against one another with swords and spears, others targeting man-sized bales of dried grass with bows and crossbows. He could hear their shouts floating on the light breeze. Armor and weapons glittered in the sunlight and flashed as the soldiers simulated battle after battle.

He caught sight of General Sicarius striding along the outer edge of his troops, their ranks a wash of brilliant red and gold, stopping now and then to commend a warrior on a particularly brilliant move or to redress some inconsistency or failure. Wherever the general walked, men stood straighter and weapons clashed with greater zeal. Eyes followed when he moved on. There were a lot of failings in Mavinor, but the abilities of the general in charge of her armies were not in question. He was a strong leader who would not tolerate anything less than perfection from his troops.

The kingdom's crisis had little to do with strength of arms or prowess in battle. Onestus was more than an administrator. His position was that of spiritual leader and guide. Those of faith remembered all too well. At one time, The Scrolls had resided within the thick and protected walls of Mavinor's main house of worship, The Author's Temple. Priests had studied those words and spread their wisdom. Kings and their armies had clear direction and shared purpose. So much had changed.

The Scrolls were being recreated. There was a careful oral

tradition running through Onestus' people. While recreation was far from complete, a great deal of the ancient teachings had been recovered, transcribed, and stored. Onestus did not doubt their veracity; his own memory was clear, and he could recite long passages without hesitation. He had contributed to the reconstruction himself.

Now he faced an important crossroad. He was childless. With no heir to the throne, Onestus knew that he needed to appoint a successor, and soon. His health was failing, and he did not wish to leave Mavinor without a leader for fear of the confusion and turmoil that might result. There were passages in The Scrolls dealing the succession to the throne. He remembered them but not well enough to recreate the words, and anything less would be unfair to the kingdom. Any error in following The Author's guidance could lead to ruin. If he acted recklessly, trusting to his memory to guide him, he would be setting himself up to fail, and it was beginning to look as if this might be his last act as king. He had to get it right.

Onestus turned at the sound of heavy footsteps beyond the entrance to his room. Talmik crossed the chamber and opened the door. Four impeccably uniformed guards stepped through. A fifth man, Kenrick, captain of the king's personal guard, stepped forward, his helm in the crook of his arm.

"It is time for the council, Lord," he said.

Onestus nodded. He drained his tea, which had grown tepid, and stood slowly. Talmik stepped forward, as if to help him up, but Onestus waved him away.

"I'll be fine," the king said to his trustworthy aide. "Bring me my raiment."

Onestus stood still and held out his arms. Talmik quickly

draped him in a robe trimmed in fur. It was a bit too heavy for the weather, but no one would question it. The extra warmth helped Onestus' joints, and he was going to need his wits about him for what was to come. If the scribes did not bring him what he needed, he'd have to find another way to save Mavinor. He wasn't certain he was up to the task.

"Gentlemen," he said, "I do not wish to be late."

He started for the door, and the guards filed in around him, Kenrick leading the way and Talmik trailing directly behind. If he stumbled or faltered, no one would see. For once their precautions were not necessary, but all of them knew it was a charade they could not keep up forever. They walked in silence, and none among them smiled.

<hr>

The Great Hall was empty when they arrived. The guards spread out and searched the huge room, checking in alcoves and behind pillars. It was mostly a ritualistic precaution, but they took it as seriously as if they had a death threat in hand. Onestus stood and watched them from an antechamber at the bottom of the stairs that led to the Great Hall. He could only imagine the number of times he'd witnessed this same scene. When he was much younger, he'd watch the guards with impatience. Now it calmed him, seeing that they did not deviate from what they had been taught.

When the hall was cleared, Onestus entered and took his seat at the head of a long, glossy wooden table. During better times he'd taken that same seat to oversee sumptuous feasts. But now the room echoed when anyone moved, and he felt alone and lost in the center of it.

Not long after he was seated, hurried footsteps sounded.

Onestus turned and watched as a small group of men entered the chamber. They were an odd lot, robed in brown and burdened with sheaves of paper, furled scrolls, and one enormous leather-bound tome. Onestus frowned. Normally his reports consisted only of the portion of The Scrolls that had been reconstructed since their last meeting. Sometimes there were many pages...other times the scribes produced no more than a paragraph from their research. They very rarely brought the source of their research before him, and his curiosity was piqued. Perhaps this time the rumors of a breakthrough had been true?

There were six in all: two scribes, two historians, and two priests. All were devout believers in The Author and in The Scrolls. All had dedicated their lives to bringing those holy documents back to their full splendor. It was tedious work. They constantly questioned the eldest and the brightest in the city, filling in missing passages, working their way from one subject to the next with painstaking care. Some passages from The Scrolls had been discovered in other works: passages recorded verbatim in epic poems or the songs of bards. Even historians from time to time recorded passages in order to study them more carefully in the context of their own work.

The eldest of the group, Cantos, bowed very low, holding the oversized book in his hands so that it nearly brushed the floor.

"Rise, Cantos," Onestus said. "Tell me that you have come to me with a new revelation regarding The Scrolls and not to read me a story."

Cantos stood and smiled broadly at Onestus. The king caught a glimpse of the smile; he almost returned it, but he held back the urge because he felt that it was always best to remain distant and watchful with Cantos. Although he was the most knowledgeable expert on The Scrolls the king had ever met, Cantos had a past. He had once allowed his greed to overcome his sense and had embezzled money when serving as a tax collector. Cantos had repented of his crime and had returned the money, but only his charisma and his value to the kingdom as a scholar had allowed him to continue in any position of importance.

Onestus liked Cantos. He believed a man could change and also that it was the very nature of faith in The Author to believe that the lessons of The Scrolls allowed a man to better himself. At the same time, as king, he could not afford to let his faith in the man cloud his judgment.

Cantos stood straight and placed the book on the table before Onestus. The king reached out and traced the letters beveled into the smooth leather. The title caused him to stare visibly.

The Chronicle of Haggiselm

Onestus glanced at Cantos.

"This is a history?" he asked.

"Not exactly," Cantos said. "It's a poem. A very long poem. I don't have to tell you of the exploits of Haggiselm. They teach of his adventures and his courage in every temple. There are shelves in the library filled with nothing but histories, stylized legends, and the lyrics of songs dedicated to Mavinor's greatest warrior."

"And yet," Onestus said, "you have brought me this single volume."

Cantos nodded. He reached out and flipped the book open to where a thick gold ribbon marked a page near the

center of the huge book. Onestus brushed Cantos' hand aside
and began to read. He began at the first stanza on the left-
hand page; he stopped reading and gasped halfway down the
right.

"Is it possible?" he asked.

At his question, the tension in the room melted away. The
scholars seated themselves close to the king, who continued
to pore over the text. Onestus read aloud so softly that none
could hear, moving his finger carefully from word to word
and racking his brain to provide the accuracy he needed...
the memory.

It was a familiar story. He knew he'd heard it told, and
he believed that he'd read it as a younger man. It told of how
Haggiselm, fearing for the future of the kingdom, had ridden
off on a great quest.

The book appeared to include the entire text from The
Scrolls, giving the account of that quest, including its purpose.
Under attack from the armies of Xamnon, in fear of losing all
that was precious to the city, the king sent Haggiselm on a
long journey, entrusting to him two objects of great power.
The first was the Medallion of Mavinor. The second was the
Ivory Sabre. According to tradition, both of these were gifts
to the kingdom of Mavinor from The Author Himself.

Haggiselm carried the items away by night and rode hard
into the Northern Mountains, where he hid the Medallion
in a place described as a labyrinth of sorts. It was to remain
there, secreted away, until the time when Mavinor needed it
most. When that time arrived, a group of thirteen men would
be chosen to set out to retrieve it, and the one who returned
bearing the Medallion would be Mavinor's next king. When
Haggiselm's task was complete, he took the Ivory Sabre but

never came back to Mavinor. It was almost as if he had disappeared, and no one knew whatever became of him.

At this point the poem diverged from The Scrolls and returned to its own rambling style. Onestus glanced up at Cantos.

"Is it accurate?" he asked.

"It is," Cantos said. There was no uncertainty in his voice, and Onestus felt a great weight lifting from his shoulders.

"This matches up with what we had, then?" Onestus persisted. "There are no gaps?"

"It is the next sequence," Cantos said. "It confirms the location of the Medallion, and it confirms the quest. It is what you have been searching for."

Nothing more was said, but the implications of Cantos' words hung heavy in the air. Onestus sat back with a heavy sigh.

"You have the transcription for me?" he asked.

A heavyset blonde man with a scraggle of beard stepped forward. He held out a single scroll that was carefully tied with gilt ribbon. Onestus took it, but he made no move to open it.

"There are copies?" he asked.

"Of course," Cantos replied. "It has been appended to the main scrolls, and copies have been secreted in the temples. We were careful, as always."

"Do not speak to any of this," Onestus said, standing more quickly than he meant to. The room spun for a moment, but he gritted his teeth and managed not to show the momentary weakness—at least he hoped he had. "I will study this and prepare an announcement."

"You will sanction the quest?" Cantos asked.

Onestus nodded. "What choice do I have? A kingdom must have a king. The Scrolls have returned their wisdom in our time of need, but to be worthy of that wisdom we must act upon it."

A tremble shot up the king's spine as he turned to exit the hall. He reached out and managed to catch himself on the edge of the table. Onestus regained his bearings and straightened. Talmik moved closer to help, but Onestus waved him away.

"We haven't much time," Onestus said. "Give me this afternoon to study what you have brought. Tomorrow I will issue the proclamation. In the meantime, I expect each and every one of you to study what resources you have and to think about those among our finest and strongest who might suit the quest. We will have to make our choices quickly, and yet there is no room for error. If we send one not worthy of the quest, he will fail. I do not believe the waning faith of Mavinor would survive such a blow. Once we have committed to this, those who doubt will be looking for the quest to falter. We cannot allow that to happen."

"Surely finding thirteen warriors won't be so difficult," Cantos said. "We have the entire city to choose from—the army—there are heroes aplenty."

"It isn't a matter of finding thirteen heroes," Onestus said, cocking an eyebrow in Cantos' direction. "It is also not necessarily true that they will all be great warriors. The key is in finding those who are called. There would seem to be obvious choices, but in issues of faith the easy way is very seldom the best."

Cantos nodded. "We will do what we can," he said.

The scribes hurried to gather up the rest of their papers

and scrolls. Talmik and the guards surrounded Onestus and formed a narrow corridor with their bodies that stretched back toward the anteroom and the stairs beyond. Two guards slipped out and checked the way, finding nothing as Onestus had known they would. He followed after them slowly, and his guards filled in behind.

Sicarius looked up as his lieutenant and right-hand man, Tarsus, stepped into the doorway and knocked gently. With an omnipresent look of intensity on his face and insignia of two golden swords crossed over one another on his military uniform, Tarsus entered the room.

"What is it?" the general grated. He was deep into plans for refortification of the city walls and not in a mood for interruption.

"There is someone here to see you," Tarsus replied. "It is Valdan, of the king's guard. I informed him that you gave instructions not to be interrupted, but he insists that it is very important."

Sicarius straightened; his expression shifted from annoyance to keen interest.

"Show him in," he said.

Tarsus bowed, and he backed out of the door. A moment later he returned, leading a tall man in the ornate armor of the king's private guard.

"I trust you are well, Valdan," Sicarius said.

"I am well," he said. "I have word from the palace that I wish to share with you."

"By all means," Sicarius replied.

"He will summon you tomorrow," Valdan said, "but not

until he has had a chance to confer with his advisors. They have recovered a new segment of The Scrolls."

"They are always recovering segments of The Scrolls," Sicarius said. "You have taken quite a chance coming to me openly, in broad daylight."

"I know, but this is urgent," Valdan said. "There is to be a quest. The king will decree it tomorrow. There are to be thirteen champions chosen; he believes that most of them will come from the military."

Sicarius smoothed the map he'd been studying idly and then pushed back from the table and stared up at Valdan.

"A quest?" he said. "For what?"

"They will seek the Medallion of Mavinor," Valdan said. "The Scrolls say that Haggiselm hid the Medallion in the Northern Mountains…against a time of need."

Sicarius frowned.

"Need? There is never peace, that much is true, but there is no more particular need now than there has been at other times. The legend that I remember said that the Medallion should be sought when…" he grew silent.

Valdan finished the sentence, "When Mavinor needed a king."

Sicarius sat very still for a moment. "This opportunity is a fool's folly," he said. "We will not support the quest. I tire of living by the words of a mythical being. Haggiselm himself was so lost in legends that we don't know the truth of his life let alone any quest he might have undertaken."

"The king is convinced that it is the only thing to do," Valdan said. "He is not well. He has tried to hide it, and he is a strong-willed man, but time is growing very short."

Sicarius nodded. "Of course," he said. "It changes nothing. The time for living in our past is coming to an end. This… fool's quest…will be the final straw."

"The Scrolls were very clear," Valdan said softly.

Sicarius shook his head, a look of disdain coming over his face. "You will tell no one of our meeting, of course?"

"Of course," Valdan said, bowing his head.

"Good. Return to Onestus and your duties. I have a great deal of work to do and very little time for it. I will see you tomorrow at the palace…when I am summoned."

Valdan nodded and backed out of the room in silence. Sicarius waited until he had left and then called for Tarsus.

"Get our officers in here," he said. "I don't care what they are doing or what other orders they may have received. They don't have to come all at once, but I need to see them all before day's end. Be discreet. I don't want word getting back to the palace that anything odd is going on here."

"By all means, general," Tarsus said.

A moment later, Sicarius was alone with his thoughts. He turned and gazed out his window in the direction of the palace. After a few minutes he shook his head, and he smiled.

Chapter Two

Onestus summoned Sicarius at the break of dawn and waited in his chambers, where his breakfast lay on a tray, mostly ignored. He wanted the general to know before anyone else in the kingdom—the general's wisdom in searching out the thirteen would be invaluable. No one knew the capabilities of the army or its heroes better than Sicarius.

In recent years Onestus had felt Sicarius distancing himself, but he'd attributed this to his own weakness and inactivity. Sicarius was a man of action, and he had his hands full defending the boundaries of Mavinor. It was no wonder he had little time for anything but routine reports. To his surprise, Onestus found that he actually missed the company of the tall, gruff, bearded warrior. It had been too long since they'd shared anything but a passing conversation. He hoped that his general felt the same.

There was a knock at the door, and Sicarius swept in, not waiting to be announced. There was a clatter of armor and weapons in the hall, and Onestus heard someone curse. He glanced up and watched Sicarius' grand entrance with a wry smile. The general walked past the guards, proudly clad in his uniform, which displayed the insignia of a six-eyed spider, the bite of which was the most venomous and lethal known to man.

"Impatient as always, I see," he said. "Good morning, Sicarius. I pray the day finds you well?"

"It found me better before my duties were interrupted, sire," he said, speaking frankly as always. "I am sorry if I have injured the pride of any member of your guard, but when I'm summoned, I expect that I am welcome. You'll pardon me for not surrendering my weapons or allowing a search."

Onestus chuckled.

"It would be entertaining indeed to see them push the attempt, old friend," he said. "Sit. I have important news, and I need your counsel. It has been far too long since the two of us spoke freely."

"My duties keep me away," Sicarius said. He bowed ever so slightly, nodding his head in respect.

"Yes," Onestus said. "There is always someone pounding at the gate, isn't there? You have done an admirable job and are to be commended. This time, though, it is not exactly a matter of war or defense that concerns me. It is a matter of faith."

"Perhaps," Sicarius said, taking a seat across from the king and reaching for a piece of the uneaten fruit on the breakfast tray, "you have mistaken me for a priest?"

Onestus laughed.

"Hardly," he said. "We have had a breakthrough in the recreation of The Scrolls. I believe it to be a sign. There are— circumstances—that make me believe this particular bit of The Scrolls has come back to us in our time of need."

Sicarius held his tongue. It was well known among his

own men that he was not a man of faith, and he believed it was high time the kingdom was run by a more practical set of rules. The kingdom's enemies were constantly at its gates, and though—in the past—its strength had been rooted in their possession of The Author's Scrolls, the recreation of those scrolls steadily ate away at Onestus' time and at his mind. It distracted him from the day-to-day business of his kingdom and his people. Sicarius stood at the gates and fended off the wolves while his king chased what Sicarius considered to be myth and shadow.

Still, it was wise for even a general to keep his thoughts to himself when they did not parallel those of the king. Sicarius believed that if he was patient, his own philosophy would show itself as truth. But he didn't want to sacrifice his position and authority in the attempt to hurry it along.

"The segment of The Scrolls that has been recovered most recently involves a warrior. You are familiar, I'm sure, with the stories of Haggiselm?"

"What boy of Mavinor did not study the epic stories?" Sicarius asked in reply. "Of course I am aware of those tales— they are part of my very being. It was stories of heroism and adventure that drew me to the military, and I admired Haggiselm more so than any of the other mythic heroes."

"The Scrolls are not myths," Onestus said, sitting up straighter.

"I did not mean to imply that they were," Sicarius said placatingly. "There are songs, stories, legends—Haggiselm was chronicled in many places other than The Scrolls."

Onestus nodded and relaxed. Then he continued.

"Then you are also familiar with the Medallion of Mavinor?"

Sicarius kept his face devoid of emotion. It would not

do for the king to realize the information had already been leaked. The king was old, and he was growing weak, but he was not a stupid man, and Sicarius was not ready to lose his source. It had taken him months of recommendations and hard work to place a man so close to the throne.

"I have heard of the Medallion, yes," he said. "It has been lost for many years."

"Not lost, exactly," Onestus replied. He lifted a scroll from its stand on the table and unrolled it. As Sicarius sat in silence, Onestus recited the recovered segment of The Scrolls. When he was done, he glanced up to catch his general's reaction.

Sicarius considered his response carefully.

"It is a compelling tale," he said at last. "One can almost picture the pass in that far-off mountain range and the great warrior secreting away the Medallion. Still, it isn't very— detailed. The Northern Mountains extend for many miles, much of which is unmapped. There are other legends of those mountains as well, and few of them end happily."

"The wisdom of The Scrolls is not always evident on the surface," Onestus replied. "It is there to be studied and then acted upon. We will be naming the thirteen beginning today. I would value your opinion as we make those decisions."

There was an uncomfortable moment of silence during which a hundred inappropriate responses rose to Sicarius' lips but were bitten back. He raised his eyes slowly and looked directly at the king.

"I will pass on the call for the thirteen to my men," he said carefully. "I will make it clear that you seek only the strongest and the bravest. If they should ask, I will explain to them that this quest is written in The Scrolls and that you believe the outcome will greatly affect the future of Mavinor."

"We are not going to make an open call," Onestus said. "We will choose the thirteen ourselves and summon them. It was in their selection that I'd hoped to have your guidance."

"I would recommend any man under my command for such a mission," Sicarius said with a shrug. "There are some more proficient than others, but their abilities are well documented. With all due respect, sire, I believe my services would be better utilized overseeing the defenses of the kingdom."

Onestus opened his mouth as if to push the issue, but he sat back. In that moment he looked older and wearier than Sicarius ever remembered seeing him. The general felt almost guilty for his lack of support, but still he held his tongue. He believed he was acting in the best interests of the kingdom and was firm in his decision. Protection was his duty and his purpose.

"I will keep this to myself, as you requested," Sicarius said, rising. "I wish you all the best in your selections."

"Thank you for your time," Onestus said. "I am certain that The Author will guide us in our decisions and that they will prove the right ones. You are right to put your duties first."

"If I may take my leave, sire?" Sicarius said. "I have an entire regiment awaiting my inspection, and the sun is rising quickly. They must be growing restless."

"Of course," Onestus said. "Do not keep them waiting. We will begin our selection this afternoon. By tomorrow morning we should be ready to summon the thirteen. I wouldn't want any of them to succumb to the heat before we have the opportunity to send for them."

Sicarius smiled, but he did not laugh. He turned on his heel and left the king's chambers without looking back.

Onestus watched the man go until he was out of sight, and then he took a deep breath and turned to Talmik, who had reentered the room. The young man stood still, waiting for instructions.

"Summon the elders," Onestus said. "Summon the scribes. Have wine and food brought to The Great Hall—enough to last the night if necessary."

Talmik nodded and turned.

"Talmik?" Onestus asked softly.

The aide turned back.

"Before you summon the others…send me Ignatus."

Talmik heeded and departed. The king stared out the window in silence, bracing himself against the coming storm of the day.

Chapter Three

Ignatus obeyed Onestus' summons immediately. The old
soldier was compact and lean. His hair was dark with a
hint of gray at the temples though he was bald on top. His
sideburns extended down to a neatly trimmed beard and
mustache. Unlike General Sicarius, Ignatus handed over his
weapons without question when asked. He stood very still,
just inside the door, waiting. Emblazoned across his breastplate was a sunburst with the letters IHS in the center. Above
the letter H was a cross, and below it the image of three
swords in a semicircle. The letters stood for Ignatus Heroicus
Sanctus, the venerable and heroic Ignatus.

"Come in, old friend," Onestus said. "We have known
one another far too long to be bound by ceremony."

Ignatus bowed nonetheless and entered the room. He
walked over to the table and took the seat that Talmik had
pulled out for him.

"I have something very important to ask you," Onestus
said without preamble. "A breakthrough was made today in

the recreation of The Scrolls, a breakthrough that is currently of vast importance to the kingdom."

"Any breakthrough is of importance," Ignatus said.

Onestus nodded gravely. "That is true, of course, but let me speak openly. I have not been well. The last year has been a difficult one for me, and it seems at times that I grow weaker with every passing day. There will come a time, and not so far in the future, that Mavinor will need a new king."

Caught off guard by the king's statement, Ignatus paused briefly. "You have many years left, my lord," he then said. "You are stronger than you believe."

"That may be true," Onestus replied, though his smile was tired and showed no credence. "Still, it would be unwise of me to trust the fate of an entire kingdom to my own failing health. Our enemies are constantly at our gates, and though General Sicarius has kept them at bay, military might alone is not going to win the day. The work we are doing with The Scrolls is slow and tedious; attendance in the temples is lower than it has been in my lifetime."

"The people are faithful," Ignatus said. "They are merely confused. It is a difficult time, and in difficult times it is leadership that turns the tide. They will turn to you."

"I hope that is true, Ignatus. But what I will announce tomorrow will test us all. We will be calling on our bravest and our most faithful. We have recovered the tale of Haggiselm. Tomorrow I will call together thirteen men chosen for a quest."

"A quest?"

"The Medallion of Mavinor," Onestus said. He let the words hang in the air and noticed how Ignatus stiffened. Then the old warrior relaxed.

"Could it be?" he said. "Haggiselm is a legendary warrior. Songs and the tales of the elders make him almost mythic. I know that the Medallion existed—that much I have read for myself—but can this quest actually be validated?"

"It is in The Scrolls," Onestus said. "The tale they tell is far more subdued than that of the old songs, but it is basically the same. The Medallion was hidden against the needs of the city in the Northern Mountains. It is clearly written that if we are to find our new king, we must recover it."

"Why do you tell me now?" Ignatus asked. "Surely I should learn of this along with the rest of the kingdom? It is a momentous occasion, and I will want to be present to wish the thirteen well."

"You know me well enough to understand why you have been summoned," Onestus replied. "I want you to lead them, Ignatus. When I said the quest should include our strongest and our bravest, I was speaking of you. You have won more honors at arms than any among us save Sicarius, and no one in Mavinor has more experience in battle than you. There is no other to whom I would trust such a journey."

Ignatus sat for a long moment without speaking. Emotions warred through the scarred and weathered lines of his face. When he broke the silence, his voice was low and filled with emotion. He did not meet Onestus' eyes.

"I have fought many long years in the army of Mavinor," he said. "I have seen men grow from children to mighty champions. I have seen great warriors fall to chance and others rise to greatness. I remember when Sicarius was but a bold youth, and I served in your guard when you first took the throne.

"In all of those years I have not rested. I have had no

family other than Mavinor's army, and no purpose other than to serve. Now I am old—too old, I think, for facing off against the young and the strong, and too wise to chance it.

"I would have come to you within the week because I have an announcement of my own. Now I fear that it is ill timed, and yet I believe it is still the correct decision. I am laying down my sword, my lord. I am far past the age when I should have surrendered my role, and I wish to devote myself to higher purpose. It is with a very heavy heart that I must decline this quest. My days of fighting and adventure are over."

It was the king's turn to sit in silence though his was tinged with shock. He shook his head as if clearing something from his ears.

"You are laying down your sword?" he asked at last. "I cannot fault the truth in what you say—if any in our kingdom has earned a rest, it is you. But it is that very dedication—that strength of spirit—that I need so desperately on this quest. We cannot afford to fail, Ignatus."

"I am not the only strong warrior in your service, my lord," Ignatus said. "I will help to train those who are chosen. I will support you and your mission in any way other than being a part of it. My decision was made long before we spoke this day, and it would be a disservice to us both if I were to rescind it out of pride—taking the place of one more worthy. If I felt in my heart that this was something I was meant for—that this quest called to me—I would lay down my life to be included. It is a sacred quest, and those who are meant to have a place in it will be chosen. I am flattered that you first thought of me, but I do not believe that you will be afforded an open choice in this. I believe that The Author will guide you."

"You are right, of course," Onestus said. "Still, I am afraid that General Sicarius is not going to be of much help, and his men are very loyal. I asked him to be a part of the choosing—to join the counselors who will guide me—and he refused."

"I am not surprised," Ignatus said. "Sicarius' mind works very differently from yours and mine. He believes in only one thing—the might of his strong right arm."

Onestus nodded. "It is more of what I mentioned earlier. Our people need something to restore their faith. We offer them stories of faith, signs of the truth behind The Scrolls, but it has been a long time since such a sign was delivered to them in any real manner. Our enemies pound our gates. The very Scrolls we were entrusted to defend have been destroyed, and many despair their ever being completely restored. It is time for something new—something magnificent.

"In our time of need the tale of Haggiselm was presented to me, and I will act upon it. I wish that you would reconsider, but I will certainly honor your wishes. I do not want any man on this quest against his will. It will be long and arduous, and to fail will not be an option. The Medallion must return to Mavinor."

"It is a quest worthy of champions," Ignatus said. "There are many I can think of who would be exemplary choices, but I think that will wait until we see what The Author brings before you. You can count on me to train those who need it and to support them in any way possible."

"Your loyalty has never been in question, old friend," Onestus said. "Your advice, as always, is sound. Sometimes

I need to stop trying so hard to rule every moment of every day and let myself be led by a higher power."

"The thirteen will be found," Ignatus said, rising. "My guess is that they will surprise you in ways we could not anticipate if we debated the subject a thousand nights."

"I hope only that you are right," Onestus said. He rose, glad for once not to feel the shaky weakness in his limbs, and clasped Ignatus by the shoulder. "We will know soon enough. I must leave you now. The wise have gathered, and I am to meet with them. We will work as long as it takes for us to name the thirteen. I am afraid that it may prove to be a very long night."

Ignatus saluted smartly, turned, and left the room. Onestus watched him go. When he was alone again, he sank back into his chair. Talmik stepped from the shadows by the window.

"We'd best be going, sire," he said.

Onestus nodded, distracted.

"I hope," he said as he rose once more, "that the last two meetings are not what I have to look forward to in the days to come. I will do whatever is needed to find the thirteen, but I can't help believing that time is growing very short."

Talmik didn't answer. He held out Onestus' robe, and the king stepped into it, showing more strength and purpose than he had at any other point that day. Without another word they exited the chambers, passed into the quietly assembled phalanx of guards, and on toward The Great Hall. The empty corridor echoed with passing and then fell into total silence.

Chapter Four

The next morning King Onestus did not awaken at dawn, as was his wont. He slept through the sunrise, exhausted from the night's efforts. While he slept, Talmik gathered messengers to the throne room. The night before, several short messages had been written, summoning the chosen to an audience with the king. They were given two full days to report, partly to allow time for them to prepare, and partly to give Onestus time to recover.

And yet there was another matter. There were only twelve men being summoned. The thirteenth still eluded them, and they needed time for the king to make his final choice. As the sun broke over the mountains and began the familiar trek across the sea toward Mavinor, the messengers mounted and rode from the palace. Talmik stood on the front steps and watched until they were out of sight.

━━━

The first messenger rode down a narrow trail just inside the city walls by the North Gate. Trees lined the way, and he rounded a corner into a short lane. Several small homes lined either side. A well stood in the center, and to the right a small fenced pen held several goats. At the end of the row, a larger home gleamed in the sunlight. Flanking the front door, two small woven banners danced lightly in the breeze.

The design on the right banner was that of two golden keys on a red background. The banner on the left bore the image of two crossed white lines in the form of an X on a blue background. A single horse stood tied to the post in front. The messenger rode up to the door with the banners flying and tied his mount beside the other. He looked back down the road and then scanned the fields to either side of the small stone structure. But there was no one in sight.

The young man unrolled the small scroll he held and strode to the door, calling out in a bold voice.

"Silex and Ferox, sons of Namon, hear this message."

He waited for a long moment, but he heard nothing. He raised the scroll and readied himself to cry out again, but before he could do so, a querulous voice floated back to him from within the home.

"I'm coming. Stop your shouting."

A heavyset man, stoop-shouldered with age and sporting a shaggy crest of gray hair that made him look like some sort of ancient predatory bird, stepped into the doorway and scowled at the messenger.

"What is it you want, young man?" he asked. "Why are you standing in my doorway yelling?"

The messenger cleared his throat and glanced down at the message.

"None of that," the old man growled. "I've little time for foolishness. Who are you here to see?"

"Are you Namon?"

"I am," the old man said.

"I am here to bring a message to your sons, Silex and Ferox. They have been summoned to appear before the king at first light two days hence."

"Why didn't you just say so? Come in."

"I'm to deliver the message in person," the young man said, "and to return straightaway with the answer."

The old man laughed. "And how would anyone know if you stopped in for a warm cup of tea before returning? You're going to have to wait if you want to talk to both of my sons. Silex is out back sharpening his sword, but Ferox, bow and arrow in hand, is hunting. He is always hunting. He will not be back until later in the afternoon—possibly after dark—unless fortune smiles on him early. He isn't fond of returning empty-handed. After all, he is considered the finest archer in all of Mavinor."

The messenger stood on the threshold of the home, watching Namon's retreating figure.

"What's your name, boy?" the old man called back.

"Nuntius," the messenger answered uncertainly.

"Well, Nuntius," Namon called over his shoulder, "you can stand out there with your message in hand all the day if you like. But if you come in and sit, I will bring Silex in from the back."

Slowly, Nuntius entered the clean, well-kept home and followed the old man through to the back, where a small kitchen faced the rear wall. The back door stood ajar, and he could clearly hear the sound of a whetstone sliding over a blade.

"Sit," Namon said. Then he disappeared out the back door, leaving Nuntius to find his way to the table where he sat, waiting.

A moment later Namon returned, followed by Silex, who stood well over six feet tall. He was broad in the shoulder and had deep brown, well-groomed hair. His eyes were intense, and he moved with grace and the economy of motion gained through years of battle.

Silex wore a leather breastplate, a rough tunic, and heavy boots. His sword rode easily at his side. Over his heart, tooled into the leather, was the same key design that flew on the banner out front. Nuntius knew that Silex had once been granted the keys to the kingdom after displaying incredible fortitude in a battle with Xamnon. His prowess as a warrior was known throughout the city, and standing so close to the man, the messenger could see that it was not exaggerated.

Nuntius stood and held his message steadily. Namon looked as if he might protest again, but Silex stilled the old man with a hand.

"Silex, son of Namon," Nuntius said. "Hear this message. You have been summoned to appear before his majesty, King Onestus, at first light two days hence. You have been chosen by a council of the wise and by the king himself to take part in a great quest.

"The tale of Haggiselm has been recovered, and by direction of The Scrolls, and therefore of The Author Himself, you will accompany twelve companions to the Northern Mountains. Your quest will be to recover the Medallion of Mavinor and return it to the king."

Silex had grown very still as the words poured forth from the messenger's mouth. His hand dropped onto the hilt of his sword. He reached out as though he might take the scroll from the messenger's hand and read it himself, as if he didn't believe. Then he thought better and took a seat at the table.

"That is a fool's quest," Namon grumbled, turning away

to start water boiling for the promised tea. "Surely you know that? The stories of Haggiselm are like those your brother tells after a bad hunt. Smoke and mist and only a skeleton of truth."

Silex turned to his father.

"You know that is not true," he said. "The Scrolls told the story of Haggiselm before it was corrupted by minstrels and poets, and if I understand this message, that story has been recovered. If I am called to this quest, I will accept. How could I do otherwise?"

"Very simply," his father said. "You could say no."

Silex looked as though he might speak again, but at that moment a loud *thump* sounded outside the back door and a cheery voice floated in through the window.

"Some help, brother! Father! Do I have to hunt, kill, skin, and cook this myself, or are you ready to help with fresh meat?"

A moment later Ferox entered. He was smaller than his brother, slender and lithe. He wore his hair longer, and his tunic was green to blend in with the forest. He wore a quiver of hand-flocked arrows across one shoulder, and a long hunting blade rode his hip. He also wore a leather breastplate, though it was lighter and allowed easier motion than the heavier armor of his brother. It bore the bright blue background and X symbol that matched the second banner in front of the home.

Ferox stopped when he saw Nuntius, who still stood beside the table.

"Who do we have here, then?" Ferox asked.

"His name is Nuntius," Namon grumbled. "He has your brother all worked up about a quest."

Nuntius cleared his throat and raised the message. Namon

shook his head and poured steaming water into three cups. He ignored his sons as well as the king's messenger and went about making the tea.

"Ferox, son of Namon," Nuntius said. "Hear this message."

The summons was repeated, and Ferox, as his brother had, stood very still when it was complete. He turned and glanced at Silex.

"You are going?" he asked.

"Of course," Silex replied. "What man of Mavinor would not jump at the chance?"

"I would not," Namon replied, turning with a cup of tea. He handed it to Nuntius, who, his message delivered, felt suddenly confused and out of place.

"And you?" Silex asked, watching his brother. "What will you do?"

"I will do as my king bids," Ferox replied. "Whatever the quest, it is an honor to be one of only thirteen chosen. And you, father," he said with a grin, "may boast that of all the men of Mavinor, *both* of your sons were selected."

"Oh, yes, I will tell everyone," Namon said. "I will tell them how you left me alone in my twilight years to fend for myself, an old and broken man. It will be a wondrous tale."

Nuntius stared at Namon. He considered setting the teacup on the table and bolting for the door before things developed into a family dispute.

"You are as broken as a strong plank," Ferox laughed, "and age has barely slowed you. You do not need us to look after you."

Namon grinned. "I never said that I did."

Silex frowned.

"This is a serious moment," he said. "To be summoned

before the king is an honor that does not happen every day or to every man. It is not a time for jokes."

"There is no better time for joking and laughter," Namon said, stepping forward to lay a hand on Silex's arm, "than when a man is about to say farewell to his sons. It is not an easy journey. The Northern Mountains are filled with danger, as are all the roads between."

"Think of the game along that trail," Ferox said. "I will have such stories to tell."

"And I will have to watch your back the entire time to be certain you don't worry so much about hunting that you forget the more dangerous enemies," Silex said.

"One can hunt more than deer," Ferox replied.

Nuntius glanced from one to the other, not sure whether to agree with either of them or simply hold his tongue.

"Return to the palace," Silex said. "Tell them that we will arrive at the appointed time and await his majesty's convenience."

"Ask them," Ferox said, "if I should bring meat for the morning meal." He laughed heartily, and immediately afterward Namon joined in.

As Nuntius turned and hurried outside, he heard Ferox and his father still laughing. He climbed back onto his mount, and the laughter grew even louder. Nuntius shook his head, turned his horse back into the lane, and took off at a trot for the castle.

———

Tonitrus spun to his left, narrowly avoiding the swinging blade of his opponent. He then brought his sword in a vicious arc that caught the other's blade from behind and drove it forward even faster. With a cry, the wielder released his weapon, which spun through the air toward the stone fence surrounding the yard.

At that moment the sound of hoofbeats clattering to a halt in the road beyond the fence startled both combatants, and they turned to look. The errant blade spun in a glittering arc toward the gate.

"Wait!" Tonitrus cried.

He was too late. A man in the king's livery stepped around the corner of the fence, glanced up and cried out in shock. The blade dropped quickly and slammed into the ground between his booted feet. The three of them—the messenger, Tonitrus, and his sparring partner and brother, Cedrus—stood as still and silent as statues. Very carefully the messenger reached out, gripped the sword by its hilt, and drew it free of the ground. He turned, saw Tonitrus standing sword in hand, and nodded toward Cedrus.

"I believe this is yours," he said, stepping forward and holding out the sword.

Cedrus, red-faced, took it and stepped back. Tonitrus glanced at him, shook his head, and then turned to their visitor.

"Tonitrus," the man said, unfurling a single page scroll, "hear this message."

When it was done, Tonitrus smiled. He glanced over at his brother, who had gone pale.

"I would be honored," Tonitrus said, "to attend his majesty as requested, and further honored to be a part of such a worthy quest."

The messenger nodded, and then turned to Cedrus.

"You are Cedrus, brother to Tonitrus?" the man asked.

Cedrus nodded. He was several years Tonitrus' junior, and it showed. He had a baby face, long brown hair, and deep brown eyes that shone brightly. Tonitrus was well regarded; he was considered by most to be the finest swordsman in the kingdom. Cedrus had been training hard under his brother's tutelage in the hope of getting an opportunity to see action. But if Tonitrus was called away, then his training would be interrupted.

"Cedrus, brother to Tonitrus," the messenger said in a clear voice, "hear this message."

"Wait!" Tonitrus said, stepping forward. He laid his hand on the messenger's arm. "You can't mean to summon Cedrus as well? He is but a boy."

"I will go!" Cedrus said, stepping forward eagerly. "I am no boy. I am a man."

The messenger continued to read the summons. Tonitrus withdrew his hand, but he did not step back.

"There must be some mistake," Tonitrus said, when the messenger was finished. "Cedrus is not up to such a quest. His training is incomplete."

"I did not write the summons," the messenger said. "I am only to deliver the words of the king and to return to the palace. You are both expected by dawn two days from now."

"I will be there!" Cedrus cried.

Tonitrus stood silent, staring first at the scrolls in the messenger's hand, then at his brother, and then into the messenger's eyes.

"If this is the will of King Onestus, then we will report as ordered. I do not care for the idea of my brother going on such a journey. He is not prepared for it, and I still believe that he is too young. If I were not accompanying him, I would stand against it—though it meant betraying my king. But if we are to go together, then at least I can continue his training and can watch over him. Thus I consent to the king's wishes."

"I don't need you to watch over me, Tonitrus," Cedrus said impatiently. "I can fend for myself. I am up to the task, and I am ready."

Tonitrus glanced at the sword that Cedrus held loosely and then over at the gate where it had landed only moments before.

"Is that so?" asked Tonitrus. "Well then, let us hope that no others are endangered by that blade before you learn to wield it properly."

Tonitrus abruptly turned and left the yard, his long blonde locks flowing in the breeze as he went inside the house. By the door hung a small banner that bore the image of a red cross on a white background, and the base of the cross was a blade. Tonitrus had borne that standard into many a battle, wearing it on his helm, breastplate, and weapons.

After hearing the door close, Cedrus glanced at the sword in his hand, and he gripped the hilt more tightly. The messenger nodded to him and left the yard to remount and ride back to the palace. Cedrus waited until he was gone, and then he turned. He raised his sword, swung it in a slow arc, and then faster. He made his way across the yard, fencing with unseen opponents. He worked hard, his breath labored. His brown eyes shone with zeal, and his brow was coated with sweat. The sun had begun its descent before he called a halt, exhausted, and decided that he had enough training for one day. After placing his sword in its scabbard, he went in the house to join his brother and begin preparations for the quest.

Og stood, staring at a four-foot-tall log about two feet in diameter. It rested atop a flat stone, and despite its height, Og towered over it. The huge, brawny warrior stood nearly seven feet in height with massive shoulders and shaggy black hair that hung below them. His beard was big and bushy. Nearby, leaning against a fence post, he rested his shield, emblazoned with the likeness of a battle axe very similar to the one in his hands.

The sound of hoofbeats floated to him from the road beyond the fence, but he ignored it. His concentration was fixed on the log. His shoulders, though not tense, were taut, and his focus was absolute. Beyond the fence, the rider dismounted with a clatter. Still, Og ignored the interruption.

A tall, thin man approached the fence. Og saw him out of the corner of his eye but did not react. The man held a rolled parchment in one hand and wore the colors of the uniform of a palace messenger. Standing very tall, the man unrolled the parchment. Og heard the stiff paper scratching. He heard the man clear his throat, but he continued to stare intently at the log.

"Og, hear this message," the man intoned.

Og ignored him. He tested his grip on the axe and smiled. It was a big weapon, heavy and destructive. He knew there were few in the entire kingdom who could wield it in battle and fewer still who could do so effectively.

The man ruffled the parchment and cleared his throat once more.

"Og, hear this message," he repeated, a bit louder.

When Og did not respond, the man walked down the length of the fence and entered the yard. Og heard him approach but did not turn. This time the messenger came up very close to Og, on the far side from where he'd stood before, as if he thought maybe the big man were hard of hearing in one ear. He rattled his paper again, and cleared his throat. Then he started to speak.

But it was all for naught. The words died in his mouth as Og moved. With speed belying his mountainous size, Og whipped the axe back, swung it in a glittering arc through the air, and slammed it into the top of the log. The log was too tall. It should not have split. The axe should have caught and stuck…but it did not. Instead, the wood split dead center, the two halves falling away. One fell directly in front of the now silent messenger who, still trying to speak, seemed unable to draw breath.

Og turned and watched as the man staggered back, fought for balance, and fell. Before he touched the ground, Og leaned over and caught him with one arm, lowering him gently. Then, after a quick, satisfied glance at the log—the log too tall for any man to split that now lay in halves on the ground—he leaned on the handle of his axe to wait.

After a few moments the messenger sat up slowly, shaking his head. He glanced up and saw Og smiling down at him. Og held out a hand and helped him to his feet. The messenger brushed off his uniform, found the paper he'd dropped, and lifted it. In a shaky voice, he read the king's summons.

"Of course I will be there," Og replied. "I am sorry if I

startled you. I was afraid if I let my concentration slip, I might not split the log—or it might damage my axe." When the man did not reply, Og added, "It was a very big log, you know."

The messenger nodded. Then he turned and walked stiffly back the way he'd come, trying not to break into a run, as Og watched him go with amusement. A moment later, the big man stood one of the halves of the split log on the stone and began to concentrate once more.

<hr />

In the great library of Mavinor, a small army of scribes worked constantly on the restoration of The Scrolls. Some pored over ancient books and records; others translated obscure texts that had been deemed relevant. Still others sat in small alcoves with the eldest of the city and also the eldest they were able to find in outlying areas, who remembered things that others did not. The interviews were carefully recorded, matched against other information for accuracy, and retained for study. Nothing was taken for granted. Multiple sources were required for corroboration before any part of the reconstructed text could be considered valid.

Cantos sat with a group of others at a long table. Scrolls in various states of decomposition, some burned, some torn, and others simply crumbling with age, were secured on the working surface. Cantos was bent over a charred strip of parchment with a lens ground for magnification when the king's messenger entered. The man stood patiently and silently to one side of the table, waiting to be noticed.

Cantos was a stout man with gray hair, a heavy beard, and deep-set, piercing eyes. His nose was long and sharp, and he had a penchant for getting lost in his work when reviewing potential material for The Scrolls. This moment was no exception. But finally, sensing the weight of another's gaze on his back, Cantos glanced up.

"Yes?" he said. "Is there something I can help you with?"

Cantos recognized the king's livery, but he hated to be interrupted when he was working. It was difficult enough to concentrate on the damaged manuscripts and find any truth without being dragged back to mundane matters in the middle of the task.

"Cantos," the man said softly, "hear this message."

Cantos sat up straight. This was no casual message from the king. The formal wording was used only in official proclamations or in a summons. He tried to think if there was something he'd done, something he'd neglected. Given his past as a tax collector who had cheated others of their hard-earned wealth, being summoned directly gave him an impulsive shiver.

When the message had been delivered, Cantos sank back in his seat. The tension went out of him momentarily, and he released a breath he hadn't even been aware he'd held. Then almost immediately his face became tinged with shock and dismay.

"You can't be serious," he said. "There must be some sort of mistake. I'm no warrior! I have work to do here—important work. If it weren't for what I'm doing, the tale of Haggiselm would still be only a bedtime story for children."

"The king suspected that you would feel this way," the messenger said. The man tried not to smile, but he failed in this regard. "He asked me to pose a question to you."

"I have no time to play games," Cantos said.

"The question is this. There are many mountains in the

North. How can you tell when you have come near to the range where Haggiselm hid the Medallion?"

"The area is described numerous times in The Scrolls," Cantos snapped. "Not all of the information has made it into the reconstruction, but there are other sources."

"And the thirteen chosen, they would know all of this?"

"Of course not," Cantos said. "The reconstruction has taken long grueling hours, and only a few…"

He fell silent. The messenger smiled.

"It is Onestus' wish that you accompany the quest as one of the thirteen, not to fight, though you will undoubtedly learn something of that fine art, but as the foremost expert on The Scrolls in Mavinor. You will be their guide—their source of information in dangerous, uncharted places."

Cantos dropped his eyes to the floor and thought. It was obvious he was hoping to find a way around the question. At last he glanced up at the messenger.

"Tell the king that I will be there," he said. "I do not believe it is the best use of my abilities, but I admit…they are going to need a guide. I will spend my time between now and then gathering any manuscripts that are small enough to be carried on a lengthy journey and might be of service to the quest."

The messenger bowed and turned. Before he was out of sight, Cantos had returned to his work.

———

The whistle of a dagger whirling through the air was followed by the solid *thunk* of that dagger striking a target made of wooden planks. A second, third, and fourth dagger followed with such rapidity that their strikes mimicked the rapping of a hammer. A well-built man with light brown hair tied back behind his head strode across the small clearing, tugged the daggers free, and slid them into a set of sheaths that hung at an angle across his chest. Just above and to the left of the blades was a symbol that had been dyed into the leather of his armor. It was an apple, split dead center by a dagger very similar to those he'd just sheathed.

As he turned away from the target, he saw a man riding slowly up to him through the trees. The man, who wore the palace colors, carried some sort of document.

"Pugius?" the man called.

"I am Pugius. To what do I owe the pleasure of your company?"

The messenger drew up short. Unrolling the small scroll, he passed on his message.

"So I'm chosen, am I?" Pugius said with a smile. "Of course I am honored to be one of the chosen. I will arrive as I have been asked, but I wonder if you could help me with something since you're here. I find myself in need of a second set of hands."

"I am to report directly back to the palace," the messenger said.

"It will take only a moment," Pugius said. "Then you can be about your business."

"What is it you need?" the man asked.

Pugius strode to a small wooden table beneath a tree. He grabbed a bit of parchment and held it up. Painted in the center of the paper was the image of a brilliant red apple.

"I am using this as a target," Pugius explained, "or I plan to. I just need to get some perspective. Do you think you could walk over there and hold it up against that backdrop?"

The messenger looked at the crude painting dubiously,

but then he shrugged. He took it and started across the clearing. When he reached the wooden backdrop, he held the painting up to it, one hand at the very top and the other at the bottom.

"A little higher," Pugius called out.

The messenger adjusted the paper. The instant that he started to turn back to ask if he had it right, Pugius moved. His hands were a blur of motion as he sent first one and then another blade flashing across the clearing. The first embedded itself between the messenger's hand and the top of the apple. The second did the same for the bottom, firmly attaching the paper to the wood. The man spun, cried out, and as he did so, one more dagger flashed through the air. It struck dead center on the apple with a loud *thunk* and buried itself nearly to the hilt.

The messenger glanced over in shock at the blade buried in the apple. He shook his head to clear it and lurched away from the target.

"I think that's about it," Pugius called out to him, smiling. "That will do."

The messenger turned and fled, leaping into his saddle and spinning his mount in a quick turn. He was off at a gallop, and Pugius stood, watching him go in amusement. Then with a quick shrug he returned to the target and retrieved his weapons.

━━━━━

Sceptrus spun his staff easily, letting it describe lazy circles in the air in hypnotic patterns. Cidivus squared off with him, his eyes glued to the whirling staff. He held his own at the ready, backing off each time Sceptrus feinted.

"You have got to learn," Sceptrus said, slashing out with

his weapon and smacking it solidly into Cidivus' thigh, "where to keep your eyes. You will never keep up with the staff. You can't gauge it or measure its intent. You must watch your opponent's waist to see which direction he will move, and his shoulders for the tell on the staff."

Cidivus grunted in pain. He concentrated even harder but still could not drag his gaze away from the whirling staff. Sceptrus feinted at the thigh, slid past Cidivus' clumsy attempt to block, and drove his staff up until he brought it to rest gently against Cidivus' temple. He smiled and started to step back, drawing his weapon with him. Then Cidivus moved as quickly as a snake, flipping his staff up and driving it at Sceptrus' chest. At the last second Sceptrus smacked it to the side.

"You need to learn not only to control your eyes," Sceptrus said, taking a step back, "but you need to work on your temper as well."

Cidivus looked ready to say something sharp when one of his servants rushed up, breathlessly.

"My lord," the boy said. "There is a messenger here from the palace."

Cidivus turned, irritated. Then his frown disappeared as the boy's words slid past his momentary ire.

"From the palace? By all means, see him in."

The courtyard where the two men had been sparring was lush. They were surrounded on two sides by gardens. Behind them, a stone paved walk led through still more trees to Cidivus' estate, which bore the emblem of a silver serpent above the entrance. Sceptrus, widely acknowledged as the best man with a staff in all of Mavinor, had been asked to come by and train Cidivus in that ancient weapon's use. Used to getting things his way quickly and easily, Cidivus was not enjoying the lesson.

The servant returned to the main gate of the estate and ushered in the messenger, a short, squat man with a bald head and a short, pointed goatee. He looked uncomfortable in Cidivus' presence, but he pulled a small scroll free and read the king's summons to Sceptrus. Humbled by the request, Sceptrus graciously accepted.

"A quest in The Author's name?" Cidivus asked. "What a magnificent honor! You say there are to be only thirteen? Then I must seek an audience with his majesty. As a man of great faith, I feel obligated to volunteer myself. How could I not?"

Sceptrus stood still as he listened carefully to Cidivus' rant. He watched him closely as if waiting for a punch line to a good joke. When it was not forthcoming, Sceptrus glared at him. Though he'd been willing to train Cidivus, he had little love for him beyond weapons. Cidivus was known to be selfish and to have openly spoken out against The Author and The Scrolls as folly. Sceptrus suspected that the messenger was not foolish enough to fall for it, but hearing the words angered him.

Then the unthinkable happened. The man pulled out a second scroll, unbound it, and repeated his summons, this time aimed at Cidivus himself, who finally grew quiet. Cidivus stepped forward and took the paper, reading it a second time to himself before handing it back to the messenger. He seemed almost as shocked as Sceptrus at his inclusion, but he recovered very quickly.

"I should not be surprised," he said. "I should merely be thankful. Tell his majesty that I will gladly answer his summons. I am certain I speak for the both of us," he turned and waved an arm at Sceptrus, "when I say that it is a great honor."

Sceptrus nodded his agreement to the messenger, not trusting himself to speak. He stood very still and very quiet until the messenger had turned away. Then he reassumed his position and held his staff at the ready. Sceptrus' eyes were cold, and none of his good cheer of only a short time before shone through.

Cidivus turned toward him, caught his expression, and shook his head.

"No. That's enough for one day," he said. "We both have a lot of planning and packing to do. I will see you at the palace in two days, my friend."

Sceptrus stared a moment longer and then turned and left without a word or gesture. He walked down the path toward the main gate of Cidivus' estate and the road beyond, carrying his breastplate, which bore the insignia of two staffs crossed over one another. Cidivus watched him go for a moment, then he smiled widely, turned, and went inside his extravagant home to begin preparations for the quest.

Chapter Five

Onestus lay very still until he heard the solid click of the door to his chamber latching firmly. He knew Talmik was outside, giving final instructions to the guards. Sleep was not going to come quickly or easily this night, but he hadn't wanted to be disturbed with offers of sleep tinctures or the incessant opening and closing of his door as they checked in on him. Better that they believed he slept soundly and left him to his thoughts.

He went over the day's events in his mind, looking for some sort of sign. He'd been so certain that Ignatus would lead the thirteen. From the moment he'd realized the quest was real, he'd envisioned the seasoned old warrior as the moral compass of the group and the steel in its spine. It was difficult to erase those images from his mind and concentrate on something wholly different.

He'd had warm tea before retiring, and he found that the breeze ruffling the curtains of his window was oddly soothing. He tried to remain lucid, wondering where the sleeplessness of a few moments past had gone, but his eyelids grew heavy. He could still almost see Ignatus seated across from him. He thought he even heard the man's voice, but it slipped away on the breeze, and darkness claimed him. Despite the stress, the weariness the day had brought overcame him, and he slept. As he fell into a deep sleep, he began to have a vivid dream, one that would leave an indelible impression on both his mind and heart.

In his dream, Onestus walks along the shore of a vast lake. He cannot see more than a few hundred yards in any direction because a thick fog has descended. He picks his way carefully along the shoreline, moving toward a glow in the distance.

Ahead he hears splashing and the sound of something grating. There are loud voices, but he can't make out what they are saying. The rocks are treacherous, and he stumbles often but manages to keep his footing. Cold, damp air mats his hair to his head and drenches his robes, but he ignores the discomfort.

In the distance the frame of a large boat shimmers through the mist and then solidifies. Shadowed figures move about its decks. Onestus can make out a pier jutting from the shore. Nets are strung over the sides of the ship and laid out to dry. Men move steadily and efficiently from ship to shore, bearing baskets of freshly caught fish.

He makes his way closer, fascinated. The fishermen do not seem aware of him, but this does not bother him. As he approaches the base of the pier, one man in particular catches his eye. He is a lean, shaggy-headed man bearing a full basket of the day's catch. His pace is steady, and his features are set in a strong, serious expression that lends an odd comfort. Onestus is about to step forward and to try to speak but stops when he notices that, though he is certain he saw a simple fisherman moments before, the man with the basket is actually wearing crude leather armor. There is a sword belted to his side, and he wears an equally crude helm with a hammered metal visor.

Onestus stands still as the man approaches. When it seems they will pass in the fog without notice, the fisherman turned soldier stops. He cocks his head as if hearing something on the wind, and then he turns, gazing directly into Onestus' eyes. As he does, he holds out the basket of fish filled to the brim and glistening in the odd, silvery light.

Something glitters in the bottom of that basket, something shining brighter than the slick scales of the fish. The man holds it out patiently, and Onestus steps forward. He cannot make out the object that has caught his attention, so he reaches into the basket. When he finds himself unable to push the fish aside, he glances up in apology and begins to pluck them out. He does not know why, but as he pulls each free, dropping it to the ground at his feet, he counts. After he removes nine, he is able to see the object of his search. He tries to grab it, but the man pulls the basket just out of reach. Onestus glances up at the man, who nods toward the remaining fish.

Onestus pulls out three more. Twelve. An even dozen fish, and at the bottom of the basket a golden medallion lies, coiled in a puddle formed by the loops of its own chain. Onestus reaches for it, but as he does the basket is gently pulled back again. The man removes his helm and Onestus sees his face clearly. The king meets that calm gaze, and the mist around him gathers suddenly. He reaches out, but the basket is nowhere in sight. The man, the ship, and the pier are obscured by a thick, chill cloud. He takes a step and stumbles, his feet slipping on the damp stone. He then pitches forward, but just before falling face-first to the ground...

Onestus woke with a startle, bathed in sweat, clutching

the blankets to his chest fiercely. He glanced around his chamber wildly, but there was nothing to see. The curtains danced idly in the breeze. The moon shone in bright and silver. He rose, wrapped a blanket around his shoulders, and walked over to the window.

The palace grounds and the walls of the city were shrouded in mist. He saw no one on the streets below. There was no lake or boat, and there were no fishermen moving about. Onestus raised a hand to his nose and took a deep breath, half-expecting the scent of fish. But there was nothing out of the ordinary, though the face of the man in his dreams was etched firmly in his mind.

He crossed the room to his desk, opened a drawer, and pulled out ink, a quill, and paper. At first he didn't know what he intended to do. But as he carried the paper to the table and sat down, he felt drawn by something beyond himself, controlled by powers he sensed but could not name. He unstoppered the ink and dipped the quill. Beginning with the strong line of the jaw, he began to sketch the fisherman, seeking the eyes he'd gazed into on that misty shore.

The king was not an artist. He had dabbled as a young man in illuminated texts and fanciful etchings, but nothing like this. This was a true likeness. This face had drifted from the mist of his dreams, and he knew he had to capture it— that there would be no rest or sleep until he had recreated it in detail.

It took a very long time to finish. His fingers were tired from gripping the pen. His wrists and the table were splattered with ink. He glanced at the window as he laid the quill aside and turned toward his bed as if to rise. Instead, he slumped forward across his drawing, cheek smudging the ink. There were hours until sunrise…but he spent them sleeping at the table, waking only when Talmik came in the door and rushed to his side.

Groggy, Onestus sat up. He was stiff but felt surprisingly rested. When Talmik tried to help him to his feet, he brushed him away and stood on his own, stretching his back.

Talmik glanced at the table and caught sight of the sketch. He picked it up, studying it carefully.

"Who is it, sire?" he asked. "It is…remarkable. I did not know you could create such a drawing."

Onestus stared at the face on the paper and frowned.

"Nor did I," he said. "I have not drawn a thing since I was a boy. As to whom that may be, I have no idea. But I believe I met him last night. In a dream…or perhaps a vision."

Talmik stared intently at the drawing and looked at Onestus.

"There is something familiar in this face," he said. "I have seen this man."

"Take the drawing to the guards," Onestus said. "Show it to them, and see if any among them knows who this might be. Spread it as far as you can. The vision was very clear, and if it is a true vision, then we need this man. I believe that when you find him, you will have found our thirteenth—the last of the chosen."

Talmik bowed quickly and headed for the door.

"Talmik!" Onestus called after him, surprised at the strength in his voice. "Before you go, send someone for food. I am hungry, and it will be a very long day. There is much to be done in preparation for the arrival of the thirteen tomorrow."

"Yes, my lord," Talmik said.

Onestus turned to his window and watched below as

the city came to life. A few minutes later, two young men laden with trays of fruit, cheese, hot tea, and bread entered, breaking the king's reverie. Onestus sat to eat with gusto; he could not remember a morning in recent times when he'd felt more alive or a time when food had tasted so good.

He was just washing down the last of his meal with tea when Talmik returned. He held the drawing in his hand, and he was out of breath as if he'd been running.

"We have found him," he said. "His name is Gobius, and he trains even now with Sicarius' warriors. But he is no hero."

"Tell me," Onestus said.

"He is a fisherman," Talmik said, "from the southern end of Mavinor, by the coastline."

Onestus grew very still and listened.

"He has only recently been accepted into the army. Gobius is strong, and he shows an aptitude for weapons, but he is rough. His training is far from complete."

"And yet," Onestus said, "he is chosen. Send the messenger immediately."

"As you wish," Talmik said. "Gobius will be summoned to arrive along with the others at first light tomorrow. He will not be difficult to find, as he is drilling in the field beneath this very window." Talmik quickly exited to dispatch the messenger, leaving the king alone with his thoughts.

Onestus rose early the next morning and dressed without Talmik's aid, slowly but more easily than he had in years. The sketch he'd drawn still rested on the table where Talmik had placed it. He seated himself, lifting it and examining it carefully. Gobius had been summoned. The king was still amazed and energized by his vision. The thought of meeting the man face to face was both exciting and frightening. What if Gobius was nothing like he'd seemed? What if he'd just seen the man in passing and constructed the dream out of desperation? There was nothing to do with the morning but wait. There was a knock on the door, and Onestus replied that it was all right to enter.

When Talmik opened the door and stepped inside the king's bedroom, he drew up short in the doorway and stared.

"Don't just stand there," Onestus said. Then he smiled. "It's going to be a day of momentous events. I thought it best to get an early start so I would have time to reflect. Bring my breakfast, and have them prepare The Great Hall. Send to the scribes for maps of any and all areas and roads between here and the Northern Mountains."

"Yes, sire," Talmik said. "And if I may say so—it is good to see you so spirited. It has been too long."

Onestus smiled broadly. "Let us hope it lasts through the day," he said. "A lot depends on my presentation of the passage from The Scrolls and on their reactions to being summoned. It is not enough that I send them off on a quest. They have to believe that they have been called, at least enough to start them on their way."

The king glanced at the drawing in his hand and then at Talmik.

"They have to believe as surely as I do."

"They will," Talmik assured him. "The quest is ordained, and such matters have a way of making their true nature known to all."

"May those words be fulfilled," the king said.

As his aide turned to leave the room, Onestus called after him.

"Have them met by the royal guard, Talmik. Before they enter the palace, they should be escorted. They are heroes, after all—the chosen. From the moment they are in sight of the palace, I want them to feel what that means."

Talmik nodded and then disappeared. When he was gone, Onestus turned to the window. The sun had only just begun to rise, and the city was still quiet. He was the healthiest and strongest he'd felt in more than a year. If for no other reason than that he would have believed. But he had The Scrolls, he had his faith, and he had been granted a vision. He had things to live for, it seemed; he had a purpose. He hoped he could live up to it with honor.

———

Thaddeus strode down the center of the road leading to the palace, his club resting over one shoulder. The muscular warrior wore leather armor, and the insignia on his chest was a stylized club much like the weapon he carried. His eyes were bright, and he had a smile for all he passed. It wasn't every day a man was summoned to serve his king. As rumors rushed through the streets like errant winds, the citizens of Mavinor gathered to watch as the thirteen made their way to their meeting with the king.

The sound of hurrying steps caught Thaddeus' attention, and he glanced over his shoulder. Coming up behind were two men, both wearing the red and gold of Sicarius' troops. He knew the first. His name was Nomis, a soldier with a lot of enthusiasm but little experience. The two had met during drills. Thaddeus slowed his steps, and the other two caught up, matching his stride as he continued.

"Surely you weren't called for the quest?" Thaddeus said, glancing at Nomis.

"We were both called," Nomis replied. He was young and earnest. "I've heard the story of Haggiselm all my life…to become a part of that prophecy is to fulfill a lifelong dream."

Thaddeus laughed. "You haven't fulfilled anything yet," he said. "It is one thing to be called to a dangerous quest, and quite another to see it through into prophecy."

He turned to the third man.

"I am Thaddeus," he said. "Nomis I know, but if we are going to share road and battle, I should at least know your name."

"Alphaeus," the man replied. He was thinner than Nomis, and he seemed nervous. He didn't look comfortable in his armor, and a sword hung clumsily from his belt. He reminded Thaddeus of a boy on his way for his first tryst, and it was all the big man could do to stifle a chuckle.

"Well met, Alphaeus," he said.

The three of them walked together down the center of the road, attracting a growing crowd. Thaddeus tried to ignore them, keeping his eyes on the palace in the distance. The sudden notoriety made him uncomfortable, and he didn't want to do anything that might worsen the situation. For one thing he didn't want to get caught up in trying to answer questions—he didn't know any more than they did. Odds were that if they'd been following gossip all morning, they knew more than him.

"How do you think we were chosen?" Nomis asked, breaking the silence. "I am honored, but surely there are men with more experience."

"I have been wondering the same thing all night long," Alphaeus said. "I've considered it from every angle, and it's beyond me. I honestly can't imagine what quality I possess that would separate me from those with whom I serve. I've hardly been with the army long enough to have my gear issued."

"The Scrolls don't follow the logic of men," Thaddeus replied. He kept his voice low and ducked his head toward his companions in an attempt to shield their conversation from those around them. "If King Onestus says we are the chosen, then there is nothing for us to do but to serve to the best of our strength and wisdom. I will admit that, taking the three of us into consideration, I am curious about the others. For now, though, I think we should remain silent and wait. Stray words have a habit of traveling very quickly, and I for one do not want to be asked why I was flapping my tongue."

They fell silent and continued on. When they reached the palace and mounted the steps, several of the king's guard descended to meet them. As they climbed, the guards fell in to either side, forming an escort.

Thaddeus slowed his steps and held his head high. Nomis and Alphaeus nearly tripped over him, but then they slowed down to match his pace. After entering the palace, their escort continued along with them until they reached The Great Hall of Mavinor.

The room had been cleared but for one long table that ran down its center. At the far end of the table, watching them calmly, King Onestus sat waiting. There were exactly thirteen other seats, six on each side and one on the opposite end from the king. Nine of them were already filled. Thaddeus recognized most of the men, skilled fighters that they were. He took in the diversity of styles and weapons they represented, nodding at those he knew.

"Take a seat, gentlemen," Onestus called out. "We have only one man left to wait for, and then we can begin. I have much to tell you before we start the official preparations for the quest."

The three took seats near the far end of the table from the king. Now there was only one place left…the very end of the table…without a tenant. There was a commotion at the door, and they all turned. A tall, gaunt man with a beard, mustache, and long, shaggy brown hair entered the room. Under his arm he carried a crudely formed helm, and an old, worn sword rode on his hip. His leather armor looked as though it might have passed through generations of fighters. His expression was calm and very serious. Though none of the other twelve had ever met him, they found themselves smiling and nodding as he approached. King Onestus, however, could only gaze in wonder upon seeing the man whose face he had sketched just the day before.

As Gobius entered, Onestus stood. The king's eyes were wide. His mouth opened as if he would speak, but he closed it again and simply stared. Gobius was just as he had appeared in Onestus' dream. His face, his build, his attire…he was the culmination of everything that Onestus had seen in his vision. Those gathered watched as Gobius crossed the room and self-consciously took the last seat at the table. Onestus dropped slowly back into his own seat, closed his eyes, and fought for composure.

Seeing the king's momentary distress, Talmik stepped from behind Onestus' chair to address the hall.

"Welcome," he said.

That single word was all it took to bring Onestus around. He shook his head as if freeing it from some sort of cobweb, took a drink from the mug of hot tea on the table before him, and cleared his throat.

"This is a wonderful day," he said. "It is a day that I have looked forward to for many long years because it is the beginning of a new day for Mavinor. The Scrolls return to us, their message a little more complete each day, and we grow and expand with them. We have tucked ourselves away in Mavinor for too long, trying to protect what we have and living in fear of our neighbors.

"To the west we have Xamnon. King Antiugus would love nothing more than to see Mavinor reduced to a pile of rubble. He has no respect for The Author or for the lessons of The Scrolls. He would see it all destroyed given the chance, and our military gets no rest—as most of you know only too well—from anticipating his next move.

"To the East, King Bardus walls himself in, even as we do, but so tightly that he seems to have forgotten the rest of the world exists. We have no hope of assistance or camaraderie from the city of Urmina. Our world is crumbling, and in this time of need The Author has given us hope."

Onestus stood again, and Talmik handed him a scroll. He unfurled it and began to read. His voice was strong, stronger than it had been in months. His words rang out and echoed through the hall as he told, once again, the story of Haggiselm. He discussed the Medallion, and when he reached the section concerning the gathering of the thirteen, he turned to those in the room.

"Each of you," he said, "has been chosen for a reason. I gathered my advisors, and we debated late into the night. We prayed fervently to The Author for guidance. We considered officers and enlisted, cavalry and infantry. We held each name up to the light of what small wisdom we possess, and we chose those who seemed—for one reason or another—to stand out.

"I know that many of these choices will be questioned. I would not be surprised if some among you question them. It is the nature of The Scrolls that, when we try hardest to bend them to what we know—to the bounds of this physical realm—we find that they are at their most cryptic. I believe in each and every choice that we have made, however; I back those choices with my faith and with all the power of my office as King of Mavinor.

"If any among you doubts this quest, you will have your opportunity to voice that doubt, but first I wish to share something, something miraculous. I considered keeping it to myself, but after giving it more thought, I realized that to do so would be a foolish mistake. For when The Author reaches out to us, His revelation is for all men, not just a chosen few—and certainly not for just one. Even if that one is a king."

There were some murmurs around the table, but no one spoke. Onestus paused and took a drink from the cup of tea that Talmik dutifully kept full and hot, managing to do so without intruding. His hand was a bit unsteady, but as Talmik stepped forward to help, Onestus waved him back.

"I am not gifted with the skill of an artist," he said. "When

I was a young man, the priests were certain I'd never master calligraphy to any acceptable level, and it was deemed a waste of time for me to attempt the illumination of manuscripts, though many of my friends grew proficient in that art. The night before last, after twelve of you had been chosen and after the one man I believed would lead you had declined my request that he be included, I had a vision. You might think it was an old man dreaming, and I would probably have agreed with you but for the way things have unfolded since.

"I dreamed that I encountered a man on a misty shore. When it seemed as though we would just pass each other like two ships in the night, he stopped and held out a basket of some sort. I began to look through it, and as I did, something shone at the very bottom. It was something round and gold, but when I reached in for it, he turned away and disappeared into the fog.

"When I woke, I drew the face of the man I encountered in my dream. I had never seen the man before, but I sent my aides and my guards into the courtyard and the fields, and they found him. I will not reveal his identity, but I will tell you that he now sits here among you as one of the thirteen chosen for this quest."

The room grew very quiet all of a sudden.

"What I'm saying," Onestus said at last, breaking the silence, "is that when we most need Him, The Author reaches out to us. When we believe there is no answer, it is provided. All that is asked of us is that we have faith."

He swept the table with a searching glance. No one moved.

"Are there any among you who would deny this call?" he asked. "Do not fear that you will be persecuted. This is not a quest to be entered into lightly, and if you decline, I swear to you there will be no repercussion. This quest must be undertaken with a clear heart and mind. It will be long and dangerous, and it is likely that not all of you will make it back. When Haggiselm made this same journey he lost all of his men, and he himself never returned to Mavinor."

The room was silent. None of those present looked at the others or shuffled his feet. They met the king's gaze, and they held their peace. After pausing to allow a response, Onestus nodded.

"It is as I expected," he said. "You have been called, and you have been chosen. You feel it, as I feel it. There is no turning back."

As Onestus sat down, a bald man in the rough robes of a monk stepped up beside the king's chair.

"With your permission, sire?"

Onestus nodded.

"My name," the robed man said, "is Olin. I have prepared quarters for all of you here in the palace. You will be outfitted for the journey, and there will be a series of lessons prepared. As you sit here, my men are scouring the libraries for accounts of the Northern Mountains. Any rumor, or story, or song, or bit of poetry that seems in some way relevant to this quest will be gathered and presented to you.

"You will receive new armor and weapons if you need them. If you do not have a mount, one will be provided. There are maps being copied for the journey. We anticipate the preparations will take three days."

Now there were murmurs up and down the table. The air was charged with energy. Onestus reached for his tea again, and this time his hand was steady. He was feeding off their emotion, and though he knew that it would cost him, he allowed himself to be carried along. He sat in silence and watched as Olin's men made their way along the table. They took measurements, asked questions, and swarmed like an army of industrious ants. The chosen were in good hands.

Finally, at Talmik's urging, Onestus rose. The hall fell silent once again, but he waved to them to continue.

"I must go and attend to other affairs," he said. "You have plans to make, and I do not want to interfere with their completion. You will see me from time to time over the next few days. May the Author guide your preparations and grant you rest."

The king turned, and his aides and guards fell in around him. The silence held until his entourage reached the far end of the hall and passed into the antechamber beyond. Then the voices of the chosen rose once more, as well as those of Olin and his men. Their words and laughter escorted the king to the stairs and buoyed him as he returned to his chamber. They had the ring of destiny.

Chapter Six

For the next three days little was said or done in Mavinor that did not relate in some way to the quest or to the thirteen. Men discussed the best routes over flagons of ale. Children and young women chose personal favorites among the champions and tried to win a moment of their time or a sign of their favor.

In the streets could be found everything from speculation to heated arguments. There was an air of hope compounded by a counterpoint of cynicism. The military, under Sicarius' control, leaned toward the latter. Its members chose to view the quest as almost an insult—a calling on magic and myth to save the kingdom when the only thing currently keeping it safe was its own might and ingenuity. Soldiers in the red and gold of Sicarius' army were quick to speak up any time the quest was mentioned and to deal roughly with those appearing too optimistic.

But this was not enough to dampen the spirits of the city. The quest was a breath of hope where none had existed, a proof of the validity of faith. More and more of the faithful found their way into The Author's Temple and the smaller halls of worship. Priests found their advice to once more have become a valued commodity. Taverns and inns found themselves overrun with evening commerce as the citizens of Mavinor, great and small, gathered to discuss the king's quest and the thirteen who had been selected.

The chosen trained daily in an inner courtyard of the palace. Few except for the members of the staff, the guard, and the king were there to witness it. Onestus had arranged to sit for an hour a day in the middle of the morning, watching their progress. He came to see these moments as the highlight of his waking hours, and he had to fight the urge to stretch that time out and neglect his other duties.

When the thirteen came together on the first day of training, they immediately started to bond with one another. Even before anyone drew a weapon, they started a conversation among themselves in an effort to get to know each other better.

"So here we are," said Silex. "I don't know about the rest of you, but I'm still somewhat overcome with emotion at the thought of being chosen for this task."

"Overcome with emotion? You?" asked his brother, Ferox. "Oh, come now. Surely you must be joking." He then addressed the rest of the group. "Trust me; my brother never lets his emotions get the best of him. But let there be no doubt that we were humbled when the king's messenger arrived at our home to summon us."

"I was quite humbled as well," said Cidivus. "Sceptrus and I were training together in my courtyard when we were summoned. It is a great honor to have this opportunity to serve our king and show our undying faith in The Author." Sceptrus glared at Cidivus but said nothing. He knew quite well that his comments were insincere and that the word *humble* was not a part of Cidivus' vocabulary.

"I think I scared the wits out of the messenger who came to me," said Og. "The poor fellow dropped right down to the ground after he came upon me while I was splitting a log with my battle axe."

"I sent my messenger running scared when I used my daggers to pin a drawing against a backdrop…as he was holding it," said Pugius to roars of laughter.

"I almost hit mine with a sword that went flying out of my hands," added Cedrus. He had hoped the remark would endear him to the more seasoned warriors, but instead they immediately stopped their laughing and stared at him. Always looking out for his younger brother, Tonitrus jumped into the conversation and changed the subject.

"Isn't it amazing," Tonitrus said, "how King Onestus dreamed of a man, sketched his likeness, and then managed to find the same man in the drawing?"

"Hardly a coincidence, is it?" said Silex.

"I wonder which one of us it is," said Og. "Surely we can find out."

"It makes no difference to me. Personally, I'd like to hear a bit more from these men," Cidivus said, nodding towards the lesser known members of the group: Nomis, Alphaeus, and Gobius.

"This is Nomis," said Thaddeus. He thought the young men might feel somewhat nervous after being placed on the spot, so he stepped in. "And this is Alphaeus. They met me on the way to the castle on the day our king summoned us."

"Thank you, Thaddeus," said Nomis. Though younger and less experienced than most of the thirteen, he wasn't as shy as one might expect. "I haven't served in the army long, but you should know that I had to battle both of my parents for the longest time in order to get in. They were dead set against my wish, so I had to wait until I was old enough to break free and go out on my own. Needless to say, they are less than thrilled that I have been called to this quest. But to me, it is the opportunity of a lifetime and one that I would not trade for anything else in the entire world."

"And you?" asked Ferox, looking directly at Alphaeus.

"I just recently enlisted," Alphaeus replied in a shy tone. "My father once served in Mavinor's army, so I am merely following in his footsteps." It was clear that he was far more introverted than Nomis was.

"Weren't you just accepted into the army as well?" Cidivus asked while looking directly at Gobius.

"Yes, that is true," replied Gobius.

"And who are you and where are you from? What's your story?" asked Og.

"I am a fisherman from the south side of Mavinor," Gobius said. "My parents are both recently deceased, and I have long wished to be a soldier. But I didn't want to enlist while they were ill and needed me to care for them. Now that they are no longer with us, I decided that it was time to pursue my dream."

"Sorry for your loss," said Silex. "Ferox and I are still lucky enough to have our father with us. It's hard for me to imagine what life would be like if he were no longer here."

"I can't imagine how your skills as a fisherman might help us on this quest," Cidivus said. The others looked at Gobius as if waiting for a response, but he said nothing. Cidivus then continued to speak in his usual supercilious tone. "Well, gentlemen, it is quite obvious that we have some among us who are less proficient in battle than others."

"None less than me," said Cantos, providing some levity. The scribe had been listening the entire time, waiting for an opening in the conversation when he might be able to chime in. "And if I were you, I wouldn't expect much out of me if my services in battle were required. I am far better suited for the library than for the battlefield." The others chuckled at his statement.

"Hey, don't they say the quill is mightier than the sword?" said Pugius, drawing even heartier laughter from the group. With that, they began to sharpen their weapons and prepare for a full day of training.

In keeping his promise to Onestus, Ignatus helped train the thirteen before they began the quest. Those who were more inexperienced drew most of his time and attention. Ignatus worked extensively with Cedrus, Nomis, Alphaeus, and Gobius. These soldiers had no insignia because they had not yet earned one. Only those warriors who had proven themselves in battle through some type of accomplishment were permitted to adopt an insignia for their arms. Ignatus was especially impressed with how far Gobius had come in such a short period of time and could not recall anyone who had made such great strides during all his years of military service. It was almost otherworldly.

The more experienced soldiers trained together throughout those three days. Cantos sat in on the training, and while he learned quite a bit as he observed, he had no intention of joining them. Instead, they would gather around him when taking a respite from their exercises. Cantos would then share some of his knowledge of The Scrolls and the roads they needed to travel in order to arrive at their destination.

Cidivus appeared to be the most distant, separating himself from the group as if he were better than any one of them. He was certainly the wealthiest, having been born into a life of privilege and residing in the most beautiful estate in all of Mavinor. Sceptrus was still annoyed that Cidivus had even been asked to join the quest, as he knew that he was a nonbeliever when it came to religious faith. Sceptrus himself was a doubter, but unlike Cidivus he truly wanted to believe. He desperately wished to overcome the obstacles he struggled with, and he hoped the quest might somehow aid him in that task.

As the others tried to connect with Cidivus, they asked him about his insignia, the silver serpent. Cidivus replied that he always preferred silver to gold and that he chose the serpent because of its quickness in its ability to strike. He even hinted that he might well have the quickest sword of any soldier in Mavinor's army. Though the others were less than convinced, no one argued the point with him lest a rift develop within the group before the quest had even begun.

Tonitrus had been keeping an eye on his younger brother as Ignatus trained him. When he saw Ignatus allow them a short break, Tonitrus approached Ignatus and engaged him in conversation.

"So sorry to hear that we're losing you," Tonitrus said. "There is no one in Mavinor's army who I admire more than you, Ignatus, and it would have been a great honor to have you lead us in this quest."

"Thank you, Tonitrus," Ignatus replied. "But it is time for

this old soldier to move on to other things. My time as a warrior has come and gone. The Author has other plans for me now. I am certain of it."

"I understand," Tonitrus said. "I have the utmost respect for you and for your decision, but I need to ask a favor of you."

Ignatus raised his eyebrows, trying to anticipate what Tonitrus would ask him to do. "Anything for a great swordsman and faithful servant of The Author such as yourself, Tonitrus. What can I do for you?"

Tonitrus told Ignatus about how he had been training not only Cedrus in the art of fighting but also his first cousins, Solitus and Arcala. Now that Tonitrus was leaving on the quest, Solitus and Arcala had no one to continue their training.

"They are young, but they are eager to learn and willing to listen," explained Tonitrus. "They have the hearts of champions, and I have nothing but the utmost confidence that they will one day serve Mavinor quite well as members of her esteemed army."

"Arcala is a woman, is she not?" asked Ignatus.

"Yes," replied Tonitrus. "But she is focused on becoming the first woman to serve in our military. I certainly would not bet against her. You'll see what I mean firsthand should you agree to my request."

Ignatus pondered for a minute, and though he had made up his mind to lay down his sword, he saw no reason not to help Tonitrus by training his cousins.

"I will do as you ask," Ignatus said. "You have my word that I will pick up where you left off with them and train them myself right up until the day you return to Mavinor.

Faithful soldiers like us, we who believe in The Author and
The Scrolls, are few and far in between. We must always look
out for one another."

Tonitrus expressed his sincere gratitude, and with that,
the break in training had ended. Without allowing another
second to elapse, Ignatus returned to where his pupils stood
and began communicating his instructions.

The days passed quickly. At the conclusion of the last day
of training, the more experienced warriors decided to call
a meeting before they prepared to embark on their quest.
Nomis, Alphaeus, Gobius, and Cedrus were called over to
the rest of the group, along with Cantos. Tonitrus was the
first to speak, and everyone else immediately focused their
attention on him.

"Before we depart tomorrow, it is imperative that we
choose someone among us to serve as leader of the group.
We all know that King Onestus had originally envisioned
Ignatus in that role, but it was not meant to be. Thus it is
now up to us to choose a leader." He had barely finished his
statement when Cidivus spoke up.

"I agree wholeheartedly, Tonitrus," he said. "A quest
without a leader is like an army without a general or a
kingdom without a king. We need someone swift and deci-
sive, someone to guide the others and to keep the group
focused on the task at hand, someone who has accomplished
amazing things on the battlefield, and whose prior experience qualifies him for the role beyond any shadow of a
doubt." The haughty tone of his voice caused the others to
look at him suspiciously.

"Someone...like you, perhaps, Cidivus? Is that what you're trying to say?" asked Sceptrus. Knowing Cidivus better than the rest, he saw right through him and wasn't about to let him get away with suggesting himself for the role. Cidivus gave Sceptrus a cold stare but did not respond to his question.

"Well, I know who I would nominate," said Ferox. "You might say I'm biased, but my brother, Silex, is the one to lead us. Who among us has more experience as a warrior than he? Who else among us was once given the keys to the kingdom of Mavinor for bravery in battling our enemies? Who among us is better at containing his emotions, never allowing them to cloud his judgment?"

"No one, no one, and no one," replied Og. "There is no denying the truth in what you say, Ferox. I second your nomination."

"I go along with it as well," said Pugius.

"Wait!" exclaimed Cidivus. "Come now, Ferox. You want your brother in charge because he will favor you and listen to you more so than anyone else would. Aside from you leading us yourself, you stand to benefit more from Silex's leadership role than anyone else."

"Not true," said Tonitrus. "Though my younger brother is joining us on this quest, I would not favor him more than the others. We know from our military training that when you're on the battlefield, every one of your fellow soldiers is your brother. I strongly disagree with you, Cidivus. I believe in Silex and his ability to remain objective. Thus I stand behind the nomination and give it my full support."

"And I as well," replied Cedrus.

"Anyone else?" asked Ferox.

One by one, Thaddeus, Sceptrus, Gobius, Nomis, Alphaeus, and Cantos nodded in agreement. That left Cidivus as the only one who did not cast a vote. It was quite evident that he would nominate only himself, but he refrained from declaring it openly lest he appear foolish by losing the vote by a count of twelve to one. "Silex it is," he finally said.

"Then it is done," said Tonitrus. "Congratulations, Silex. You are officially the leader of the thirteen in our quest for the Medallion of Mavinor."

"I humbly accept this honor," replied Silex. "I hope only that The Author will guide me in this task and that He will afford me every grace I need to fulfill it."

"He will," Cantos assured him. "He always does."

On the fourth day, rested and trained as well as they could be for a journey into relatively unknown territory, with companions none of them had ever traveled with before, on a quest to retrieve a legend, the thirteen rose early and enjoyed a quick and very complete breakfast in the Great Hall.

Onestus joined them, and over the course of the meal several others appeared: priests, scribes, and even political figures. Pachaias, Chair of the Tribunal, had come along with the rest of the magistrates: Pontius, Theophilus, Annus, and Aramus. Notably absent from the meal was General Sicarius, whom Onestus had asked to attend and speak a few words. That honor fell to Ignatus instead. The old warrior reported in full armor. His helm and shield were polished to a fine sheen, and his leather gear shone with oil and care. All eyes turned to the man with the sunburst on his breastplate, and he began to speak.

"It is a fine day," he said after surveying each of them in turn. "It is a fine day to set out on a quest worthy of the greatest of champions. It is the right time to have a new purpose and to make a new beginning not only for yourselves but for all of Mavinor. It is the rarest of opportunities to give glory to The Author and to bring the Medallion back to Mavinor, where it truly belongs. It is my hope that all of you will seize this opportunity and make the most of it, knowing that it was given to you not only by our great king but by The Author Himself. May The Author be with you, and may He guide and protect you during your quest for the Medallion."

After Ignatus' speech, Olin gave them a rundown on the equipment that had been prepared. The food disappeared, and at last the words ran into silence. The time for thinking and dreaming of the road had passed; it was time to mount and ride.

Onestus rose, finally, and smiled. He held out his hands and raised them, beckoning the thirteen to follow suit.

"The time has come," he said. "If you would all join me in a moment of prayer?"

Thirteen heads bowed mostly in unison, with Cidivus hesitating at first but then following the lead of the others. The facial expressions this gesture concealed were as varied as the constellations in the night sky, with some smiling broadly, others stern and serious, and still others nervous and anxious.

"Be strong in The Author and in His mighty power. Put on His armor so that you can take your stand against the forces of evil. For a struggle will arise, one in which the powers of this dark world and the spiritual force of evil will conspire to destroy all that has been created. Therefore put on the full armor of The Author so that when the day of evil comes you may be able to stand your ground. Stand firm then, with the belt of truth buckled around your waist, with the breastplate of righteousness in place, and with your feet fitted with the readiness that comes from The Author's grace. Take up the shield of faith, with which you can extinguish all the flaming arrows of the forces of darkness. Take the helm of salvation and the sword of hope and defend this world against those who would destroy it. Solicit The Author with all kinds of prayers and requests, knowing that He is with you in this mighty struggle until the very end. Be firm, have faith, and hope in The Author!"

The prayer seemed to bring energy and radiance to the room. As the thirteen turned toward the door, the king's guards formed a human corridor from the table in the Great Hall to the exit, stretching out to the main entrance of the palace. The chosen marched solemnly down the center of it all. They did not look to either side, nor did they speak. The gravity of the moment rode securely on their shoulders as they walked by the throngs of people who had gathered.

At the base of the steps, their mounts were held by a group of young men in the king's colors. Packs were slung over the back of each horse, and as the thirteen approached, all but Gobius walked confidently in the direction of their mounts. Fisherman that he was, Gobius' humble background had made it impossible for him to own a horse. But as Olin had promised, one had been provided for him. Olin led Gobius to his mount, and when he arrived at it, Gobius turned and saw Onestus at the top of the stairs. The king smiled and nodded ever so slightly, and Gobius smiled and nodded back.

Then the thirteen swung up into the saddle and turned

away from the palace. The route to the North Gate of Mavinor was lined with citizens and soldiers. As they moved along the road, the group pulled together. They formed up two abreast, riding slowly. Their heads were high, and even those among the people who doubted or were outright opposed to the quest held their silence.

Cidivus rode slightly in front of the rest, immediately showing his refusal to defer to Silex as leader. His mount was a magnificent black stallion, half a hand taller even than the massive warhorse that bore Og. He had waved aside all offers of outfit from Olin. His packs were not as large as those of the others, but they were ornate, tooled and gilt. His saddle shone with inlaid silver, and his armor gleamed. Everything he carried with him bore the insignia of his chosen symbol, a silver serpent. He smiled at the crowd as they passed, waved to the ladies, and made as big a show of that one short ride as humanly possible.

Silex and Ferox rode directly behind him. The two remained serious, and Silex kept his helm down, covering his face. He did not want to spoil the moment by allowing his disdain of Cidivus' manner to show. There would be plenty of time on the road to set ground rules and voice opinions. This moment belonged to the city, to King Onestus, and to The Author.

Behind the first set of brothers rode Cedrus at his elder brother's side. While Tonitrus rode easily, Cedrus scanned the crowd nervously. He glanced first to one side and then to the other. More than once his horse shied as he lost concentration and nearly bumped shoulders with Tonitrus' mount or came too close to Silex, riding ahead.

A dark haired and slender woman broke from the crowd

as they neared the gate. She stood a few feet closer to the road than did the rest, and she had eyes only for Cedrus. Tonitrus saw her as well, and he called to Silex, who in turn called for Cidivus to halt. The thirteen stopped their forward motion. Their horses stamped and snorted, not liking to be halted so soon after setting out. A murmur ran through the crowd.

Cedrus ignored them all. He swung down from the saddle and stood in the street just for a second. Then the woman was moving, running toward him, and he caught her up in his arms.

"Magdala," he said.

They embraced tightly. She was shorter, and the hug lifted her from her feet. She buried her head in his chest, and they stood that way for several breaths before he pushed her back gently to arm's length.

"I will miss you," he said simply. "I will think of you when I wake in the morning, and you will be the last thought to cross my mind when the moon rises in the sky. I will count the days until I return."

Magdala looked down, and then she pulled a scarf from around her neck. Stepping closer again, she wound it around his arm and tied it so that its bright red color shone in the morning sun. Then she gazed into his eyes, tears streaming down her face.

"And I will miss you. There will be no comfort for me in Mavinor until you return."

"Take comfort in our quest," he said. "Take comfort in The Author's Temple. Pray for our return and our success."

She nodded, not trusting herself to speak.

The horses shied again, and the murmur in the crowd grew louder. Cedrus shook his head as if waking from a dream. He hugged Magdala a final time, kissed her quickly on the lips, and then turned. He was back in the saddle a moment later, and they resumed their ride to the North Gate.

Magdala watched until Cedrus was no longer in sight. The tears dried on her cheeks, but she did not wipe them away.

The rest followed behind the two sets of brothers. Og stood out from the crowd, riding his huge warhorse. At his side rode Gobius. The fisherman sat easily in the saddle. His face was serene; his gaze was locked on the horizon or some point beyond it. Though he was one of the least experienced among them, he exuded an air of confidence that no one seeing him could deny.

Behind Og and Gobius rode Sceptrus and Cantos, who began to engage in conversation about The Scrolls. Cantos soon learned that Sceptrus had been struggling with his faith. He wanted to believe, but his doubt was difficult for him to overcome. Cantos spoke briefly about The Scrolls and promised Sceptrus that they would discuss them more extensively during the quest.

Rounding out the pairs were Pugius and Thaddeus, with Nomis and Alphaeus at the rear. When Thaddeus saw who was behind him, he immediately asked Pugius to halt for a second. Wanting to keep an eye on the younger, more inexperienced soldiers, he told Nomis and Alphaeus to go ahead. Pugius yielded and joined Thaddeus at the end of the line.

In this manner they reached the North Gate of Mavinor when the sun was approaching its zenith. Where they passed, there was silence. Behind them, when they had dropped from sight, the speculation had begun. Few expected to see them return. Odds were laid in the taverns on who, and how many, would survive. Patrons wagered on whether they would reach the Northern Mountains and whether they would succeed in their quest. By far the worst odds were reserved for those betting on success.

The guard towers that flanked the road at the gate were fully manned. Despite his obvious disdain for the entire operation, Sicarius had been letter-perfect in providing escorts and guards outfitted in their finest gear. He stood by, watching the thirteen as they rode on. Tarsus stood alongside him, and as he looked toward his general, Sicarius muttered that the thirteen had zero chance of success in obtaining the Medallion. There was little doubt in his mind that none would return and that they were foolishly risking their lives to search for something that did not exist.

Onestus, who had ridden ahead by a different route, waited atop the right-hand tower. He did not halt the group for a final speech. He stood very still and watched as they passed beneath him, each saluting in turn. It was a solemn moment that quieted the crowds far back into the streets so that only the distant murmur of those who were too far away to see could be heard.

On the far side of the gate, the road stretched off across a plain and then wound in toward the long stretch of dark forest known as the Tenebrae. That forbidden place, a place that few had ever dared to enter, separated the north road from Xamnon. The road wound round the extremities of the Tenebrae, but there were other roads leading into the interior. It was on those roads that the thirteen would travel despite the lurid tales of what awaited them beneath that black canopy of trees.

Watching from the city walls, Onestus was suddenly

glad that the road curved out of sight before they made their entrance into the forest. The memory of them riding slowly, erect and proud, was the one he needed to sustain him. He watched until they were nothing but tiny black dots against the glare of the sun. The gates were closed at last, and the crowds dispersed. The quest for the Medallion had begun.

Part II

Chapter Seven

The thirteen spread out and paired off as they rode slowly away from the city. The gates had long closed behind them, and though they had been traveling only for most of a single day, it felt as if worlds separated them from anything familiar. The two sets of brothers rode smoothly together, falling into familiar conversation easily. Gobius rode in silence with Og, and Cidivus was flanked by Nomis and Alphaeus, who were awed by the majesty of his mount and his armor. Up ahead, the black line of the forest they knew as the Tenebrae stretched into the distance, dark and intimidating.

"I can't believe we're going in there," Alphaeus said, staring at the monstrous trees. "All my life I've been told to stay as far away from the Tenebrae as possible. Now we're riding straight into it."

"If half the stories I've heard are true," Ferox commented, glancing over his shoulder with a sly wink, "we could be in some serious trouble."

"Frightened?" Og asked with a grin.

"Hardly," Ferox said. "I'm a hunter. I follow where the game leads. I don't know much about the Tenebrae, but I do know that even at the outer reaches, deer are scarce. I've seen sign of bear while hunting in that area, and there were other signs that were unfamiliar to me."

"I don't believe in fairy tales," Og said. "I have killed a bear before and can do so again. Anything else I will treat the same." He rested his hand on the hilt of his great axe as if to punctuate his statement.

"Most fairy tales start with a grain of fact," Cantos cut in. "There are numerous references to the Tenebrae in The Scrolls and in the reference material being used to recreate them. Heroes and champions of Mavinor have ridden those paths before, and those who returned brought some very strange tales."

"You've read them?" Gobius asked.

"Of course," Cantos said. "I've done nothing but read and translate for so long that I see scrolls in my sleep. Much of the information is very old, however. The older the tale, the longer it's been cycling through poets, bards, and scholars. Storytellers tend to embellish the details. A pack of wolves becomes hell hounds. A bear becomes an ogre. You have to expect the ordinary but be ready for the extraordinary."

"I suppose you'll have much to tell us then throughout the course of our journey," Ferox said.

"Indeed I will," Cantos said. "I have nothing much to offer here but words and knowledge. If we run into a bear, I can keep out of the way, and our friend Og here is confident he can kill it. If we run into an actual ogre, well, I know how the last person who claimed to meet one defeated it. That's what I mean by being ready for the extraordinary."

As the thirteen continued, Cantos shared more stories with them. He told them tales of the forest, some strange and unsettling, and others so obviously fabricated that they could only laugh upon hearing them. It calmed them, and by the time they turned from the main road onto the wide path leading into that dark wood, the smaller cliques had expanded until they rode as a group, joking and occasionally poking fun at one another.

But once they rode into the shadows of the first of the great trees, the stories and laughter faded to uneasy silence. The air among the trees was thick, and it weighed heavy on their shoulders. It was stagnant and pungent with the scent of rotting moss and leaves. On the main road they'd had a soft breeze, but inside the Tenebrae the air did not move.

"It feels...dead," Silex said. "I have felt this sensation before, on a field of battle, when all the killing was done."

"Pleasant as always," Ferox said.

No one laughed this time, and even the young hunter seemed to have no energy or enthusiasm for joking. Og rode with his hand firmly wrapped around the hilt of his axe, and Thaddeus drew his club from the leather thong that held it to his saddle, swinging it in what might have seemed random patterns but was really a calming exercise. A preparation—though he couldn't have said for what.

"Well," Pugius said at last, "this is going to be a cheerful ride."

When Cidivus spurred his mount, it lurched and then trotted forward. Before any of the others could stop him or protest, he'd turned the next corner in the road and was out of sight. They all hurried their pace. The afternoon was falling away to deeper shadows, and they knew they'd have to find a place to make camp soon.

"Cidivus," Silex called loudly. He was clearly annoyed that Cidivus had made a unilateral decision to go ahead of the rest.

There was no answer. Silex and Ferox rounded the bend first, and they pulled up so suddenly that the others nearly plowed into their backs.

Cidivus sat still with a petrified look on his face, his mount motionless in the center of the road. He stared off into the trees on the left, and his hand was on the hilt of his sword, though he hadn't drawn it yet.

"Cidivus," Silex repeated, spurring his mount forward. "What are you doing?"

Cidivus spun. He held a finger to his lips, and his eyes were wide. Silex stopped and followed the motion of Cidivus' hand as he pointed in the direction he'd been staring. Beyond the first line of trees a huge, looming shadow rose toward the sky. It was difficult to make out what it was in the dim light, but what they saw appeared to be a long neck, rising at an angle to end in a huge rounded head.

"What do you suppose that is?" Ferox asked.

Tonitrus, who now sat alongside Silex and Ferox, followed their gaze. He squinted and then relaxed in his saddle. A moment later he started to laugh. Both Silex and Ferox turned toward him, surprised by his frivolous reaction.

Tonitrus paid no attention to either. He shook his reins and walked his mount off the road and into the trees, heading straight for the great shadow. It loomed over him but made no move to attack. When he disappeared into the trees, Og shrugged and followed.

A few moments later they all dismounted in a large clearing. They could just make out a long line of shadowy structures like the first one they'd seen stretching off into the darkness. What they'd first thought to be a neck turned out to be a long, stout wooden pole. At the end, beveled like a great bowl, was the rounded tip of a catapult. The battle engine rested at its uppermost point as if it had been fired, left behind, and forgotten.

"How did you know?" Og asked, stepping up beside Tonitrus, who was examining the catapult with interest.

"They are left over from the last attack of Xamnon," Tonitrus said. "I have heard of them before; it just took me a moment to realize it. These must have been sitting here since they pulled back."

Cidivus, slightly embarrassed, joined them. "There must be a dozen of them," he said. "They stretch out of sight into the forest."

Gobius gazed at the huge cup. At the edge of the clearing sat a pile of boulders. He glanced at them and then back at the siege engine.

"They are still pointed at the city," he said. "I know they are not loaded or armed, but it bothers me to think that they are just sitting here and that someone passing by as we are could load and fire them. Who would be hit? What damage might be done?"

No one spoke for a moment, and then Thaddeus stepped up to the machine and pushed on its wheel. It rocked slightly and then settled back. He turned to Gobius.

"We can turn them," he said. "There should be enough

light left, and if we all pitch in, it won't take long. Consider it a fond farewell to Mavinor."

"I prefer 'until we meet again,'" Cidivus said. "Still, you have a point. I'd hate to be standing in my court and have a stone from one of these weapons crash down on me or one of my servants."

They gathered quickly, splitting into groups to muscle the huge, heavy siege engines around so that they faced into the center of the forest. It was hard work, but it soon became a competition. In the end, the teams led by Og and Thaddeus won the day, tying at four catapults apiece. They had broken into teams of three, and in such a contest, the bigger, stronger men had a decided advantage.

Cedrus, who had quickly found himself the odd man out, wandered back to the first catapult and examined it carefully. It was quite large, an engineering marvel. There were similar siege engines in Mavinor, but none built on such a grand scale.

He glanced at the piles of stones lining the clearing. They were big, but he thought if he put his back into it, he could lift one. He tested the ropes and found them solid and without visible signs of rot. Without further hesitation he grabbed the huge crank, and with all his strength he began to cock the huge machine, hanging onto the lever for dear life as it clicked from notch to notch. The pressure was tremendous, and more than once he thought he might lose his grip and have it slap him to the ground or even break his arm. He concentrated, and at last he felt the solid *thunk* of the last cog dropping into place. He stepped back quickly, but there was no danger. The huge wooden arm was bent back and held by the rope and the locking mechanism. The cup at the end of the arm rested about the height of his chest.

It took him a few moments to regain his breath. He looked over at the others. They were all laughing and wrestling the other catapults around in tight circles. Each group tossed cat-calls at the others, and none had glanced back toward Cedrus or the machine he'd just armed.

The stones were heavier than he'd thought they would be. He studied the pile and chose what seemed to be the smallest. He bent his knees, squatted, and lifted the stone. It came away from the pile easily, and it wasn't until he had it about waist high that he started to feel the strain. He staggered back, nearly stumbled, then spread his legs wide and planted. When he was sure he was not going to fall and be pinned beneath the stone, he turned slowly and began the arduous walk across the small clearing to the catapult.

It took longer than he'd expected, and by the time he finally rolled the stone onto the edge of the wooden cup, his legs felt like jelly. His arms and back were coated in sweat. He tried to put the stone in carefully, not wanting to jostle the mechanism holding the arm, but it was too much for him. The stone rolled over the lip and fell into the cup with a loud *thump*.

Cedrus had lost track of what the others were doing. The effort of first cocking the great battle engine and then carrying the stone across the clearing had taken all of his concentration. When the stone fell into place, the sound caught Gobius' attention, and he turned to see what had caused it.

"What are you doing?" he called, turning and starting back toward Cedrus. "Why would you arm the catapult?"

"Relax," Cedrus said, staring at the stone and fingering the hilt of his sword. "I'm just curious. I've never seen anything like this. Have you? Did they have siege engines on the fishing boats? I just want to see what it can do. It's not aimed at the city."

"But what *is* it aimed at?" Cantos asked, hurrying after Gobius.

Now they were all headed back toward the first catapult, staring at what Cedrus had accomplished.

"What difference does it make?" Cedrus asked. "It's pointed into the forest. Trees? A hillside?"

"It matters *because* you don't know," Gobius said calmly. "Remember when we decided to turn them away from the city? Our thought was, 'What if someone came along and just set one off?' There's no way to know where the stone might land, and no way to know who might be injured or killed. It isn't safe."

"Tell me you are not curious," Cedrus said. His eyes were bright, and his hand was still on the hilt of his sword.

"There will be no launch this day," Tonitrus said, stepping up beside his brother and laying a hand on his shoulder. "Gobius is right. It isn't safe, and it isn't what we are here to do. If there is an enemy waiting for us in that forest, the last thing we want to do is announce our presence with a flying boulder."

Cedrus looked as if he might protest, but his shoulders slumped and he turned away.

"You have no idea," he said, "how hard it was to draw that cursed thing back or how heavy that stone was. If you knew, you would cut the cord yourself."

They all laughed at this.

"Perhaps if you'd set your shoulder to the same task as the rest of us," Og boomed, "you'd have no energy for such foolishness. Come; we have little time to set a proper camp, and I am starving. This has been more work on the first day of our journey than I anticipated in the first week!"

There were murmurs of agreement, and Cedrus reluctantly turned away from the great siege engine, leaving it cocked, loaded, and ready.

"I suppose," he said, "that I will have to satisfy myself with wondering."

"That you will," Silex said. "Now let us make a fire, eat, and get some rest. We need to be back on the road early. I don't think we'll make good time through the forest in the hours of darkness, so we need to take advantage of whatever daylight these trees allow us."

At this, they all set about making a fire, choosing spots for their bedrolls, and quietly getting to know one another. Cantos and Sceptrus spoke more about The Scrolls, with Cantos answering several questions that had always bothered Sceptrus. Gobius bonded with Cedrus, to whom he had taken a liking. He was impressed with Cedrus' zealous attitude, and though he was more than a little impetuous, Gobius knew that Cedrus' heart was in the right place. Nomis and Alphaeus spoke almost exclusively with Thaddeus, who had become a role model and even an idol for both of them. Silex, dutiful leader that he was, was already making plans for the following day. He consulted with both Ferox and Tonitrus; the three of them examined the maps that Olin had provided them. Og and Pugius conversed while Cidivus sat alone, isolated from the rest. When it was time for slumber they set a watch, with Thaddeus claiming the first hour.

Cedrus, sitting on the ground and leaning his back against a tree, stared off toward the line of catapults. They were now dark shadows against the darker night. When Og snored, it came out as a whistle, like the sound of a great stone flying through the air. It caused the young warrior to smile as he sat there and eyed the catapult he had loaded earlier. Looking down, he pulled out of his bag the scarf that Magdala had tied around his arm, a token of remembrance for him during their time apart. He stared intently at its deep, bright red color, clutched it tightly, and held it up to his face. As he inhaled its scent and gave it a soft kiss, he tilted his head back and drifted off to sleep.

Chapter Eight

The next morning they ate a frugal breakfast, packed quickly, and returned to the main road. Though they knew that the sun had risen, they could make out nothing of its light. The road was gray and dingy, cloaked in shadows too thick even to have structure. It was more like twilight than first light, and the weight of it dampened their spirits. They rode in silence, with Silex and Ferox on point and Og, accompanied by Gobius, bringing up the rear. They stretched out, not feeling particularly companionable, and settled in for a long, gloomy day's ride.

"It's not natural," Cantos said. "I mean I've read about this—how the branches of the trees are so thick the sun can't penetrate, but I had no idea it would be so dark."

He never finished the sentence. The silence was sucked from the moment in the updraft from great wings. A cry, hideous and loud but dying in the heavy air before it could echo, drove through them like daggers of ice. In the second they were paralyzed, it struck.

From the trees above a great shape swooped down, gripped Cantos by his shoulders with huge talons, and shot back toward the trees with a powerful sweep of dark wings.

"Get to the middle of the road!" Silex cried. "Form up!"

"What was that?" Nomis cried. "What was it?"

"Shut up and get into the middle of the road," Cidivus said.

More dark shapes plunged from the trees, but they were moving fast. It was difficult to make them out in the shadowy light. Whatever they were, their wingspans were easily fifteen feet.

"It's too dark," Og cursed. "I can't see the things."

"Owls," Ferox said, just loudly enough to be heard. "They are giant owls."

A very human cry from above reminded them of Cantos. They gathered into a clumsy circle in the center of the road. Their mounts were terrified; they held them only with difficulty. Those with more experience had weapons drawn. As the huge owls dove from the trees, they dodged and swung wildly, unable to do anything more than prevent themselves from joining Cantos as victims. The swords of Silex and Tonitrus, the club of Thaddeus, the battle axe of Og…none of these was able to find its mark as the monsters continued to attack relentlessly.

"Cover me!" Sceptrus cried.

Ferox drew his bow. His horse shied, but he held on tightly with his knees and notched an arrow with practiced ease. He saw a shift in the shadows, and let fly, already drawing a second arrow as the first one struck something with a muffled *thump*. There was an unearthly scream of pain and a frantic rustle of feathers, but whatever it was did not fall.

Sceptrus was out of his saddle and moving. Another huge owl dropped from the sky, but he heard it coming. He spun and brought his staff in a whirling arc that caught the creature full in the face. It fluttered, almost fell, then shot back toward the treetops. Sceptrus never slowed. He ran to the base of the tree where Cantos had disappeared, planted the end of his long staff between two roots, and vaulted upward. He caught a low limb with one hand, followed through with the momentum of his leap, and swung up. Then he leaped again, catching a branch higher up, and he disappeared into the dark foliage.

The others tightened their circle. Now that they knew what they were dealing with, it was easier to keep watch. But the owls were big, and they were fast. Their thick feathers were jet-black with occasional dark gray stripes. Rather than making it easier to see, the stripes blurred when they moved, shifting so quickly that they distracted anyone watching them.

"Stay close!" Tonitrus cried. "They can't get at us if we watch one another's back."

All but Ferox heeded his call. The hunter scanned the trees above. He could not see the owls, but he was used to searching shadows for motion.

"Watch my back," he called. Then, glancing up into the trees, he cried "Sceptrus!"

There was no answer. It was as if the trees had swallowed first Cantos and then his would-be savior without a trace. Ferox kept his bow bent and his eyes open. For the moment the owls had ceased their attacks, but none of them believed it would last.

"Owls are territorial," Ferox said, keeping his voice low

but speaking loudly enough that they could all hear him. "If we can get them out of the tree and get back on the road, we should be able to ride beyond their territory. I don't think they'll follow."

"What kind of creatures are they?" Nomis asked. His tones were hushed, as if he thought speaking up would bring the same fate down on him that had befallen Cantos. "I have never seen a bird so large."

"Didn't your parents tell you stories?" Cidivus spat. "These can only be the monsters they call the Surnia. I can't count the number of times my mother's helper told me that if I didn't get into bed and keep quiet, the Surnia would sweep from the sky and carry me off to the Tenebrae. I thought it was just a fairy tale, but apparently that's not the case."

"My parents weren't fond of frightening me," Nomis replied. "Particularly at bedtime."

Cidivus spat again and scanned the treetops. All of them remained in a tight formation as they faced their first major test in the quest for the Medallion.

As they grouped themselves and watched the sky, trying desperately to pierce the darkness overhead and locate their attackers, Sceptrus climbed. He swung up easily, remembering the trees he had climbed as a young man and the hours he had spent in training with the staff. As he rose, he used his weapon, ramming the end into the crook of a branch to lever himself up to the next perch.

He heard the rustle and cry of one of the great birds above. The branches he climbed were too close together to allow the creature to dive in after him. He kept as close to the trunk as he could, and without thinking about what he was doing he continued to climb.

"Cantos?" he cried. "Cantos? Can you hear me?"

"Yes! Yes," came the frantic reply. "Yes, I can hear you."

There was the sound of a struggle above, followed by a crash of leaves and branches. Something dropped, splayed out over the branch to Sceptrus' left. He glanced, saw with sudden clarity that it was Cantos, and he moved. He balanced on the branch, took a step away from the trunk, and reached to steady the scribe before he fell to his death.

It was the opening the Surnia had been waiting for. With cunning beyond what Sceptrus had given it credit for, the bird had baited him. It lunged, huge beak driving like the twin blades of giant swords. Sceptrus caught the attack out of the corner of his eye. Instead of falling back, he spun his staff and drove it up tip first into the great owl's maw. He pressed down into the branch beneath him, trusting his balance, and put his strength into the strike. He felt the wood bite deep as the creature scrambled back, and he pursued. He drove the staff into the bird's throat and then yanked it back. Turning to where Cantos clung to the branch like a drowning rat, Sceptrus held out his hand.

"For The Author's sake," he cried. "Take my hand. You have to get in close to the trunk."

At first it seemed that the scribe would not be able to comply. He clung to the branch with a death grip. Then the Surnia cried in pain and rage, and he moved. He took Sceptrus' hand, stood, and lunged toward the trunk of the tree, just as something dark and swift shot past, its talons gouging huge chunks out of the branch where he'd lain moments before. The branch shook, and only Sceptrus' tight grip in dragging Cantos back toward the trunk saved them from falling.

"We have to get down fast," Sceptrus said. "Can you climb?"

"I have no idea," Cantos said.

"Well it's a good time to find out," Sceptrus said. "Go. Stay as close to the trunk as you can. I'll stay just above you. If it returns or tries to shake us free, I'll stop it."

Cantos glanced down. He could see nothing through the murky shadows beyond the next branch, but he gathered his courage. He swung around, dropped toward the next branch, and caught the one he stood on with both hands. There was a moment of imbalance, and then he righted himself. Taking no time to think about it, he repeated the process, dropping farther into the shadows.

At that moment the Surnia dove, but Sceptrus was waiting for it. As it dropped toward where Cantos scrabbled down the tree, Sceptrus leaped. He whipped the staff around the great bird's neck, and as it snapped around, he gripped it on the other end, putting a choke hold on the Surnia that sent it careening away from the tree, fluttering madly and dropping rapidly.

The creature screamed in surprise and fury. Sceptrus wrapped his legs around it and yanked back on his staff. No matter how it struggled, it could not gain altitude. Sceptrus continued his descent, pressing his body as tightly against the trunk and branches of the tree as he possibly could.

"Here!" Tonitrus cried. "Cantos, over here!"

Cantos glanced upward. He could see nothing, but he heard the struggle going on in the air above. He remembered the sickening sensation in his stomach as the great owl lifted him from his saddle. He remembered the terror, and he froze for a moment. Then he dashed across the clearing toward the ring of horses. He kept his head down and his legs churning. It would do no good to watch over his shoulder...if one of the great birds dove at him, he would be caught. He had no weapon to stop it. His one chance was to make it over to the horses, get back into the saddle, and draw the sword he only vaguely knew how to use, trusting in the others to guard his back.

There was another cry from above, and the shadow of the bird with Sceptrus astride careened into view. It dove at an odd angle, apparently unable to pull out of it, and Sceptrus clung with all his might. A second cry sounded higher up, but as that bird dropped, drawing a bead on Sceptrus, Ferox took aim and fired. This time he knew where the bird would be, and his shot was true. It drove into the Surnia's breast. The creature tumbled back, flapped wildly once, and dropped like a stone.

Ferox already had another arrow notched.

"Sceptrus!" he cried. "Jump!"

Sceptrus released his hold on one end of the staff, whipped it back around, and drove his boots into the owl's back. He dropped in an arc to the road, rolled in a quick somersault, and was back on his feet, weapon at the ready.

Ferox let the arrow fly. This time his shot embedded itself in the Surnia's eye. It screamed and whirled out of control. The shot wasn't immediately fatal—the beast's strength was incredible. It slammed into trees, tried to regain its equilibrium, and struck out at anything it saw with its good eye. Sensing an opening, Og slid off his warhorse and dropped to the ground. He ran at the creature with a roar, his great axe lifted high. The Surnia heard him and spun, snapping out with its beak, but Og charged fearlessly. He swung the axe in a high arc and caught the Surnia, even as it attacked, driving his blade into and through its skull.

"To the horses," Silex cried.

Cantos fumbled his way into his saddle, and Sceptrus sprinted quickly to his own mount. Og dragged his axe free of the Surnia's corpse. He stood for a moment, looking down at it, and then turned to join the others.

"Get in the saddle and keep moving," Silex called out. "Ferox, do what you can to cover us. Sceptrus, ride near Cantos."

They drew into a tight formation and started down the road again. They heard rustling overhead, but no more of the birds attacked. There was a final piercing cry, but none of them looked back. As they rounded the next bend the road opened up a little, and they spurred their mounts to greater speed.

They didn't stop until after midday, when the clearing and the Surnia were far behind. Silex called a halt when he saw Cantos leaning over into the neck of his horse as if ready to pass out. His arms had been bruised and scarred by the talons of the owl that had attacked him. His body was torn and scraped from descending the tree.

They found a small clearing with a tight overhead cover of branches and tucked their horses in underneath. After the animals had been brushed and fed, they ate another small meal, conserving their supplies.

Cantos lay on the ground and closed his eyes as Sceptrus came and sat beside him. Cantos heard him and opened his eyes.

"Thank you," he said. "You saved my life."

"You'd have done it for me," Sceptrus said, grinning.

Cantos shook his head. "Would and could are two very different words, my friend. I owe you one, and don't think I'll be quick to forget it."

"Get some rest," Sceptrus said. "You're going to need it."

Cantos groaned and closed his eyes again. Sceptrus leaned against a tree and scanned the branches overhead.

"And just think," Pugius said, dropping down beside them. "It's only the second day."

Chapter Nine

The next morning they were back in the saddle and on the road. This time they kept a tighter formation, with Silex and Ferox riding point, Thaddeus and Og watching the rear, and the others between. Each watched the trees to either side of the road more carefully, glancing up nervously from time to time. There was no further sign of the Surnia, but none of them—least of all Cantos—felt comfortable beneath that sun-blotting mass of foliage.

As they rode farther into the Tenebrae, the shadows deepened. The road was clear, but it had not been traveled for a long time. The silence was eerie, and it felt wrong somehow to break it, so they rode quietly, making slow but steady progress. It was dark, but not so dark that they couldn't see or required a torch. In some way a grayish illumination filtered through the trees and branches, differentiating day from night by the slightest of margins.

Eventually the ground to the right of the road began sloping upward. What had been flat forest on both sides gave way to rocky outcroppings as the road wound its way around a small mountain. To the left, the forest remained as thick and impenetrable as ever. On the right, they passed stone cliff walls that were peppered with batches of scrub and roots. Stones had rolled into the road over time, dropping from the heights above, but no one was there to clear them away. The thirteen picked their way through the rubble carefully.

With the peak of the mountain breaking through the trees, there was a little more light than what the thirteen had experienced thus far in the Tenebrae. The top of the mountain was overgrown with bent, scraggly versions of the trees surrounding them. There was less moisture in the stony soil to sustain them, so their branches were unable to stretch out over the entire road. The thirteen were grateful for the light but only vaguely interested in the mountains themselves.

Then Silex rounded a corner and slowed, holding up his hand. His mount shuffled a few steps to the side, and Ferox drew up beside him.

"What is it?" Tonitrus called out.

"I'm not sure yet," Silex replied. "There's an opening in the rock here—not a cave exactly, but larger."

Slowly they all rode around and stopped in the center of the road. At this point the cliffs were a good fifty yards removed from the main path. A trail lined with rounded stones led away from the road and ended at a dark, yawning doorway in the side of the mountain. There were carvings in the stone to either side, but there was no evidence that there'd ever been an actual door closing the entrance. It was difficult to tell whether the opening was natural and merely decorated by men who'd found it thus or if it had been cut and widened, shaped into something more.

"What manner of man would choose such a place to live?" Sceptrus asked. "The forest is bad enough, but this?"

"It's not necessarily anyone's home," Cantos said. "It's most likely a place where men have come to worship or to camp on long hunts. Without reading the inscriptions it's impossible to know for certain. It's not listed on any of the maps. There is something mystical here, though, something very old."

They all felt it. Something ominous and powerful hung in the air around the dark portal they faced. There was no sign that anyone had walked the trail between that black hole and the road in recent times, but the carvings were enough evidence for them that someone had once called the place home—or at the very least had found reasons to visit frequently.

Silex turned to Cantos.

"Can you translate the symbols? Can you tell us who might have created this place or what its purpose might have been?"

Cantos dismounted and handed the reins of his horse to Ferox. He and Silex walked down the path slowly, studying the placement of the stones. When they reached the entrance to the cavern, Cantos stepped to one side, reached out, and traced the symbols with one finger. His brow wrinkled in concentration, and he worked at the letters, brushing aside dirt and dust carefully.

"It's very old," he said at last. "I can't say for sure. The language is familiar, but the characters are archaic. I can't be certain what it says."

"Surely you have some idea?" Tonitrus said. He too dropped from the saddle to the road and approached the cavern. "It's right off the main road. There must be some way to figure out why it was significant."

"I can make out only a few words," Cantos said. "This here," he rubbed at a faded sequence of lines, "appears to refer to a test or a trial. There is another word that I believe might be *sabre*, but too much of it has worn away over the years."

Thaddeus snorted.

"It's a hole in a mountain," he said. "This isn't the Northern Mountains, and it isn't our concern. We have a purpose, and it awaits us farther down this road. We should ignore this cavern and move on."

"Don't be so hasty, my friend," Cidivus said, dropping from his saddle and approaching the cavern's entrance. "This was left here for a reason. How can we know that something we are meant to have isn't secreted away inside, waiting for us to find? Are you ready to take that chance?"

"I am," Thaddeus said flatly. "We are wasting time."

"I want to see what's inside," Cidivus said. "It won't take long to have a quick look, and then we can be on our way."

Silex was hesitant to approve at first, but then he acquiesced to Cidivus' wish.

"It's as good a place as any to rest," he said. "There's more light here than most of the other clearings we've passed. I have no objection to your peering inside the cave, but don't be long. Thaddeus is right that we need to be back on the road as quickly as we can."

They tied the horses in the clearing. Og and Thaddeus set about feeding the animals, and Ferox slipped into the trees in search of water or game, if there was any to be found. Cidivus stood before the cavern's entrance and glanced over his shoulder.

"Anyone care to join me?" he asked.

Nomis stepped forward, as did Cedrus.

"You should not go in there," Tonitrus said. His words were directed at the group, but everyone knew they were meant for Cedrus, who flushed with irritation.

"I am not frightened of a cave," Cedrus said.

"Wait," Nomis said. He followed Ferox into the forest but returned only a moment later. He held a long branch and a handful of twigs. He carried this to his horse, fumbled in his pack for a moment, and brought out a strip of linen embedded with wax. He used this to wrap the kindling onto the end of his improvised torch. A moment later he'd pulled out his flint and fanned the torch to flickering life.

"We won't find anything inside if we can't see," he said with a shrug.

Cidivus nodded, and Cedrus grinned. Before anyone else could offer an opinion or an objection, the three stepped into the shadows and disappeared from sight.

Tonitrus was irritated at Cedrus but didn't go in after him lest he embarrass his brother by making him feel as if he needed a chaperone. Instead he strode to the cave entrance and took a seat to one side, his back against the wall. Og followed suit, choosing the opposite side of the doorway. After a moment they all settled down in one fashion or another to wait and see what if anything was to be found in the cavern. For a few moments they could hear the echoes of voices from what seemed a great distance, and then the small clearing fell silent.

About twenty minutes later, Ferox returned with several dark-furred hares slung over his shoulder.

"Dinner, I think," he said, dropping his small load. "The

pickings are not good around here, and they spook easily. Makes me wonder who or what else hunts these woods."

"Let's hope we don't find out," Cantos said. "The Surnia were enough for me."

"I'd wager we'll see our share of strange things and difficult enemies before we're done," Pugius said. He was seated against a rounded stone, tossing his knives across the road at a knot in one of the trees on the far side. The handles of the blades stuck out from the bark in a tight group. "It would almost be a disappointment if the greatest challenge we faced was owls."

"Speak for yourself," Cantos said. He turned to say more, but just then a bloodcurdling cry rose from the mouth of the cavern, followed by a second, deeper shout, and the pounding of footsteps on stone. Tonitrus and Og were on their feet in seconds, turning toward the cavern. As they drew their weapons, Nomis dove through into the light, stumbling and sprawling headlong. Cedrus was right on his heels, though he managed to keep his feet. Moments later, pale as chalk and walking slowly, as if in a daze, Cidivus stepped through the opening and staggered. He might have fallen, but Og reached out and gripped his arm, steadying him.

Tonitrus spun across the entrance, sword in hand, waiting for whatever might have been chasing them. But nothing happened. Nothing came racing out of the shadows; there was no sound at all from the cavern. After a moment he glanced hesitantly over his shoulder. Nomis, who had risen, stood very still. Cedrus shook his head as if trying to clear it of some sort of cobweb. Cidivus had broken free of Og and wandered across the road to stand and stare off into the trees.

"What happened?" Silex asked. He went to Nomis and

put his hands on the younger man's shoulders, shaking him gently. "What did you see?"

Nomis only shook his head. His eyes were clear again, and he was steady on his feet. Cedrus was the same, though he glanced nervously back at the doorway every few seconds.

"What is in there?" Tonitrus demanded, still unwilling to give up his post at the dark entrance to the cave. "What is following you? I told you not to go in!"

Cidivus turned and walked back across the road.

"You are wasting your time," he said. "There is nothing following us. No one is going to charge out of the shadows. We should move on."

"That's not an answer," Pugius observed. He whipped his arm forward and sent the knife he held flipping across the road. It came to a quivering halt in the center of the now pockmarked knothole.

"It's the only answer I'm giving you," Cidivus snapped. "I suspect you'll get the same out of those other two. I am not sure what happened, exactly, in that cave, but I can tell you that I have no words to describe it, and if I did have those words, I would keep them to myself. It was…very private."

Thaddeus studied Cidivus for a long moment and then shrugged.

"I think we should be on the road. We have wasted too much time here already."

"Agreed," Silex said. "We still have several hours of what passes for daylight here. I don't know what happened to you three in that cave, and I'm not certain that I want to know. But I do know that I don't want to be making camp anywhere near it."

There was no argument to this, so they mounted and hit

the trail. Ferox bagged the hares quickly, filling a small game sack, and slung them from his pommel.

"At least," he said, kicking his heels into his horse's flanks and taking point again, "we'll eat well tonight."

As the others followed him onto the road and away from the strange cavern, Tonitrus pulled his brother off to the side for a moment.

"That is the first and last time on this quest that I will be letting you out of my sight," he said to Cedrus. The young man stood silent with a sheepish look on his face as Tonitrus motioned for him to go ahead and join the others.

Cidivus brought up the rear. He sat in the center of the road, staring at the dark entrance. The rest were out of sight before he started forward. He continued for a while at a trot. It wasn't until Thaddeus dropped back to see what was keeping him that Cidivus finally picked up his pace, staring one last time in the direction of the cavern before turning away.

Chapter Ten

After the cavern, the cliffs to their right had slowly dropped away, sloping down to gentler, rolling hills. The road spun away into the deeper forest, and once again their light was all but cut off. Even the fire Ferox made to cook the hares could do no more than create a small circle of brightness in that huge pit of shadow. They dined in silence and slept early. Before the dim light had seeped into their camp to compete with the glowing coals of the fire, the thirteen were up and packing their saddlebags.

They broke camp and rode out in silence. By midday the nature of the trees had shifted. The branches were more spare, and the light filtering in was slightly brighter. It cheered their spirits, and by the time they were ready to stop and eat, Nomis and Cedrus were joking again.

The place they chose to stop was a large clearing in which several trees had been felled. As Og admired the style and the economy of the cuts, noting how incredibly clean they were, there was a loud flapping noise. All of them dove for cover.

The attack of the Surnia still haunted them, and they scanned the clearing and the sky overhead, weapons drawn.

But there was no invasion of dark forms from above, just a piercing cry that caused their ears to vibrate. As they all watched from whatever cover they'd found, a large black raven dropped down on to the stump of one of the fallen trees. It ruffled its feathers and turned its head in a slow semicircle.

"See you," it croaked. "See you all."

At first no one moved. The notion of a talking bird was ludicrous, and despite what they'd already encountered in the Tenebrae, they weren't ready to accept it. Finally, Og rose from where he'd dropped behind a fallen log. The big man brushed leaves and grass from himself in disgust and started inching closer toward the raven.

The bird watched him approaching. It ruffled the feathers on one wing again and poked its beak in beneath it, grooming itself and ignoring Og.

Around the clearing, the others stood and approached slowly. None of them was in a hurry to get too close to this new apparition, whatever it was.

"Did it really talk?" Sceptrus asked.

"Unless we all share some strange form of madness," Cantos said, "it did. Birds can be trained to speak. I've heard of hunters in Xamnon who slit the tongues of such creatures, allowing them to mimic speech. It's no more than a parlor trick."

The raven cocked its head and glanced over at the scribe.

"Parlor trick?" it crowed. "No tricks."

They all grew still once more, amazed at what they were seeing and hearing.

Og was still the closest of them.

"Maybe I should see," he said, "if it is able to talk with its head separated from its shoulders."

He pulled his axe and swung it experimentally through the air. The raven glared at him but showed no fear.

"Big," it said. "Big man, little bird. Going to hurt me? Going to make feathers fly?"

It was more than Og could stand. The big man rushed the stump, axe drawn back for a huge swing. The blade whistled through the air.

"Wait," Silex called out. "We don't know what it is or where it came from."

It was too late. Og's blade ripped through the spot where the bird's neck waited. Only the raven wasn't there. It launched in a fluid dive to the right, wove around another stump, and perched itself on top.

"Slow!" it croaked. "Too big, too slow. Still talking."

Og's axe, finding only empty air instead of its chosen target, had whistled around and spun him off balance. He staggered, regained his equilibrium, and turned back with a snarl. Og then lurched toward the raven's new roost with a roar. This time he held his swing, keeping his eye on the target. Og and the raven glared at one another as the big man circled the trunk. The raven lifted one foot and then the other, tracking its attacker cautiously.

"Big," it observed, "and slow."

Og lost control and lunged forward. This time he spun his axe in such a way so as to fool the raven, leaving it unsure of which direction the swing was going to come from. With a quick flick of his wrist he lashed out with an uppercut swing from right to left. The raven screeched in fear but managed to dodge the huge battle axe at the last second. Og then followed up quickly with an overhead swing, but he was slightly off, and the axe buried itself in the tree trunk. The shock of that strike dislodged the flailing bird, and it dropped to the ground flat on its back.

"Yes!" Og cried. He quickly removed his weapon from the stump, but before he could raise his battle axe to deal the raven a lethal blow, the solid *thunk* of an arrow striking the tree trunk drew him up short. They all spun to see where the arrow had come from, but they stopped, dumbfounded, for the second time in only a few short moments. Even Og seemed to have forgotten the flopping raven.

Across the clearing stood what might have been a man, except that it was not. The creature was tall and slender. Wings that sprouted from its shoulders glittered in the sunlight. Its eyes were so blue that they glinted like chips of ice or shards broken from the sky, even from across the clearing. It held a bow loosely in one hand, and a quiver of arrows was clearly visible poking up between its wings in back.

"Who," Og said, trying to control his voice, "or what… are you?"

The others moved up beside and around Og. They walked slowly, as if afraid a quick motion might startle the being confronting them. Ferox, his own bow in hand, scanned the trees behind and to either side, trying to ascertain if the newcomer was alone.

"I am Orius, leader of the Legans. I cannot allow you to harm the raven."

Og stared at Orius and then turned to meet Silex's gaze. As he turned, three more of the creatures, two male and one female, stepped from the forest. Each held two swords, one in each hand. They were spread out along the edge of the clearing, and though they made no move to attack, there was no doubt that their position was strategic.

Og lifted his battle axe again, but Silex had reached him at last.

"Wait," he said in a low voice. "We don't know who they are or what they want. We can't go attacking everything that appears along the road, and I for one would at least like to know the odds of winning a battle before joining it."

Og shrugged him off, and for a moment it looked as if he might attack regardless of what the others said or did. Then with an effort of will he controlled his anger. Silex stepped in front of him and stood, gazing at Orius.

"We are travelers, making our way through the Tenebrae," he said. "We seek no trouble and mean no harm."

"Your actions speak differently," Orius replied calmly. "Your large friend offered harm to one of nature's creatures without provocation."

"Without provocation?" Og retorted.

"It is only a bird," Orius replied. "It offered only words. That is not sufficient reason for an attack. You would have ended its life...why? Because it insulted you?"

Og started to speak, but then he bit back the words and lowered his eyes. He could think of nothing to say that would not make him sound ridiculous. The raven had hopped back up onto the stump and stared at him, but Og paid no attention to it.

"Why have you come?" Silex asked.

"We protect the natural order," Orius said. "It is our duty to defend The Author's creation and to offer succor to creatures in need. We have tracked your progress for some time but until now have seen no need to interfere. The Surnia attacked you, so you acted in self-defense."

"I didn't see you jumping in to prevent the Surnia attack on our party," Tonitrus observed. "Or are we not considered a part of nature?"

"We are commissioned by The Author to protect only nature," replied Orius, "and to refrain from intervening in human affairs. I'm afraid that it is not our role to protect you as you travel through the forest." He then continued to address the group, and the calm tone of his voice never shifted.

"Regarding the Surnia, you traveled through their home. They attacked for food and to protect their territory. You successfully defended yourselves. That is the natural order. But what was about to happen here," he indicated the raven, who sat on the stump glaring at Og, "was not a part of the natural order. The bird cannot help its nature."

"It talks," Og said. His voice sounded almost petulant, but no one laughed. "*That* is not natural."

"It talks, yes," Orius replied. "Perhaps this is not natural in the land from which you traveled, but here, nature has its own rules. We are chosen to uphold nature's rules, wherever and whatever they may be."

"We understand," Silex said. "Again, allow me to state that we mean no harm and seek no trouble."

"Nor shall you have it," Orius replied, "but we cannot allow harm to come to the raven."

Silex placed a hand on Og's shoulder.

"No harm will come to the bird. We were ignorant of your race and your purpose. We have a purpose of our own, prophesied by The Author Himself and passed to us. We require only passage."

"The roads of the Tenebrae are open to all travelers," Orius replied. "If you pass through without causing harm to the forest, we will have no trouble."

"What about hunting?" Ferox asked. "I have already taken hares and will require other game as we pass through."

"It is the natural inclination of man to hunt for sustenance," Orius replied. "This is a part of the natural order and is thus permissible as far as we're concerned."

Og eyed the raven. It was obvious he'd like nothing better than to take a sudden swipe at it, but he kept his peace.

"Then," Silex said, "we are well met."

Orius inclined his head and then gestured at his companions.

"These are my fellow Legans," he said. Orius introduced them as Chaelim, Apteris, and Volara. "They aid me in protecting nature from harm and intrusion. We may meet again before you pass out of the Tenebrae or maybe even somewhere else during your quest. I believe that your intentions are honorable, but you must refrain from unprovoked attacks on nature during your journey. We will watch over you."

"I don't take well to threats," Silex replied. "Know that we will not hesitate to do whatever it takes to see us through this quest. Our success is vital to our king and our homeland, and we will not be deterred."

"I do not mean to issue threats. We have no issue with your quest," Orius assured him. "We seek only to serve and protect nature. That is my only reason for watching you during your journey. I wish you luck and bid you farewell, warriors of Mavinor."

Without another word, Orius turned and melted back into the trees. Silex turned, but before he could catch their movement, the others followed. Now the thirteen stood alone in the odd little clearing along with the raven, which remained on its stump, staring at them.

"Is there no place in this forest that a man can just sit and rest?" Og asked.

"Big, slow, and tired," the raven said, cocking its head to the side.

"Let it be," Silex said. "We need to stop pitting ourselves against the Tenebrae so single-mindedly. The Surnia attack has us on edge, and we go for our weapons now before we have fully assessed the situation."

"It's just a bird," Og growled.

"Is it?" Gobius asked, stepping closer to the raven and eyeing it curiously. "If so, then those I've encountered previously have been singularly uncommunicative. It doesn't seem to be mocking us."

"Mocking him," the bird said, cocking his head toward Og again.

Gobius laughed. "Fair enough," he said.

The bird turned its attention to Gobius. It watched him for a moment and then croaked a final word.

"Friend?"

Gobius nodded, but before he or any of the thirteen could reply, the bird launched itself into the air and shot up through the trees. It circled them once and then, as quickly as it had appeared, it was gone.

"I've had enough of this place," Tonitrus said. "I say we get back on the road. If the maps we have seen are accurate, we should be nearing the far edge of the Tenebrae, and I—for one—will not be sorry to see it falling away behind us."

"Agreed," Silex said. "They don't seem to be posing a threat, but I don't much like the notion of these strange winged guardians watching us from the shadows. The sooner we get out from under these trees the better."

"Where did those things come from?" Cidivus asked.

"The Author," Cantos replied. "It is written in The Scrolls that The Author created winged beings to watch over nature since the beginning of time. Though their names are not mentioned, I can only surmise that the Legans are the ones appointed with that task."

"Then you've heard of them before," Cedrus said.

"Yes," Cantos replied. "But trust me when I say that I was no less shocked to see them than the rest of you. I've told you before that we need to be ready for the extraordinary, but nothing could have possibly prepared us for that encounter."

They gathered their things and climbed back into the saddle. None of them was able to do so without scanning the trees on all sides. Each felt the weight of unseen eyes and the underlying malice of the forest itself. Even the things that seemed good were warped in ways that were impossible to determine.

They rode off at a good pace, moving down the road in silence. None spoke; Og in particular sulked. There were no more attacks or strange encounters. As it had darkened on their way in, the way became lighter as they neared the far edge of the Tenebrae. Even their horses sensed it. They had more spring in their step, and they were filled with a nervous energy as if sensing the impending escape from the gloom and shadows.

When the trees finally thinned and they broke out into the open, they stopped, one after the other, until they stood crossing the road in one long, straight line. The path through the Tenebrae ended abruptly at the foot of a long, narrow bridge that stretched into the distance. Beneath it the ground dropped away so suddenly and so completely that from where they stood they could not see the bottom. Misty clouds hung low over the far end of the bridge, obscuring it from sight. It was as if their trail led into space and disappeared.

The bridge itself was constructed of wood and ropes. It looked sturdy enough, but at the same time it was obvious that it would sway, and there was no way to tell what condition it might be in closer to the middle.

"The Black Hollow," Cantos said softly.

Silex turned to him.

"You know of this?" he asked.

"I do," Cantos said. "The bridge has been here a very long time. When Haggiselm passed this way, the bridge spanned the Black Hollow, and he crossed it. But I expected that the bridge would be more solid and that the distance across would not be so great."

"It's like riding into a dream," said Pugius.

"Or," said Cantos, "into a nightmare."

They fell silent as they stared out across the void. Nomis and Alphaeus shivered. They turned and glanced back the way they'd come, as if they were considering whether they really wanted to leave the Tenebrae behind. Thaddeus rode up alongside them, meaning to comfort the two younger and less-experienced soldiers whom he had decided to watch over throughout the journey.

Somewhere in the forest a raven cried. The bridge beckoned like a doorway into another world. All of the thirteen gazed in wonder toward the other side of the Black Hollow, not knowing whether they could make it across or what dangers awaited them on the other side. But what they did know was that there was no turning back. Having been chosen by King Onestus and called by The Author Himself to complete this task, they could only go forward, trusting their fate to that of divine providence.

Chapter Eleven

The bridge that stretched across the Black Hollow bowed in the center and swung gently in the breeze. It was wide enough for several men to walk abreast, easily wide enough to accommodate a horse. The problem was in getting the animals to chance the shaky footing.

"Are you sure there's no other way across?" Tonitrus asked. "Maybe if we follow the rim we'll find a path that winds down and back up the far side?"

He started forward to study the cliff and the bridge. Tonitrus went only a couple of steps before his mount reared suddenly, forcing him to grip the reins more tightly. The animal fought him, and he barely managed to remain seated, whirling first one way and then the other to scan the area. There was no way to see what lay beneath in the Black Hollow. As Tonitrus stared down into the abyss, there was nothing to be seen but complete and utter darkness.

Then, as he lifted his gaze back up at the bridge, he saw them. Wrapped around the supports on the near side that they gripped with long, sinuous coils were several snakes. They were rather large and clearly not at all daunted by the sight of men and horses. Immediately they reared up, meeting his gaze coldly and swaying from side to side. He drew his sword and backed his mount slowly, keeping a wary eye on the serpent creatures.

"Look out!" Cedrus cried. He drew his own weapon and started forward.

"Hold!" Silex yelled. "Hold back."

Cedrus ignored Silex and continued moving, not willing to leave his brother to face the creatures alone. Tonitrus, who had continued to back away slowly, heard the clank of Cedrus' weapon and glanced over his shoulder.

"Stay behind me, brother," he said. The others drew their weapons and began to step forward as well.

"Wait," Silex said. He rode forward until he was even with Tonitrus. "We have only just agreed not to dive into every new situation with weapons drawn. I don't want to break that vow before the end of the day it was made. These creatures have made no effort to attack or even obstruct us as of yet."

"But," Tonitrus said, "they're snakes."

"I beg your pardon?" a voice said.

The voice was low and sibilant. It wasn't a hiss exactly, but it wasn't human either. It vibrated and teased around human tones, coherent, but barely. It sounded absolutely foreign to the thirteen, and it froze them in their saddles.

The creature on the right side of the bridge coiled up its post so that it wove back and forth a good three feet above the top and on eye level with Silex.

"We are not snakes," it said.

Silex, who watched the creature carefully, was close

enough to see the truth of its statement. Their bodies were long and serpentine. They had fangs, but their jaws were also lined with razor-sharp teeth not found in snakes. They appeared to be intended for tearing meat or ripping flesh. Their eyes glittered, bright with intelligence. The creatures also seemed to have a hood of sorts that fanned out, making them look even larger than they already were. Unlike the others, the one that spoke had two horns emerging from the top of its head.

"What…who…are you, then?" Silex asked.

"I am Cerastes," the creature said. "We, the Colubri, inhabit the Tenebrae. We are many, and we watch the roads carefully. We have known of you and your quest from the moment you entered the forest.

"Our kind has lived in this forest and near this bridge for the entire length of our existence. It is not often that we encounter humans, and we need to be wary of their presence. Surely you understand why we must watch our territory and keep a close eye on intruders."

Silex nodded. He made no move to get closer to the thing, and though he kept his tones low and calm, he studied Cerastes carefully. The Colubri were varied in size, with some no longer than a man's arm and others stretching ten to twelve feet in length. At their widest point, the bigger ones could be as thick as a man's leg. Their coloration varied but ran to the colors of the forest. If they had not been waiting, wrapped around the bridge, then they would have been virtually impossible to spot against the backdrop of the Tenebrae. The camouflage would have allowed the Colubri to take the thirteen by complete surprise, just as the Surnia had done earlier.

"We seek to cause no trouble," Silex said. "My companions and I simply need to reach the far side of the hollow. We are looking for another way—perhaps a path that leads down through the valley below? The bridge seems unsafe for travel by horseback."

"It is a strong bridge," Cerastes said. "It is also a very old bridge. Many travelers have crossed over it to the road beyond. It is the only way. If you wish to cross the Black Hollow, then you must use the bridge."

"There is no way down into the hollow?" Tonitrus asked, cutting in. "No road that leads to the bottom that could be traveled on horseback?"

"You might make it to the bottom," Cerastes replied. "There are trails. Many have tried before you. If you enter that dark place, however, you will not make it up the far side. The valley is not empty—it is the home of The Beast. She sleeps, and it would not be wise to wake her. The Beast will never allow you passage, and strong as you might be, you cannot kill her. The Black Hollow belongs to her, and none have ever passed."

"Beast?" Silex asked. He turned back to Cantos. "Have you heard of such a thing?"

Cantos did not ride closer. He stared openly at the creatures on the bridge, unable to look away, and he was trembling in his saddle. Silex waited only a moment before he called out more sharply.

"Cantos!"

The scribe turned slowly, his gaze lingering on Cerastes and finally snapping up to stare openly at Silex.

"Sorry. I am afraid of snakes. I have been since I was a

child." He turned back to Cerastes for a second and said, "I know you are not actually snakes, so please accept my apologies." Then he proceeded to answer Silex's question.

"I have heard of a great evil in the Black Hollow. But what I have heard was not in any history. It is mentioned in legends and in song. In all the old stories, heroes crossed a bridge. It is as Cerastes says. None has ever entered the Black Hollow and lived, or if they did, they did not return to tell the tale."

"It looks safe enough," Cidivus said. He pointedly ignored the Colubri and Silex as well, riding up to the bridge as if he owned it—or as if he should.

"It is wider by twice than the road we've been on since we entered this seemingly forsaken forest. I say we bid our scaly friends farewell and cross over."

Cerastes stared intently at Cidivus as Silex held up a hand to wave him back.

"Wait, Cidivus," he said. Silex then turned toward Cerastes. "I am glad for your counsel, but if you have been aware of our presence since we entered the Tenebrae—why do you appear to us only now?"

"Most travelers on this road ask themselves the same questions you have when they arrive at this bridge," replied Cerastes. "Many do not get the counsel we have provided, and still more have chosen to ride through the Black Hollow rather than heed our warning. I wanted to be certain that you knew the danger waiting below and that you would at least be aware of what lies down there before moving ahead. It is what we do. We aid travelers."

Silex met the creature's gaze levelly. He wanted to believe that Cerastes was sincere, but something inside told him it would be a mistake to do so. Still, he didn't want to say or do anything to antagonize the Colubri.

"Thank you, Cerastes," Silex said in a dubious tone. "We need only safe passage. I would ask that you and the Colubri back away from the bridge. I believe that the bridge offers enough for our horses to fear without the necessity of passing between you and your companions. I wouldn't want them to be any more frightened than they already are."

Cerastes made a sound that might have been a susurrus laugh or even a hiss of irritation. He nodded his head, his mouthful of teeth flashing in the dim light, and then he unwound himself from the support post and dropped heavily to the ground. His companion did the same on the other side. Suddenly there was motion all around them, and their horses shied away again. The Colubri made no move to approach. Instead, they pulled back away from the path and the bridge.

They didn't exactly slither. Their head remained erect, and they glided. Their bodies bunched in the center, raised, and then rolled forward in slow loops. The thirteen sat still, watching, until the serpentine creatures turned and gathered.

"I wish you a safe trip," Cerastes said. Despite his lack of the proper frame for the motion, he pulled off a semblance of a bow. Nothing about his voice, his words, or his actions put the thirteen at ease. There was no expression, no emotion. The gesture might well have been made by a creature carved of stone.

"How do we get the horses across?" Tonitrus asked. "The bridge isn't steady. I don't think they will stand for it."

"For a group of warriors," Cidivus said, barely able to contain his arrogance, "you are remarkably cautious."

He turned without another word and urged his mount toward the bridge. The black pranced the first few steps, uneasy, but then stepped onto the bridge.

"You should walk the animal," Tonitrus called. "You are risking both your lives."

Cidivus ignored Tonitrus and started across the bridge. The black was sure-footed, and though the structure swayed from side to side, the animal kept up a steady pace. There was no strain on the bridge—it was constructed to hold the weight. They all watched, tense in their saddles, as Cidivus rode expertly across. It seemed he would make it without incident, but at about the two-thirds point an errant breeze kicked up and the swaying motion increased. Silex shook his head, annoyed once again by Cidivus' arrogance and his insistence on always being first. This time he thought for sure that it would cost him dearly. Cidivus' fate was hanging in the balance over the Black Hollow, and there was nothing that any of the thirteen could do about it.

"Stay still," Tonitrus cried. "Wait for the wind to die down."

Cidivus either did not hear or did not heed the advice. He dug in his heels and sent his mount lurching toward the far side of the hollow. At first it seemed he'd be fine. Then, as Cidivus dragged cruelly on the reins, trying to force the animal against its will, the black stumbled. It looked as if it would go down, and Cidivus, as if noticing the drop off to either side, suddenly clutched the animal's mane and held on for dear life.

The horse slid and shuffled to the side, fighting for footing. Cidivus folded down over its body, still clutching tightly. Tonitrus dropped from his saddle and headed for the bridge, but he hesitated before stepping onto it. He didn't want to cause any more motion or scare the already unbalanced animal. Silex held Tonitrus back, and at this point it was clear that Cidivus was entirely on his own.

Then, when it seemed horse and rider would plunge over the side and disappear into the shadows of the Black Hollow, the black righted itself. It lurched up, leaned forward, and surged across the remaining few feet. With a sigh of relief from the others, Cidivus rode onto solid ground, clutching the horse's neck so tightly that he looked as though he might have to be pried from the saddle. His arrogance was gone, melted away in the terror of near death. He did not even sit up straight to gaze back across the void.

"Author be praised," Silex said. He studied the bridge for a long moment, taking its measure, and then he glanced over to where the Colubri still watched. The serpent creatures were gathered, coiling one over the other, their heads lifted and swaying. The sight of it was mesmerizing. It was difficult to tell where one ended and the next began. They coiled in and around one another like some intricate, bewildering puzzle. The Colubri watched the remaining twelve with interest but made no move to come closer.

"We can't risk repeating that," Tonitrus said, turning to Silex. "It is only by The Author's grace he lives. There is no way that luck can hold for the rest. If we don't want to lose anyone to that dark pit, we have to either find another way down and through the valley, past this beast we've been warned about, or try to cross on foot and lead the horses."

Silex nodded and then rode closer to Tonitrus so that

he could lean in and speak in low tones. Ferox came up and stood right by his brother's side.

"I agree, but I won't trust our backs to those creatures," Silex said. "They may not be snakes, exactly, but nor are they men. I question the sincerity of Cerastes' words, and I can't help but think that the Colubri may have ulterior motives."

"Then we should send the horses first," Ferox said. "Some of us can remain behind and be the last to cross, watching the rear for trouble. Perhaps the three of us can assume that responsibility."

Silex agreed with his brother; he turned toward the others.

"Cedrus, Nomis, Alphaeus," he called. Silex then spoke to them in a faint enough tone that the Colubri could not hear him. "I want you to take your horses across. Keep a good distance between the animals, and don't let them startle one another. Cidivus can watch them on the far side. Then you can return here and walk our horses across. Once you do, pull them up and tie them away from the bridge. The rest will follow. If there is trouble, we may be moving quickly. Don't block our way, and be prepared for anything."

Cedrus looked as if he might protest, but then he thought better of it. He nodded, dismounted, and took his horse by the reins. Alphaeus and Nomis followed suit, and moments later the three had begun the slow trek across the bridge. They moved carefully, coaxing the nervous horses forward. When the wind set the bridge in motion, they slowed, stopped, and then continued. It took quite a bit longer than Cidivus' crossing, but it went without a hitch, and the three made their way back across.

"Take my mount," Silex instructed, "and those of Tonitrus and Ferox. The three of us will remain here for now."

Cedrus glanced at the snake creatures again without expression and then nodded. He took Silex's mount, turned, and led it to the other side. Nomis and Alphaeus did the same for Ferox and Tonitrus, and Thaddeus accompanied them. Og did not look pleased about being sent across with the younger warriors, but he grudgingly heeded Silex's orders. There was a moment when Og's warhorse shied, backing and nearly panicking Thaddeus' gray, but the big man brought the animal under control by brute strength, holding it still until it calmed. When the danger had passed, they all continued. Cantos, Sceptrus, Pugius, and Gobius then led their horses across one by one. At last, only Silex, Tonitrus, and Ferox remained on the near side of the bridge.

"You are more careful than I would have believed possible for warriors," Cerastes said, slithering forward slowly.

"Given what we faced in the Tenebrae, such caution is necessary," said Silex.

Cerastes dipped his head in another odd bow. As before, it was absolutely impossible to tell what kind of emotion lay behind the action. The creature's face was devoid of all expression.

"Understood," Cerastes said. "Don't worry. We will watch this end of the bridge for you. The Beast in the Black Hollow should not be awakened, and as you have already discovered, the Tenebrae holds many dangers and challenges for those who pass through. We pride ourselves on providing warnings and on diverting as many as possible who would otherwise become The Beast's prey."

"Very well," Silex said. "Now, I'm afraid my companions

and I must be on the road. Our way lies across this bridge and beyond, and our time is limited. Thank you once again for your counsel."

There was no response, which gave Silex an uneasy feeling. He thought about waiting for the Colubri to retreat back into the forest before walking across the bridge with Ferox and Tonitrus. His instincts told him something wasn't right, but he ignored them. Instead he led Ferox and Tonitrus onto the bridge, and the three started across. Silex watched ahead while Tonitrus scanned the air and mist around them. Ferox stood in the back and watched the rear for signs of trouble. The Colubri made no move to follow them onto the bridge, but the two who had wound themselves around the support posts at their approach returned to their positions, watching the travelers' progress with unblinking, serpentine eyes.

At first it seemed the passing would be as uneventful as the others. The three moved quickly and efficiently. The bridge was a long one, but they didn't have to lead horses. It wasn't until they were nearly across that Ferox, still scanning the way behind them, glanced over the edge and let loose a cry of alarm.

"Run!" he screamed.

Silex and Tonitrus were trained to battle. They didn't stop to think or to ask why; they turned and sprinted toward the end of the bridge. As they ran, Ferox spit out what he'd seen between labored breaths.

"Colubri," he gasped. "They are hanging underneath from the ropes that support the bridge, sawing at them with their teeth. They mean to drop the whole bridge into the Black Hollow—with us on it!"

"I knew it!" Tonitrus growled. "I really hate snakes. Always have."

As he spoke there was a huge, grinding, tearing sound. Ropes whipped through the air, released from the strain of supporting the bridge's weight. The bridge behind them swayed, dipped, and then dropped with sickening speed. They scrambled, grabbing whatever hold they could as the structure collapsed, dropping planks and supports into the Black Hollow. As the ropes behind them snapped, they swung toward the cliffside at a dizzying pace.

"Hang on!" Silex cried.

The bridge swung down and crashed into stone and dirt and brush. The three held on for dear life, dragged along the wall and battered by the stone and rubble. When the shaking mass that had once been a bridge settled, they dangled several yards below the lip of the hollow. The ropes they hung from were taut. They creaked under the weight of the ruined bridge and the three dangling warriors, but they held as they had held for hundreds of years.

"Climb!" Pugius cried down to them. "Climb for your lives!"

Silex looked over at Ferox, who was alone on the left side. Wanting his younger brother to climb to safety before him, he urged him to go ahead. Ferox dug the toe of one boot in between the planks of the bridge, and, using them as a ladder's rungs, started upward. His hunts had taken him through the hills, into the tops of trees, and across all manner of terrain. He was slighter of frame than the other two and more limber. He made good progress. After what seemed only moments he crawled over the rim of the hollow, hauled up the last foot or so by Og, who gripped him firmly with his strong right hand to pull him to safety.

Tonitrus and Silex moved much more slowly. When Ferox's weight shifted off the bridge, it canted to the side and slid a few feet across the face of the cliff, nearly dislodging Tonitrus, whose heavier armor and weapons weighed him down. Silex, seeing the imbalance, cried out.

"Hang on! I'll go to the other side."

He worked his way across to the far side of the bridge, and as he went, the dangling remnant of the bridge crept back across until it was straight up and down once again. Then Silex started slowly up.

"Match me!" he called across to Tonitrus, who gritted his teeth, dug his boot between two planks, and levered himself upward. The two continued to climb, first one, and then the other. They climbed in such a way so as to keep the bridge from swaying. Each time they pulled up, the ropes creaked under the strain, barely holding. Ferox and Cedrus called down to their brothers incessantly, offering words of encouragement and exhorting them to hold on. But it was becoming quite clear that the bridge would not hold long enough for Silex and Tonitrus to climb to safety.

Realizing what was about to happen, Gobius dashed to his horse. He dug through his bags and came up with a length of stout rope. He took it and tied two loops about six feet apart, near the center. When Gobius had tested the knots, he hurried back to the side of the cliff.

"I have an idea," he said, turning to the others. "But we're going to have to work together, and we're going to have to work fast. Sceptrus, give me your staff."

Sceptrus handed the stout rod over willingly enough. Gobius, in turn, handed it to Og.

"Hold one end. Thaddeus, grab the other."

The two men did as Gobius instructed, though their expressions were confused. Gobius directed them to lower the staff. He slid under it and hooked his legs over it, bent at the knee with his ankles crossed.

"Lift me," he directed them curtly, "and then lower me over the edge."

Gobius held the rope tightly and concentrated. When Og and Thaddeus lifted the staff, he dangled from it, balancing easily and surprising the rest with this ability. Gobius recalled his many years as a fisherman, when he would hang from the rigging of a ship in order to adjust the sails.

"Get me down to them," he said. "If we can get each one to grab a loop of this rope, we should be able to grip the other ends and pull them up."

As they figured out what he hoped to do, the others began moving more quickly. Og and Thaddeus knelt at the lip of the chasm, and Gobius slowly slid over it. The others gathered behind, holding the two big men firmly to keep them from becoming overbalanced. The ends of Gobius' rope dangled over the staff, where Cedrus and Ferox held them tightly.

"No," Silex called up. "It's too dangerous. Go back!"

Gobius paid no attention. He worked his way slowly downward, even as the two climbed to meet him. Og and Thaddeus watched carefully, lowering themselves until they lay flat on the top of the cliff. The rest gripped their boots and anchored them as they extended Gobius as far into the hollow as their strength and their reach allowed. Their arms strained, but Og and Thaddeus were strong enough to hold on.

Just as it seemed he'd fall short, Gobius worked the rope loose slightly and swung a loop over to Tonitrus. He made a one-handed grab that nearly caused him to lose his balance, but then he pulled the rope in close to the bridge. Gobius swung the other end of the rope to Silex, who took it and gripped it carefully.

"Pull me up," Gobius cried. Og and Thaddeus gritted their teeth and pulled. Gobius inched his way up, using his hands to help lift. It was slow going. It wasn't that he was too heavy, but the angle for lifting was a difficult one. From where they lay face down on the ground, it took all that Og and Thaddeus could muster to draw their companion upward.

Gobius was patient, and his strength never wavered. They hauled him up the last few feet, but before he was even standing, he called out to the two below.

"Grip the rope," he said. "Let go of the bridge. We have you. Grip the rope and we'll pull you up."

They all grabbed the rope then, half on each side. As Tonitrus and Silex held on with their remaining strength, the group lifted them to safety, dragging them the last few feet onto the cliff top with a final lurch that left half of them on the ground and the rest heaving for breath, exhausted.

Silex lay on the ground, gathering his strength. As he did so, his anger grew. He rose, turned, and stared back across the hollow. The mists had risen higher, and it was difficult to see the far side. Still he was certain he saw Cerastes' glittering eyes glaring back at him over the dark expanse. Silex stared directly back at him.

"Did I mention," Tonitrus asked, stepping up beside Silex, "that I hate snakes?"

Silex shook his head. "This journey tests us," he said. "At every turn, we are faced with something new. I should have seen through them. Something told me not to trust them."

"There is no way you could have known," Tonitrus said. "Those who wrought the destruction were hidden from our sight the entire time. That is just how snakes operate, isn't it?"

Gobius joined them, and Silex turned to him.

"I owe you my life," he said.

"No," Gobius replied. "It was all of us. The prophecy holds true—the thirteen were necessary. Each of us was chosen for a reason. I think, all things considered, that it is a very good day and that we should be grateful for The Author's grace in surviving this grave danger." The rest nodded in agreement, and Cantos in particular looked pensively at Gobius.

On the far side of the ruined bridge, Cerastes dropped from his perch once more, stared out over the chasm, and hissed in frustrated fury. Then he and his followers slowly slithered from the clearing, passing from sight, back into the darkness of the Tenebrae.

Chapter Twelve

As the thirteen continued to stare back across the Black Hollow, Silex turned and motioned to his companions that it was time to move on. Although no one said anything, he was certain that they were all wondering the same thing that he was. If they succeeded in their quest, how were they now going to cross the Black Hollow on their way back to Mavinor? It was a question that he could not answer and was not ready to face, especially given the fact that he was still somewhat in shock from nearly falling to his death. There was no going back now, even if they wanted to give up on the quest. Silex thus shifted his focus to what lay ahead. He gathered himself and remounted, and the others followed his lead. They didn't know what to expect, for this side of the Black Hollow had been obscured from view by a thick mist, one that seemed as though it perpetually hovered overhead. But now it was time to see exactly what that mist was concealing.

As they entered the forest, it became clear that there were

just as many trees as there were in the Tenebrae. But the trees didn't stretch as high overhead, and their foliage didn't block the sunlight as effectively. It was like waking from a very long dream into the light of a new day, and it buoyed their spirits. They sensed that the darkness of the Tenebrae was long behind them now and that whatever it was that lay ahead would not be nearly as daunting.

"There should be only a few miles of forest left," Cantos said, riding up to travel at Silex's side for a while. "You can see that it's thinning. Before long we should start rising into the hill country."

"It's good to have the added light," Silex replied. "I think it's safe to say that not even the Surnia would be successful in launching a sneak attack in this stretch of forest."

"Something to be thankful for," Cantos said.

As the forest thinned and they were able to see beyond the tops of the trees, one gigantic trunk came clearly into view. It dwarfed everything around it, far exceeding anything they'd ever seen. They slowed and stared as their approach emphasized the absolute grandeur of it.

"By The Author," Pugius said, stopping in the center of the road and almost causing Nomis to plow into him from behind. There was a rough moment when Cidivus' great black bucked and looked as if it might kick. He brought it under control almost distractedly.

"I've never seen its like," Ferox said. "I've traveled every forest within a day's ride from Mavinor, and I can assure you that there is no tree that comes even close to measuring up to this one."

They rode slowly forward as the trees to either side fell away. The monstrous tree rose from a clearing, its trunk as big around as a house. Though they craned their necks and shielded their eyes from the sun, there was no way to make out where the uppermost branches ended and the clouds began.

"You could build a house in those branches," Cedrus said. "Several houses, for that matter. How did it grow so large— and why? What *is* this place?"

They all turned to Cantos at this point, and he shrugged.

"As always," he said, "there are stories. I had no idea the tree was here—but I have heard of its existence. The Scrolls speak of a great tree being the very springboard of life and that it grew in The Author's garden. I can only conclude that this must be it."

"It's not hard to believe it," Thaddeus said, staring into the seemingly endless foliage above.

As they rode closer, the tree filled their sight. Its branches were alive with greenery. Birds flew in and around its boughs, and it seemed that the light of the sun where it struck bark or leaf reflected and glowed. Later they would agree that it was their fascination with the tree that nearly caused them to miss one of the most marvelous sights a man ever could see.

It was Alphaeus who saw it first, but he was too shocked to move. He stopped and stared as the others continued to ride toward the tree. Nomis, who rode beside him, started to go in front of Alphaeus. But he noticed that his companion wasn't looking at the tree, so he followed Alphaeus' gaze. Upon doing so, Nomis stopped dead in his tracks as well.

When Nomis spoke, it broke the spell, but he spoke softly. Alphaeus heard him. Ferox heard as well, because he had the best ears of them all. He didn't know what Nomis said, and that also contributed to what happened next. Ferox reacted a bit more slowly than he might have, and he was still trying to tear his concentration from the impossibility that was the tree.

"Author preserve me," Nomis said softly. "It can't be true."

Off in the distance but well within sight was a magnificent unicorn. It was as large as Cidivus' black, but it shimmered like pearl. It wasn't white, exactly. There was a luster to its coat that rippled with the hint of color that was never still long enough to resolve into one hue or another.

"Don't move," Ferox said, louder than Nomis had been and loud enough for the others to hear, but not loud enough to startle the creature watching them from a distance.

It stared at him as if curious, but it showed no sign of fear. Ferox turned his mount to face the unicorn. By this point the others had caught on that something out of the ordinary was happening and had turned in confusion.

First they saw Ferox. He had leaned forward in the saddle, his knees drawn in tight as if ready for a race. His arms were taut, and he appeared to be whispering to his horse.

"What is the matter?" Cidivus asked. Then he turned too and immediately fell silent.

They all stared in wonder. The unicorn regarded them with a calm, liquid gaze. Its eyes, larger than those of a horse, did not look equine. Even from a distance they gave the impression of intelligence and sentience. They seemed almost human. The horn was easily three feet in length. It was long, slender, and spiraled. The tip came to a sharp, wicked point. It was beautiful, and the very sight of the creature sent a chill down their spines and raised bumps on their skin.

A talking raven, winged guardians of nature wielding

weapons, giant owls that preyed on man, serpent-like creatures that were able to speak, a beast residing deep in a dark chasm, a great tree—all of these things were beyond normal experience. What they'd encountered in a very short span of days was remarkable, and yet it all paled in comparison to that single moment. The unicorn watched them calmly, and they stared back in utter amazement...until Ferox moved. He took off like a bolt of lightning. There was no warning, and his passing spooked several of the horses, sending them rearing into the air. He stretched out over the neck of his horse, becoming one with the animal, streamlined and supple.

But as fast as he was, before he could cross the hundred yards separating him from the unicorn, it turned and disappeared. Ferox never looked back. He gave chase. His mount leaped the gnarled roots at the base of the huge tree, whipped around the corner, and was out of sight before the others managed to settle their horses.

"What...what was that?" Sceptrus asked.

He sat very still on his horse, staring at the point where Ferox had vanished. Cantos rode up beside him, also staring.

"It was a unicorn," he said softly. "It was an impossibility— a legend. It is said that there is one left in the entire world and that it is the last of its kind. But I never believed it was true. Though briefly mentioned in The Scrolls, the unicorn is described mostly in the odes of ancient poets. I don't know how it's possible for this creature to still exist."

"Could there be more of them?" Cedrus asked.

"I don't think so," Cantos replied. "I think that, just like the great tree, the unicorn is another sign. It's a symbol of the truth—that what The Scrolls tell us is the truth and that our quest and our faith are not vanities. They are signs of The Author's creation and of His infinite greatness."

"Or," Cidivus threw in, "it's just a horse with a horn." The others glared at him, and he caught himself, albeit too late. "Do you think Ferox will catch it?" he asked, hoping to move the conversation quickly along.

"I don't even know if I hope he succeeds," Cantos replied.

They dismounted and made a quick camp, watching all the while for Ferox to return or for another sight of the unicorn.

The minute his horse took off, the world around Ferox disappeared. He flew across the space separating him from the unicorn and yet it felt as if he stood still. He met its gaze, saw worlds of expression in its ageless eyes, and then it was gone. He was moving quickly enough to see it cut around the far side of the tree and launch into the brush; he dug in his heels and followed.

He'd never seen anything so beautiful, and he wasn't even certain why he was chasing it. He was a hunter, and those were the instincts that had set him in motion. But he was not hunting the unicorn. He wanted to see it—to touch it—to know all that there was to know about it. He wanted to match wits with it and win—or at least come up even. He wanted to run with it—or to at least feel his horse run with it.

But he could not. No matter how he maneuvered and directed his mount, the unicorn was too fast. It ducked in and out of trees and brushed so close to branches and low-hanging foliage that Ferox was hard pressed to stay in the saddle as he pursued. The unicorn remained just far enough out of range that all Ferox could make out was the hair of its tail or the tip of its horn—that magnificent horn.

Finally Ferox stopped. He didn't want to get too far away from the others, and he knew if he chased any deeper into the forest, he'd be in real danger of losing his bearings. He'd hunted long enough to know that mad flight through the woods was a bad idea. He stared off after the unicorn...and it stopped. The creature turned and stared directly at him with those deep, wondrous eyes. It shook its head and whinnied, but the sound was like no horse he'd ever heard. It rang clear, almost like silver bells. Ferox swore to himself that it had spoken, but then he wasn't sure. It was as if his ears were too dull to hear, his mind too dull to understand.

Then the unicorn turned, and it was gone. It was so quick that, had he blinked, it would have seemed as if the creature disappeared into thin air. Ferox sat for a long moment, staring at the last spot where the unicorn had stood. Then very slowly he turned away.

Ferox followed his own trail back and arrived to find that the others had set camp. Day was turning to dusk, but there was something in the air—the scent of the leaves, the way the sunlight rippled over the branches, and the trunk of the magnificent tree—something that made them feel good and alive.

"Well?" Silex said. "Where is it? Surely you haven't let it get away, brother?"

Ferox glanced up. Normally he'd have had a quick retort, but his mind was miles away.

"I have never seen anything so fast," he said. "I have never seen anything so beautiful. I could not have caught it, and I doubt that—had I the inclination or courage—that I could kill it. It led me on a good chase, and then it disappeared."

"Who cares?" asked Cidivus. "It is but a horse with a horn. I don't see why it is so special. You act as if it is a sign of some sort when it is merely a coincidence."

"There are no coincidences," Silex said. "This quest was prophesied, and the events that take place on this journey are all a part of The Author's plan. I am sure of it."

"You believe that, do you?" Cidivus asked. "You believe that it's all set in stone and that we're just playing out our parts on stage in some grand play directed by The Author Himself. I'm afraid that I can't see it that way."

"Really? Is that so?" asked Tonitrus.

Cidivus responded to him directly. "There would be no reason to pick us—to choose men of particular abilities—if there were no danger of failure. Thus I cannot possibly believe that this is all somehow predestined. We set our own path and choose our own destiny. Do we not?"

"Yes, Cidivus, but only to a certain degree," Gobius said as he rose and walked away from the group. He stopped at the base of the tree and stood, staring out into the area where the unicorn had disappeared. Then he turned to face the others. "We do choose our own path, but there is indeed one that has already been set for us.

"The Author calls each and every one of us to perform certain tasks as we pass through this world. He has set a path for us, but in the end it is for us to decide whether we want to go down that path or to take another one. If we take another one, then we must accept the fact that we will be on our own, for then we have chosen to separate ourselves from The Author and from His grace. But if we choose to walk down the path that He has set for us, then we will walk alongside

Him. That is not to say that we will not face difficult obstacles, but they will be easier to overcome if we are on the right path. It is inevitable that we will all meet challenges, but we must show resilience and mettle in overcoming them, just as we have so far on this quest. While I know that it is possible we could have failed, I can tell you that these circumstances are not at all random. There is a purpose to everything, from our near disaster on the rope bridge to our sighting of the unicorn. It is imperative that you, Cidivus, and all of us for that matter, understand and believe that to be the truth."

Cidivus snorted softly, turned away from Gobius, and began polishing his sword. The others sat in silence, reflecting deeply on what Gobius had just said. Cantos in particular directed a pensive glance toward the man who had just spoken as if suspecting him of being someone else. His wisdom was so unbecoming of a simple fisherman, and Cantos couldn't help but think that there was something more to Gobius than what he and the others saw on the surface.

For the first time since starting out from Mavinor they didn't feel as though danger was imminent. Beneath the branches of the great tree they rested, and they regained their strength. As each man drifted off to sleep, he heard a strange, clear whinny in the distance. But none of the thirteen dared to rise and chase after it. They took turns keeping watch, switching every hour. As dawn approached and it came time for the last watch, Ferox rose to relieve Silex and caught his brother in a rather contemplative state.

"What are you thinking about, brother?" he asked, catching Silex by surprise.

"A lot of things," Silex replied. "But mostly I cannot stop thinking about father."

"So it is with me as well," said Ferox.

Silex continued. "I can't help but remember what he said to us, about leaving him all alone in his twilight years, an 'old and broken man,' as he referred to himself."

"Ha!" Ferox said, keeping his voice low so as not to wake the others. "We both know he was pulling our leg. That's father for you. He knows quite well that he is strong for his age and does not need anyone to care for him. There's no reason to feel guilty, Silex. Let's face it. We were called, and we answered. This is our duty to our king, our kingdom, and to The Author. Refusing that call was never an option, at least not with us."

"You are right, brother," Silex answered. "Though I agree with you, I still wonder about him and how he will fare with neither of us there."

"He'll be fine," Ferox assured him. "There is nothing to worry about."

"I hope you are right," replied Silex.

"You have enough to be concerned about as our leader," said Ferox. "Don't worry about father. If we could speak to him now, I'm sure he'd want you to focus on your role. In fact I can hear him yelling, 'Get it together, boy. They're counting on you!'"

Silex laughed, and then he turned toward his brother. "You are absolutely right. That is just what father would say if he were here."

"Get some rest now," Ferox told him. "I will keep watch the last hour."

"Very well," Silex replied. "By the way, are you alright? I could see that you were deeply affected by something when you returned from your chase of the unicorn. I know how badly you wanted to catch it."

"I will be fine," Ferox said. "Now go and rest."

As Silex went off to catch one last hour of sleep, Ferox stared off into the distance, wondering if the unicorn would return and whether he could once again catch a glimpse of the creature. It never did, but that didn't stop him from believing that he and the others would cross paths with it again.

Chapter Thirteen

The thirteen rode out at sunrise, rested and refreshed. The forest grew thinner and thinner to either side of them. The huge tree stretched up behind them, and they knew it was going to be a while before they lost sight of it. Somehow it was a comfort for them to know it was there.

The land had been fairly flat in the forest, but as they moved farther away, they climbed and descended a series of rolling hills. Climbing steadily, each ascent lasted a little longer than the descent on the far side. Near noon on the fifth day of the quest, Alphaeus, who'd been riding with Thaddeus and extracting wisdom from his mentor, spotted smoke swirling up into the sky.

They grouped more tightly and rode slowly forward. Ahead, a range of hills rose to the right of the road. The first line of hills was covered in trees and rocky cliffs, but just beyond it they could make out the tips of roofs and the rounded walls of a tower. It was from there that the smoke was rising. Before they came within a mile or so of the tower, the road cut off to the left. On the right was a wide wooden bridge of strange construction just beyond a somewhat narrow body of water.

The bridge was attached on the far side, lying parallel to the shore. On the near side, where they sat staring in consternation, there was only a winch and a cable assembly. Silex rode forward, and Og joined him, fascinated by the mechanism. The big man dropped to the road and walked over to the winch, examining it carefully.

"It's ingenious," he said. "The bridge releases on this side and can be dragged across to the far side by cables and locked into place. Unless it is released, there is no way to draw it to this side without breaking the cable. And the water—do you see it? It was fashioned by hand. This is not a river...it's a moat!"

"But what is it protecting?" Silex asked.

He turned and stared down the length of the waterway in either direction. There was no end or other crossing in sight. The moat curled around the hills they faced on either side and seemingly disappeared.

"This is the direction we are supposed to travel," Silex said, turning to the others. "Our way lies through these hills and beyond."

"We could make our way around the outside of the moat," Tonitrus said, dubiously.

"It's too far," Silex replied. "It seems as though it could take weeks."

At that moment Thaddeus called out to them softly.

"We have company."

They all turned to the moat. A very short man in leather armor emerged from the trees on the other side, riding a rough, dusky pony. He had a helm of iron and wore a short, curved sword on his belt. The man stopped just beyond the edge of the trees and stared across at them. Then in a booming voice that belied his diminutive stature he called out.

"Who approaches Mizar?" he asked.

Silex strode to the edge of the moat.

"We come from Mavinor, on the far side of the Tenebrae. We have crossed the Black Hollow and seek the Northern Mountains. Our way leads through your hills. We come in peace and ask only safe passage through your land."

The tiny man made no move to come closer or to release the mechanism on the bridge. He turned and disappeared into the trees, leaving them to stare at the place where he and his mount had been moments before.

"Now what?" Cidivus asked.

"Now we wait," Silex said. "We can't turn aside and go well out of our way without at least taking a chance at passing through the hills."

"He looked like a child in armor," Cidivus said. "Yet I don't trust him. I think we should be ready in case he returns with an army of tiny soldiers."

"I'm not ready to assume he's our enemy," Silex said, "but what you say makes sense. It would be shortsighted of us to ignore the possible danger, particularly after what we've survived thus far. At the same time, they have no reason to trust us either. We have to be careful not to give the wrong impression if we expect them to allow us to cross over."

Silex directed them to pull back from the moat. They waited a short distance down the road for the small man to return. When he came back, he had two others with him. One of them was slightly taller than the other two but still much tinier than the average man. All of them rode hill ponies, and all were armed.

The taller man rode out to where the road met the bridge on the far side. Silex moved up to the edge of the moat, and the two studied one another for a long moment.

"So," the man said, "you wish to pass through the hills of Mizar?"

"It is our hope to do so," Silex replied. "Our way leads through the hills and beyond, where the road leads into the Northern Mountains. We are on a quest from the kingdom of Mavinor."

"A quest?" the man said thoughtfully. "That is a word I have not heard used in anything but story and song."

"I assure you that I am telling the truth," Silex said. "We ride in peace and mean you no harm."

"I am told you survived the Tenebrae," the man said. "Is this true?"

"It is," Silex replied. "Though I must say it has not been an easy journey."

"I suspect that is understating the truth," the man said, laughing. "I am Minstro, citizen of Mizar. If you will trade stories of your journey, I will grant you passage."

"That seems a very fair offer and one I will gladly accept," Silex said. "I am Silex, citizen of Mavinor. These are my companions who, along with me, were selected by King Onestus to embark on our quest."

"Very well," Minstro replied. He then waved his two companions forward. After exchanging a few hasty words, the three dismounted and began to release the catch that held the swinging bridge in place. Working together they spun the ratchet that, by a clever feat of engineering, maneuvered the length of the heavy bridge out across the water.

"Stand back," Minstro called out.

Silex stepped back from the water, and the bridge swung the final few feet. It met the mechanism on Silex's side with a loud snapping sound. The bridge had locked into place, and though the bulk of it floated in the center of the moat, it held steady nonetheless.

"It is now safe to pass," Minstro called out.

Silex nodded and turned to the others.

"Let's go," he said, "before they change their minds."

The thirteen approached the moat slowly and one by one crossed the floating bridge into the land of Mizar. When Og, who brought up the rear, had crossed, Minstro sent one of his companions to the far side to release the bridge. There was another snap as the mechanism released its hold, and after the little man returned to the near side, Minstro and his other companion spun the ratchet to draw the bridge back across. A few moments later it was latched in place, and the Mizarians climbed back onto their ponies.

"I will escort you into the hills," Minstro told them with a grin. "My fellow soldiers will ride on ahead and announce your arrival. As I said, we don't get much company, and most who request to pass through our land are denied. We are generally a private folk. The moat helps us to maintain that privacy against the intrusion of outsiders."

"We are honored to be allowed into your land," Silex said.

He introduced the other twelve, and they all nodded or made their own short greetings. Each was eager to get moving and to see what they would find in the hills. The cities that they'd known since their births were very similar to Mavinor. They had heard tales of other peoples and of different places, but until very recently that's all there had been—tales. Now they rode into the hills with men the size of children, fresh from a meeting with a unicorn under an awe-inspiring tree. Their world was expanding more rapidly than any of them was comfortable with, but the lure of new experiences was too strong to resist.

Minstro rode slowly into the trees, and as they followed him, they found a road just beyond the tree line leading upward. The slope wasn't too steep, but it was constant. As on the road, they'd climb for a while, then drop down, and then climb again, moving into steadily higher altitudes.

Eventually they began seeing small structures to the right and left of the road. The smoke they'd first seen from across the moat rose from several chimneys, and the scent of cooking meat filled the air. As they passed, groups of the small hill people gathered to watch. Some stared intently, while others pulled back from the road and retreated fearfully toward their homes. They were undoubtedly as fascinated by the large group and their mounts as the thirteen were of their diminutive hosts.

They passed through a village and then entered a larger town. Minstro didn't stop in the center as Silex had expected. Instead he led them on to the outer edge of the streets where a single building larger than the rest towered over the homes and small businesses.

"This outbuilding was constructed many years ago," Minstro told them. "We had three men who visited here for an extended time, and they built it so they'd have a roof over their heads. It's been used on a couple of occasions for a feasting hall, but I can allow you to spend the night here. For such a large group it's not much, but at least you won't be sleeping in the open."

"We thank you," Silex said. "It's been a while now since any of us has had anything but stars and clouds for a roof. It will be nice to get cleaned up and to rest. We won't be able to stay long—our quest is urgent—but we thank you for your hospitality."

Minstro looked disappointed when Silex said that they'd soon be on their way, but his grin returned quickly.

"There will be a feast tonight," he said. "Everyone will want to meet you, and we will want to hear your stories. There will be music and dancing. We will trade with you, entertainment for entertainment, before you set out once more."

"We gratefully accept," Silex said. "For now, though, we should rest and tend to our horses. If we are going to be up feasting, we should conserve our energy and be worthy of the hopes you pin on us."

Minstro bowed low.

"The doors are open," he said. "Make yourselves at home. There is water in a well out back and hay for your horses. I will return at sunset to escort you to the feast."

A moment later their small host was gone, and the thirteen stood beside their horses, staring after him. They could see crowds of tiny folk gathered in the streets not far away, vying for the chance to get a good look at them.

"Let's take care of the animals," Silex said, "and be sure to get some rest. I have the feeling our hosts aren't going to want us heading off to sleep very early this evening, and I don't want to get too late a start in the morning."

"I'm not looking forward to watching their dances or

their entertainment," Cidivus said. He could barely contain his discomfort. "They are...strange."

"I'm sure you seem strange to them as well," Pugius assured him. "And I am fairly certain that they do not want to see you dance."

Cidivus shot an icy glare in Pugius' direction while all the others broke into infectious laughter. Without further words they cared for their horses, wiping the animals down carefully, brushing them, and doling out the food their hosts had left for their mounts. Their hosts may have been tiny men, but they understood horses and their care. Everything the thirteen needed was at hand, including a trough with water and a good supply of fresh hay and oats. Working steadily, they finished the work quickly.

The building was tall with wide wooden doors. Inside was a single large chamber. There were three chairs, a table, and a scattering of other furniture, all crude and handmade. There were no beds, but there were pallets covered in straw, and the group arranged themselves across them quickly. It was still early in the afternoon, but with the exception of the night under the great tree, they'd not had a serious rest since leaving Mavinor, and they were tired.

Nomis placed himself near Thaddeus, and though he was as sleepy as any of them, he lay staring at the ceiling with his hands behind his head.

"They're fascinating, aren't they, Thaddeus," he said softly. "The little people? How long do you reckon they've lived up here? Who built that moat? It must have taken them years...I mean, how big could their spades be?"

Thaddeus opened one eye and stared intently in Nomis' direction.

"Yes, they are fascinating. Very interesting little people with a wide range of stories I'm sure. But right now I'm certain of only one thing."

"What's that?" Nomis asked. He raised himself up on one elbow and glanced eagerly over at his companion, ready for any discussion of the Mizarians.

"I'm absolutely certain," Thaddeus said slowly and intently, "that if you don't lie back and go to sleep, I'm going to be forced to knock you unconscious so that I can drift off and join you."

Nomis snorted and lay back, but he dared not speak again. For the moment they were all content to enjoy their host's hospitality and to dream of what might await them at the coming feast.

The first of the thirteen to awaken after their afternoon nap was Cedrus. When he saw that the others were still asleep, he stepped outside and took Magdala's scarf from his bag. After lifting it to his nose, he was elated to find that, after almost five days, there was still a trace of Magdala's scent. He envisioned her praying in The Author's Temple for his safe return, looking up to the sky with those beautiful brown eyes of hers. He planted a soft kiss on the scarf, and as he admired its deep red hue, he realized that the color of the scarf was reflective of the color of the fire in his heart, which burned deeply for the love of his life.

Upon hearing the others arising from their slumber he quickly placed the scarf back in his bag. Cedrus grabbed his sword, walked inside, and turned to his brother.

"Tonitrus, while we are waiting for Minstro to return and

escort us to the feast, perhaps we can get in an hour or so of training. I have a good feeling that today is the day that I will finally beat you in a sparring match." The others looked at Cedrus in disbelief, knowing full well that Tonitrus was the most gifted swordsman in all of Mavinor.

"Boldly spoken, brother," replied Tonitrus. "Very well, then. No doubt it's as good a time as any to get some training in. Let's go to work and see if your actions can back up your words. If anyone else would like to join us, he is more than welcome."

The brothers went into an open area on the side of the building where they were shielded from the view of the hill people. They did not want an audience for their training, and it proved to be the perfect spot for a sparring session. Nomis and Alphaeus wanted to join Cedrus though they were hesitant to do so at first. But after Thaddeus encouraged them to take advantage of this opportunity, they followed right behind, eager to glean as much knowledge from Tonitrus as possible.

After going over several maneuvers, Tonitrus worked with them and corrected their errors numerous times on turns, cuts, and transitions. All three listened attentively, and whenever Tonitrus instructed them to redo a mistake, they complied without resistance. As expected, Tonitrus saved his harshest criticism for his younger brother, for whom he held higher expectations. Finally, the lesson wound down, and Cedrus and his elder brother were ready to spar. Nomis and Alphaeus went off to the side to watch, while Og and Cidivus came over to see how Cedrus might fare in backing up his words. Gobius, who had been off alone praying for the past hour, also arrived in time to view the sparring session.

The brothers drew their swords and crossed them over

one another. Tonitrus asked Og to officiate by giving the signal to begin. The big man accepted, and after he indicated for them to start, the sparring match was on. Cedrus went on the attack immediately and sent Tonitrus back on his heels. But the seasoned warrior used his advantage in size and strength to push back and repel his younger brother. As Tonitrus went on the offensive and swung his sword from right to left, Cedrus ducked and rolled on the ground in the opposite direction. Without missing a beat, Cedrus got back to his feet and started to charge at Tonitrus again. The expert swordsman was clearly caught off guard and went back on the defensive. Once again, Tonitrus found himself on his heels, doing everything he could to fend off Cedrus' attack. He began to see that with each passing battle the pupil was edging ever more closely to the master.

But Tonitrus again used his strength to push Cedrus away, and this time he managed to knock him flat on his back. He thought it was over, but when he went to finish it, Cedrus twisted his body sideways and swung out his leg, knocking Tonitrus' feet out from under him. Just as he did before, Cedrus transitioned seamlessly back to his feet and brought his sword downward in a whirling arc toward his brother. Tonitrus managed to raise his sword and defend himself, but the force of Cedrus' blow was too much. The sword went flying out of Tonitrus' hands, leaving him on the ground in a helpless position.

Amazed by what just happened, Cedrus stood still for a few seconds and admired his accomplishment. But he failed to place the point of his sword against Tonitrus' body to claim victory. As he let his guard down for that one brief moment, Tonitrus quickly shot up and grabbed his right wrist. Tonitrus lifted Cedrus' hand upward, holding the young man's wrist in a vice-like grip, and he managed to twist Cedrus' arm behind his back. The maneuver forced Cedrus to drop his weapon. Tonitrus then pushed his brother face first to the ground and seized Cedrus' sword. As Cedrus rolled over in an attempt to get back up, Tonitrus was already waiting for him. He placed the tip of the sword against his younger brother's neck, completing the most improbable of comebacks.

Having won the match, Tonitrus dropped the sword in disgust and walked away from his brother. As he retrieved his own weapon, he began to berate Cedrus for letting his guard down.

"When will you learn, brother? How many times do I have to tell you to never let your guard down until the fight has ended? Your tendency to celebrate victory before it has been realized may one day cost you your very life on the battlefield! You tell me that you are no longer a boy but a man? Then if that is the case, it is time for you to start showing the wisdom of a man and let go of your childlike foolishness!"

As Tonitrus walked away, the rest stood in silence. Og, Nomis, and Alphaeus left one by one while Gobius went over to Cedrus and helped him to his feet. With a snide look on his face, Cidivus slowly marched toward Gobius and Cedrus. The young swordsman appeared downtrodden over committing such a grave error, and even after he bent down to pick up his sword, his chin remained at his chest as he stared straight down at the ground where he had just been lying.

"Perhaps," Cidivus said to Cedrus, "if you spent more time honing your craft and less time sniffing your girlfriend's scarf, this would not have happened. Better luck next time, my friend." He then haughtily turned his back and went to join the others.

Cedrus was startled by Cidivus' words, completely caught

off guard that one of his companions was even aware that he had Magdala's scarf in his possession. He grew very angry rather quickly, but before he could retort, Gobius held him back.

"Pay no attention to those words," Gobius said. "Giving in to your anger will get you nowhere. It is a mere waste of time and effort."

Cedrus heeded Gobius' advice and went back to staring down at the ground. "When will I ever learn?" he said.

"Don't worry, Cedrus," said Gobius. "You showed great fortitude and strength in your match today. I must say that I was quite impressed."

"Far more impressed than my brother, I'm sure," replied Cedrus. "He's right, you know. I keep making the same mistakes over and over again."

"Your time will come," said Gobius in a comforting tone. "You are still quite young, but you will be ready when you are needed most. Your brother does not mean to belittle you. He is merely testing you, pushing you to see how much you can take."

"I know," Cedrus replied. "I realize that. It's just that I can't see myself ever being as great as he is. Being the younger brother of Mavinor's greatest swordsman is not easy."

"I can only imagine," said Gobius. "But I can assure you, The Author does not expect you to be your brother. He expects you to be the person He has called you to be. As long as you respond to that call, there is no reason to be disappointed in yourself. Hold your head high and keep moving forward. It is a gradual process, one that none of us can complete overnight. You will get there, Cedrus, and when you do, you'll see what great things you can accomplish."

Comforted by Gobius' words, Cedrus lifted his head and

cracked the semblance of a smile. As Gobius placed his hand on Cedrus' shoulder, they walked back together to find the others awaiting Minstro's arrival.

Chapter Fourteen

Just before sunset Minstro returned to escort them to the feast. In the distance the thirteen heard the low beat of a drum, and when Silex stepped out the door, he saw the glow from fires in the direction of the village.

"They have gathered in the square," Minstro said. "They have been preparing food since late afternoon. There will be roasted meat and stew, vegetables, ale and sweet wine."

"Do you always eat so extravagantly?" Silex asked him.

"Almost never," Minstro replied. "Very little changes here from day to day. Your coming is the most excitement we've had in many months. I'm afraid Mizar is dull compared to the Tenebrae and the other exciting places you've visited."

"Sometimes safety and quiet are their own reward," Silex said. "Most of what you call adventure I would gladly trade for something far more calm and serene, especially after what we've been through on the first week of this quest."

The others trickled out and gathered on the trail in front of the tall building. All of them towered over Minstro, who gravitated to Pugius' side. The two of them had spoken at length on the journey in from the bridge, and Minstro seemed eager to learn more about the expert knife thrower with the dry sense of humor.

"Has the feast begun yet?" Pugius asked.

"No," Minstro said. "They will not eat until we arrive, and the elders want to meet you. My people are very cautious. They don't allow many outsiders in, and they seldom allow any of our people to venture out into the world. Their wish is to remain secret; if no one knows we are here, then no one will start to want what we have for their own."

"It's a sound philosophy," Tonitrus said. "It has apparently kept you safe for a very long time."

"Yes, but…" Minstro silenced himself, as if thinking better of his words. "We should go."

Minstro and the thirteen walked down the road toward the village. The hill people were watching them from darkened windows or shadowed doorways. As they walked down the main street, they saw the flames of fires ahead and heard the music more clearly, but there was no crowd gathered as of yet. Once the group arrived at the site of the feast, the music slowed and then ceased altogether. The thirteen stepped into the firelight, towering over the objects they surveyed, with Minstro at their side.

The silence was thick and uneasy. Silex moved nearer to the fire, and as he did so a group of gray-haired little men exited the shadows across from him. They kept the flames between themselves and the newcomers, and while they did not appear in any way unfriendly, neither did they make any particular gesture of good will.

"Greetings," Silex said. "I am Silex of Mavinor. We would

like to thank you for your hospitality and for allowing us to pass through your land. The repose we enjoyed this afternoon was much needed and will undoubtedly help us as we continue our quest."

A very thin old man hobbled slowly around the fire. Red-gold highlights from the flames danced up and down his silvery beard as he walked. Though he was old, his eyes were bright and keen. He stopped a few feet from Silex and leaned his head back so he could meet the taller man's gaze.

"I am Orn," he said. "I am eldest in this village and can speak for my people." Glaring in Minstro's direction, he continued to address Silex. "Unlike those who sometimes presume too much, it is I who make the decisions regarding whether we allow certain visitors into our land. It is not our way to allow strangers among us. It is a matter usually discussed over time and with careful thought and consideration."

"We are sorry if we have infringed upon you in any way," Silex replied. "We sought passage only in order to shorten our journey. We do not wish to be an imposition, and we offer no threat."

Orn studied him for a moment, and finally he nodded.

"You seem to be good men with honorable intentions," the elder said. "You are welcome to our hospitality. We will gladly share what we have, but we must ask that you be on your way at sunrise tomorrow. We can escort you as far as the bridge on the north side of Mizar."

"It is a generous offer," Silex said, "and one we accept gratefully."

"Will you introduce your party, then?" Orn asked.

Silex began to acquaint Orn with the rest of the thirteen. As he did, he recounted a few of their deeds, adventures, and misadventures along the way. When he reached the part where Cantos had been stripped from his horse by the Surnia and how Sceptrus had vaulted into the branches to rescue him, the citizens of the village began filtering into the street and gathering around the fire. They paid very close attention to Silex, seemingly hanging on his every word. Finally, when the tale of the giant owls was complete, Orn stood to speak.

"Minstro told us you had tales to trade, but we had no idea that we were in for anything like this. We look forward to hearing more about your quest, but for now let us eat! There is an abundance of food and drink, and some of our young people would like to entertain you. There will be plenty of time later for rest before you continue your journey tomorrow."

They were led to benches beside which a few small, low-slung tables were lined up, laden with food. The benches were so low to the ground that they had to be pulled away from the tables since it simply would not have been possible for the thirteen to sit with their legs underneath. Drinks had been poured, and Pugius was the first one to accept his ale from Minstro. He laughed aloud when he realized that while their guests were drinking from small flagons, he had been handed a whole pitcher.

They took their seats, and moments later they found themselves surrounded. First it was children, so tiny that Og could easily have held one in his hand. They sat in a semi-circle before the bench. The adults gathered and filled in behind them. As he sat beside Pugius, Minstro beamed as if he'd been given a great gift or had been presented with an honor of some sort. After everyone took a seat, Silex passed the torch to Tonitrus, who told the story of the Black Hollow and the Colubri.

When he finished, Cantos then took center stage and told the tale of the talking raven that had taunted Og only to be rescued by the Legans. Of all of them, Cantos was best able to weave a story together, drawing on his years of reading and study. Even the other twelve found themselves captivated before he was done, when he finally spoke of the great tree and the legends surrounding it.

They tried to get Ferox to tell of his mad chase after the unicorn, but he was strangely quiet and recalcitrant. Not wanting to force him, they ceased in their exhortation. Seeing that it was an appropriate time, the elders then asked the thirteen to direct their gaze toward an open area where presumably the entertainment was to take place.

Many of the younger Mizarians rose and, while blushing at first, danced to music played by several adults. There were the drums that the thirteen had heard earlier, which they now saw the Mizarians beating with their hands. There were harps that stood as tall as the tiny minstrels who plucked their strings and yet still only came up as high as Og's waist. There were miniature lutes and thin, five-holed flutes carved from the reeds by the moat. Impressed by the sweet sounds of the symphony, the thirteen began to clap their hands and tap their feet. That is all except for Cidivus, whose look and demeanor indicated that he wanted nothing to do with the Mizarians or the feast they had prepared.

———

When the music was over, the thirteen continued to mingle with their hosts. Og soon found himself surrounded by a large group of the little people, who could only marvel at his great size. He entertained them by picking them up with one hand and allowing them to take turns sitting on his shoulders.

Minstro gravitated toward Pugius and asked him about his technique in throwing daggers. He practically begged Pugius to put on a demonstration for him and his friends, so Pugius had them set up three apples across a wooden table. Standing a good forty feet away, Pugius quickly fired three daggers in succession, one right after the other. Before Minstro and his friends even saw all of the daggers leave their sheaths, they turned to see each apple split dead center.

"Just like the image on your breastplate," Minstro said, standing in complete awe of Pugius' ability.

"Well," Pugius responded, "now you know why I chose it as my insignia." He then smiled and winked at Minstro as he went to retrieve his daggers.

"Perhaps you can teach me, Pugius," Minstro suggested. "I can assure you that I am a quick study."

"This is an art that takes years to master," replied Pugius. "You're bound to hurt someone or even yourself if you try to master it based on the minimal amount of training I can give you before we leave tomorrow." He saw the disappointment in Minstro's face, and not wanting to leave the young man feeling dejected, Pugius told him that he would return to Mizar another time to teach him the skill. Minstro nodded his head but sadly looked at the ground as Pugius walked away.

─────

Thaddeus sat, taking it all in, with Nomis seated on his right and Alphaeus on his left.

"I am still in awe that I am here," Alphaeus stated.

"Why?" asked Nomis. "This is incredible. Who could have guessed that we would have had such amazing adventures

already in just the first week of the quest? I am eagerly anticipating what lies ahead for us."

"Don't be too eager," advised Thaddeus. "You are still
learning your craft. Let's hope you're ready by the time an
opportunity comes along."

"Oh I am ready, Thaddeus," Nomis replied. "I am ready—
trust me."

The big man smiled and nodded ever so slightly. He was
fond of both Nomis and Alphaeus and determined to do all
he could to bring them along as they matured into courageous warriors. Just as Thaddeus was thinking about their
next steps in training, Alphaeus commented on the fact that
he and Nomis still had a long way to go.

"I still don't understand it, though. Why were we chosen?
Of all the seasoned soldiers whom King Onestus could have
picked for this quest, why did he choose you and me, Nomis?
Why?"

"I don't know," Nomis replied, "and I honestly don't care.
I'm just thankful he did."

"As I've told you before," said Thaddeus, "The Scrolls
don't follow the logic of men. On the surface it may appear to
be strange that you were chosen. But rest assured that there is
a reason for it. You may not be the best fighters, but you may
have been chosen for your strong faith, your character, your
determination…there are many possible explanations. Only
The Author knows. We, however, do not need to know. All
we need to know is that we were called to this task, and we
must do what we can to live up to that call with honor. If we
do that, then no one can ask any more of us."

Nomis and Alphaeus slowly turned away from Thaddeus
to witness the activity going on all around them, but inside

they were really reflecting on the great warrior's words of wisdom.

Sceptrus, Cantos, Gobius, and Cedrus walked over to where a great crowd of Mizarians had gathered. Curious about the commotion, they soon saw that Cidivus was standing in the center of the group, telling stories of the current quest. Apparently he had decided to seize the opportunity to proclaim his prowess as a warrior to the hill people. Cidivus had them mesmerized as he spoke about how he was the one who single-handedly used his sword to fend off the giant owls, how he sent the Legans retreating back into the woods, and how he saved his fellow companions when they were nearly swallowed by the Black Hollow.

The little people were captivated by his tales, and all eyes were fixed upon the man in silver and black. As Cidivus drew his sword and showed them the silver serpent coiled around its handle, he began swinging it left and right, demonstrating his quickness and bragging about how none in all of Mavinor could ever match it. Having had enough, Sceptrus stepped forward and joined Cidivus in the center.

"So you are the quickest in all of Mavinor? Is that so? I suppose you can prove this to the good people of Mizar?"

Though caught off guard by Sceptrus' dare, Cidivus could not run the risk of appearing cowardly after the tales he had just unabashedly proclaimed. "But of course," he answered.

"Very well, then," said Sceptrus. "Let's have a friendly competition, Cidivus. Just the two of us…my staff versus your sword. If you manage to knock my staff from my hands, then I will concede your self-proclaimed title. Does that sound fair?"

"Fair?" asked Cidivus. "Of course it isn't fair. A staff versus a sword? You must be joking. Did you land on your head when you jumped from the tree after rescuing Cantos in the Tenebrae?"

"I can assure you that I am in my right state of mind," Sceptrus said. "Perhaps you are afraid of losing your sword and proving your claim to be false?"

"Not at all," replied Cidivus in a defiant tone. "I accept your challenge. Although I should warn you that I do not intend to knock the staff out of your hands. Rather, I shall demonstrate both quickness and accuracy by slicing it perfectly in half."

"As you say," answered Sceptrus as he brought his staff into a defensive position. Cidivus drew his sword and stood at the ready. They circled as they faced off with each other, and the Mizarians watched in wonder, anticipating a spectacular showdown.

Cidivus attacked, but he didn't come even close to touching Sceptrus. He then lunged again and again, but Sceptrus was too quick. Almost immediately, it was evident that Sceptrus was toying with Cidivus, playing a nifty game of cat-and-mouse. Cidivus' anger began to grow just as Sceptrus knew it would. He remembered the lesson he had given him in the grand courtyard alongside his mansion and how Cidivus' quick temper got the best of him when he didn't get his way. Now, he knew that he could use this against him, and Sceptrus planned to take full advantage.

The next time Cidivus lunged, Sceptrus dodged and tapped Cidivus on the thigh with his staff, repelling him. That only enraged Cidivus even more, and as he charged once again, Sceptrus spun to his right and brought his staff around in a huge arc, whacking Cidivus square in the buttocks as he drove past him. This gave rise to rousing laughter from the hill people, and Cidivus' face turned beet red.

At this point, Cidivus was determined to win any way he could. He pretended to lose his footing, and as he fell to the ground, he held himself up with his left hand. As he rose, he used that same hand to clench a fistful of dirt. After turning toward Sceptrus, he attacked yet again, but this time he feigned with the sword and threw the dirt toward Sceptrus' eyes.

Still, Sceptrus was quick enough to duck beneath the dirt as it flew by him. Cidivus had already begun his swing of the sword, expecting that Sceptrus would be blinded and thus unable to dodge him this time. But having outsmarted him, Sceptrus thrust his staff outward toward Cidivus' right forearm as the sword was on its way down. After striking the forearm, Cidivus lost his grip on the weapon, and Sceptrus retrieved it to complete his victory.

Cidivus angrily demanded that Sceptrus return his sword, and Sceptrus held it out toward him with a smile. "Remember," Sceptrus said, "that quick as you may be, there is always someone quicker." Cidivus grabbed the sword forcefully from Sceptrus' hand and turned his back on him. Cidivus then placed it back in its black scabbard as he pushed his way through the crowd, refusing to acknowledge anyone as he stormed away.

The Mizarians began to gather around Sceptrus and congratulate him on his victory as Cantos looked on and smiled. Gobius looked over at Cedrus, who was smiling broadly as well. Cedrus was glad to see Cidivus get what had been coming to him, and he recalled what Gobius had said earlier about giving in to anger. As he returned Gobius' gaze, he felt his admiration for the noble fisherman growing more by the day.

$$\equiv$$

Finally, when the moon was high in the sky, Silex rose from the table where he had eaten and made his way to where Orn sat with the rest of the elders.

"It has been a wonderful night," he said. "We have enjoyed your food and your company, and we hope you have enjoyed our stories as well. But I believe it is time for us to turn in if we are to be on our way at first light. We don't have a lot with us, but we have some items for trade—I wonder if we might barter for food and supplies before we depart?"

"Of course," Orn said. "We pride ourselves on preparation, and we are always sure to store extra items in anticipation of hard times. We have ample supplies for trade and seldom have the opportunity to acquire anything new."

The old man turned.

"Minstro!" he called. "Escort our visitors back to their quarters. The morning will be here all too soon, and we must see them on their way."

Minstro's smile fell at the mention of their departure, but he was quick to do as Orn had bidden him. Silex and his men followed as Minstro led them off through the merry crowd toward the road leading out of the village. While the Mizarians had been shy and withdrawn at their approach, the opposite was true as they departed. There was now an abundance of smiles and laughter across the firelit square. Children followed the thirteen and called out to them as they left. Nomis and Alphaeus returned their chatter. Most of the older warriors just waved and smiled, their minds already turned toward rest and the journey ahead.

Minstro kept pace with Pugius, taking at least three steps for every one of his and pelting him with an endless string of questions about his adventures. Pugius, who'd taken a liking to the young man, did his best to entertain his curiosity, though he was also beginning to grow a bit weary.

"I wish that I could go with you," Minstro said, his gaze far away. "I would ride out of here in a moment if you'd have me."

"It's a dangerous road," Pugius said. "You're far better off remaining here with the rest of the hill people. Didn't you tell me that you seldom leave Mizar?"

"If by seldom you mean never," Minstro said, "then you are correct. They would never let me go—the elders. They would tell me of my duty and warn me of what might happen if those outside Mizar saw me and wondered where such a small man might come from. They would say I was putting everyone in Mizar at risk for my own selfish ends."

"They may be right," Pugius said. "Surely things must have happened in the past to cause them to believe as they do?"

"I don't care," Minstro said. "It isn't fair that what happened long ago should dictate how I live my life. I want to go with you, Pugius."

He turned his face upward to look Pugius right in the eye, and there was such a burning hunger in it that the bigger man nearly stepped back.

"I can't let you do that, Minstro," Pugius said. "We were chosen for this quest—destined to fulfill it. Our number was decided in prophecy, and it is not my right to change that prophecy. It would also be wrong of us to take you along in defiance of your village elders. How can we do such a thing when they have shown us such grace and hospitality?"

Minstro turned away. Pugius suspected the young man was on the verge of tears, and he refrained from saying anything more, not wanting to make the moment any worse for him. They walked on in silence, and when they reached their quarters, Minstro disappeared quickly without a word. Pugius stood outside the door and scanned the road for a moment. He shook his head and went inside.

Cidivus was already sleeping, or at least pretending to. Cedrus suspected that he might have been faking it in order to avoid facing the others so soon after being embarrassed by Sceptrus. Nonetheless, they all quietly returned to the corners they'd chosen earlier in the day. Pugius lay awake for some time before dropping off, wondering if he'd see Minstro the following morning and hoping he'd not hurt the boy's feelings too badly.

The others, however, fell asleep rather quickly, worn out from the day's events. Gobius especially descended into a deep sleep, after which he found himself caught up in the most vivid of dreams.

In his dream, Gobius walks through a deep, thick forest. He doesn't recognize his surroundings, yet it doesn't trouble him. Something lies ahead. He doesn't know what it is, but he senses it is something important. With great anticipation he hurries his steps.

Gobius walks on a trail that winds between tall trees. The trail ahead is clear and seems to glow with light from a hidden source, but the trees appear as blurred walls of shadow. No matter what direction the path turns, the only thing he can make out is the light and the essence of something more, just beyond his sight and growing brighter around each bend.

He hurries again before slowing his pace out of caution. When it appears as if no danger is lurking, Gobius begins to run as quickly as possible. With his hair whipped against his shoulders and sweat beaded on his brow, Gobius strains for more speed, but some aspect of the air surrounding him seems to cause time itself to stop ticking. The faster he runs, the slower the trees to either side pass through his peripheral vision.

Then the path opens up ahead. He churns his legs, fighting for traction. The closer he comes to the clearing, the harder it is to move forward. In that clearing something flashes. Whatever it is, it is brighter even than the light that now burns all around him. He can't make out the trees, but it doesn't matter. All that matters is that clearing and whatever is in it that is emanating such a luminous glow.

He reaches the edge of the clearing and can move no closer. A majestic unicorn stands in the center; it glances at him, eyes deep and liquid, seemingly searching his soul. It lowers its head, crops the grass, and then shivers. The gesture is so much like that of a regular horse that Gobius almost forgets what he has just seen. Then it glances up at him again.

The resistance of the light lessens. Gobius is able to move again, but he fights the urge. After allowing a few seconds to elapse, he takes a very short, tentative step forward. The unicorn shivers again and paws at the ground. It does not look up. Gobius' heart races. The animal is so breathtakingly beautiful that Gobius can't help but stare in complete admiration. He takes another step forward. With each passing moment, movement becomes easier. He tries to control his motion, to hold himself back, but the closer he comes to the unicorn, the stronger is its pull. As he moves forward he becomes bathed in sweat from the effort of fighting, first to move toward the creature and then to prevent himself from approaching too quickly.

He stumbles, and the unicorn shies away. It tosses its head, and in that instant Gobius sees that long, slender, spiraling horn for the wonder that it is. As the animal rears, Gobius catches sight of its flashing hooves. Still he steps forward again and again. As he comes closer, the unicorn drops its head, its horn nearly within Gobius' reach. He reaches out to touch it ever so slightly...

Then in an instant the unicorn whirls and is gone. Gobius lunges after it, but as it leaps from the circle of light, shadows roll in, swallowing it as though it had never existed. Gobius drops to his knees and falls face first to the ground. As he turns his head, he feels the cool grass against his cheek, and tears begin streaming down his face. Though he does not know exactly why, he feels an enormous sense of loss. As he gathers every ounce of strength to push himself back up off the ground...

Gobius woke to silence broken only by the snoring of his companions. The moon had dropped from the sky, but the sun had not yet topped the trees outside. The darkness was as close to complete as it ever came, and Gobius sat up slowly, shaking his head. He ran a hand back through his hair and began to rise, staying as quiet as possible. Moving very slowly he stepped outside into the cool night air.

Gobius' heart was beating rapidly, and in his mind he ran over the dream again and again, trying to gain understanding. Even the way the unicorn had tantalized him with its horn was full of vague innuendo, and he couldn't shake the memory of the need to reach out to the creature, to touch it.

The darkness began to subside as the hint of sunrise frosted the tops of the trees. As the sun rose and the area around him grew brighter, Gobius tried to imagine that light as the light of his dream. He studied the shadows, hoping to get a glimpse of white—or to catch the long, spiraled image of a slender horn. But there was nothing to see. As time passed he grew calmer. His heartbeat returned to normal, and he was able to breathe easier. Gobius then decided to make the most of this quiet time by beginning to pray, taking full advantage of the rare opportunity for solitude and reflection…rarer still when one is traveling with twelve companions.

When he finished praying, Gobius was hungry, so he lit a fire and found water for tea. He started cooking breakfast, stepping out now and then to look out into the woods, still hoping to see something that reminded him of his dream.

The others, catching the scent of bread toasting near the fire, rolled over and sat up. They shook the sleep off quickly and prepared themselves for a new day, one that would see them continue their journey. The sun had just about fully risen, making it light enough to see far off in the distance. Everything around Mizar had a golden-orange sheen of color and life.

Silex came out and stood near Gobius, glancing at him quizzically.

"Up early today, are we?" Silex asked.

"Yes," Gobius replied. "I couldn't sleep. I had strange dreams and needed time to ponder them."

"I see," Silex said. He looked out toward the trees, seemingly contemplating something important.

"What is it?" Gobius asked.

"Nothing," Silex answered. "I'm just wondering what else

lies ahead of us, that's all. The challenges we've faced thus far
have been daunting to say the least. I hope only that whom-
ever or whatever else we encounter on our quest, we can
come together as a group and fulfill the task we have been
called to fulfill."

"We have so far," Gobius said. "There is no reason to
think otherwise. We cannot afford to doubt ourselves or each
other. Surely the road before us will not be an easy one to
travel, but we must believe that we will stand together and
rise to the challenge. If we have faith in The Author and in
each other, then nothing will deter us."

"I agree with everything you just said, Gobius," Silex
replied. "It's just hard sometimes to put it into practice…
especially…"

"Especially…" Gobius interrupted, "when you are the
leader of the group. That is what causes you to feel more anxiety than the rest of us. You feel that the outcome of this quest
rests almost entirely on your shoulders, and understandably
so. But know, Silex, that you have a group of strong, capable
men behind you. Do not believe for one second that you
alone should bear the burden of this quest. We share it with
you. Don't forget that."

Impressed by Gobius' insight, Silex looked into his eyes
and nodded in agreement. "Thank you for the support,
Gobius. That means a lot to me. And please know that I
have not forgotten, nor will I ever forget, the way you risked
your life to save me from falling into the depths of the Black
Hollow. I owe the fact that I'm still here to you and you alone."

"No," said Gobius. "Not to me alone, but to the rest of us
as well…and to The Author."

"Yes," Silex said. "And to The Author." Upon finishing his

reply, Silex noticed someone coming up the road. He called out to the rest of the thirteen. "I believe we have company, gentlemen. I think it's time we had our meal and got ready to depart. Unless my eyes deceive me, the Mizarians are approaching with some sort of cart, and I believe they will expect us to be on our way as promised."

Silex turned and watched as the Mizarians drew nearer. The group consisted of men and women with a few children by their sides. There were two small but obviously powerful ponies pulling a wagon loaded with provisions. The others came out to stand with Gobius and Silex as their hosts approached, eating their breakfast and watching as the wagon came to a stop.

Orn was among those who had come to see the thirteen on their way. The tiny old man held out his hand and smiled as Silex stepped out to meet him.

"I trust that you slept well," Orn said. "It is good to see this place in use again, even if it's only for a short time."

"Know that we appreciate everything you have done for us," Silex said.

Orn nodded. "We brought you some supplies. We have been storing away for a long winter, so a surplus is available. I hope you will accept what we offer. We met this morning, and we have packed more than you asked for. It is still not much, but you have an arduous journey ahead, and though we have not traveled far from our own land in many years, I do not believe you will find supplies easy to come by along the way. You will almost certainly face grave dangers as well, for generations of my people have handed down frightening stories of the lands north of Mizar. These two are our largest ponies. They can't keep up with your mounts at a gallop, but on the road they should be able to pull the supplies. When you have depleted the load and can release the cart, let them go. They will find their way back down the road."

Silex glanced at the ponies. They were larger than any he'd seen in the village, and they appeared to be moving the cart with little trouble. The thirteen had not done any galloping in the Tenebrae, but Silex wasn't familiar with the road ahead.

"Cantos?" he said. "Will we have occasion to move swiftly on the next leg of our journey?"

"Not according to the information I have," Cantos replied. "We will be entering another forest soon, though it should not be as deep or dark as the Tenebrae. I believe we will have time enough to use up most of the supplies, or at least enough to transfer them to our own mounts before we hit any sort of open plain."

"Then we accept," Silex said. "We have some gold, and we will pay for what you have given us, but it is far too generous."

"You have given us tales to tell and retell by the fire for years to come," Orn replied.

Pugius, who had been standing behind Silex, stepped forward to address Orn.

"Excuse me, Orn," he said, "I don't mean to interrupt, but I was wondering if you've seen Minstro this morning? When I last spoke with him, he seemed a little upset. I was hoping to have a chance to say farewell before we depart."

Orn looked around at the cart, perplexed.

"No," he said. "Now that you have mentioned it, I don't know that I've seen the boy since last night. He's a very impetuous lad—a bit high strung. It could be that he just doesn't trust himself with a good-bye."

Pugius nodded but didn't look convinced.

"When you are ready," Orn said, "we will escort you to the moat. You'll need us to operate the bridge so you can cross over."

Silex smiled with gratitude.

"It won't take us long to be ready," he said. "We've eaten, and most of what we have with us is already packed. We'll tend to the horses, and then we'll be prepared to depart."

Orn dismounted slowly. He turned to a young woman who had ridden by his side.

"Celia," he said, "go back and see if you can find Minstro. It's rude of him not to bid our guests farewell."

The girl nodded. She glanced at Silex, smiled, then blushed and urged her pony out of the small formation and back down the road. Its hooves kicked up a small cloud of dust as she disappeared back in the direction of the village.

Orn walked over to the building and took a seat on the bench in front of it. Two younger Mizarians carrying weapons took up positions to either side of him. They looked almost comical standing guard, but the thirteen nodded at them each time they passed and began gathering their possessions and packing their saddlebags.

In less than half an hour they were ready to ride out. The girl, Celia, returned, but she was alone.

"Minstro has not been seen since last night," she said. "I looked everywhere that I could think of but couldn't find him."

"It is fine," Orn said, rising and returning to his pony. "There will be plenty of time to discuss the boy's manners with him once our guests have been seen on their way." His guards then formed around him while the thirteen mounted and assembled around the wagon. They formed up as Alphaeus and Nomis took positions closest to the wagon. They had taken a liking to the ponies, so they agreed to work together to manage the animals and the supplies for the first leg of the journey beyond Mizar.

As they took to the road, Silex and Ferox rode up front alongside Orn, with Orn's guards flanking them. The others filled in behind.

"When you return to Mavinor," Orn said, "I hope you will stop and share the rest of your story."

"If there is time," Silex said, "we will do so, and gladly. Our quest is of great importance to our king and our kingdom. We have a lot of things in our favor, but time is not one of them."

"I understand," Orn said. "If you are successful, perhaps your king will send you—or others like you—to make contact with us again. Sometimes I think the young ones, like Minstro, have a point when they say that we have been locked away in this village for too long, hidden from the world and cringing at the thought of discovery."

"Your situation is not so different from our own," Silex said. "We have enemies, and we remain close within our walls. If it were not for the urgency of this quest, we'd be there still and would never have known you even existed. Perhaps The Author is working to bring us all together."

"I do not know of this 'author' you speak of," Orn said, "but I would like to learn more about these beliefs you hold. I think, perhaps, we have more than just stories to gain from your people if the opportunity arises."

Cantos, who rode close behind, chimed in at this.

"Since this quest has been foretold, it seems likely that

we were meant to meet. If that is true, than it can hardly just have been to share stories and gain supplies. I have to believe that before this quest is completed, you and your people will have played a part in it."

They rode on in silence, reflecting upon Cantos' words, until the slowly flowing waters of the moat came into sight. Orn sent three of his men ahead, and by the time the thirteen arrived at the bank, the bridge had swung across and had latched on the far side. Silex leaned over and clasped Orn's hand, meeting the old man's gaze a final time.

"Be well," Silex said. "If we meet again, I suspect there will be much to talk about."

"May your 'author' watch over you," Orn said.

Silex turned and started across the bridge. The others followed. As Pugius passed the elder he stopped just for a moment.

"When you see Minstro," he said, "tell the boy that I am sorry I did not get to see him before we left. If I can, I will visit him on the return journey. He's a good boy."

Orn nodded. "I will tell him. I'm sure he'll be fine in a few days. He has always wanted to escape. I think seeing you coming from afar and leaving again so soon was more than he could bear."

Pugius said nothing. He turned his mount and followed the others across the bridge. The ponies pulled the wagon to the other side of the moat, and when they'd climbed onto the far bank, the bridge was released, floating back across. The thirteen paused, waved to their hosts, and then turned back to the road, heading for the forest in the distance at a slow trot. As they did, each of them wondered what might await them on the next leg of their journey.

Part III

Chapter Fifteen

After leaving Mizar, the thirteen followed a long, curving road that led into a bright, open forest. It was nothing like the Tenebrae. There was a lot of light, and the colors were very vibrant. The shadows were deep, but they were just shadows—not an extension of some deeper darkness. The group was almost cheerful as they moved ahead, the ponies pulling the cart with their new supplies bringing up the rear, flanked by Nomis and Alphaeus.

The road was well cleared, with open space to either side. Beyond that space the trees were thick and the shadows thicker. Though there was no appearance of danger, some areas of darkness seemed fluid. Now and then a patch darker than the shadows passed, flickered, and disappeared deeper into the forest. Once or twice a few of the thirteen turned almost in time to catch the motion, but they never saw enough to be certain that something was lurking among the trees.

Still it was enough to make them a little nervous. As they

moved farther down the road, the canvas cover in the back of the supply wagon rippled once. It rippled a second time. One of the crates then tipped on its side, even though there was nothing uneven in the road. Alphaeus noticed, but he didn't say anything at first. He rode up closer to the cart and leaned over its side. A moment later the canvas moved again, and Alphaeus leaned in, gripped it, and yanked it free.

Several things happened at once. The ponies shied, and the cart lurched toward the side of the road. Nomis cried out as the cart came at him, and the canvas tarpaulin flew into the air as Alphaeus tossed it up and drew his sword. He lunged forward and was about to plunge it into the center of the cart when a high-pitched voice cried out.

"No! Stop!"

"What is it?" shouted Silex. "Surround the wagon!"

The thirteen wheeled and spread out in a circle. Nomis recovered quickly and gripped the ponies' reigns, holding them in check. In the cart, scuttling back away from Alphaeus, was a very frightened Minstro. Alphaeus pulled his sword back at the last second, and Minstro breathed a sigh of relief.

"Minstro?" Pugius said. He rode closer. "What in The Author's name are you doing here?"

Silex dismounted and walked over to where Minstro was sitting. He leaned in, held out his hand, and helped the young Mizarian to his feet. Then he pulled him over the rail of the wagon and down to the ground.

"What are you doing here?" Silex asked. "Your people will be worried about you by now, as were we all when you didn't come to say farewell."

"I couldn't bear it," Minstro said. "I couldn't bear the

thought of all of you bringing your wonderful stories to Mizar and then riding away again so soon, leaving me there to rot in that tiny, boring village. I have waited for something like this all my life—a chance to be a part of something great, to move beyond Mizar's boundaries and explore what the world has to offer. I had to come."

"But you cannot," Silex said firmly. "We were chosen for this quest. Our number is set in prophecy, and we cannot burden ourselves with watching out for you through whatever dangers we may encounter."

"I don't need you to watch out for me," Minstro said.

The little man straightened up to his full height, though he was still only about even with Silex's belt.

"I have my weapons, and I'm trained in their use. I have been a part of the Mizarian Guard for more than five years. I can take care of myself. All I ask is that you allow me to travel with you."

"You have got to be kidding," said Cidivus.

Silex was about to speak again when Pugius stepped forward.

"It's a long way back to the bridge," Pugius said. "We're going to lose a lot of time if we escort him back, and I don't feel comfortable sending him alone. If you'll agree to let him ride with us, I'll take responsibility for watching out for him. He can share my portion of the food and the watch."

Silex stared at Pugius for a moment, and then he turned to the others.

"Pugius has a point. We would lose two full days' ride if we turned back," he said.

"I say we let him walk back on his own," Cidivus said.

"No one asked him along, and he will be more of a hindrance than a help to us. What could possibly happen to him walking along the forest path back to Mizar? Besides, as he says, he's trained to take care of himself, and we're closer to his home than to our own—if any of us knows this area, it should be him."

Minstro glanced up at Cidivus, his eyes filled with sadness.

"I am sorry for inconveniencing you," he said. "I did not intend to become a burden on anyone, and I'm sure that I can make it back on my own." He then turned and walked in the other direction.

"Hold on!" Pugius exclaimed. "I said that I would look out for him, and I meant it. Do you not trust me to protect him? I will accept the responsibility. How can any of you possibly know whether he might not be a help to us before all is said and done?"

"I could drive the wagon," Minstro said. "I can cook a little, and I do know some tales of this forest."

Silex shook his head impatiently. He glared back down the length of the road toward Mizar and then sighed.

"Under the circumstances you propose," he said to Pugius, "I am in agreement. It is a burden that we don't need, and I won't pretend to be happy about it, but the course of action that makes the most sense is to continue on. I expect you to keep him from interfering with our task. I expect you," he turned to Minstro, "to pull your weight. Cooking is a good start. Caring for those ponies and that wagon, and helping Ferox to keep it stocked is better still. Don't make me regret this decision."

"You won't be sorry," Minstro said, his voice fierce.

"I already am," Cidivus said, snorting and turning away in disdain.

Pugius turned to Minstro with a grin.

"Don't pay any attention to him. He's been too long away from his fancy dinners and feather bed." The others smirked as Cidivus pretended that he had not heard what Pugius had said.

"Thank you, men of Mavinor," Minstro stated. "If you made me go back, I don't know what I would do. The elders would most certainly punish me. They believe that if one of our number ventures out into the world he will draw too much attention to Mizar. They have been sequestered and hidden away so long that they believe the first time they open the gates the world will swallow them up and destroy them."

"They may be right," Cantos said. "There are a lot of unfriendly people and creatures in the world."

"They needn't worry about me," Minstro said, scowling. "I'm never going back. Out here I may be considered an oddity, but at least I'll be doing something meaningful. I'll see places they have heard of only in stories and do things I've dreamed of but never had the chance to accomplish."

"For now, you'd better get back into that wagon," Silex said. "There will be plenty of opportunities for adventure, but right now we have to make up some lost time."

Minstro clambered back into the wagon, this time taking the reins of the ponies in hand, and the group started traveling down the road deeper into the forest. As he flipped the reins to get the ponies moving, Minstro glanced into the trees, and for a second he was certain he saw something large and dark flit past…something darker than the surrounding shadows. He stared after it, but the movement wasn't repeated. With a shake of his head he turned his attention to the wagon, swinging it into the center of the road between Nomis and Alphaeus.

Pugius glanced back for a second and gave Minstro a sly wink. The accomplished warrior couldn't help but smile, knowing how thrilled Minstro was to finally have the chance to journey out into the world and leave the safe haven of his small village behind. He admired the little man's determination, and as strange as it seemed, Pugius actually felt glad that Minstro decided to stow away with them.

—————

The forest opened up around them, vast and seemingly filled with life. Yet they did not encounter any creatures other than the game that Ferox was able to bring in for sustenance. Minstro rode among them in silence. Pugius glanced over at him from time to time, and Nomis leaned in now and again to ask a quick question. Some of the thirteen were still somewhat irritated at the unexpected burden, especially Cidivus, and they weren't quite sure how Minstro was going to work into their plans.

The silence was finally broken when Cantos realized that he had a question to ask Minstro. "I'm curious," he said. "Can you tell us more about the 'frightening tales' of the lands north of Mizar, the ones that Orn referred to before we departed? Is that why your kingdom is surrounded by a moat for protection? All of us are of course aware of the dangers that reside in the Tenebrae, but we haven't encountered anything like that on this side of the Black Hollow. What exactly do you know?"

Minstro glanced up. He seemed reluctant to speak, but

when he caught the sincere interest in Cantos' expression, he loosened up.

"This land that we are now traveling through supposedly belongs to the Strya," he said. "Though I have never seen them, our elders tell us they are very dangerous. Under no circumstances are we ever permitted to come in this direction."

"Strya?" Cantos repeated. "I can remember reading about them somewhere."

"Really?" Minstro asked.

"Yes," Cantos replied. "Are you surprised?"

"Well…" said Minstro, pausing a moment to gather his thoughts. "I just never believed what the elders told us about the Strya. I've always been convinced that they will tell us anything to keep us as close to Mizar as possible. That's why I didn't say anything about them to you before. My friends believe everything Orn says and have thus grown very fearful of the outside world. Me, on the other hand…I can't be fooled that easily. I refuse to let them scare me to the point that I would never consider crossing the bridge over our moat."

"I see," Cantos said. "Well, I can tell you this. The Strya do exist, though I didn't know that this was where they resided. Can you tell us anything else about them? What exactly did the elders say?"

"They claimed that the Strya are half man, half animal," replied Minstro. "Their upper body is that of a man, but from the waist down they resemble a horse or a deer, only with two legs instead of four. They are very fast and very strong. They supposedly wear only a sash of leather around their midsection for clothing, and they wield all kinds of weapons, from spears to slingshots. Oh, and they have horns on the tops of their heads like goats. They have been known to use these horns as weapons, charging at their enemies when the situation calls for it."

"Oh come now," Nomis scoffed. "I agree with you, Minstro. That very much sounds like the sort of thing the elders would make up to frighten children."

"An odd thing to say," Ferox tossed in, dropping back to join the conversation, "when one has already encountered talking ravens, giant owls…"

"And the unicorn," Cantos said thoughtfully, finishing Ferox's sentence for him. "Let us not forget that magnificent beast."

In the trees to the right of the road, just out of sight, a dark flash flickered across the shadows. None of them noticed it. The darkness paralleled their path for a short period and then faded into the distance once again. Minstro spoke no more of the Strya, and Cantos seemed lost in thought as if trying to remember something important. The road ahead sloped down into a long valley, and the woods to either side grew denser. It was late afternoon, and the shadows in the valley were thickening. Silex raised his hand, and they stopped once more, studying the road ahead.

"I don't like it," Tonitrus said. "If I were going to set a trap, this would be the place, and with the light failing, it's all the more dangerous."

"I think we can make the far side before dark," Silex said. "We'll have to pick up the pace, but if we can get there, we'll make camp and set a watch."

Tonitrus didn't look convinced but nor did he argue.

"Tighten up the formation," Silex called out. "The road is narrower ahead, and we need to get through this valley before nightfall and set camp. I don't want to be caught down there when the darkness begins to set in."

Minstro brought the wagon up to the center of the pack, and the others closed around him. Og and Tonitrus brought up the rear, with Silex and Ferox out front and the others filling in on either side of the wagon. They started slowly and then picked up speed, rolling steadily down the slope toward the floor of the valley. As they reached the valley floor and leveled out, Silex noticed someone, or something, up ahead. "Halt!" he yelled out.

Silex continued to stare ahead, and the others took a few steps forward until they were even with him. They looked out into the distance and saw what he had seen, the sight that had caused him to bring their progress to a sudden standstill.

"What is that?" asked Cidivus.

"I'm not sure," Silex replied. There were three shapes in the distance that appeared to be men, moving about and seemingly unaware of the presence of the thirteen. "But we need to travel this way, so let's proceed slowly and in a way that they would perceive as nonthreatening. Remember what I have said before: there is no need to draw weapons until we deem it absolutely necessary. Is that understood, Og?"

"Understood," the big man replied after a slight growl.

Silex led them closer, and as they drew nearer they could plainly see that the creatures moving about were not men. Instead, they matched the description of the Strya that Minstro had related just moments before. All were amazed, especially Cantos, who could not believe what he was seeing. After all his years of studying texts and reassembling The Scrolls, he was now witnessing their content come to life before his very eyes. The others just gazed in wonder at the

creatures that they would have considered to be only mythical if not for the fact that they were now almost face to face
with them.

At that point the Strya became aware of the presence
of the thirteen. They looked at them with blank stares and
made no move to advance toward them or retreat. When the
thirteen got within twenty yards of them, Silex again called
for the rest to halt.

"Stay here," he said. "I'm going to approach them and let
them know that we mean no harm and only seek passage
through their land."

"I'm going with you," Ferox said.

"Fine. Just stay a step behind me and let me handle
things," Silex replied. "I want everyone else to remain here.
They may feel threatened if there are more than two of us
approaching. Don't do anything to make them think we are
a danger to them."

As Silex and Ferox approached, Silex called out with a
friendly greeting. "Hello," he said. "I am Silex of Mavinor.
We are on a quest, having been sent by our king to retrieve
something of great importance to our kingdom. We offer no
threat and merely seek passage through your land as we head
toward the Northern Mountains."

The Strya did not react to him. They said nothing and
made no sudden movements. It was bizarre, and Silex did not
know quite what to do. He called out to them again, thinking
that they may not have been able to understand him. "We
are travelers and seek only safe passage through your forest
kingdom. Can you understand what I am saying?"

At that very moment, loud inhuman cries rose all around
them, and nearly two dozen of the creatures burst from the

trees, leaping and bounding forward with incredible speed and dexterity. They had the back legs and hindquarters of animals but stood erect, their torsos resembling men, with hair from temple to waist. Their muscular arms were wrapped in leather bands, and they wore what appeared to be some sort of sash or loincloth around their midsections. They carried weapons; several had swords, and one carried a large axe. Others had twin blades or spears.

"Well," shouted Og, "is it permissible to draw our weapons now?"

"Yes," screamed Silex, "and form up around the wagon!"

"So much for extending our hands in friendship," said Ferox.

The thirteen circled the wagon, drawing their weapons and preparing for an attack. Tonitrus and Silex shouted commands as they circled, one before and one behind the wagon, directing the others to defensive positions as well as they could on such short notice. Quicker than lightning the Strya moved in on them, and there was nothing left to do but fight for their lives.

Og let out a bellow and charged a pair of Strya trying to flank him. He feinted left and then swung his great axe in a circle back toward the attacker on the right, slicing him at the waist and dropping him to the road. The other one leaped aside, and Og spun to face off with him. Nearby, Tonitrus engaged a taller Strya bearing a sword and shield. The creature wasn't as polished with the weapon, but it was fast, and its odd stance and gait made it difficult to gauge its next move. Still, Tonitrus managed to cut off its left hand, causing the shield to drop to the ground. He then killed the Strya by driving his sword deep into its midsection.

Cedrus moved ahead to fight alongside his brother as other Strya began to close in. He quickly found himself in trouble, but Tonitrus bailed him out by felling two more of the creatures as they surrounded Cedrus. Tonitrus then shoved his brother away and told him to stay back, all while swinging his sword to fend off their attackers.

In the wagon, Minstro fought his own battle with the terrified ponies. He held the reins in one hand and pulled his sword from the wagon's floor where he'd had it stashed. Pugius kept an eye on him as he went to help the others. Nomis and Alphaeus slashed and hacked at the Strya to either side, but their inexperience showed, and they barely held their own. Cantos had pulled back, and Sceptrus, who was looking out for him, fought alongside Ferox and Cidivus to keep the creatures away. Cantos drew his sword, but he held it clumsily.

Thaddeus, Og, Tonitrus, and Silex cut a bloody swath through the Strya. Thaddeus swung his club with such force that he knocked several of them on their backs, while Og continued to battle his other attacker, ultimately decapitating it with a powerful, swift swing of his great axe. Tonitrus and Silex wielded their swords masterfully, and it was clear that the Strya lacked the technical skills to stand toe to toe with them. But the Strya remained dogged even as their number dwindled rapidly.

Gobius fought valiantly. He was not as experienced as the others, but he was quick and strong. When Ferox rushed to the left to cut down a Strya about to attack Cidivus from behind, two of the creatures swung out and separated Gobius from the pack. He pierced the first Strya with his sword, but instead of bolting, the second one darted in. It lowered its head with a snarl and charged Gobius' mount. The horse screamed as the Strya drove its horns in deep and yanked its head back, opening a huge, mortal wound in the animal's side. It spun and reared, hooves flashing, but the Strya was able to duck out of reach. When the horse's hooves returned to the ground, its front legs buckled, and Gobius was nearly thrown from the saddle. He slid off to one side, placing himself between the horse and the creature that had gored it. The second attacker, wounded but still upright, lunged at Gobius from the side and distracted him.

The two Strya then managed to turn Gobius around, forcing him farther and farther from the center of the battle. The rest of the thirteen had not yet noticed his fallen mount. Gobius fought on, worried about his wounded horse and frustrated that he could not win his way back to where his comrades were anchored. Then from out of nowhere, a third Strya joined the two others who were attacking him. Gobius gritted his teeth, timed his swings, and managed to cut a slash across the leg of his already wounded adversary, who limped off into the trees with a snarl. It still left him outnumbered, and the two healthy Strya bore down on him, working in tandem. Though he fended them off, he was tiring, and they sensed it. He was also too far down the road from the rest of the group for any of them to reach him in time if he were in need of help.

Finally his legs gave out, and the Strya knocked him to the ground. Just as it seemed as though they would easily finish him off, a loud sound cracked through the battle like a chisel into a frozen lake. It was like the scream of an angry horse, and yet it was not. There was something feral and powerful in the sound—something uncannily sharp and jarring.

There was a flash of silver white, and as Gobius was about to be skewered on the blade of the Strya, his attacker was suddenly yanked from the ground. Gobius turned and saw that the unicorn, its eyes flashing like fire, had caught the Strya on its horn. With a jerk it lifted it from the ground, reared back, and threw the creature as if it were a feather, sending it in an arc toward the nearest of the trees. As it flew through the air, the Strya left a long trail of blood droplets falling to the road.

There was no time to think. The second Strya spun on the unicorn, and as it did, Gobius swung his blade in a smooth arc and cut the creature's head from its shoulders. Its body dropped like a rock to the ground, blood pouring from the void where its head had been attached.

Gobius glanced at the unicorn. It had taken up a wide-legged stance, its horn low to the ground, and faced the wagon. He marveled at the creature's beauty and the remarkable strength of its muscles. The horn—long, sharp, and spiraled—ran with the Strya's blood, which flecked the animal's brilliant white coat. Gobius recalled how he had desperately wished to make contact with the unicorn in his dream. Now he was standing just a few feet away from the beast, staring directly into its piercing eyes.

Then a loud shout from Silex broke Gobius' reverie. He immediately turned and sprinted into the battle, joining the rest of the thirteen in fighting off the remaining Strya. The Strya were falling back; having lost half their number, they were no longer a match for the mounted warriors. But in that moment, more quickly than anyone could follow, a lone Strya launched from the edge of the forest.

Without a sound it leaped toward the wagon. The creature jumped so high off the ground that it cleared Nomis, who dumbly stared at the spot it had occupied only a second before. It landed directly in the center of the wagon, avoided Minstro's wildly swinging sword, and grasped the little man around the waist. After ripping the sword from Minstro's hands and quickly tossing it aside, the Strya leaped to the edge of the wagon, paused there for the slightest moment, a moment when time seemed to stand still and all those present were watching, and then sprang again. This time it barely cleared Alphaeus, who was unable to swing his blade for fear of striking Minstro.

Then the Strya bounded into the trees and was gone. It had happened so quickly that none of the thirteen could react. They heard Minstro's scream of terror and saw the creature darting off with him into the trees. Most of the Strya began to fall back quickly, as if they'd accomplished what they'd set out to do. But some remained to continue fighting and keep the thirteen at bay.

Pugius immediately streaked to the side of the road where Minstro had disappeared and looked as if he might dash into the shadows in pursuit. But Silex yelled out to him.

"Not now!" he said. "You'll never catch him, and if you go into those trees alone, they'll cut you off."

Pugius knew that what Silex said was true. With a cry of frustrated rage he spun his mount and charged after the last of the fleeing Strya. He leaned low over the neck of his horse and spurred it to extra speed. Before the creature could dash off into the woods, Pugius drew one of the daggers from the sheaths across his back and whipped his arm forward. The blade caught the Strya at the base of the neck, buried itself to the hilt, and drove the creature forward and down. It pitched onto its face, skidded and rolled, and came to a stop just at the edge of the trees.

It was the last one. All of their attackers were either dead or had retreated into the forest. The thirteen drew in close around the wagon to tend to their wounded as Gobius stood beside the ponies, steadying them. They waited, poised, but the Strya were gone. All that remained were the corpses in the road.

Nomis had a cut on his arm that was bleeding steadily, and Alphaeus had a bruised thigh where one of the Strya had tried to gore him with its horns. He'd managed to spin and catch only the creature's temple, avoiding a wound that would have meant certain death. Still, the force of the collision felt like being battered with a rock. Thaddeus immediately tended to Nomis, bandaging his arm to stop the bleeding.

As the shock of the moment wore off, the thirteen became aware of another oddity. Squared off against them, head still lowered, the unicorn stood in the center of the road, a fallen Strya to either side of it. The creature did not look tired, but it was wary. Its eyes gleamed, and the dying sunlight glimmered along its flanks, catching in the flecks of blood on its horn, which reflected like a dark mirror. Not willing to take any chances, Silex drew his sword and stood at the ready.

"What do you suppose it wants?" Cedrus asked. His mount was tight against the wagon behind Silex and Tonitrus, and his expression was full of uncertainty.

"It saved me," Gobius said. His voice was calm and filled with an odd tone—tinged with awe. "I was cut off. Without the horse I was at a disadvantage, and I found myself in the most vulnerable of positions. The two that were on me would certainly have killed me had it not been for the intervention of the unicorn."

He stepped forward. Silex and Tonitrus, whose mounts

stood at the front of the group, moved aside to let him pass. Gobius walked ahead slowly but steadily, his gaze locked to that of the unicorn. He was careful not to make a sudden movement, but he sensed as well that it would be a mistake to show fear. As he approached, the unicorn shuffled its feet, pawed at the ground, and then slowly raised its head from the fighting stance it had held since joining the battle. It shivered in an equine gesture and tossed its head, sending its mane flowing back over its shoulders in a cascade of pearlescent light.

"Be careful," Og called out. "I saw what it did to the Strya."

"I don't believe it means us any harm," Gobius said. "If it did, it would not have saved me. I was as close as the Strya, and if it had wanted to kill me, then it would be my body you'd find by that tree."

Gobius continued across the clearing and stopped just a foot or so from the unicorn's nose. He watched it for a moment, studying its features, and then, slowly, he held out his hand. The creature snorted once, and then, as if it were the most natural thing in the world, it stepped closer, lowered its head, and nuzzled his hand. Gobius stroked it gently; the unicorn did not shy away or show any fear. The rest stared in wonder, especially Ferox, who had longed to touch the beast himself.

"You're going to need a mount," Silex said.

"I believe that I have one," Gobius responded. He made no move to mount the unicorn, but he laid his hand on its shoulder, and it stood peacefully at his side. If it had not been for the creature's size, beauty, and the great horn protruding from its temple, it might have been any other horse being gentled by its rider.

"Maybe you do," Silex said in awe. He then turned his attention to the two who had been injured in the battle. "Nomis and Alphaeus, how are you doing?"

"Nomis will be fine," Thaddeus said as he finished bandaging his wound. "Thankfully the creature's sword only nicked him rather than penetrating deeply."

"I'll be alright as well," said Alphaeus. "I think my leg will be sore for a while, but I'll deal with it."

Then the gravity of the moment hit them, and the adrenalin drained from their taut muscles and overtaxed limbs. The sun was already low in the sky. Flies had begun to gather around the dead Styra littering the road, and blood stained the grass and the packed earth.

"What are we to do about Minstro?" Nomis asked.

"What are you talking about?" retorted Cidivus. "That is not our concern. He was the one who left Mizar without permission from the elders, stowing away and joining our quest even though he was never invited. He put himself in his own predicament, and now he will have to find his way out of it."

"We can't possibly leave him as a captive to those monsters," Pugius said.

"If you'd done what you had promised to do," Cidivus replied, his voice dry and angry, "then we wouldn't be in this position, would we? I thought you were going to look out for him—see that no harm came to him. That was one of the most short-lived watches I've ever witnessed."

Pugius snarled and started toward Cidivus, but Silex moved between them.

"We can't afford to fight among ourselves," he said.

"I'm sorry, Silex, but I can't just leave him out there," Pugius said. "He doesn't stand a chance. I was the one who took responsibility for him, and thus the burden of rescuing him is on me. You should keep moving. I will search for Minstro, and if I succeed, then I will look to catch up with you down the road. If not, then you'll have to fulfill this quest without me."

"Well said, Pugius," remarked Cidivus, his voice icy. He then addressed the others. "Minstro is not our concern. We were chosen for this quest, and there can be no deviating from it. If Pugius wishes to chase the Strya and look for Minstro, then I say let him go. There are enough of us here, enough seasoned warriors, to finish what we have started. If Pugius never makes it back, then we have to remember that it was his choice to go off on his own."

Gobius, who'd been listening to the conversation while standing off to the side with the unicorn, began to speak. He addressed Cidivus directly, his voice carrying easily though he was several yards away. They all turned to face him.

"You are wrong," he said. "This is a quest, yes, and we were chosen for it. There are reasons for all things that The Author sanctions, and this quest is no different. But if you set your sights on the final goal and ignore everything and everyone around you, then you cannot possibly succeed. This is not a question of whether saving Minstro will aid or hinder our quest—it's a moral question—a question of our worth.

"It does not matter that we did not invite him to join us. He was a friend to us before he followed, and we accepted him into our group. When Cantos was taken by the Surnia, there was no thought of leaving him behind. We went to his aid, and we did not move on until all were safe.

"If we were to turn away from Minstro and abandon him to the Strya, then we would be no better than the monsters themselves, showing ourselves to care more for the quest and our own safety than the welfare of an innocent young man."

"He is not one of our own," Cidivus said. His voice bore a lot less conviction, and as he said it, he turned away.

"As much as any other he is," Gobius said. As he spoke, the unicorn stepped beside him and lowered its head so its neck brushed his shoulder. It was an amazing sight, and it almost conveyed the notion that the unicorn was agreeing with what Gobius had just stated.

"Gobius speaks the truth," Silex said, stepping forward. "If we are to live our lives according to The Scrolls, then we must be ready to set an example, even when that example interferes with our own ends. I agree with him that we must do what we can to get Minstro back safely. If there is one lesson I have learned in all of my years serving in Mavinor's army, it is that you never leave a fellow soldier on the battlefield. Thus I have made my decision. Despite the risk involved and the time we will lose, we will join Pugius and go into the forest to find Minstro. Now gather your weapons and get ready to ride."

"For all we know," Cidivus said, "he could be dead by now. I can't believe you're having us ride into that forest, Silex!"

"Enough!" Silex replied. "If you do not wish to help in this task, then you, Cidivus, may go on alone if you so choose. Sooner or later you need to decide whether you're part of this group or not. I am beginning to lose patience with you. If we're going to succeed in this quest, then we will succeed together. Anything less than complete collaboration with one another will almost certainly result in failure."

There was no more speech. Cidivus relented in his protest, but it was clear from the expression on his face that he was not at all happy with the decision that was made. Still, he went along with it rather than go off on his own.

After taking a quick inventory of their supplies, they

packed their weapons and prepared to enter the forest. Gobius spent a moment mourning his fallen mount before going to join his companions. As he turned back, he met the unicorn's gaze, looking directly into its deep, piercing eyes. He approached it, and as he did, it stepped toward him deferentially. Gobius caressed its neck briefly before walking toward the forest, and the unicorn walked beside him.

Chapter Sixteen

Ferox took the lead as they left the road and entered the forest. The veteran hunter had the most experience as a tracker and was the obvious choice to guide the thirteen in their search for Minstro. Before leaving, they'd dragged the wagon off the road and out of sight. They moved as quickly as possible, but after they'd gone about half a mile, it was obvious that the Strya had spread out. Their trail grew colder and slower, making it more difficult for Ferox to track them.

As Ferox slowed, Gobius felt his mount grow restless, and then, with a sudden impatient toss of its head, it leaped forward. Gobius was startled by the sudden lunge, but the unicorn somehow compensated for his alarm and kept him balanced. The unicorn stopped in front of Ferox, legs planted wide.

"What is it, Gobius?" Ferox asked. He'd been leaning down close to the ground, checking signs.

"I'm not sure," Gobius said.

As the others watched, the unicorn half-turned and tossed its head in the direction they'd been moving.

"I think she's trying to tell us something," Gobius said.

The unicorn tossed its head a second time and then spun. Without hesitation it started through the trees at a fast trot. The others spurred their mounts in pursuit.

"Get that thing under control," Cidivus barked. "We're going to lose the trail completely."

"I think she knows where to go," Gobius called back softly.

"That beast looked as if she was ready to joust with us back there, and now you want to follow her off into the woods?" asked Cidivus. "If indeed she knows the way to where these Strya are camped, how do you know she's not aligned with them? We could be heading straight into a trap."

"If the unicorn were in league with the Strya, Cidivus, then somehow I doubt that she would have killed one of her own when she saved Gobius, don't you?" asked Silex. "We'll follow her lead, and quietly. With the trail having gone cold, what other choice do we have?"

Cidivus might have said more, but the ride became complicated at that point, winding in and around the trunks of trees, and he needed his concentration to remain in the saddle. His black stallion, wonderful on the open road, was tall, and Cidivus found himself fighting to avoid low-hanging branches that posed no threat to most of the others.

Gobius didn't look back. He leaned over the unicorn's neck and pressed his cheek to the animal's mane, which was soft as silk. They moved steadily deeper into the forest until, finally, the unicorn slowed to a trot, a walk, and then stood still. The others filed in around Gobius until they were all gathered in a small clearing.

"What now?" Tonitrus asked. "Where are they?"

Ferox nodded into the trees.

"There, I'd say. See the flicker of firelight? There's someone ahead, and not that far off."

"We need to get a look at that camp," Thaddeus said.

"I'll go," Ferox said.

He slipped out of the saddle before anyone could protest. Somehow, even as he was in the process of dismounting, he managed to draw his bow and arrow. Then he disappeared into the shadows of the trees and was gone in an instant.

The unicorn stood very still, placid even. Gobius stroked its neck, wishing he had a clearer way to communicate with the creature. He was beginning to believe that they'd picked up quite a bit more than just a new mount by acquiring the unicorn. He wondered just how intelligent she might be and what it was that led her to him.

Ferox returned quickly, and they dismounted to gather around him.

"It's them," he said. "They have a fire, and they are gathered loosely around it. They have Minstro tied like an animal, hung by his legs from a tree branch. I don't believe they're aware that we've followed them. In fact, they seem entirely unconcerned with the thought of attack."

"I'd like to show them some concern," Og growled.

"We're not here to start another war," Silex said tersely. "We need to get Minstro out of there as quickly as we can and then find our way back to the road and to our supplies. We're going to need a plan."

"I've got an idea," Pugius said.

Cidivus snorted. "Right! And that would be our best bet for a plan, seeing as how you did such a wonderful job protecting him in the first place."

"Let him talk," Tonitrus said. "There isn't much time."

"If he's dangling from a rope, then I can break it," Pugius said. "I should be able to hit it with a dagger from the shadows and then get in to catch him as he falls."

"It's too much for one," Sceptrus cut in. "I think your plan is sound, but if you can get that rope cut, it's going to take your concentration to do it. I can get in and out of there with some quick staff work, grab Minstro as he drops, and be out the far side. If we move quickly, we'll have the same advantage of surprise that the creatures had on us before."

Silex thought about it for a moment and then turned to Gobius.

"What do you think?" he asked. "If we are to succeed in this, then we'll need to rely on your mount to lead us back the way we came."

"I think she will do it," Gobius said. "We'll need a second line, though, in order to stop any Strya who pursue Sceptrus and Minstro. If we give them the time they need to get back here to the horses, then I'm confident that the unicorn will lead us back, and we should be able to outdistance the Strya easily."

"And what if she leads us off into the forest?" Cidivus asked, unable to contain the venom in his voice. "Or what if, seeing the Strya, she's suddenly overcome with the need to kill more of them, and we end up in another major battle, here in the dark in the middle of their territory?"

"It's done," Silex said. "We're here, and it's the best plan of action we have. We've got to make it work. Ferox, you go with Pugius and Sceptrus. Og, Thaddeus, and Tonitrus, the four of us will follow shortly after as the second guard. We'll hold our ground until the three of them have passed back through, then we'll follow. Gobius—while I'm gone, you'll be in charge. If we do not make it back here, do not come after us. Return to the wagon, and we'll find our way back as best we can. If and when we all reassemble at the road, we will continue on and up, out of the valley, until we find a defensible position to camp."

When he stopped, they were all silent.

"Questions?" he asked.

No one spoke, though Cidivus was livid that Silex had placed Gobius in charge over him. Ferox led Pugius and Sceptrus through the shadows and into the trees. Silex, Og, Thaddeus, and Tonitrus followed a few moments later, weapons drawn. Gobius urged the others to turn their mounts and prepare for a possible quick exit. There was no way to know what to expect when the others returned, and the silence was so thick it seemed hard to breathe.

"What now?" Nomis whispered.

"Now," Gobius said softly, "we wait, and we pray, and we trust in The Author to guide us."

"I thought we were trusting in the unicorn," Cidivus spat. Then he, too, fell silent, and they waited.

<hr />

Ferox moved slowly through the trees, brushing branches aside and indicating to Pugius and Sceptrus where to step without rustling leaves. The Strya seemed to be celebrating. They were loud, and the sound helped to mask the approach of the rescuers. Minstro dangled near the edge of the large clearing from an overhanging branch. Every now and then one of the Strya bounded near and swung him. Their seeming laughter was braying and abrasive, loud and without concern.

"What are they doing with him?" Sceptrus whispered.

"I don't know," Ferox said. "He was hanging just like that when I was here the first time."

"I don't even want to think about it," Pugius said. He turned and glanced at the fire in the center of the clearing. "But whatever they're looking to do, we cannot allow it to happen. We need to get Minstro back safely and leave these hideous savages behind. Let's get moving."

"I'll cover you as well as I can," Ferox said. "I'm going to set up a diversion. Once it starts, I'm out of here, so you'd better move quickly. You know the way back?"

Pugius nodded. Sceptrus rose and stretched slowly, being careful not to make any sudden movement that might give them away. He stood, planted the end of his staff on the ground, and turned to Pugius.

"You'd better make it count," he said. "When I start moving in, I'm not going to be able to take a second shot at grabbing him. If he's not loose, then I'll have to leave him."

"I won't miss," Pugius said. He had a dagger in each hand, and his gaze was locked on the swinging length of rope, gauging the distance and the rope's slow back-and-forth motion. He probably had only the one chance, but he held the second dagger at the ready just in case. If he had to, he thought he might be able to follow Sceptrus through and cut the small man down, though he wasn't certain he could get out again if he did.

"Let's do this," Ferox said. "Give me a count of fifty. I'm going to take a few of them out and draw their attention. When you see the first one drop, make your move. I'll see you back with the others."

Then he was gone, and Pugius returned his attention to the moment and to the swinging rope.

The Strya continued their revelry, unaware of their visitors. They were either very confident in their ability to elude pursuit, or it never occurred to them that they might have been followed. No guards had been set. A moment later, as Pugius counted fifty and drew back his arm, there was a whistling sound from the far end of the clearing. One of the Strya, caught mid-bound as he danced around the fire, fell victim to the first arrow, taking it right through the center of its throat.

At first the others didn't notice. The wounded Strya danced in a jerky circle that seemed part of its natural motion. It wasn't until a second and then a third Strya fell, blood gushing and arrow shafts protruding from their bodies, that the uproar began. The others rushed first toward their fallen comrades and then, slowly grasping the direction of the attack, turned toward the spot where Ferox had fired the arrows. He was long gone, and as they rushed off in pursuit, Pugius drew back his arm and let the dagger fly. It spun end over end, and just as it seemed as though it would miss its mark, the rope reversed its swing and the blade sliced cleanly through. Pugius had timed it perfectly. Minstro, half delirious from the rush of blood to his head and the sudden cries of the Strya, gave out a yelp. He dropped toward the ground like a stone, bound and unable to lower his arms to try to break his fall.

Sceptrus ran, planted the end of his staff into the ground, and whipped through the air. He flipped once, clearing some gathered logs, and landed, one arm extended, catching Minstro around the waist before he hit the ground. Without hesitation Sceptrus tucked the little man under his arm, turned, and sprinted back into the forest. One of the Strya, glancing back, witnessed the rescue and began to give chase. But it didn't get far. Pugius let the second dagger fly, and it caught the Strya in the center of its chest, driving it back. The creature fell to the ground, clutching the hilt of the blade, while Pugius whirled and followed Sceptrus back into the forest.

They ran as fast as they could without looking back. If the Strya followed and caught them before they reached the horses, they were doomed. Their only hope was distance and speed. Sceptrus panted and strained under Minstro's weight. More than once he collided with a passing tree trunk, but each time he fought through and continued onward.

Behind them, the Strya were frenzied. Pugius heard them crying out to one another and crashing through the trees, but they didn't sound as if they were close behind. Then the forest opened up ahead, and he heard Og's voice.

"Hand him to me!" Og yelled.

They made better time once Sceptrus handed Minstro to the bigger man, who tossed him over one shoulder like a bag of grain and ran as if the extra weight was completely insignificant. They reached the clearing, and Minstro was handed off again, this time to Tonitrus, who drew him up and cut the ropes from the little man's wrists with a quick thrust of his knife. When Minstro's hands were free, Tonitrus lifted him onto his horse's neck.

"Hold on!" he ordered. Without waiting to see if Minstro could comply, Tonitrus kicked his heels, and his horse dove off through the trees.

Pugius and Sceptrus continued onward, and soon Ferox joined them. Silex, Thaddeus, and Og stayed back to watch their trail. The Strya did not follow, and, miraculously, they all made it back to the clearing unscathed, where Ferox, Sceptrus, and Pugius remounted.

Gobius led the way out of the forest, the unicorn winding

its way through the shadowed trails and scattered trees with eerie precision. There was no hesitation in the creature. Once in motion, it flowed like a river dancing over and around stones. As the moon rose and offered its light to the forest, the thirteen burst through onto the road, dismounted, and hurried to pull the wagon back out of the trees.

"Do you think they'll follow?" Tonitrus asked.

At that moment, as if hearing his words, a strange horn sounded. It was answered by another and yet another. The air came alive with the sound, and the thirteen froze, just for an instant, staring at one another.

"Forget the wagon," Silex barked. "Cut the ponies free."

Nomis and Alphaeus leaped to do as he commanded. When slapped, the ponies turned and bolted back down the road. The thirteen grabbed at the bags and bundles, dragging them onto their horses and binding them in place as quickly as possible. The sound of the horns continued, and it was clear that the Strya were getting closer.

"They're coming," Ferox said.

Silex nodded. Gobius sat astride the unicorn, which didn't appear disturbed by the tumult descending on them.

"Do we stick to the road?" Alphaeus asked. His fear was obvious, and Cidivus looked at him contemptuously.

"Only if you want to die," Cidivus said.

"We don't have time for this," Silex said. "We have to pick a direction, and we have to pick it now."

"Most of the pursuit is on the left, the direction we came from," Sceptrus said. "We have no idea what is off to the right."

"We can't go back," Tonitrus added. "It's too far to get to anywhere that might be safe, and we have no idea how many of them there are."

Silex turned to Gobius. He glanced at the fisherman turned warrior and then dropped his gaze to the unicorn. As if aware of his scrutiny, the creature tossed its head nervously and stamped its feet.

"She's lived here longer than we have," Silex said. "She got us this far."

"Not again," Cidivus said. "Are you kidding?" he asked. A glare from Silex showed that he was not.

The others looked around, their expressions varying from shock to nervous anticipation. There was no time to argue over it, and in the end it was Gobius—or perhaps the unicorn itself—that made the decision. With a final toss of its head, the creature spun and leaped into the trees to the left side of the road. Its speed was incredible, shifting from a dead stop to nearly a gallop in what seemed only a few strides. Taken by surprise, the others kicked their own mounts into action and gave chase. Og grabbed Minstro with one hand and pulled him up onto his warhorse as they darted off.

It was dark, and they couldn't make the speed they otherwise might have mustered. Only the white flash of the unicorn ahead led them safely through the trees and brush. There were paths, but they were much narrower than the road, and they wound in long curves and shot off at odd angles.

Behind them the sounds of pursuit grew louder. Despite their lack of mounts, the Strya were fast, and they were pouring out of the cracks in the forest, following the call of the horns. The pounding of their hooves on the earth rattled like thunder. The thirteen dashed through the forest, unable to mark their path or their direction, and continued to follow the unicorn in its flight.

No matter how quickly they fled, the pursuit gained on them. The voices of the Strya carried through the darkness, loud braying calls and screams of anger. And then there was something else. Another sound rose, at first competing with the howls of the Strya and the pounding of their hooves, but then louder.

"Water!" Silex called. "It's a river! We're running straight at it."

Cidivus growled in anger. "I knew it!" he cried. "I told you that we shouldn't be blindly following this creature. Look at where it has led us!"

"It's too late to argue," Tonitrus said. "Ride on, unless you'd like to wait here and explain why you're angry to those beasts on our tail."

They pulled up on the bank of a wide river that flowed swiftly around a bend off to their right. There was no way to tell how deep it might be, and the far bank was nothing but a shadowed silhouette.

"What do we do?" Cedrus cried. "They'll be here in moments."

As if in answer, the unicorn plunged into the river with a sharp cry and set off for the far shore. The current caught it, and it was swept downstream, but it kept its head high, and Gobius, clinging to it tightly, was carried along. Silex did not hesitate.

"Ride!" he yelled. He spurred his horse into the river, and one by one the others followed. The horses were frightened and they cried out loudly, snorting and churning their legs to keep afloat. Their riders clung to manes and saddles, holding on for dear life as they swam for the safety of the far bank.

Behind them, the cries of the Strya and the blare of horns

reached the river's bank. Arrows and spears dropped around them, but in the darkness none found its mark. Within moments the thirteen were swept down the river and away. Ferox turned, staring back to where they'd entered the water. The Strya ran up and down the bank, splashing and crying out. They flung weapons, but none of them plunged into the river to follow after them.

Ferox turned and called to the others, almost laughing despite the danger.

"They aren't following," he said. "I don't believe they can swim."

The current carried them around the side of a cliff face—the same slope that the road rose up and over had they stayed on it. The thirteen fought hard to make it to the far shore. The water was moving faster, and as they rounded that bend, they were caught in what seemed to be rapids. There was a roar that had been muffled by the cliff, a sound much louder than just water rushing down a river. It was Og, positioned up front, who figured it out first.

"Waterfall!" he cried. "There's a waterfall ahead! We have to get out of the river!"

The unicorn forced its way toward shore. At first it seemed the water would be too deep, but the creature found its footing. Where the river whipped around the cliff, it drew away from the farther shore, and the water was shallow. The unicorn shivered and fought its way back to its feet. With a lurch it dragged itself the remaining distance to the shore. Almost before it was on dry ground, Gobius was in the process of dismounting and clawing at his pack for rope.

Og struggled, but ultimately he exited the water right behind Gobius, with Minstro still clinging—terrified—to the warhorse's neck. Og rode onto the bank, dropped from the saddle, and pulled Minstro down.

As Gobius reentered the water with his rope, Og went to assist him. They fought the current to grab for the reins of the other riders and drag them to safety. Cidivus and his black powered ashore, and as they rode up the bank, Cidivus leaned forward and clutched the animal's mane tightly. Og called after him to help, but Cidivus either didn't hear him or ignored the plea, and there was no time to waste on him.

The others came ashore in a ragged pack. Gobius used his rope to help pull them in one by one. The last was Nomis, whose mount found its footing a little farther down the bank. He had just begun to sit up straighter and ride up onto the shore when the horse slipped. It screamed and tilted, nearly losing its balance. Nomis leaned over its neck in a panic, clinging like a drowning rat to the struggling animal.

The ground was slick beneath the horse's feet, mud giving way as it fought to get back onto the rock and shale that could support it. Gobius and Og used all the strength they could muster to keep Nomis from drifting away, and Thaddeus waded into the river to help them. They called out to Nomis, exhorting the young man to hold on. But he was petrified. Behind him the water roared over a steep fall. If he was swept back any farther, he'd be lost.

"Don't let go!" Og cried. "I'm coming in after you."

The big man was much more unswayable than the others, thus he was better able to stand against the drag of the current. As he drew near to Nomis and the floundering horse, he felt the bottom of the river going soft, and he slowed.

Nomis was unable to do anything but cling to the neck of his mount. The horse's ears were back, and the whites of its eyes showed nothing but terror. It struggled to right itself, but without good footing, the struggle did more harm than good, and it slipped back a yard very quickly. Og let out a roar and surged forward. Somehow he managed to grip the horse's reins. He leaned back, putting his weight and strength into it, and the horse stopped sliding. A moment later, Thaddeus was on the other side, also gripping the reins. At first all they could do was hold steady.

"Take my hands," Gobius cried out.

He was only a few steps behind the two larger men. Gobius was very steady on his feet, despite the current. His time on the boats and near water stood him in good stead. He gripped Thaddeus' free hand in one of his own and took Og by the other. The three began slowly and laboriously to walk backward toward the shore.

At first the horse was dead weight. Its eyes were wild, and despite the anchor the three provided, it could not find its footing. Then, suddenly, a hoof caught on the slippery riverbed. Then a second. The animal surged forward, and the three pulled.

"Harder!" Gobius cried out. "Get it nearer to the bank."

They made steady progress, and a few moments later, though it seemed like years, Nomis' mount finally found its footing and fought its way up the bank. He clung to the horse like ivy as it rushed ashore. Silex grabbed the reins before it could spook or run, while Alphaeus and Sceptrus reached up and dragged Nomis free.

Gobius helped Og and Thaddeus back to the shore, and they gathered, drawing the horses into a circle. Ferox, who had made his way back up the stream to check on their pursuit, returned shortly thereafter.

"They are gathered on the shore," he said. "They're moving up and down the river as if they're looking for something, but they aren't crossing."

"The Strya can't swim," Minstro said.

The small man spoke cautiously, as if he was nervous about the reaction his words might incite. "That is why our kingdom is surrounded by the moat. It has kept them away all these years, or so the elders have said."

Everyone grew silent at this, and then Cidivus spoke.

"You tell us this now?" he said. His voice was as cold and brittle as breaking ice. "You tell us this now, as if it were not important? No warning to speak of—nothing about how we might escape if they came at us. We were nearly killed, once in the ambush, and once saving you…this is all your fault!"

Without warning, Cidivus dropped from his mount and drew his sword. He lunged toward Minstro, who stood still and panic-stricken, too tired and frightened to react.

"Leave him alone!" Pugius cried. He drew two daggers from their sheaths and leaped to head Cidivus off before he could reach Minstro. Most of the others stood in shocked silence, but Silex was too quick for both men. He stepped around Minstro and then directly between Cidivus and Pugius.

"There is no one at fault here," he said. "Minstro had no way of knowing that we were riding into a trap. He's lived his life in the confines of his kingdom. Without his stories of the Strya, we would not have even known that they existed. And certainly none of us, except perhaps the unicorn, was aware that we were heading straight for a raging river."

"He should not be with us," Cidivus growled. "He cannot protect himself, and he has nearly gotten us all killed."

"You don't look any worse for wear," Pugius said. "A little damp perhaps, but tell me, Cidivus, how your life is in danger more now than it already was."

Cidivus moved again as if he intended to attack, but all the fire had gone out of his anger. He glared at Pugius a moment and then down at Minstro. As if realizing how ridiculous his assault on the tiny man might appear, he turned away, sheathing his blade with an angry twist of his wrist.

"Keep your pet away from me," he said to Pugius. "I'd hate for him to get hurt."

"What next?" Tonitrus asked, turning away from Cidivus in disgust. "We can't go back to the road, that's for sure."

Silex turned to Cantos.

"Any idea what route we might take from here?"

"The falls ring a bell," Cantos said. He glanced back at the river; he seemed lost in thought for a long moment.

"Where the falls drop off, the river breaks to the right," he said at last. "From the bottom, if we followed the river, we'd eventually cross the road again and be back on our original route. But I think there is another way."

"I'm thinking any way that takes us far from that road is our best option," Ferox said. "I'm not looking forward to another meeting with our hoofed friends any time soon."

"At the bottom of the slope, to the left," Cantos said, "I believe we'll find a second road. It winds around that peak," he pointed directly ahead, straight, instead of turning with the river. "On the far side is a great valley. If the maps are correct, we should be able to cross through there and reach the Northern Mountains, still hitting the entry point we originally set out for. It's not longer—it's actually shorter—but the route through that valley is a dangerous one. All of the scrolls I've studied have warned against it."

"What is it called?" Og asked. "Surely such a place has a name."

"Mortuus Valley," Cantos said softly. "Some have called it the 'Valley of Death.' It is a long stretch of sand, scrub, and stone. There is no water to speak of, at least none that I know. It will not be an easy crossing, but I don't believe that the Strya will try to ambush us there."

"Then it is settled," Silex said. "Tonight we will camp, dry off, and find food, and tomorrow we will descend along the side of the falls and make our way into Mortuus Valley."

No one spoke, but the mood was anything but cheerful as they gathered their soggy supplies and moved into the forest. They found a spot with a stone ledge to their back and started a fire. As usual they set a watch, but no one slept well. The fight, flight, and rescue from the waterfall had left them exhausted, nervous, and wary. They lay, staring up at the stars, waiting for the darkness to pass and thinking ahead to the valley and the next leg of their journey. In the distance now and again they heard the horns of the Strya. But they were faint, and eventually they faded altogether.

From the deepest shadows, pale eyes watched them in silence. No one noticed this scrutiny, and eventually the eyes faded back into the denseness of the forest and disappeared.

Chapter Seventeen

The thirteen broke camp before daylight and made their way slowly down the incline by the waterfall, walking the horses and being as careful as possible on the steep slope. There was little conversation. They hadn't had much rest, and the hot tempers and wild events of the previous night hadn't faded. But as the sun rose, they made the turn at the base of the cliff and began to move into the land beyond.

Silex felt a sense of relief. They had just overcome their biggest hurdle yet and were now one step closer to the Northern Mountains. He hoped that they could leave yesterday's contentious quarrels far behind, for he knew that as the journey went on, the obstacles would become only greater. As leader, he was determined to keep their petty grievances with one another from causing the entire quest to implode.

"We'd better fill the canteens before we move into the valley," Silex warned. "As Cantos said, there will be no water to be found there."

The thirteen sat astride their mounts and stared into the

wasteland. They turned and hurried to stockpile as much water as they could. They'd lost most of their supplies in the rush across the river, and the remaining canteens and water-skins weren't going to hold much. When they had all they were equipped to carry, they set back out on their journey. The thirteen kept their pace slow but steady in order to prevent the animals from overheating and to preserve both energy and water.

Almost as soon as they made the turn into the valley, they felt the heat of the rising sun. It rose from the baked earth and sand, extending out from where they stood and glistening off the white stone crags rising along the way.

"We need to watch for shelter," Ferox said. "If it's near the time to camp and we see shade, a cave, or an overhang, it will behoove us to stop. A place as desolate as this is nothing to trifle with."

"You'd better believe it's nothing to trifle with," Cantos added. "There are plenty of stories of adventurers who made their way into Mortuus Valley only to never return. That is why it came to be known as the 'Valley of Death.'"

"What happened to them?" asked Cedrus.

"I have no idea," answered Cantos. "Perhaps they died from thirst, overexposure to the heat...or maybe some sinister evil resides here as well."

"Great. Just what we need," said Cidivus.

As they rode on, the thirteen broke into smaller groups. Each time they stopped to eat or to take a rest out of the growing heat, Pugius pulled Minstro to the side and began training him in the art of throwing daggers. The smaller blades were something the diminutive would-be adventurer could handle more easily, and he took to them with a natural ability that made Pugius smile. Cidivus watched in disdain when Pugius showed Minstro how to hold the dagger and demonstrated the proper throwing motion. But he said nothing more about his opposition to including Minstro in the quest, knowing full well that nothing would ever come of it.

Eventually they came to a ring of stones tall enough to provide shade no matter what the direction of the sun. It was late afternoon—there was time left to travel, but the horses needed care, and the steady heat had drained the energy and will from all of them.

"I think we should camp here," Silex said. "Chances are we aren't going to find a better location before dark, and we might not find shelter at all farther down the valley."

No one argued. They hadn't had a good, solid rest since leaving Mizar, and they were badly in need of one given the events that occurred since their departure. Thus they set camp, tended to their mounts, and began to unwind.

Gobius and Cedrus continued to bond as the tall fisherman shared several stories with the curious young soldier. While not experienced as a warrior, he had a wealth of tales of boats, sailing, and fishing, and he continued to dazzle Cedrus with his extraordinary, almost eerie, knowledge of life and spirituality. Cedrus listened attentively and often asked questions, which Gobius was all too happy to answer.

Sceptrus wandered off to sit alone in the last of the afternoon sun with Cantos.

"How are you holding up, friend?" he asked. "Not just physically but mentally. I wondered if the situations we've encountered have done anything to shake your faith."

Cantos smiled. "Never," he said. "In fact, it's been just the opposite. Every time we encounter another challenge and overcome it, I feel my faith grow even stronger. I feel The Author's presence more and more, guiding us and protecting us. Don't you, Sceptrus?"

"I wish that I did," Sceptrus replied. "At times I feel as if it's all slipping away from me or that what I believe, or at least try to believe, is just a smoke screen to prevent me from taking responsibility for my own life."

"Well, make no mistake about it," said Cantos. "You are responsible for your own life. All of us are. But that doesn't mean we can't have faith in a supreme being who we believe can help us along the way, as long as we allow Him to do so. Having religious faith does not equate to relinquishing one's responsibilities."

"Can I tell you something?" said Sceptrus. "Something private, which you promise to keep only between us?" He turned around to make sure that none of the others was within earshot.

"Of course," said Cantos.

"I think that one of the obstacles to my faith has been my moral shortcomings," Sceptrus expressed in an almost somber tone. "I'd rather not get into specifics, but I am not exactly proud of my past. I am a man who has made many mistakes and has regretted each and every one of them. That is yet another obstacle that I am dealing with."

"You are aware of my past, aren't you?" asked Cantos.

"No," Sceptrus responded. His facial expression changed as his curiosity was now piqued.

"Well," said Cantos, "many years ago I had another role in the kingdom. Aside from my duties as a scribe and scholar of The Scrolls, I also served as a tax collector. I still believe that

I was chosen because, presumably, a scribe who had undying faith in The Author was beyond reproach and would carry out the responsibilities with the utmost integrity. But in the end the opposite proved to be true. I soon learned how easy it was to steal taxpayers' money without being caught, and though I resisted the temptation many a time, I eventually weakened and gave in."

"I had no idea," said Sceptrus.

"Well," replied Cantos, "you are young, and this may be a little before your time. But anyway, it was a grave scandal that caused me to lose nearly everything I hold dear. I begged for forgiveness, both from King Onestus and from The Author, hoping and praying that I might receive a second chance. Onestus, good man that he was and still is, forgave me. Still, he had little choice but to relieve me of my duties as a tax collector. I was allowed to continue in my role as a scribe, and for that I am forever grateful to the king."

"Amazing," said Sceptrus. "I never could have guessed that you had such a past."

"I know," Cantos responded. "Still, my point is this. Do not allow your shortcomings to impact your faith. We all make mistakes, both small ones and big ones. The bigger ones merely require more atonement. Even when you stumble, The Author is with you. Do not let your actions separate you from His love, Sceptrus. You'll never find happiness if you continue to do so."

"You make it sound so easy," said Sceptrus, his eyes sparkling.

"Well, it's not," Cantos stated. "I know this as well as anyone. And I will gladly help you as you make the same journey yourself."

"Thanks, Cantos," Sceptrus said gratefully.

"It's the least I can do for a man who saved my life," replied Cantos. "Oh and by the way, since you also asked about my physical well-being, know that I am still a little sore from the attack of the Surnia, not to mention everything else we've endured. But I think I'm holding up alright for an old man." He smiled as Sceptrus laughed.

Tonitrus huddled with Silex and Ferox as they made plans for the next day. According to the maps given to them by Olin, they were not all that far from the Northern Mountains. Once they arrived there, they knew that it would be the most difficult terrain yet to navigate. Not only would they have to ascend dizzying heights, but they also needed to locate where Haggiselm had hidden the Medallion. It had all the appearances of trying to find a needle in a haystack, but that is where they knew that Cantos' wisdom and guidance would be needed more than ever.

Cidivus sat alone, watching the others go about their business. As he sat, he idly flicked tiny rocks from an outcrop of stone in the wall beside him. Inside, he was stewing. Cidivus despised Minstro and was still angry with Silex for his decision to include him. He hadn't spoken to Pugius since their confrontation back at the river, and he still resented Sceptrus for making him look like a fool in front of the Mizarians. Cidivus couldn't stand to hear any more talk from Cantos or Gobius about The Author and how they needed to have faith that He would lead them in fulfilling the quest. As he watched Og and Thaddeus drill, he told himself that if the rest were anywhere near as intelligent as he was, then they would put their faith in the strong right arms of men who bear destructive weapons and not an invisible deity residing in the sky. He cared even less about his companions now than he did at the beginning of the quest, and he resolutely declared to himself that he would continue to watch out only for his own welfare and personal interests. The others would have to rely on their "Author" to save them.

As the moon rose, Cidivus volunteered to take the first watch. This alone raised eyebrows, for Cidivus had never done so before. But the others agreed to it, and it was decided that Gobius would relieve him for the second shift.

It had been a long, dry day, and Cidivus believed that Silex had been stingy with the rations. They'd filled all their canteens, and surely they would find water or reach the far side of the wasteland before they ran out. It was enough that he had to deal with their constant mewling about having faith in The Author without dying of thirst.

All of their supplies were gathered in one area where they would be more protected from the elements. Silex had been portioning out the water, keeping a careful eye on it so there would be plenty for the animals and enough to keep them moving forward. Angering Cidivus even more was the fact that Minstro, whom he still blamed for all of their trouble with the Strya, was taking one of those shares.

Like a slithering snake, Cidivus moved stealthily through the camp, stopping several times when one of his comrades stirred in his sleep. Eventually he reached the carefully stowed water bottles, and he grabbed the first one he came to. Without another thought to those around him, he upended the bottle. It was all but empty when footfalls behind him caught his attention. Before turning to see who it was, Cidivus took one last gulp and tossed the bottle contemptuously back onto the pile.

"There is very little left for the journey we have ahead of us," Gobius said in a soft tone. There was no accusation in his voice.

"I guess you'd better wake the others and have me flogged then," Cidivus replied.

"I'm concerned only with the well-being of the group," Gobius said, unperturbed. "You have far more experience than me on military campaigns, so I am certain you understand."

A dozen caustic replies rose to his lips, but Cidivus bit them back. Something in the other man's calm demeanor irked him, but he didn't want to wake the others if there was any chance he'd get away with his selfish act.

"We can't be far from water," he said gruffly.

"But you can't know for sure," Gobius said, speaking in a low-pitched voice.

"Well, why can't you tell us?" Cidivus said sarcastically. "Don't you know? Hasn't 'The Author' provided you with an answer yet?"

"When will you learn, Cidivus?" Gobius replied, shaking his head. "The journey of faith doesn't always provide such answers to us. It is like walking through a long, dark cave with a torch. You can see only a few feet in front of you at a time. You have no inkling of what may lie ahead down the path. So all you can do is prepare yourself as best you can. That is what Silex is trying to do as our leader."

"That same leader nearly got us all killed back there in the forest," Cidivus responded. "The decisions to include Minstro on our quest, to amicably approach the Strya, then venture into the woods to rescue the dwarf after he unwittingly allowed himself to be captured...these were all foolish and misguided."

"I'm sure you believe that you can do a better job and that we'd be better off if you had been leading us all along," Gobius said. "However, the fact is that Silex was chosen. You can accept that or continue to resent it, but you can't change it. Have you not noticed that you have been the sole source of internal conflict among us throughout this quest?"

Cidivus did not respond. He merely scowled at Gobius and turned away.

"Look, Cidivus," said Gobius. "I know that you are a non-believer and that you may well have agreed to join the quest for all the wrong reasons. But given my faith, I do believe that you too are here by The Author's will. That may seem impossible for you to comprehend, but I have no doubt whatsoever that this is the case. I hope and pray that you discover for yourself what that reason might be. Going forward, you can either help us or hurt us. The choice is yours, my friend."

Cidivus had no response to Gobius' eloquence. He merely looked at the ground and walked right past him, going to where his bed had been arranged. Gobius then assumed the watch as Cidivus retired for the night. After crawling under his blanket, Cidivus pondered Gobius' words for a little while before drifting off to sleep. As Gobius patrolled the camp, he glanced down at him, just for a second, and then continued on, hoping that his message had somehow penetrated the heart of the band's black sheep.

While Gobius was keeping watch, Cedrus shifted and turned in his sleep. His breathing grew rough for a second but then calmed. As his mind shifted from the pitch darkness of deep sleep, he began to dream…

The streets of Mavinor are brightly lit. The market is filled with flashing colors and the laughter of children. The light wavers as Cedrus steps into the street and passes through the market. Something draws him toward the center, where the city's water is supplied by a large stone well. No one who he passes speaks to him or acknowledges his presence. He sees people he knows, but they look right through him. He ignores them as well.

Ahead, the well comes into sight, and his heart skips a beat. Magdala is seated by the fountain. She is looking the other way, but even from behind he knows it is her. She rises as if sensing his presence, but she doesn't turn. She walks past the fountain and stops at a booth selling brightly colored cloth.

Cedrus draws closer. Magdala fingers a piece of cloth, bright red in color, almost wistfully. The woman behind the counter says something, and Magdala blushes. She turns and backs away. Then without warning Magdala spins around and dashes off through the market.

Cedrus reaches out toward her. He tries to run and follow, but it feels as if his legs are knee-deep in mud. He tries to cry out, but no sound seems to come from his tongue. Finally, he is able to move, and he begins to run. He runs as fast as he can, as if his very life depends on it. By then he barely has Magdala in his sight, but he continues to pursue her and feels himself gaining ground. She makes her way down an alley and turns a corner up ahead. Though Cedrus is hot on her tail, he is forced to stop dead in his tracks as a large crowd turns to walk down the alley from the other side. He fights his way through as best he can, bumping arms and shoulders with several of them. When he finally turns the corner, there is no sight of Magdala. Cedrus scans the area and looks everywhere for her, but she is gone. Suddenly he is totally overwhelmed by sadness, as if he has lost her forever. Cedrus shakes his head and bends over, placing his hands on his knees. As he closes his eyes and begins to cry...

Cedrus woke with a startle, a tear rolling down his cheek. He sat up very quickly, glancing around to see if anyone was watching. But the others were still asleep, and Gobius was on the other side of the camp with his back to him. The image of Magdala stuck with Cedrus. He'd felt something wrong—something beyond his ability to correct—in her flight. It had been only a dream, but it was impossible for him to dismiss. He rolled over and lay back down, but he didn't sleep. When the sun rose, he joined the others but made no mention of his dream, though he couldn't shake it from his mind.

The thirteen chanced a small fire for breakfast and cooked a quick meal. It was likely to be a long day's journey, and they had no idea if they would be as lucky the next time they sought shelter. They began to gather their supplies, with Nomis and Alphaeus passing the saddlebags around to their owners.

"There is water missing," Alphaeus called. "Someone has been into the water supply."

They gathered around, and Alphaeus held up the bottle from which Cidivus had drunk the night before. He swung it by its strap and stared around at the others in confusion.

"This was first in line," he explained. "It was full last night when we went to sleep. Now it's all but empty."

Silex stepped forward and took the bottle from Alphaeus, turning to the others.

"Who did it?" he asked. He swept them all with his gaze, lingering a bit longer on Cidivus than he did on the others.

No one spoke. Cidivus looked over at Gobius, who stared right back at him. Yet he too remained silent.

"The rationing of the water is not voluntary," Silex said at last. "It is necessary, and if we have to, we will enforce it. Most of you are veteran warriors who should know better. I thought that all of you would, but then, I thought a lot of things before yesterday."

When they all held their silence, Silex sighed. "Okay then," he said. "Tonight we will begin to double the guard. One will watch the perimeter, the other the water, until we are able to replenish our supplies or reach the far side of the desert."

"It was him," Cedrus said, pointing directly at Cidivus. "It had to be."

"Did you see him do it?" Silex asked.

"No, but I can assure you that he did. Who else is selfish enough to commit such an act?" Cedrus asked.

"Who are you to accuse me?" Cidivus said, reaching for his sword.

"Enough," Silex said. "If you did not see him do it, Cedrus, then you cannot possibly know if he did. We may as well put this behind us and get moving."

Cidivus glanced at Gobius, surprised that he hadn't exposed him as the culprit. Gobius looked Cidivus in the eye but not in a way that was judgmental. In fact, it was almost serene enough to put Cidivus at ease. They locked stares for a brief moment before walking back to the horses.

The thirteen mounted, turning once more into the desert and aiming toward the Northern Mountains, a wavering, hazy line of purple on the horizon. They rode at a steady pace but did not push the horses. Despite the urge to quicken the pace on the wide open plain, they knew that doing so might cause their mounts to give out.

"Distances in the desert are deceptive," Tonitrus said. "Those mountains look barely a day's ride from afar, but they might be five."

"Very true, Tonitrus," replied Cantos. "Who knows? They might even be farther than that."

Silex was about to comment when his mount suddenly shied to the side and reared, nearly unseating him. Something was wrong. The horses sensed it, and the thirteen began to scan the surrounding area. There was nothing in sight but sand and rocks.

"What do you suppose is happening?" Cedrus asked.

"I don't know," replied Og. "But it can't be good."

The big man barely finished his statement when the ground beneath them began to shake. The thirteen immediately suspected an earthquake, but as they looked around them, they saw five massive holes form in the sand. Something was sucking the sand below like furious maelstroms. But as the sand descended below the earth, something else rose up. They heard a hideous, chittering scream as five huge, ghastly creatures came to the surface. They had heads like giant locusts and the bodies, claws, and tails of a giant scorpion. They opened their mouths to reveal razor-sharp teeth that could pass for those of a lion.

"By the Author!" exclaimed Cantos. "Cyporsks!"

"What are Cyporsks?" cried Nomis.

"There's no time for that now!" Silex yelled. "Split up and form three groups of three and two groups of two. In this way we'll confront each of them and fend off their attack. Ferox and I will square off with this one here. Let's go, brother!"

As Silex and Ferox approached, the monster began lashing out with its tail, looking to impale the brothers with its poisonous stinger. When it became obvious that they could not make headway in advancing on the creature, Ferox drew his bow and shot an arrow in so quickly that it seemed almost magical. The arrow flew directly into the terrifying monster's right eye, and Silex, seeing his chance, yanked hard on the reins and drove his heels into his horse's flanks. His mount lurched to the left just as the giant stinger pounded into the earth with incredible force.

But he was still unable to get close enough for an attack. The creature turned so that it could see Silex with its good eye. As it continuously launched its tail toward him, it was only a matter of time before the stinger lanced Silex or his mount by sheer luck.

Ferox shot again, but the monster moved at the last second, and the arrow went wide. Silex knew that he had to give his brother a clear shot, and he came up with an idea. He spurred his mount to the right and began to circle the beast. As he raced around it, the Cyporsk turned and followed him with its left eye. Ferox, always in tune with his brother, quickly deciphered the plan. He held up his bow, drew back, and waited. The Cyporsk now had its back to him, but as Silex baited the creature, it began to turn in Ferox's direction. As soon as the left eye came into view, Ferox fired. His shot was incredibly accurate, as the arrow plunged deep into the center of its other eye.

The monster was now blinded, making it a vulnerable target for Silex. He aggressively charged the beast, ultimately driving his sword down into and through its body. It collapsed to the ground, writhing in pain as Silex continued to press down with his sword. As Ferox ran up beside him, they both watched as it breathed its last breath.

While Silex and Ferox were executing their strategic attack, Cedrus had been backed up against a boulder by one of the monsters. He'd batted away the creature's questing claws twice, but it was too strong, and on the second block his weapon was knocked free. Its stinger dripped venom and rose, but before it could strike, Tonitrus threw himself at it from the side. Flashing his sword with incredible speed, he managed to lop off the stinger two tail segments below its tip. It seemed to float in the air just for a second before dropping to the sand with a gruesome *thump*.

The Cyporsk spun, and Tonitrus met the attack. He whirled, blade slicing in a wide arc, and the first of the monster's pincers snapped, dangling uselessly as it screeched and lunged.

"Look out!" Cedrus cried. The creature whirled and shot its remaining pincer straight at Tonitrus' head. The motion was incredibly quick, but Tonitrus reacted with even greater speed. He dropped beneath the blow, swung his sword straight over his head, and cleanly cut the remaining claw from its flailing arm.

"Stay back, Cedrus!" Tonitrus growled as he drove forward to ram his blade deep into the creature's chest. There was a horrible cracking sound as the tip of his sword broke through the monster's outer shell. Tonitrus was almost buried under its stumbling weight as Cedrus cried out to his brother. But at the last second he ducked and rolled, escaping what could have been a crushing death.

Cantos and Sceptrus were backed into a small crevasse by a third Cyporsk after they rounded the corner of the stone outcropping to their left. It attacked viciously, but Sceptrus, using his body as a shield, brought his staff to bear and managed to divert the huge pincers. He blocked three attempts in quick succession and actually managed to bat aside the stinger as it almost skewered Cantos, who cowered back against the stone. But there was no way to win the battle. The staff could work only as a defensive weapon against the monster.

Pugius, who'd drawn Minstro into a small cave-like opening, fired off a pair of daggers at the creature, hoping to distract it long enough for Sceptrus and Cantos to escape. The blades sank into the beast's exoskeleton but could not pierce deeply enough to have any significant impact.

"Here!" Minstro cried.

Pugius turned in surprise to find Minstro holding out his sword. It was considerably heavier than a dagger but much smaller than a normal sword. Pugius took it by the blade and hefted it.

"Hurry!" Minstro urged.

Pugius sized up the situation quickly. The huge scorpion's stinger was poised for another strike. If it landed, either Cantos or Sceptrus would be killed. Pugius drew back his arm, stepped into the throw, and let out a loud grunt.

The tiny sword whistled through the air. At first it seemed it would go too high, but the extra weight pulled it into a much shorter arc. Just as the Cyporsk flexed to snap its stinger down, the sword bit deep, whirling in and through shell and flesh. The stinger was lopped off, and the blade spun on past. The monster reared in pain and slammed down. As it did, Og let out a huge bellowing cry and rushed in from the side.

The creature was too distracted to notice the new threat.

The huge man's axe rose and fell, driving in behind the Cyporsk's head. It fell almost immediately, flopping on the ground as Og stared down at it. As he stood there, Cantos and Sceptrus stepped up beside him, and they watched the hideous beast shiver and twitch in its death throes.

Nomis and Alphaeus were fighting their own battle. A fourth Cyporsk skittered over the sand at them and they split, moving to either side.

"Distract it," Nomis cried. "If we stay together, it will get one of us for sure. But if we confuse it, perhaps one of us can get close enough to strike."

The monster moved forward and buried its stinger in the earth less than a foot from where Alphaeus sat in his saddle. He drove his mount to the right, and Nomis went left, darting in to swing his blade at the creature's claw. It slapped at him; with a cry of surprise and pain he was driven from the saddle. His mount took off, and Nomis lay stunned and vulnerable.

Alphaeus saw him and tried to draw the creature away, but it sensed weakness and moved in for the kill. Then, as if appearing from thin air, Thaddeus stepped between Nomis and his would-be executioner. The big man stood his ground, but he made no attempt to advance. Rather, he waited for the Cyporsk to make the first move. When it launched its stinger directly at him, he spun with a grace belied by his great stature, ducking just to the side and driving his club in a whipping arc that crushed the segmented tail with a sickening crunch.

Thaddeus didn't hesitate. As the beast reared, he launched himself with a battle cry that rang from the stones around them and drove the club down on the creature's head. The hard shell cracked, and gore splattered Thaddeus from head to foot. While the monster was dazed, he began to swing the club mercilessly, pounding the beast into oblivion. When he finally stopped, the Cyporsk shuddered but once before crumpling in a lifeless heap.

Behind them, the last of the creatures moved in on Cidivus. When he'd seen them rise up from the ground, Cidivus had turned his mount, trying to go back and around the stone outcropping in order to escape. He'd made it only a short distance when the Cyporsk dropped down before him, leaving him no choice but to draw his blade. Now cornered, Cidivus attempted to use his snakelike quickness to evade the monster. As it launched a pincer at him, he drove it aside with his sword, barely avoiding the back swing as the creature resumed its attack. He blocked two more quick assaults and actually started to grin.

"Not so terrible, are you?" he grated, swinging his blade again.

He was too focused on the pincers and thus didn't see the tail rising…twitching…readying for the strike. Gobius, who had now come to Cidivus' aid, saw exactly what the beast was looking to do. The unicorn sensed his intent, and it dashed forward. Gobius drew his blade and held on tight. He wasn't as experienced a rider as many of the others, but the unicorn worked with him. It left the ground in a long, fluid leap, and Gobius, trusting to its balance, swung his sword in a Herculean hack. It severed the tail, leaving it dangling from the monster's body. The unicorn, aware of the proximity of the poisonous stinger, lurched to the side.

Cidivus glanced up, saw the danger that he'd been in, and froze just for an instant. In that second the Cyporsk spun, screeching with pain. Now enraged, it swung out its heavy pincer and struck Cidivus on the side of the head. The blow stunned him, and he nearly fell from the saddle. The black backed away, nervous and skittish. But being a trained war-horse, it didn't break and run.

The unicorn spun as well, and with Gobius clinging to it, dove back into the battle. The wounded Cyporsk moved erratically, making it difficult to target. Gobius swung several times, but he could not get a clean shot at the pincers, which were still snapping and flailing about. He heard the cries of the others and knew they were rushing to his aid, but they might be too late. He had to finish things and do so quickly.

Cidivus lay half-unconscious across his horse's neck. He sat up groggily and tried to focus. His blade had dropped to the ground, and he fumbled at his belt for his dagger, though it would be far too small to be of any real use.

Gobius tried again to cut through one of the front appendages and managed a hit. His blow half-severed the pincer, causing it to hang uselessly. But the pain maddened the creature further, and with its last strength it whirled.

The unicorn acted. Without urging from Gobius, it drove forward, hooves grinding into the sandy, rocky soil. The great horn drove into the Cyporsk's chest and lifted it off the ground. As the unicorn pressed on, it jacked the monster up and drove it back. The beast toppled, and Gobius felt himself leaving the ground once more as the unicorn continued up and over, pounding its hooves into the creature's dying body.

And just like that it was over. The thirteen spun wildly about, watching the rocks and the sandy expanse of the desert, but no more of the creatures appeared. Gobius slid from the unicorn's back and ran to Cidivus. Cidivus tried to push him away, but he was dazed, and Gobius managed to get him down from his mount and to lay him against a stone.

Cidivus' face was swollen where the pincer had struck. His eye was black and almost shut. He shook his head slowly from side to side. Silex came over to him, holding a waterskin.

"Drink," he said. "You've taken quite a blow."

Cidivus took the water. It was impossible to read his expression, but it almost seemed that he sneered. He turned the waterskin up and drank deeply until Silex snatched it back. Then Cidivus began to cough.

When he got his breath back, he glanced up with his one good eye and caught sight of Gobius.

"That's twice," Cidivus said.

He looked as if about to say something more, but Gobius smiled and motioned for him to keep quiet. "I'm glad I could help," Gobius said.

Alphaeus and Ferox rode out to gather up the horses that had been scattered, and the others checked weapons, packs, and supplies. Nomis, who'd recovered from his fall, wandered around the far side of the rocks and called out to the others.

Silex and Tonitrus ran to him. Where Nomis stood, staring at the rocks, a small pool of water glistened in the sun, fed from an underground stream.

"You think they were guarding it?" Tonitrus asked. "Or did we just happen to wander up at feeding time?"

"I don't know," Silex answered, "but I think we need to fill our waterskins and get out of here before anything else shows up for a drink."

They gazed in the direction they'd been heading. There was a small range of hills ahead.

"Is that a tree?" Nomis asked.

They all stared for a moment, and Tonitrus shook his head. The heat rose from the ground in waves, blurring their sight, so it was difficult to make out what was real and what was a mirage.

"It might well be," Silex said. "But it's too hard to tell from here. We need to get everyone mounted and moving."

Og, Nomis, Alphaeus, and Cedrus filled the water bottles and skins while the others packed their equipment. Cidivus looked awful, but he was up and moving and insisted he could ride. He was more subdued than usual, though Silex thought it was only because it hurt his bruised face to speak.

Within an hour they were riding across the wasteland again, the carcasses of the Cyporsks already growing pungent in the sun and the heat. They watched carefully in all directions, but nothing moved, and after a while they began to relax a little.

"What exactly were those monsters back there?" asked Cedrus. "Cantos, had you ever heard of anything that looked so abominable?"

"As I said earlier," Cantos said, "they are called Cyporsks. They're part insect and part scorpion with the jaws of a lion. I have read those stories, but of course I never imagined that they were anything but poetic exaggeration. And I certainly could not have known that they resided underground in Mortuus Valley. I suppose they may be the reason why so many adventurers have gone missing when passing through, and why this place came to be known as the 'Valley of Death.'"

"I'll never forget them," said Thaddeus. "The pincers, the razor-sharp teeth, the stingers…I can't imagine a beast being more dangerous."

"A good bit less dangerous now," Pugius noted with a sly

grin. He slapped Minstro, who was mounted before him, on the shoulder. "Isn't that right, Minstro? If not for this man's sword, I could never have cut the stinger off the one attacking Sceptrus and Cantos."

"I suppose we owe you one now, Minstro," Sceptrus said, smiling.

Minstro blushed bashfully and held his silence. He glanced over at Cidivus. The little man still did not feel comfortable around all of them, Cidivus in particular, and he was a bit ashamed of how little use he'd been to them so far on the quest.

"I too might be dead," Pugius continued, "if you hadn't thought quickly enough to give me your sword. Thanks again, my good friend."

The battle had left them exhausted, and though they rode steadily, it was several hours before they were close enough to know for sure that there were trees on the hills ahead.

"It is the end of the wasteland," Cantos said. "We should start seeing grass and plants soon, possibly some game."

"Author be praised," Silex said. "I'm sure I speak for all of us when I say that we'll be thrilled to leave this desert behind."

"I've seen enough of this place to last me a lifetime," replied Og.

They continued in silence, climbing slowly into the hills. At last they found a hollow with trees on both sides, and Silex directed them to stop. They made camp quickly and efficiently, setting their watch and eating without a fire. All of them were exhausted, and they didn't want to take a chance on attracting anything or anyone to their camp.

Before he dropped off to sleep, Cidivus turned to watch Gobius, who knelt in prayer beside a tree. He rolled over on his good side and lay back, reflecting on all that Gobius had said to him and done for him.

As the moon rose, darkness closed in on them, and they rested. In the distance, but not so far now, the Northern Mountains rose over them like silent sentinels.

Chapter Eighteen

They passed a couple more days in the hills as they advanced toward the Northern Mountains. Tonitrus had been right in stating that distances in the desert can be deceptive, for they were farther away from their destination than it had appeared. As they drew closer, the mountains rose above them, tall, majestic, and sobering. The thirteen advanced toward them cautiously and in silence for the most part. Without even noticing he was doing it, Cantos moved toward the front of the group. When they came to a seldom-used road twisting around the side of a cliff and sloping upward, he stopped.

At first the others didn't notice. They continued riding slowly up the trail. It wasn't until Ferox and Og, who'd been bringing up the rear, drew even with him that the group slowed and came to a stop.

"What is it?" Pugius asked, turning back. "What do you see?"

Cantos stared up into the mountains. His eyes were open very wide, and he studied the peaks rising on either side of the road as well as the road slicing up between them. He remained silent a few moments longer and shook his head as if waking from a fog.

"I've seen this road and these hills in The Scrolls. I know this place. It's just that I never imagined I would one day see it in person." Cantos pointed up and to the right.

"If we follow the trail up through those peaks, we will be walking the same route as Haggiselm. We are so close. This is the exact mountain range. I could not mistake them after the descriptions I've read."

"You are certain?" Silex asked.

Cantos nodded. "If we follow this road to the right, we will climb until we reach the entrance to the labyrinth where Haggiselm supposedly hid the Medallion."

They all turned at this. The thirteen sat and stared upward in silence for a good few minutes. It finally hit them that their goal was now within reach.

"We need to keep moving," Silex said. "We have to find a place to camp, and we need water."

"I am trying to remember what I know," Cantos said. "I believe that there is water nearby."

"It is on this part of the journey that we need your guidance more than ever," Silex said. "What you have read, what you know, no matter how scattered the details, is all we have to go on. We could ride through these mountains for years and not come across the entrance to the right cave."

"I will do what I can," Cantos said. "When we make camp, I will consult the records I brought with me."

"I'll help," Gobius said.

Cantos nodded absently. They traveled upward around the cliff and to the right, after which the road straightened. As they continued, it widened. Here and there they saw a patch of brush, and the higher they climbed, the greener their surroundings became. Finally, the thirteen reached a point where they looked above and saw a line of trees. A couple of them also heard a faint sound.

"What's that?" Sceptrus said.

"Water," Ferox said with a grin. Soon they were all able to hear the sound of a stream bubbling over stone. To the right of the road was a clearing surrounded by trees that appeared to have been trimmed back to create an almost perfectly round void.

Ferox stopped and dismounted. Before anyone could utter a word, he walked into the clearing and disappeared through the trees on the far side. A moment later he returned, smiling.

"There is water," he said. "And plenty of it. I believe we have found our camp for the night."

They wasted no time dismounting, tending to the horses, and refilling every available waterskin from the stream that rolled gently downward from the side of the mountain. As they drank the cool, clear water, their spirits lightened considerably. They laid out a small fire, being careful to keep guards set in either direction on the road. Ferox disappeared shortly after they arrived, and before the sun had completely dropped over the horizon, he reappeared with a small deer slung over his shoulder.

Og and Thaddeus helped him with the animal, and within

a short time they had skinned, dressed, and butchered it, setting large slabs of meat to roast on spits over the fire. The food satisfied them so completely that the road behind them seemed to fade from their thoughts, at least temporarily.

Nonetheless they did not relax their vigilance. At least three stood guard at any time, and as the others drifted through conversations into rest and then sleep, the guards patrolled, checking in with one another and watching every side of the encampment. There had already been too many surprises.

As they drifted off, Cantos stared up at the peaks above him. In his mind he continued to reflect upon maps, poems, and ancient stories. It seemed to him in that moment that he could imagine Haggiselm riding up the trail a few yards away. The proximity to places he'd only read and dreamed about caused his heart to race. He closed his eyes and fell into a deep sleep filled with dreams of mountain peaks, tall pine trees, and the entrance to a grand cavern.

The night passed without incident. They rose, had a breakfast to rival the previous night's dinner, and topped off their water bottles. There was no indication they'd be without water in the mountains, but after the wasteland, they were taking no chances. Once mounted, Silex called Cantos to his side.

"What do you recommend?" Silex asked. "There is only one road here, but I suspect before long it will come to an end."

"I believe it will," Cantos replied without hesitation. "I have given it a lot of thought, and I am nearly certain that all of the texts mention branching to the right and up the second peak. If we pay attention, we should be able to find the same road that Haggiselm followed."

"Good enough for me," Silex nodded. "Lead on."

Cantos turned his mount toward the mountains and rode slowly forward. The others fell in behind him, spreading out and taking up stations to watch the peaks to either side as well as the road behind.

They climbed through the first two days and on into late afternoon of the third. Twice the road forked, and both times Cantos bore right. Just before the sun dipped behind the peaks in the distance, they came to a point where the trail forked in three directions. Two of the paths wound up the mountain vaguely right, while the third bore left and appeared to cut in between two cliffs. Cantos drew up and surveyed the landscape with a look of bewilderment on his face.

"What is it?" Silex asked.

"I'm not sure," Cantos said. "I don't recall a mention of a triple fork in Haggiselm's journey."

"Go with your instinct, then," Silex said. "We can only trust that you will find what we are meant to find."

"All of the accounts say that Haggiselm consistently bore to the right," Cantos said. "They always implied that there were but two paths to take. Still, I suppose it's possible that there were three or more at times."

"Given what you have said, it seems as though we should take the one that appears to lead as far right as possible," Gobius said.

"I think you're right, Gobius," replied Cantos. "That would be this one here."

"Let us go then," said Silex.

There was a snort of derision as Cidivus spurned his mount and pushed around them. He took the fork to the right and was out of sight in seconds.

"Impatient as always, I see," said Tonitrus.

They followed behind Cidivus, slowly and cautiously. Not too far up the trail they reached a long, straight stretch of road. At the top, Cidivus sat on his mount, staring at the face of the cliff.

Silex hastened his ascent, and the others followed suit. A few moments later they gathered around Cidivus in an almost circular, cleared area. The cliff face opened up into a jagged cavern door that stood at least ten feet in height and was wide enough to accommodate two horses side by side. Deep in the depths a light flickered.

"What is this place?" Cedrus asked. "Is this the cavern? Could this be where the labyrinth is located?"

Cantos dismounted and stepped forward. He walked to the dark opening and studied the stone walls to either side, looking for a mark or an indicator. There was nothing. Then he stood dead center and stared into the darkness.

"I believe this is it, though I honestly can't be sure," he said. "We have followed the route that historians have recorded. It has brought us here."

"The last time we entered a cavern," Cidivus said, "it did not end well."

"We will go in slowly," Silex said. "This time we all go. We can tie the horses out here, but we are going to need torches in order to navigate our way."

"I don't think so," Cantos said.

He waved at the cavern entrance. "I don't know where

it's coming from, but farther in is light. It's as if a campfire is burning."

"Is there mention of a fire in the labyrinth?" Thaddeus asked.

"No," Cantos said. "There is very little information available on what happened after Haggiselm entered and where he hid the Medallion."

"Sounds like we're in for an interesting search," Og said.

"Indeed," Cantos agreed. "But all we can do is to go where The Author—and our hearts—will lead us. It is this part of the journey that will test our faith more so than any other."

"We will enter," Silex said. "We have come too far to sit out here and debate whether we've come to the right place. If we have not, then we'll know soon enough. Someone had to light that fire inside the cavern; let's see if we can find out who it was."

Some were hesitant to dismount and follow Silex, but after Tonitrus turned and glared at them, they quickly jumped from their horses and prepared to enter the cavern.

"Ferox, you and Cantos come with me," Silex said. "Alphaeus, Nomis, and Thaddeus will follow, and the rest will file in three at a time. Og, you and Sceptrus will bring up the rear...keep your eyes open and watch our backs. That light doesn't seem to be too far down, so whatever—or whoever—it is, we're going to find out sooner rather than later."

They all nodded except for Cidivus, who shook his head and rolled his eyes. But even he kept his thoughts to himself. In those few moments their world shifted. They'd started out weeks before with a purpose in mind, but that purpose had seemed distant and unreal. They'd traveled many miles, believing they were ready to face destiny. But until they stepped through the entrance to that cavern, the true gravity of it had not settled so solidly into their hearts. It was one thing to chase destiny across deserts and through dark forests but quite another to meet it face to face.

They started in slowly. Cantos walked slightly ahead of the others. He did not draw his sword, but Silex and Ferox kept their weapons at the ready. The light below them flickered and danced. There was no sound but the echoes of their footsteps as their boots scraped the stone floor.

"Are you alright, Minstro?" Pugius asked, speaking quietly enough that none of the others could hear.

"I'm ready," Minstro replied. "This is why I came, Pugius. This is why I'm here. Let's go."

When they'd descended about fifty feet, Silex held up his hand to stop those behind him. The passage ahead branched right and left. The flickering light glowed on the left, and Silex looked over at Cantos, almost as if to ask which direction they should go.

Cantos shrugged and pointed silently toward the light. Silex nodded and walked ahead. He stepped up to the corner, took a deep breath, and glanced hurriedly around into the light. Then he ducked back as if confused, and he leaned out again. This time he stepped around the corner, his blade dipped toward the ground.

Cantos followed Silex slowly, and the rest stepped up behind them. As each man rounded the corner, he stopped and stood very still, staring. Unwilling to wait his turn, Cidivus pushed through the others and stepped around the corner.

"What is it?" he said softly. The others motioned to him to keep quiet.

Silex took one step forward and then another. He found himself walking down a path that led to a fire burning at the far end. The fire centered a circular chamber, and around that fire, seated in chairs of carved wood painted with gilt and encrusted with crystals and jewels sat three women. They watched the approaching men with calm, almost ethereal expressions on their faces. They did not speak, nor did they rise. They sat in silence and waited as the thirteen entered their chamber one by one and stood across the fire from them.

"By The Author," Thaddeus said.

"Cantos, who are they?" asked Tonitrus.

"I'm afraid I have no idea," Cantos responded.

Silex stepped forward and addressed the women, who gave all the semblance of goddesses sitting on majestic thrones.

"If we are intruding," he said, "then I apologize for us all. But may I ask who you are and why you are residing here, deep in a cavern in the Northern Mountains?"

There was a tinkle of laughter, bright and clear, and the woman seated in the center, directly across the low burning fire from Silex, sat slightly forward. She had silver-blonde hair, almost white, and if her features had not been so youthful and full of life, she might have appeared ancient. Her eyes even from a distance flashed a bright, sapphire blue.

"We are the Seers," she said. "The Seers of Fate. We have been waiting for your arrival, Silex of Mavinor."

"How is it that you know my name?" Silex asked with a look of astonishment on his face.

"We know all of your names," the woman replied. "We know all about your lives. We know your stories. We know your quest, and we have awaited your arrival with great anticipation."

"Then," Cantos said, stepping forward, "this is the entrance to the labyrinth?"

The second Seer, seated to the left of center, replied.

"No, Cantos. This is not the Labyrinth of Secrets," she said.

"The Labyrinth of Secrets?" Cantos replied.

"Yes," the second Seer said. "The place where Haggiselm hid the Medallion. It is the Labyrinth of Secrets that you seek."

The thirteen fell silent, and though Cidivus was as mystified as the rest of them, he could not help but cut in. "Who are you—really?" he asked. "What is this place?"

"We were sent by no one of this world, Cidivus," the third woman said. She was slender, with the same white-gold hair as the others. She was not as tall, but her eyes were wider, and she turned to face Cidivus calmly. "We were sent by The Author to aid you in your task. We serve Him and Him alone. We have been blessed with the gift of prophecy, and we are here because we knew that you would come."

"So," Cidivus said, stepping forward, "we are to believe that you've just been here all this time, waiting for the thirteen of us to wander in? That's your story?"

"Cidivus!" Silex said. "Who are you to question them? Leave this to me."

"After you, leader," Cidivus said with a sarcastic tone. As he fell silent, Silex turned to address the Seers of Fate.

"If you have words of prophecy that can help us along our way, we would be honored to hear them. We have traveled many miles, and we have overcome many obstacles to arrive here. I feel that we are near our goal, but it appears we have lost our way."

"You are not so far astray," the woman on the left said softly. "Sit. We will consult, and we will see what is revealed. What we learn we will gladly share."

Cidivus rolled his eyes again but kept his silence. The thirteen spread out, taking seats on a ring of stones facing the Seers. The women waited until their guests were settled and then turned to one another.

Forming a small circle on the far side of the fire, they joined hands. The dim light danced on their hair, making it shimmer and ripple with captured luminescence. The flames in the fire, which had burned low as the thirteen entered, began to rise and dance, obscuring their view and lengthening the shadows in the already dark cavern. The air seemed to take on a life of its own, streaming over their skin and through their hair. If the thirteen could have held their breath, they would have. Somewhere in the midst of all of this the first woman threw her head back, faced the heavens, and began to speak.

"Seek," she said, "and ye shall find. Knock, and the door will be opened to you."

Her words hung in the air like smoke and then danced away, replaced by the crackling of the fire. She lowered her head until she faced the other two and, as if by some mental command, they took a step to the left, bringing the second woman around to face across the fire.

Her voice rang out clear as a bell.

"What is good lies in the center."

As the sound of her voice died away, the Seers circled a final time so that the last of the three faced the thirteen.

Her eyes, even in the darkness and across the fire, seemed to glow with a brilliant white light. It obscured her features and spread to blur those of her companions.

"Only the sentinels can lead you home," she said.

Her words echoed briefly, and then the chamber fell to silence once more. The flames of the fire burned lower, and the three women released each other's hands. They seemed almost to shrink as they fell back and sat in their chairs. For a long moment no one spoke. Once again it was Cidivus who broke the silence.

"That's it?" he asked, incredulous. "You have messages for us from The Author Himself, and all we get is cryptic nonsense and riddles? How can this possibly help us?"

Cedrus laid a hand on Cidivus' arm in an attempt to hold him back, but Cidivus shook it off. They stared into each other's eyes for a brief moment and looked as if they might come to blows with one another. But as Silex and Tonitrus came to stand between them, Cidivus turned away and started toward the entrance to the cave. Gobius moved as if to follow, but Silex shook his head.

"Let him go," Silex said. "We will speak with him later. I will not allow anyone to dishonor the Seers by arguing or fighting."

The fire had died down, and the women sat watching them from the far side. The strange glow that had surrounded them had faded to a shimmer, but their presence still brought an unearthly sensation.

"Can you tell us anything more?" Cantos asked, stepping forward. "We are grateful for your assistance and for the wisdom you have imparted, assuming that we prove wise enough to make use of it. But we have strayed from our course, and I do believe we need something more concrete to lead us in the right direction."

"You would have come to us eventually," the first woman said softly. "Your path leads through these caverns, and the prophecy is vital to your success. That much I know. But I am afraid that is where our knowledge ends. The rest, Cantos, you will have to figure out on your own."

Cantos nodded. He dropped his chin to his chest, deep in thought.

"Does any of it mean anything to you?" Gobius asked.

Cantos shook his head. "No, Gobius, I'm afraid not," he said.

"We thank you," Silex said, stepping closer to the fire. "We are grateful for any assistance that we can obtain during this quest."

"What we have given you is all we have to offer, Silex," the first Seer said.

"I understand," Silex replied. "We will leave you now and continue onward. If I may make one last request, please pray for our success, and may The Author be with you."

"And also with you, Silex of Mavinor," the second Seer said. "Consider your request granted. You shall have our prayers as you strive to find your way. Remember always that you are chosen."

Silex nodded and turned. He gestured to the others, and slowly each of them approached the fire and bowed to the Seers. Then they made their way back up the passage and out into the late afternoon light. Cidivus stood on the far side of the small clearing outside the cavern. Hearing their approach, he quickly turned around.

"Did you hear enough nonsense then?" he asked. "Did

you get a large enough serving of gibberish for us to continue? I can't believe we wasted our time on those three crazy women."

"I've had about enough from you, Cidivus," Cedrus said. "I'm sure that I speak for all of us when I say that." He began to move toward him, but Gobius came over to hold Cedrus back.

"That's enough!" Silex said sharply. "As I've said before, we can't fulfill this task if we continue to fight among ourselves. The Seers said that we are not that far from our destination, and the closer we get to the Labyrinth of Secrets, the more we will need to act as a unit."

"Don't worry, Silex," said Tonitrus. "I'll personally see to it that any further discord is dealt with swiftly and severely."

"I'll assist you with that," said Og, holding up his battle axe to make his point.

"Very good," said Silex. "We will backtrack to the forks in the road, and we will consult what information we have… then we will continue. Our goals have not changed, and we should be thankful that The Author has chosen to gift us with clues, regardless of how cryptic they might seem."

"Cryptic?" Cidivus said. "Knock and the door shall be opened? I learned to do that when I was a boy."

Silex's glare silenced him; Cidivus shook his head and looked away.

"Let's get moving," Silex said. "We can get back to the triple fork before nightfall. We should be able to find a place to camp before it gets too dark."

They mounted in silence. Cantos was lost in thought, and Sceptrus rode close at his side, a look of concern on his face. The others spread out, keeping watch as they had since reaching the mountains, with Silex and Ferox on point and Thaddeus bringing up the rear with Og. They eventually reached the fork in the road without incident.

"It's possible," Cantos said, almost as if talking to himself, "that when Haggiselm came through here, there were only two branches to the road. The Scrolls have so clearly said to stay on the right-hand path—it's hard to believe that after being correct so many times they would cease to lead in the right direction."

Silex nodded. "It's as good a theory as any. But it is clear to me now that we were meant to follow that road, though it did not lead to the Labyrinth of Secrets. The Author led us to the Seers, and now He will lead us to the Labyrinth."

"But which of the other roads will we take?" asked Pugius.

They all looked to Cantos.

"Well," he said, "I can only surmise that we should take the middle road. If my theory is correct and that third branch did not exist when Haggiselm passed this way, then the middle road would have been the one on the right."

"Sounds logical to me," said Ferox.

Cidivus sneered but remained silent. The group started up the center trail, moving very slowly. Rocky crags rose to either side, and they didn't want to inadvertently pass some cleverly concealed entrance or overgrown cavern. Once or twice they came to openings in the cliff faces, but none was deep enough or tall enough to lead to the Labyrinth of Secrets. As the day wore on, frustration began to set in.

They found a clearing large enough to make camp, but it wasn't as sheltered or as spacious as the one they'd found the previous night. There was also no spring nearby. They were forced to tie off the animals along the cliff side across the road from the camp and to split the guard duty, so fewer of them could sleep at any one time.

After setting a small fire and making a quick meal, they found themselves exhausted, mentally and physically. The words of the Seers weighed heavily on their minds. The messages had been short and simple, so simple that one would think it easy to make sense of them.

Cantos found a flat rock and arranged his things around it. He pulled out the scrolls, fragments, books, and notes he'd brought with him and prepared to go through them yet again, looking for something he'd missed. He first pulled out a quill, a small bottle of ink, and a blank sheet of paper upon which he carefully recorded the prophecies of the Seers.

"Are you afraid you'll forget the words?" Gobius asked, dropping to sit cross-legged beside the stone.

"I won't forget them," Cantos said, "but I want them close at hand, and I don't want to have to think about them. I am wondering if they don't contain some obscure reference to something I've already been over. I'm hoping I'll see—going back through all of it one more time—exactly what they are trying to tell us."

"They were telling you that there are three crazy women who live in a cave," Cidivus snapped. "Only they just didn't come out and say it."

"How many times do we have to tell you that enough is enough?" Cedrus said, rising.

Cidivus turned, not even bothering to stand, and regarded the younger man. "Enough of what?" he said, almost dismissing Cedrus' words. "I can't help it if all of you have lost your minds. Mine, on the other hand, is not so weak."

Cedrus growled deep in his throat. He still hadn't forgotten how Cidivus had mocked him for keeping Magdala's scarf. He was also quite certain that it was Cidivus who had stolen water on their trek through Mortuus Valley. Up until now, with help from Gobius, he had been able to contain his anger. But this time he had been pushed over the edge. After weeks of putting up with him through the many obstacles they had faced on the journey, it finally all caught up with Cedrus. He was on the far side of the small clearing. Looking directly at Cidivus, he began to lunge.

"You have no respect!" Cedrus cried. "You have no love for anything or anyone but yourself. You are here for one purpose and one purpose only, and that is to seize the opportunity to succeed Onestus as King of Mavinor. That is all you want, Cidivus. That's what it's always been about for you. Is that right?"

"So you say, Cedrus," Cidivus said. "Why don't you just go back to sniffing your girlfriend's scarf?"

Cedrus ran at him, but before he could reach Cidivus, Gobius rose from his seat near Cantos, and Tonitrus joined him. They jumped between the two men and caught Cedrus by his arms.

"It's not worth it," Tonitrus said. "Let it go. You can't change what the man thinks by fighting. We have had a long day—and a very long journey leading up to it. Get some rest. When the sun rises, everything will be clearer."

"Oh yes," Cidivus cut in. "Clear like the words of your three lady friends. 'In the center lies what is good.' Do you suppose she is talking about some sort of sweetmeat, Cedrus? Perhaps the center is filled with honey, or maybe something even sweeter? I bet your girlfriend would know the answer to that. Too bad she's not here with us."

As the words rolled off Cidivus' tongue, Cedrus felt his blood boiling uncontrollably. His adrenalin levels skyrocketed, and he tore loose from Gobius and Tonitrus, making a beeline for Cidivus. Cidivus quickly rose to his feet as Cedrus charged and tackled him to the ground. Cidivus rolled him over and sat on top of him, but Cedrus rolled again and knocked Cidivus off. As they stood to face each other, Cidivus made a fist with his right hand and swung with all his might toward Cedrus' jaw. But Cedrus ducked and landed a left hook to Cidivus' side, being careful to avoid his breastplate. As Cidivus doubled over in pain, Cedrus raised his knee to the forehead of his nemesis, knocking him back several feet.

As Cedrus charged once again, Tonitrus grabbed him by the back of his tunic. It happened so quickly that Tonitrus overreacted. He swung Cedrus away from Cidivus with more force than he had intended, catching him off guard. The younger man went spinning off across the road in the direction of the horses, clearly out of control.

As Tonitrus watched in horror, Gobius tried in vain to catch Cedrus before he landed. But he was too late. Cedrus turned in a half-circle, barely avoiding Silex's horse, and with a cry he pitched over backward, straight into the stone side of the mountain. The horses shied, and for a moment they obscured him from view.

"Cedrus!" Tonitrus cried. He scrambled across the road, brushing the horses aside, and stood very still, staring. Gobius was at his side in a moment, and the others, even Cidivus, gathered behind them.

Cedrus lay on the ground, staring straight up into the darkening night sky over the mountain.

"Cedrus?" Tonitrus repeated, taking a step closer.

Cedrus rolled to his feet quickly, but he didn't smile or speak. He turned back to the mountain, almost gazing in wonder.

"What?" Tonitrus asked. "What is it?"

"I…I'm not sure," Cedrus said.

He rubbed the back of his head and stared at the cliff side. Cedrus stepped forward, placed his hand on the stone, and pushed. Nothing happened, and he stepped back.

"When I fell and hit this," he said, "it didn't feel quite like stone. It gave…Something moved."

"What do you mean?" Gobius asked. "Did you hit your head?"

"I did," Cedrus said. "It should have hurt a lot more than it did, but as I fell into the stone, something gave way. It was the strangest sensation."

Cedrus, Tonitrus, and Gobius stepped to the cliff and began pushing the stone. At first there was nothing—and it seemed that Cedrus must have imagined it, but then Gobius kicked a protruding boulder, and there was a deep grinding sound.

"There's something here," he said.

A moment later the three were pushing on the large stone, but it barely moved. As they continued their efforts, it began to slide inward toward the cliff face. Then, slowly, the stone ground to a halt and stopped. They pushed harder, but nothing happened.

"Looks like that's as far as it will go," Nomis said.

Og stepped forward. He rolled his massive shoulders and eyed the boulder.

"Step aside," he said.

The three eyed him skeptically. Though Og was a mountain of a man, the three of them had given the stone every ounce of their strength. Still, they moved away to make room for him. Og knelt, pressed his hands into the stone, and then worked his boots into the gravel and dirt behind him. He closed his eyes for just a moment, bunched his shoulders, and then, with a mighty roar that scattered the horses and even caused his companions to step back, he drove his heels back and his arms forward. At first, nothing happened. Then, with a grinding, crackling sound, the stone began to move again.

At first it rolled slowly, but as Og grunted and redoubled his effort, it moved faster. Soon it had swung in and out of sight, and he drew back, staggering at the release of pressure.

"What in The Author's name is that?" Ferox said softly.

"It's an entrance," Cantos said. As he stood, staring at the dark opening, his eyes opened wider. A moment later he was laughing as the others stared at him in consternation.

"What is so funny about a hole in the side of a cliff?" Cidivus asked impatiently.

"It's not a hole," Cantos corrected him. "It's a door. And that isn't why I'm laughing."

They continued to stare as Cantos regained his composure. When he could speak without bursting into new gales of laughter, he pointed a finger at Cedrus and grinned.

"It was certainly not the traditional method," he said, "but I believe one might say…you knocked."

It still took a moment for what he was saying to sink in, and then, slowly, the others started to grin as well. Cidivus walked away in disgust, but the others felt a lifting of the discouragement and frustration of the day. Cantos was right, of course. Cedrus had knocked into the stone door, and it had moved. It had been too heavy for Cedrus to open—so it seemed that in its own way the mountain had answered.

"Knock and the door will be opened," Cedrus said, rubbing the back of his head.

"What next?" Thaddeus asked, staring into the darkness.

"Next we rest," Silex said. "In the morning we enter, and we find out if this is truly the doorway to the Labyrinth and the way to the Medallion."

They all nodded, but they didn't walk away immediately. None of them doubted—none but Cidivus, and he was already wrapping in his cloak and dropping to the ground to sleep a short distance behind them. The rest slowly followed. As Cedrus and Gobius walked together, Cedrus apologized for failing to control his anger.

"I'm sorry, Gobius," Cedrus said. "I feel as if I've let you down. I promise that it won't happen again."

"It's alright, Cedrus," Gobius said. "Besides, I'd say you learned your lesson, albeit the hard way," he joked. Cedrus continued rubbing the back of his head as Gobius placed a hand on his shoulder and smiled.

As Cedrus went to lie down, Gobius looked back and saw Cantos, still staring at the doorway. He walked toward him, slowly advancing until he was beside the curious scribe.

"What is it?" Gobius said.

"I have a feeling that this is it," Cantos replied. "I know it is."

"I feel it, just as you do," Gobius said. "I truly believe we have reached our destination, Cantos."

Cantos looked at Gobius, nodded, and then looked back at the entrance to the cavern. "If so," he said, "then let the search for the Medallion and for our new king begin."

Part IV

Chapter Nineteen

Silex had arranged it so that he would have the last shift of the watch that night. He did this purposely so that he could spend an hour or so quietly reflecting before leading the others into the Labyrinth of Secrets. As he stood before the entrance, staring into the darkness, he heard footsteps behind him.

"Good morning," Gobius said.

Silex, immersed deep in thought, didn't answer at first. He finally turned to Gobius. "Good morning," he said.

"I sense that you're somewhat preoccupied," said Gobius. "You're anxious about leading us in there, aren't you?"

"Sometimes I feel as if you see right through me," said Silex. "Well, I've been thinking long and hard about the events of our quest to this point. I can't help but question some of the decisions I've made, and I'm trying to learn from those mistakes. Once we enter the Labyrinth, there is no room for error."

"There is no reason to doubt yourself," said Gobius.

"Remember what I told you before. All of us share the burden of this quest with you."

"Yes, I remember," Silex said. "I am grateful for those words, but I'm afraid they cannot ease the burden instilled in my mind."

"Do you ever take a respite from analyzing everything?" asked Gobius.

Silex laughed. "Never," he said. "I am always thinking. I'm afraid that thinking and fighting are the two things I do best."

"Then you should know that your ability to reason is a double-edged sword, Silex," said Gobius. "While it may have helped you in so many ways throughout your life, it is not always admirable to follow where your head leads. Sometimes you need to let go and follow your heart."

"I'm not sure I even know how," Silex said.

"Look at your brother," Gobius said. "You can learn a lesson or two from him. Don't you see how he follows his instincts without even giving it a second thought? That is all you need to do. Stop overanalyzing every situation. Just push forward and don't look back, without regret and without second-guessing your decisions. Unless you learn to do so, your life can never be all it was meant to be."

Silex said nothing. He merely stood still and pondered Gobius' words. As the others began to rise, Gobius said one last thing.

"When we enter that cavern, I would suggest that you lead with your heart as well as your head. If you can do that, then we will accomplish our goal. I am sure of it."

Gobius started walking back toward the others, and Silex followed after taking one last moment to think things through. They prepared breakfast and enjoyed a hearty meal, finding their appetites restored by the discovery of the cavern entrance. They ate with gusto and spoke excitedly among themselves. By the time the sun had begun to rise over the trees, they stood before the open doorway into the mountainside.

They had lights at the ready, and all were eager to get on with the quest. Before they entered the darkness, Silex turned to them.

"I think this would be a good time for us to thank The Author for bringing us this far. Despite the trials and dangers we have faced, we all stand here together, ready to fulfill the task assigned to us. May The Author guide us and keep us as we aim to carry out His will."

All but Cidivus bowed their heads at this. They prayed silently, each communing with The Author in his own way. It was easy to forget everything they had overcome while they were enduring it. But in that moment of silence the miracle of it all shone through, and it ignited a zealous fire in their hearts. Now more than ever they were ready to achieve what they had set out to do.

As they lifted their heads, Silex addressed them again. "We have to mark our trail so that we can find our way back out. If we blunder in blindly, we may find that we've come all this way only to be lost—and die—in this maze.

"Gather stones—as many as you can carry. We will stack them where the passages fork to mark our way. While we are inside, we will stick together. There will be no breaking off to search alone. Agreed?"

"So we will proceed as children, then," Cidivus said. "Perhaps we should all hold hands to be certain we stay close and safe."

"Perhaps we should leave you behind, Cidivus," Cedrus said. "I say we take a vote on it."

"I think you can convince me to go along with that one," Pugius said.

"And I as well," said Sceptrus.

"No," Gobius said. He looked at Cidivus and then at the others. "We need each other now more than ever. We cannot afford to be at odds with one another, especially now, as we stand on the verge of arriving at our destination. I know there has been discord in our group, but we need to leave our hostility on the doorstep of this cavern. The time for fighting among ourselves must now come to an end."

"Gobius is right," Silex said. "There will be no vote. We came this far as a group. Dissolving our number, even by just one, is not an option. All of us received and accepted the call to this quest. And so we will enter the cavern together, mindful of the Seers' words and watchful of each other's back. Each and every one of us depends on the others for protection, and we have no idea what we might be walking into."

No one spoke.

Silex lit one of the torches they'd readied and then stepped into the cavern. Behind him, the others began to follow. But after only a few steps they stopped, and there were mutters and cries from the doorway.

The horses had been tied off across the road. That is, all except the unicorn. Gobius had never thought to restrain it in any way—he didn't know what would happen if he tried. Now it was pressing Nomis and Alphaeus into the walls of the cavern unceremoniously, nosing its way through the group. Apparently it had decided that they weren't going into the Labyrinth of Secrets without it.

Gobius immediately went to the creature's side. He had his hand on its neck, trying to push it gently back. But the animal, much too powerful to be restrained by a single man, ignored him.

"What is she doing?" Silex asked, bewildered.

Gobius stepped back and stared at the unicorn. It turned and met his gaze as if in answer, and he shrugged.

"It looks as though she wants to come with us," Gobius said at last. "I'm not sure that we can do anything to prevent it."

"Very well," Silex said. "The Author knows she's helped guide us before. With any luck she'll be able to do so again." He turned away and started into the Labyrinth. Cantos and Ferox went in right behind him, and the others followed.

Unlike the passageways leading into the cavern of the Seers, these were very high and wide enough for an entire band of men to walk side by side. There were strange rock formations jutting from the ground and long rock spires decorating the ceiling, which was supported by two large stone columns.

As they proceeded, they found sconces embedded in the walls, and a few of them still held oil. Silex and Ferox lit them as they passed. The passage led, initially, to a simple fork—right and left. Cantos was about to follow the instinct that had guided him since they'd reached the mountains, but it was then that the unicorn pressed forward. It stood in front of the right-hand passage, blocking it off, and though they tried, they could not move her.

"I think she is trying to tell us not to go that way," Gobius said at last.

Silex leaned, dropped a small handful of pebbles by the left-hand passage, and turned to Gobius.

"We have said all along that the events we've experienced on this journey have happened for a reason. It is not an accident that the only such creature any of us has ever encountered beyond a fable has chosen you, Gobius. My heart tells me that the unicorn would not lead us astray. Hence we will go as she has directed us."

Cidivus snorted but otherwise kept silent. The others lowered their heads for a moment of silent prayer. When they'd finished, Silex turned again.

"Let it begin," he said. He stepped into the left-hand passageway, and the others trailed behind.

They walked for what seemed hours. They came to more forks, some with three, four, or even five directions to choose from. Each time they stopped, prayed, and watched to see if the unicorn knew where to go. For each passage they entered, they left a small pile of pebbles in the same position at the doorway. More than once they found themselves at a fork they'd already passed through and realized they had looped back. When this happened, they used a slightly different arranged group of stones to mark their second choice. Only twice more did the unicorn directly intervene, and over time they came to realize that while it may not have known the way, it may well have been preventing them from taking a path that led to danger.

It was difficult to gauge the passing of time, but when they were fairly certain that the day must have been drawing to a close, they stepped from a passageway into an even larger, more open chamber. The sound of bubbling water echoed from the ceiling and walls, and as they walked into the open space with their torches, they could make out a subterranean lagoon spreading across the far side.

Nomis started toward the water, but as he crossed the center of the chamber, a thunderous, echoing croak sounded.

It was so sudden and so loud that it startled Nomis, who stumbled back with a sharp cry that also echoed. Around the chamber, more rumbling croaks began to ring out. Silex stepped forward and held up his torch to see what it was.

Seated on the stone floor, just beside the dark water of the lagoon, sat a large horned toad. It was the biggest such creature Silex had ever seen. As he watched, its throat bulged, growing like a waterskin being filled. When it seemed that the creature's throat would explode, the air rumbled out in another booming, resounding croak.

"Toads," Silex said. "By The Author...they are huge!"

They stood staring at the oversized creatures, which sat in a rough line between them and the water of the lagoon.

"Are they dangerous?" Alphaeus asked. "Those horns..."

"I have never heard of their like," Cantos replied. "Still, I can't imagine what danger they may pose."

Og strode forward toward the water.

"I'm getting a drink," he said. "After all we've been through, I will not be turned aside by such as these."

It seemed as if the toads would let him pass, as if they did not mind his presence. Then, just as he drew near the water, passing directly between two of them, the one to his left slapped out with a hideously long tongue. The toad drove it against the stone ceiling and retracted it quickly, like the sharp crack of a whip. Og cried out, drew his battle axe from his belt, and turned to face the creature. He raised the weapon, ready to bring it down and smash the blade through the toad's odd horned head. But the blow never fell.

From out of nowhere the Legans emerged from the shadows as silently and stealthily as smoke. One of them reached up almost effortlessly and grabbed the hilt of Og's axe. The big man carried through his swing, but the axe slipped from his hand, and the Legan, holding the weapon before him, stepped back. The others watched in complete amazement, first shocked by the appearance of the Legans and then astounded by how easily one of them had pulled the axe from Og's massive hands.

Their leader, Orius, stepped forward.

"You have been warned before," he said. He spoke directly to Og, but his words carried to the others, all of whom directed their attention toward him. "Why would you raise your weapon to a helpless creature?"

"Helpless?" Og growled. "Did you see what that thing did with its tongue? Do you see the size of it and hear the noises it makes? We needed to reach the water, and it startled me."

"They would not have prevented you," Orius chided. "There are insects crawling on the ceiling above you. The creatures feed on them to survive. If you had merely walked to the water and not disturbed them, you would be drinking freely. You cannot judge everything worthy of death just because it gets in your way."

"I..." Og fell silent a moment. Then his face flushed once again. "My axe," he said. "I need my axe back."

The Legan, Apteris, who had taken Og's axe, backed away a step and eyed the big man warily.

"This is not your first warning," Orius said. "You do not wield your weapon wisely."

"You know about our quest, Orius," Silex said. "If you knew we were here and that these creatures were in danger, then you must be aware of all that we have faced. You have followed us all along, haven't you? All the way from the Tenebrae, through the lands we've traveled, right up until our arrival here at the Labyrinth of Secrets. You know then how we have been attacked by a great number of creatures wishing us harm or even death. To send one of us onward without a weapon to defend himself would be unjust and not in accordance with the nature of beings who are commissioned by The Author to protect His creation."

Orius considered Silex's words for a moment and then nodded slowly.

"You speak the truth," Orius said. "Apteris, return the weapon to the giant."

Apteris, much less certain than his leader, hesitated. Og turned to the creature and stood with his hand out, waiting. Grudgingly, Apteris returned the battle axe.

"Since you are here," Cantos said, stepping forward to face Orius, "can you guide us toward our goal? The Labyrinth is long and complex, and we've already looped around it more than once."

"We cannot," Orius said with finality. "You know that our purpose is solely to protect nature from unwarranted harm. As I've told you before, we are not to involve ourselves in the affairs of humans. You are on your own in navigating the Labyrinth."

Og stared at the toad beside him. Testing Orius' claim, he stepped past the nearest of the creatures, knelt, and cupped his hands in the cool water. The toad paid him no attention; its gaze was directed upward. As Og stood, the toad shot its tongue out again and snagged an unseen insect with a wet slap. Og flinched, but this time he kept his hand away from the haft of his axe.

"Do not forget our warning, warriors of Mavinor. And may The Author be with you," Orius said.

Silex and the others had already begun to move toward the lagoon. By the time they turned back the Legans were gone, having disappeared as silently as they'd arrived. The thirteen glanced around the cavern, but there was nothing to be seen.

"I don't trust them," Og muttered.

"You're just upset they took your axe so easily," Pugius joked.

Og shook his head. They all filled their waterskins and rested, leaning against the wall opposite the lagoon, far away from the giant squatting toads. As far as the creatures were concerned, the thirteen might not have even existed.

"A lot of passageways lead out of here," Ferox said, breaking their silence. "I have to say that if we're planning on trying them randomly and leaving pebbles along the way, then we may need a few more stones."

"I thought," Cantos said, "that we'd be able to keep our bearings. Remember the words of the Seers? 'In the center lies what is good.' We somehow need to find the passage that leads to the center."

Cidivus had been uncommonly silent. Without warning he rose and crossed the clearing. As he went, his eyes never moved from a passageway to the left of the lagoon. He stopped just outside that tunnel, staring into its shadowed depths.

Silex rose and walked over to stand beside him.

"What is it?" he asked.

"A light," Cidivus said. "I was staring at one of those ghastly toads. Beyond it was this passage, and I saw a very faint light."

Silex stared into the tunnel. He saw nothing, but he believed Cidivus. There was no reason not to.

"It might be a sign," Silex said.

"But it also might be one of the torches we left burning behind us," Sceptrus said.

Silex turned back to the others.

"Let's get moving. Someone mark this opening. If we find ourselves back in this chamber, we'll know to go a different route. For now, something is telling me to go down this passageway."

"I'm with you," Cidivus said, as the others stared at him in amazement, surprised by his sudden change in attitude.

They gathered their equipment and supplies, and after carefully marking the entrance to the passage, they ventured into the darkness. After going only a short distance, Ferox spoke up.

"That's odd," he said. "The ground—it's slanting upward."

"How can you tell?" Og said, almost irritated. "It feels level to me."

"It's turning as well," Thaddeus chimed in. "We've already curved slightly to the right."

Og grumbled but held his silence. A little farther in the incline increased, and they could all feel what Ferox had sensed immediately. They were climbing upward into the mountain. A glow rose ahead, and Silex stopped, holding up a hand to halt the others.

"Whatever it was Cidivus saw," he said softly, "I think we're about to find it. Be ready with your weapons but not too quick to use them."

They continued forward. The passageway curved more sharply to the right. There were fewer openings on either side. They rose and curved in toward the center of a huge, looping spiral. Then the glow became brighter still, and they stepped around into light so bright they had to blink and cover their eyes.

When their sight cleared, they saw a woman standing in

the passageway before them. She was tall and slender with long, sweeping jet-black hair that washed over her shoulders and down her back. Her eyes were dark as well, though small pinpricks of light glinted in their centers like chips of diamond. She wore a long gown and sandals that laced up her calves, one of which showed where the gown was slit on the side. The sight was so unexpected and so incongruous that they were stopped dead in their tracks, awestruck.

"Welcome," the woman said. "I have been expecting you."

"Greetings," Silex said, stepping forward. "I am Silex. My companions and I…"

"Are on a quest," she said.

Silex fell silent. Cantos stepped forward.

"Who are you, my good lady?" he asked. "And how do you know about our quest?"

"I am Lilith," the woman said, her dark eyes flashing. "I have come to do what the winged guardians would not. I have come to help you find what you seek. It has been many years since Haggiselm walked these very corridors. It is time that the prophecies are fulfilled."

Cantos stood his ground and studied her.

"Forgive me," he said. "The name Lilith is familiar to me, but I can't seem to put it into context."

"I am older than I look," she said. Her voice was soft, but it carried, and it was filled with the strength of authority. "My name is older still. If you study the ancient scrolls long enough, you will find those who have borne it."

Cantos frowned. Her comment was cryptic, but she appeared to pose no threat.

"You know where Haggiselm hid the Medallion?" Silex asked.

"I have come to lead you to it," she said. "If you will follow me…"

She stood, waiting. Cantos turned to Silex, who shrugged. Several of the others stared openly at Lilith, obviously besotted, captivated by her beauty. They could not overcome the shock of meeting such a beautiful woman deep in a mountain, so far from any civilization.

"We have come a long way," Silex said. "If you can lead us to what we seek, we will be eternally grateful. Our king awaits us, and the journey home promises to be as long and difficult as that which led us here."

"If you trust me, I will see that this segment of your journey goes more smoothly," she replied.

Silex turned and studied the faces of the others. None of them seemed inclined to ignore the woman, and no viable alternative presented itself other than returning to the lagoon and the toads.

"We will follow you," Silex said. "Lead the way."

Lilith smiled. She turned and disappeared up the passageway they'd been traveling. Silex fell in behind her, and the others followed. As they moved upward and deeper into the mountain, Gobius dropped to the rear of the group. The unicorn seemed reluctant to come with them. He studied the animal for a long moment, meeting its deep, soulful gaze.

As he turned and moved on, he heard the unicorn trailing behind him, but its footsteps were slower. It hung back, just out of sight. Gobius hurried his steps and caught up with Pugius, Minstro, and Thaddeus, who were bringing up the rear. Now and then he glanced back over his shoulder, and though he heard the occasional clop of hooves on stone, the unicorn remained well behind.

They did not speak as they ascended the passage, which wound on and up slowly, each loop imperceptibly shorter than the last as they drew closer and closer to the center. Lilith did not tire though they walked for what must have been hours. She moved with a steady, graceful gait that mesmerized those walking right behind her. They followed without hesitation, and eventually, as the loops of the tunnel grew tighter and tighter, they came in sight of another glowing light.

Quite suddenly and unexpectedly Lilith sped her steps. By the time the others noticed, she'd rounded the bend ahead of them. She was out of sight, having disappeared into the shining light ahead.

"Wait," Silex called out. He broke into a trot, and without thought the others did the same. Their minds felt fuzzy as if they'd been dreaming or in a daze. But the longer Lilith was out of sight, the clearer their thoughts became. By the time they realized following her blindly into that light was foolish, it was too late.

They all stumbled into a round chamber. It was large and had several doorways leading into it. Lilith was nowhere to be seen. Torches circled the chamber, nearly blinding them after their long trip up the mountain.

"Lilith?" Silex called out. "Where are you?"

Alphaeus let out a cry of sheer terror. For a single heartbeat the world froze. They spun first to Alphaeus and then to follow his gaze. Dropping down from above at dizzying speed was a nightmare. Huge, faceted eyes glared at them, and a stout, bulbous body, enormous and bloated, served as backdrop. It was a spider, black and huge, and in the bright light they could clearly make out an hourglass-shaped red mark on its back.

"Run!" Silex cried. He pushed Alphaeus ahead of him toward the nearest passageway as the others followed. They bunched together, too close for the smaller doorway they entered, and immediately fled the chamber. Thaddeus and Og stood their ground just for a moment, weapons drawn. But as soon as the others had cleared the room they backed in after them, turned, and dashed away.

"Where did she go?" Cedrus cried. "Do you think that thing took her?"

He never finished his sentence. Before the words left his lips, they reached a point where the passage slanted suddenly and steeply downward. Those in front tried to slow their steps, but the others crashed into them, unaware of the danger, and to a man they fell forward into the darkness.

As they rapidly descended, each of them, even Cidivus, prayed for The Author's intercession. They knew how far they'd climbed, and the passage beneath their feet slid off into the dark as if it would drop them to the base of the mountain—and their deaths. Then without warning they struck something soft that broke their fall.

"Ferox! Cantos! Og! Are you all here?" Silex cried.

"Here," Og said, first to regain his voice. "But I'm stuck. What is this? Where are we?"

They all struggled but found themselves held fast. As their eyes became accustomed to the darkness, they were able to make one another out in the gloom. A quick roll call established that the thirteen were all present.

"Where is Minstro?" Pugius cried.

"And the unicorn," Gobius said. "She must be up there alone, facing off with that creature!"

"I don't know," Sceptrus said, "but if we don't get loose from whatever this is that's holding us, it's not going to matter to us for long."

"It's a web," Tonitrus said.

"What?" Silex called. "Your voice is echoing."

"It's a web!" Tonitrus repeated, speaking in a louder and much more deliberate tone. "It must have been woven by that monstrous spider."

These words brought another round of frantic struggling, but they were unable to free themselves from the sticky, clinging fibers.

"Where is that thing?" Cidivus called out. "Can anyone see it?"

There were no shadows above them—and there was no sign of the huge spider. There was also no sign of Lilith.

"No, I don't see it," Silex said. "Still, we may not have much time. See if you can retrieve your blades and cut yourselves free."

They worked in silence, each man struggling to reach his own weapon or anything that might free an arm or a leg. As they listened for the spider's inevitable attack, the only sounds they heard were the frenetic grunts of their combined, fruitless efforts to escape impending doom.

———

When the spider had dropped from above and lunged after the thirteen, Minstro had only just rounded the corner into the chamber. Instinctively he'd spun and rushed back down the way they'd come. When he realized he was alone, he hesitated. He could run back to the chamber and try to join the others, but if they had fled the chamber as well, he might just walk into the waiting jaws of the spider.

He slowed his descent and eventually found a branch to his right that he'd not noticed on the way up. Minstro ducked into the passage, slid along the wall, and dropped to the floor. Sitting with his back to the wall, he tried to remain silent.

The darkness around him was full of sounds. For a moment he heard what seemed to be voices, but they faded. Minstro heard his own breathing echoing from the stone around him. Sweat trickled down his face, but he ignored it. He did everything he possibly could not to move for fear that the monster would find him.

Then he heard another sound. It was a soft clop, almost like an object striking a flat stone. Something wisped along the side of the tunnel, and Minstro shivered. Was it the skittering legs of the spider? Was it the sound of the giant black widow spinning a web? Was he being watched in the darkness by eyes sharper than his own? He tightened the muscles in his legs and prepared to spring as the sound repeated itself.

Then something snuffled softly, freezing him. Minstro very nearly fled, but something in the sound was comforting and familiar. Somehow he knew it wasn't the spider, but what?

It was the unicorn. It suddenly appeared, looming over him. A moment later he was on his feet, pressing his face into the soft fur on its side. The unicorn allowed this for a moment and then, stepping back, it nudged him with its nose.

Minstro stared up at the creature.

"What do I do now?" he asked as he faced the unicorn, almost wishing that it could answer him.

The unicorn didn't make a sound, but it shivered as if trying to tell him something. Then it turned and headed down the passageway. The tiny man stood, staring after it. He turned back the way he'd come, and then, closing his eyes and offering a silent prayer, he followed it, all the while hoping that the unicorn wasn't just wandering, lost in the dark.

They moved quickly into the blackness of the cavern. There were no torches, and after a while Minstro stepped forward and jogged, one hand brushing the unicorn's flank so that they didn't get separated. They turned right and angled up slightly. Ahead, the glow became visible again, though much dimmer than it had been.

The unicorn slowed suddenly, and Minstro nearly tumbled between its legs. They rounded another corner, and in the shadows ahead, Minstro could make out something moving. It was impossible to tell what it was from where he stood, and he pulled back in fright. The unicorn didn't hesitate. It moved forward and a moment later it whickered at him, as if calling to him to hurry.

Gathering his courage, Minstro drew the dagger Pugius had given him from his belt. As he slowly stepped forward, a voice whispered from the darkness.

"Minstro…is that you?"

He hurried in the direction from which the voice came. Soon he saw a shadowed silhouette in the form of a man and discerned that it was none other than Ferox. The expert archer was caught tight in a sticky, stringy web. Minstro glanced up and then shuddered. He saw that the thirteen had fallen a great distance, and though the great, intricate spider's web had trapped them, it was the only thing that had prevented their being crushed on the stone floor.

"Do you have a blade?" Ferox asked.

"I do," Minstro said. The little man brought the dagger up and sawed furiously at the web near Ferox's feet. He was barely able to reach it, but after only a few moments he cut Ferox's legs free, and the warrior's feet touched the floor.

Minstro then freed his right arm, enabling Ferox to draw his blade and hack his other arm free by himself.

"Quickly," he whispered. "We have to get the others out of the web."

They worked frantically, slashing first one and then another of the thirteen free. Minstro found Pugius next, and the two cut Cidivus loose. Ferox freed Og and Silex. In very short order, they had all gathered just beyond the web chamber in the hall where the unicorn waited.

"You, my little friend, have saved all our lives," Silex said to Minstro. "We will never be able to thank you enough."

"None of us will ever forget," Pugius said, laying a hand on the small man's shoulder. "Thank The Author we allowed him to stay with us and then rescued him from the Strya." He glared in Cidivus' direction as he said this.

"I will," Cidivus said unexpectedly, freezing Pugius and the others.

"There's little time to talk," Silex said. "We have to find that thing and kill it. If Lilith is still up there, we'll find her and save her, but something feels odd about all of this. I barely remember our journey from the moment we began following her to the moment that thing dropped from above."

"How did you find us, Minstro?" Thaddeus asked. "Where are we?"

"The unicorn," Minstro said. "She brought me to you." He then articulated as best he could the way in which it had led him.

"So," Gobius said, "at the end of this passage, if we turn left and climb back, we'll be in the room where we saw the spider?"

"I believe so," Minstro said.

"This time we'll be ready," said Og.

"If you can be ready for a thing like that," Nomis said uncertainly. "That creature was big as well as fast. It's not going to be easy to kill, even if we know it's there."

"The Author will watch over us," Tonitrus said. "Look at us. We are still standing here after falling nearly to our deaths after having been chased by a giant spider, and who knows how many other things that should have killed us all? We are destined for this, and we will find a way." As he drew his sword, the others followed his example, and they found themselves inspired by Tonitrus' unwavering tone and unflappable demeanor.

The unicorn whinnied at them, and as it turned, it led them back toward the main passageway. They followed quickly, brushing strands of web from their clothing and moving as quietly as possible. Silex, Gobius, and Tonitrus took the front, while Og, Thaddeus, and Cidivus brought up the rear. Minstro hurried along beside Pugius, the dagger still clutched in his hand. He carried himself with an air of confidence and determination that he had not shown before. Having rescued all of his companions, Minstro knew now that he truly belonged. For the first time on this long journey he felt like part of the quest and a major cog in the wheel of destiny.

Chapter Twenty

They reached the top of the passage without incident. This time they were alert, turning at even the slightest sound. They watched above them as well as the passages to either side the entire way, but there was no sign of the giant spider.

The unicorn had taken the last hundred feet at a trot, rounding the corner into the chamber beyond. The thirteen hurried their pace, doubling their concentration as they left the relative safety of the passage and stepped into the chamber where they had first encountered the monster.

"Where is she?" Gobius cried. "The unicorn...Where did she go?"

He turned dazedly, staring first at one passage and then at another, looking for any sign of the missing creature. The passages were all dark, open maws.

"That's the one we were chased into," Ferox said, pointing to his left.

"That still leaves several more," Silex said. "So which one do we take?"

Suddenly there was a wild, angry scream from the passage directly across from the one they had just entered. They immediately dashed into it, heedless of the possible danger. Silex and Gobius led them, with Tonitrus and Ferox trailing and the others not far behind.

They didn't have far to go. Ahead, in yet another circular chamber, the unicorn had been backed against the far wall. The huge black widow danced and swayed in front of it. Bands of silk had twisted around the unicorn's legs, and though it fought valiantly, keeping its attacker at bay with the wicked spike of its horn, its movements were hampered by the clinging fibers. The unicorn's skin was coated with frothy sweat, and its eyes were wide and crazed.

Ferox drew an arrow and fired without thought, already reaching for a second as the long, sharp shaft penetrated the spider's abdomen. The creature screeched and wheeled, backing so quickly that the threads between it and the unicorn threatened to topple them both.

"Spread out," Silex cried. "Don't let it get its bearings!"

Pugius and Minstro backed against the wall, scuttled to the left, and almost in unison threw two daggers that caught the spider where its uppermost legs attached to its body. It scampered toward the far wall of the chamber and then turned to face them. As it did, Ferox let loose another arrow, which embedded itself in the monster's jaws, and it reared up, legs flailing.

Silex, Og, Thaddeus, and Tonitrus charged while the others stood their ground. They drove straight at the spider's underbelly, weapons drawn. The thing was so huge that they were able to spread out, ringing the creature and driving in, first one and then another. They attacked relentlessly and swung their weapons with all the strength they could muster. But the black widow was too quick. It dodged them repeatedly and exposed its venomous fangs to freeze them whenever they attempted to close in.

Cidivus drew back from the rest and stood against the wall, watching in dark fascination. His hand rested on the hilt of his sword, but he did not draw it. He watched the others and waited to see if the right moment presented itself when he could join the attack and be a hero.

Gobius held back as well, but his eyes were bright, and he held his sword firmly with both hands. He studied the battle raging in front of him and the walls around the chamber. Gobius saw the unicorn free itself from the last of its silken bonds, and he caught its gaze just for an instant. But as the unicorn escaped, something dreadful occurred. The huge spider quickly pivoted away from Silex, Og, Thaddeus, and Tonitrus so that it faced the opposite direction. They perceived it as an opening, but it was a trap. As they rushed in, the creature exposed its spinnerets and shot silky strands in each of their directions. The black widow managed to catch each of the warriors around the legs and bring them to the ground, and then it began to draw each of them closer. As it did, the monster spun around and once again exposed its fangs, which were waiting for the opportunity to inject the spider's lethal venom.

Gobius knew he didn't have much time, so he returned his attention to the wall behind the spider. In a second he saw what he needed. Gobius darted toward the far wall while the creature was preoccupied, focusing its attention on devouring Silex and the others. As he arrived at the other side of the chamber, he leaped and reached out with one hand. Gobius let his mind drift back to his time as a fisherman, hanging from the rigging of a ship and swinging high above the deck. He landed on the ledge he'd spotted from across the chamber and drove upward with one boot. Placing his other foot and his free hand on the wall, he launched himself upward into the air, giving all the strength of his mind and body to that one single moment.

The spider was oblivious to Gobius' onslaught as he gave a battle cry and dropped onto its back. He held his sword high above his head, both hands on the pommel, blade down, and drove it in behind the spider's head. He didn't stop as it bit into its body. He put all his weight behind it, driving the steel in deep.

The spider shrieked. It was an inhuman, keening wail. It lunged to the side, reared up, and tried to shake Gobius free. But he clung to it, holding tight to the sword and pressing it deeper and deeper into the creature's torn flesh.

It seemed just for a moment that it would overcome even this wound. But then, as it careened to the side a final time, its legs buckled. Gobius clung to his blade a moment longer, and then, as the spider rolled, he rolled as well, sliding off the side of its body to the floor. He quickly got to his feet and backed away, still holding his sword drenched with the monster's blood.

Pugius, Minstro, Ferox, and Cedrus cut Silex and the others free of their silken constraints. Gobius circled back to stand with them, and when all had been cut loose, they pulled away with their weapons still drawn. The unicorn stepped forward and nudged the spider with its horn, but there was no life left in the beast. Then, without warning, the thing began to shrivel. It crumpled in on itself as though its center had been sucked out by some great vacuum. All around the body what dim light there was darkened until nothing lay on the floor but a shadow. As they watched in fascination, it crumbled seemingly to dust.

Gobius grabbed a torch from one of the holders on the wall and moved forward. He made it only a few steps before he stopped with a gasp.

They all stepped forward and stared at the prone form of a woman. She lay face down, and as Silex crouched and turned her over, they saw that it was none other than Lilith, who'd led them up the center of the mountain. Her skin was very pale, and as she lay on her back, her dark hair pooled around her head and shoulders.

"Leave her," Silex said at last. "This was her home, and this is where she would have left us to rot, our quest unfulfilled. It is a fitting tomb."

The others offered no protest. They stared at Lilith's corpse one last time before turning away. Then they passed through the chamber where Lilith had first attacked and went down the winding trail up which she'd led them.

———

After arriving back at the lagoon, they fell to the ground beside the water, washing away the spider silk that clung to them like ivy. There were still half a dozen passageways that they hadn't tried yet. Gobius stood and walked slowly around the chamber, studying each of them. He was tired, but his mind and heart raced. They'd been tested again, and just as each and every time before, they met the challenge and overcame it.

Silex stood and surveyed the pathways, and Cantos walked up beside him.

"There's no way to know which one leads to where the

Medallion is hidden," Cantos said. "There are still so many, and with each passage having several forks, the possibilities are endless."

The others noticed the look of concern on Silex's face. His body language was full of uncertainty, and they couldn't help but wonder if even their leader was beginning to lose hope. As they stood silently, Gobius continued to examine the passageways. He looked toward the unicorn, almost begging for it to show them the way. But it just stared at him with sad eyes. Clearly it was as lost as the rest of them.

"I'm starting to wonder if our destination even exists," Silex said, his voice weak and his tone somber. The others lowered their heads as Gobius called out to them.

"We can't afford to doubt ourselves," he said, his voice fierce. Seeing that even Silex was beginning to grow weary, he stepped up and took the lead. As Gobius stood in the entrance to the largest of the remaining passageways, he saw that it led neither up nor down—at least as far as he could make out. It was wide enough for three or four men to walk side by side. "Let's try this one," Gobius said.

Cantos followed his gaze and then shrugged. "It's as good a choice as the others," he said.

Gobius knelt by the entrance and, in keeping with their plan, marked it with a small pile of stones. Then he stood and walked into the passageway.

They followed Gobius in, advancing slowly and watching carefully. The path continued in an almost perfectly straight line until it widened at a triple fork.

"Seem familiar?" Cedrus asked.

Gobius scanned the openings, trying to discern the best option. As he did, Silex called out.

"The middle one," he said. "Remember? What is good lies in the center."

"Yes!" Cantos exclaimed. "I was about to suggest the one on the right, but I think Silex is on to something."

"I'm telling you, that's the way," Silex said. This time his voice was full of confidence, and Gobius smiled at him. Then, as the unicorn strode up beside Gobius, they led the others into the center passageway.

The walls were symmetrical, and as they progressed, the air around them grew brighter. The path started to widen until at last they came to an even larger opening. There was a very dim light beyond the portal. Silex and Gobius stepped forward first.

The room was huge. It dwarfed the chamber of the lagoon, stretching up into the guts of the mountain until the ceiling was lost in shadow. The chamber was roughly circular, and starting about forty feet inside, a ring of stone monoliths loomed like towering sentries. The ring appeared to be perfectly round, and each of the stones was positioned directly across from another as if facing a mirror.

The thirteen stepped into the chamber and stood very still. Slowly, Nomis and Alphaeus moved to the left and right, finding torches resting in their holders along the walls and lighting them. It took them a moment to get sparks from their tinder. The others stood, waiting.

As the golden glow of the torchlight licked its way up the walls, the pillar directly before them became more clearly visible. At about eye level, a circular design centered by a unicorn was chiseled into the stone.

Cidivus suddenly broke free from the group. He rushed to the pillar, gazed at the symbol, and let out a short laugh.

He immediately began circling the stone, running his hands over its surface and kicking at the dirt at its base. Silex shook his head and turned to the others.

"Spread out," he said. "Search the chamber. See if you can find a clue that might lead us to the Medallion. If this is the right place, then it could be hidden near any of these pillars. If you find writing or symbols, call out for Cantos."

They separated slowly. As they stretched out around the ring, they realized that there were exactly twelve stones. Silex moved to the pillar beside Cidivus, whose initial enthusiasm faded as his efforts revealed nothing.

While each of the other twelve went to examine a pillar, Gobius held back. He stood beside the unicorn, his companion throughout so much of the journey. Gobius glanced around the stone ring, but he no longer saw the monoliths. He no longer saw his companions, and though he sensed the unicorn nearby, he no longer saw the creature. The world shimmered, and the center of the chamber grew brighter.

Suddenly, Gobius senses that he is no longer in the cavern. He smells the damp air of the docks by Mavinor's southern shore. He sees the gentle, rolling waves and hears the flap of sails in the wind. Gobius begins to walk, and as he moves, he feels the stony beach beneath his feet.

Ahead, someone approaches out of the mist. As Gobius continues forward, he looks down and realizes he is carrying a basket loaded to the top with fresh fish. When he glances up, he sees King Onestus stumbling down the shoreline toward him. As the two meet, the king studies his face and gazes down into the basket of fish. Though he doesn't know why, Gobius feels inclined to hold the basket out toward Onestus. Without warning the king snatches it away and overturns it, shaking the fish free and sending them to the ground in a silvery, glittering cascade.

In the center of it all Gobius catches sight of a flash of gold. He reaches out, trying to catch whatever it is. But despite the fact that everything is moving in slow motion, as if time itself has stopped ticking, Gobius is too late. He anxiously drops to his knees and begins groping for the object of his curiosity as Onestus stands and watches. But all Gobius can feel is the cold surface of stones. The mist grows thick, and suddenly everything around him disappears. There is no sight of Onestus, the fish, or even the sea itself. Gobius' heart begins to race. His breathing grows heavier. He remains there, kneeling, and begins to pray to The Author. He closes his eyes and desperately petitions for a return to peacefulness and serenity. He doesn't know where that flash of gold has disappeared to. He doesn't know what it is or why it had attracted him so strongly. Still he prays, and still he clings to hope with every ounce of his being. Soon his heart rate slows, and he grows calmer. Then, as he opens his eyes…

His vision cleared. Gobius found himself back in the chamber with the others. He was kneeling in the center of the ring of stones, and a voice, soft but clear, whispered to him from his memory.

"What is good lies in the center."

He stared at the ground in front of him, and then, fixing in his mind the image of the golden object falling from the basket of fish, he reached down and began to brush at the dirt with his fingers. As the visions flashed through his mind, he worked more quickly, clawing at the earth, oblivious to the pain it brought to his hands.

Soon his nails scraped across something smooth and

solid. He worked around its edges, ignoring the others, who were equally unaware of his efforts. Each searched one of the standing stones, pressing their fingers into cracks and kicking at bases, looking for any indication of secret compartments, trap doors, or even loose spots in the dirt. Cidivus was frantically moving about, evidently more eager than any of the others to locate the Medallion.

Gobius worked the object free of the earth and lifted it into the light. It was a small chest. The workmanship was exquisite, etched designs on clasps of silver. He leaned back and held the chest up to view it more clearly.

One by one the others noticed that something was happening. They immediately halted their own efforts, turning to watch as Gobius slowly unfastened the clasp on the small chest. It seemed to take much longer than it should have, but then, as the rest of the thirteen gazed in wonder, Gobius flipped the lid open.

None of the others could see what he saw, but they caught the expression of pure rapture on his face. Silex was the first to step away from the pillars and begin the slow walk to the center. The others followed one by one. When they surrounded Gobius on all sides, they looked down and saw him reach into the chest. Gobius retracted his hand and drew forth a long glittering chain. He turned, and as he did, they gasped in unison. Dangling from that chain was a golden medallion. As they drew near they saw that on one side it bore the image of a unicorn and on the other The Scrolls.

"By The Author," Cantos said. "You've found it."

Gobius met Silex's gaze, and without hesitation stepped forward to meet him, holding the Medallion out. Silex made no move to take it. Instead, he stepped closer and peered at it. The two locked stares, and the others, still silent, gathered around. Only Cidivus hung back, his expression dark and unreadable.

Finally, Silex took the Medallion from Gobius' hand and held it up so that all could see.

"You have found it," he said at last. "The prophecies have come full circle; the Medallion has been recovered and will return to Mavinor, its rightful home. The only question I have for you, Gobius, is…why would you give it to me?"

"You were chosen to lead the thirteen," Gobius said. "Thus it is you who should have it and bear it on the return trip to Mavinor."

"No," Silex said. "I may have been chosen by all of you to lead, but I have come to realize that it is not I who has been chosen by The Author. Clearly, there is only one among us destined to bear the Medallion, and that one is you, Gobius.

"It was you who the unicorn chose to befriend. It was you who hung over the edge of a cliff to save me and Tonitrus from the depths of the Black Hollow. It was you who led us in our rescue of Minstro and our escape from the Strya. It was you who plunged into the river to save Nomis at the falls and to bring the rest of us safely to shore. It was you who risked his life to slay the beast-woman, Lilith, again saving us from certain death. And perhaps, most important, it was you and you alone who found the Medallion. Your wisdom, your prowess, and the plenitude of other virtues you possess prove that it is you, my friend, who has been chosen by the Author to carry this Medallion back to Mavinor. It is you, Gobius, who I will be honored to call…my king."

The silence grew thick with emotion as Silex stepped forward once more and slid the chain over Gobius' head, letting the Medallion drop against his chest. Pulling back, Silex dropped gently to one knee. Around him the others followed suit, some offering silent prayer, others merely staring at the glittering Medallion in silence.

Cidivus stood behind the others; none but Gobius could see him. He did not genuflect but turned away instead, seething with anger. Cidivus strode across the chamber to where they'd left their supplies, leaving the others to rise and then to gather around Gobius. Gobius stood very still and allowed each man his opportunity as one by one they stepped forward to examine the Medallion. The gravity of the moment finally hit them. Their long journey through unknown lands and uncharted territory was complete; their mission was now fulfilled. The Medallion was returning to Mavinor, where they would be welcomed as heroes and forever remembered as the men who restored faith and hope to a kingdom whose fate was becoming less and less certain.

Finally, when Thaddeus, who was last, had his moment with the Medallion, they turned to walk over to where Cidivus was waiting. Gobius packed the small chest carefully, wrapping it in a bit of cloth that Nomis brought over to him. He tucked the Medallion beneath his tunic. The chain was strong, and he did not fear that it would break. After all they'd been through…after seeing the prophecy proven true again and again…he knew in some way that it was safe where it was.

Chapter Twenty-One

After picking up their supplies, they prepared to move out of the huge chamber, but something startled them—the sound of hooves beating on the ground, a sound that became louder and louder by the minute.

"Get back," Silex warned.

As they backed away and drew their weapons, a look of shock came over their faces as several Strya began to enter the chamber. The creatures were far more cunning than they could have ever imagined. The Strya had been tracking them all along, ever since they left the forest to make the trek across the valley and into the Northern Mountains.

The others turned to Silex, but rather than lead them into battle he looked toward Gobius. The future king of Mavinor quickly recognized that it was now his place to lead. He drew his sword, gazed first at the men to his right and then to those to his left. With a look of intensity he stepped forward, let out a battle cry, and began to rush the Strya. As he did, Ferox let arrow after arrow fly, and Pugius and Minstro whipped out their daggers. The unicorn lowered its horn and followed its master while the others charged right behind, wielding their weapons, ready for battle.

Gobius managed to drop one of the invading Strya with a quick slash to its midsection. Silex, Tonitrus, and Cedrus followed right behind, facing off with the creatures and whirling their swords through the air with speed and precision. Og let out a bellow and made one great sweep with his battle axe, taking out three of the creatures with a single blow. The unicorn chased several of the Strya around the chamber and scattered them among the stone monoliths.

As some of the Strya charged Sceptrus and Cantos, Sceptrus spun his staff masterfully, almost hypnotizing the creatures. Then, quicker than lightning, he lashed out at them, knocking their weapons from their hands and striking their faces and bodies with his staff. His blinding speed allowed him to exert such great force that they immediately dropped to the ground, stunned and vulnerable.

But one Strya had eluded Sceptrus and began sneaking up behind him. Cantos caught sight of it, and as he looked down upon the sword he held tightly in his trembling hand, he began to rush forward. The beast held a dagger, and the closer it drew to Sceptrus the higher it raised its hand, pointing the blade toward the ground and ready to plunge it into Sceptrus' back. Finally it moved into a position where it could reach Sceptrus with one thrust of its arm and let out a loud scream. This startled Sceptrus, causing him to whip around with his staff in a defensive position. But before he could even blink, the Strya dropped like a rock, Cantos' sword lodged in its back. Sceptrus smiled at Cantos, who pulled his sword from the creature's body, looked up, and said, "I told you I wouldn't forget what you did for me."

Tonitrus warded the Strya off easily, and his younger brother, fighting beside him, held his own as well. Cedrus slashed one on its arm and another on its waist, driving them back. When the one on his left charged yet again, Cedrus was waiting for it. He thrust his sword and caught it in its midsection, killing it almost instantly. But the other one lunged and took a wild swing with its sword, forcing Cedrus to bend his body backward in order to dodge it. As he did so, he lost his balance and began to fall. Unable to regain his footing, Cedrus quickly found himself in trouble.

The Strya sensed an opening and moved in for the kill. Tonitrus, who was already engaged with another attacker, spun and lifted his right foot in a roundhouse kick that knocked the creature's weapon from its hands. He managed to cut down the Strya he was facing off with and then went after the one looming over his brother. At this point the beast had retrieved its blade and began to do battle with Tonitrus.

Tonitrus went on the attack and immediately had the Strya retreating toward the wall. When it ran out of room, Tonitrus moved in and swung his blade from right to left, aiming it at the Strya's head. But at the last second it ducked and crouched. As Tonitrus finished his swing, he brought the sword up over his head in one fluid motion, perpendicular to the ground, and hacked down at the creature. It defended itself successfully by holding up its sword, but Tonitrus came right back at it. He continuously lifted his blade and pounded it down on the Strya's weapon as if smashing a stone with a sledgehammer. Finally the creature dropped its sword, and Tonitrus dealt it a lethal blow.

Thaddeus drove into a crowd of Strya, whirling his club in intricate circles and driving it into the bodies of his attackers. He carved a path through the enemy, and for a moment he disappeared entirely from sight. Alphaeus and Nomis followed him, and as each dropped one of the Strya, they rammed through the horde and saw that Thaddeus had stumbled. He was now pressed back to the wall with the Strya clawing and raking at him, and he was having trouble regaining his balance.

With a cry, Nomis charged. Alphaeus followed only seconds later. Their momentum carried them forward, and before the Strya pinning Thaddeus to the wall were aware of the threat, Nomis and Alphaeus were on them. Nomis dropped one with a quick thrust of his blade. But as the creature fell, it turned, glared at him, and gripped the weapon, holding it tightly inside its own body. Nomis cried out and tugged at the sword, but the creature fell back, and the sudden pull of its weight dragged Nomis with it. Alphaeus slashed the throat of a second Strya and turned to face a third. But as he did, another one came up behind him.

"Alphaeus!" Thaddeus cried. He pressed a boot into the wall behind him and drove into the melee, but it was too late. The Strya reached around, raked a dagger across Alphaeus' throat, and the young man dropped away, an expression of shock masking his normally cheerful features.

Nomis fell over the top of the Strya he'd killed. He finally dragged his blade free, but he couldn't keep his balance. He spun and tumbled backward, losing his weapon as he crashed to the stone floor. They swarmed over him, and though Thaddeus fought bravely to the boy's side, it was too late. Soon Nomis too was dead, and Thaddeus was left fighting for his own life and crying out to the others to rally.

The rest of the thirteen had remained close together. The unicorn charged ahead, first one way and then back, attacking the Strya with its horn. Pugius and Minstro used the darting unicorn to shield them as they flashed into the open and moved in Thaddeus' direction. Seeing that he was in trouble, Pugius wasted no time. He got into position behind a rock as four Strya were moving in to gang up on Thaddeus. The rock was roughly three feet in height, and he had Minstro hide behind it. Pugius held a dagger in each hand and had two others in sheaths. "Look at me," Pugius said to Minstro. He unsheathed the daggers and handed them to the little man. "Hold them loosely, just like this." Pugius directed Minstro to hold them by the hilt, with the blade pointed toward Pugius, and loosely enough that someone could easily slide them through his fingers. Without uttering a single word, Minstro did what he was told.

Then, quicker than anyone could see, Pugius' hands whipped forward and released the daggers. They spun end over end as they approached two of the Strya, and embedded themselves deep into their tailbones. The Strya arched their backs and dropped to their knees, teetering on the brink of death. But Pugius wasn't done. When the daggers had been released, he was already bringing his hands downward toward Minstro. In one fluid motion he grabbed the blades from Minstro's hands and brought his own hands up and in toward his body, as if rowing a boat. Again, like a blur of motion, he thrust them forward, hurling the daggers at the other two Strya. They had turned when they heard the others shriek upon getting knifed in the back. As they gazed down at their fallen comrades for just a second, the daggers were already whirling toward them. Before they could even look up, the blades buried themselves in the beasts' chests. They were no longer a threat to Thaddeus as they clutched the hilts of the daggers and fell to the ground.

Minstro had peeked around the rock to see all four

Strya taken out by Pugius. He smiled and started clapping his hands, but the rejoicing was short-lived. Two other Strya saw what had happened and charged Pugius. Without his daggers he was helpless. They encroached on him, weapons drawn, as he pulled Minstro behind him. But just as one of them leaped onto the rock Minstro had been hiding behind, it pulled up and toppled over. Pugius looked down and saw an arrow in the base of its spine, and before he could even glance up at the other Strya bearing down on him, Ferox had already dropped it with a precision shot. As Pugius breathed a sigh of relief and looked across the chamber at Ferox, the archer winked, drew his bow, and turned his attention back to the ongoing battle.

Despite the help from Pugius, Thaddeus was still grossly outnumbered. Finally, Gobius saw that Thaddeus was cornered, and he directed the others toward him. They did all they could to plow through the remaining Strya, but the progress was slow. Thaddeus found a small recess in the wall behind him. With that at his back, he swung his club with all his might, swatting the Strya aside like flies.

Thaddeus fought valiantly, but he had too many of the creatures to fend off. Just as he tired, dropping to one knee and lowering his club to the ground, a lone Strya came at him with a spear. Gobius arrived just in time, stepping in front of Thaddeus and driving his sword through the creature's upper body. The rest of the Strya re-armed and began facing off with Silex, Og, and the others.

As Gobius went to pull his blade free, it stuck just at the last moment. He then glanced up and saw one of the Strya bearing down on him, causing him to stumble back. Thaddeus was still on the ground, and though the unicorn caught wind of what was happening, it was surrounded and unable to get to Gobius' side.

The lone Strya charged at Gobius relentlessly, brandishing a sharp, pointed dagger. It thrust its arm forward as it came within reach, just before Gobius was able to free his sword from his most recent victim. Gobius felt it make contact with his chest, and he was driven back into the stone wall by the force of the attack. Then, over the creature's shoulder, he saw Cidivus step closer and drive his blade into the Strya's back. It never saw the attack coming, and as Cidivus pulled back his sword, the Strya fell lifelessly to the ground.

Gobius looked down at his chest. It hurt, and he saw that his tunic was stained with blood. But he shielded this from Cidivus, telling him to go back and help the others. As Gobius drew his tunic up and gingerly rubbed the spot where he thought the Strya's dagger had pierced him, he found nothing but a bruise. The Medallion dangled freely beside it. Because his skin had not been pierced, the blood on his tunic could only have come from the creature that attacked him. Still, Gobius wondered how this could possibly have happened.

The only explanation was that the Medallion had deflected the blow. But Gobius could not understand how that dagger could hit the single spot on his chest that was fully protected. There was no scratch or mar on the surface of the Medallion, and still he had to believe that he stood there—alive—because of its obstruction. Though he knew that common sense should tell him this was the case, his memory told him otherwise. He now realized the full extent of the Medallion's powers...that he who bore it would be blessed with invincibility.

Thaddeus got up and ran over to him. "Are you alright?" he asked. Gobius nodded and picked up his sword, and together they went to join the others to close out the battle. One by one the rest of the Strya fell until none was left. As they scanned the corpses littered throughout the chamber, they caught sight of Nomis and Alphaeus and immediately rushed to their side.

"They are gone," Cantos said almost at once, kneeling between the two and checking for signs of life. He dropped his chin to his chest and offered a silent prayer. Thaddeus knelt beside him, looking at Nomis and then at Alphaeus. Soon the tears were flowing down his cheeks, and he buried his face in his hands.

As Gobius walked over and placed his hand on Thaddeus' shoulder, the brave warrior looked up at him. Thaddeus wiped the tears from his eyes and mentioned how he had taken it upon himself to watch over them throughout the quest, to see to it that no harm came to them. He was leading them in their journey to become the heroes they wanted to be, to emulate the man they came to idolize. But in the end, in a cruel twist of fate, it was they who gave their lives to save him, leaving Thaddeus virtually inconsolable.

"What can we do?" Ferox asked. "We can't leave them here to rot in this chamber."

"Here," Og said.

There was a crevasse in one of the walls, and he examined it. It was partially covered in rubble, and Og immediately began to dig. Tonitrus moved to help him, and between the two they quickly cleared a large opening in the wall.

The others nodded at Thaddeus as he hoisted Nomis and Alphaeus into the air, one over each shoulder, and carried them to the makeshift tomb. There he laid the bodies side by side, crossing their arms on their chests and gently closing their lifeless eyes. When the bodies were in place, they all took turns paying their last respects and replaced the rubble until the crack was filled.

Gobius drew them all into a circle, and they prayed as a group. Even Cidivus bowed his head as they humbly and fervently beseeched The Author.

They were a solemn group as they left the tomb and made their way back toward the lagoon. They were alert now, watching ahead and behind. Their trail was still clearly marked, and they followed it in a daze. They'd come so far without losing any of their number that to have lost two so suddenly had stunned them completely.

They made it through to the lagoon without incident, refilled their water bottles, and returned to the first corridor, the one they'd originally followed in. Ferox took the lead, reading the stones they'd placed and directing them through the maze. They trudged in silence, hoping to see the first spark of sunlight shining into the passageway. But the spark never came.

After an hour of twists and turns that became almost impossible to follow, they lost their bearings and could no longer retrace their steps. As they encountered one fork after another, they couldn't recall whether they had already been there or not. When they finally stepped through an opening that looked familiar, they found themselves standing in the chamber of the lagoon, facing the giant toads once again. They stopped dead in their tracks as Gobius turned to Ferox.

"Could we have misread one of the markers?" he said.

"I'm nearly certain we followed the trail exactly as we marked it," Ferox said. "I designed the system myself."

"We must have made an error," Silex said. "We'll have to double back and try again."

Ferox didn't look convinced, but they turned and followed Gobius back into the same tunnel they had arrived through. An hour later, after painstakingly checking each of the small piles of stones, they came out by the lagoon once again, and this time the silence was much heavier.

"The Strya," Ferox said. "They must have moved the stones, knowing that we would be trapped here and unable to find our way back. Without a clearly marked trail to the surface, we could wander down here for years."

"It's over," Cidivus said. "That's it. We've come all this way to find the Medallion only to be snared in this forsaken labyrinth. No one will ever come for us, and no one will ever find us. We'll never see Mavinor again."

None of the others lashed out at him this time. It was as if they were agreeing with him, conceding his cynical outlook to be more than justified. They were tired and hungry, and hope was fading quickly. One by one they threw down their supplies and seated themselves in a semicircle, facing the lagoon. Some buried their faces in their hands while others simply stared into space.

"Wait!" Gobius said.

"What is it?" Silex asked.

"The Seers," Gobius replied. "There is one prophecy remaining. Remember? 'Only the sentinels can lead you home.'"

"But what does that mean?" Cantos said.

Gobius turned toward the water and drew his sword.

"What are you looking to do?" Silex asked.

"Attack the toads," Gobius said.

"You can't be serious," said Sceptrus.

"Trust me," Gobius replied. "Follow my lead."

Gobius charged across the chamber and directed his sword at the nearest of the immense subterranean amphibians. He raised his voice in a battle cry. Behind him, the others charged the creatures reluctantly with weapons drawn, as if preparing for a monumental slaughter.

As Gobius closed in a voice rang out, and he felt his arms held in a vice-like grip. Immediately he relaxed, allowing his weapon to drop to the ground. When he turned, he found himself face to face with Orius.

"We meet again," Gobius said. "I knew you would come."

The others came to a dead stop as Gobius and the tall winged creature stared into one another's eyes.

"Why have you done this?" Orius asked.

"We are in need," Gobius replied. "I'm afraid that you are our only hope."

"This is growing tiresome," replied Orius. The rest of the Legans stood by, holding their weapons tight and eyeing Gobius' companions very closely.

"You must help us," Gobius said. "You are the only ones who can."

"I have told you time and again that we do not involve ourselves in the affairs of men," Orius said.

"Yes, I know," said Gobius. "But this time it's different."

"What is different?" asked Orius.

"The unicorn," Gobius replied. "She is the last of her kind, and she is with us. She herself does not know the way out of the Labyrinth of Secrets, and if we can't escape, then she will die here with us."

Orius looked Gobius directly in the eye and then turned his attention to the unicorn. The other Legans held their positions, waiting for Orius' instructions.

"You do realize that if we help you, then we will be going against the law, against our very nature as it was decided by The Author," Orius said.

"I do," Gobius said. "But tell me, Orius. Were we created for the well-being of the law? Or was the law handed down for the well-being of all creation?"

Orius didn't answer. One of the other Legans, Volara, then stepped forward.

"He is right," she said. "If we are truly the guardians of nature, then we must save the unicorn. We have no choice."

Orius hesitated at first, but then he nodded in agreement. "Very well," he said. "Chaelim, Apteris, Volara, you may return to our realm. I will lead the unicorn and her companions out of the Labyrinth."

One by one the other Legans melted into the shadows. Orius watched them leave and then turned toward Gobius.

"Let us go," he said.

Chapter Twenty-Two

Orius led them into the same tunnel they'd taken on their own, but three turns in, when the stones indicated the leftmost of three passages, he took them straight ahead. They had no choice but to trust him as he continued to flap his wings and glide through the air of the tunnel. Almost none of the passageways he chose bore the proper stone markers, and as they neared the surface, they saw that the Strya had not been content with just re-arranging the stones—they'd kicked and cast several aside, removing all indication of the proper trail.

Ahead, echoing through the mountain, a great booming sound rose. It was slow and rhythmic, and the sound shivered through the walls.

"What is that?" Ferox asked.

No one answered, and they picked up their pace. The pounding grew louder as they moved closer to the surface until it reverberated off the stone walls and actually shook the floor. It was a deep, resonating BOOM, like the footsteps of a huge beast plodding along inside the mountain.

"There is one more turn," Orius said. He led them to the right fork of a last break in the tunnel and picked up speed as he streamed around the bend.

They were barely able to make out his words. The thundering noises had become so loud that each pounding crash shook the walls around them. Bits and pieces of stone broke loose and tumbled to the floor at their feet. They looked around for Orius, but he was gone. It was evident that from here they were on their own.

"Run!" Gobius cried.

They took off at full speed, dashing through the passage and trying to ignore the threat of the tunnel crashing in on them. Up ahead they saw the thin glow of the sun's light leaking in through the entrance to the cavern. As they drew nearer, Gobius caught sight of the source of the booming sounds, and he cried out.

"It's one of the Styra! He's trying to bring the columns down."

Standing just a short distance away from them, one of the hooved creatures held a hammer even larger than Og's battle axe. It had been slamming the hammer over and over again into the center of the columns, leaving the stone chipped and cracked. After glaring at them for just a moment, the beast pulled back and gave one final, mighty swing. Then he threw the hammer aside, screamed in rage, and quickly turned to flee. But before it could escape, Ferox drew an arrow and caught the Strya in the small of its back. The creature dropped to its knees, and as it turned to glance back at Ferox, he drew one more arrow and shot it right through the beast's throat to finish it off.

Just as the arrow found its mark, one of the pillars snapped in the middle and started to buckle. With a cry and an incredible burst of speed, Thaddeus sprang past Gobius and rushed at the pillar. As it bowed and threatened to snap, there was a huge grinding sound. The pressure of the weight from above threatened to crumble the pillar to dust and bury them all alive.

Thaddeus slammed into it with his shoulder. He dug his boots into the floor and pushed. At first it seemed to make no difference at all. Then, as he drove forward and arched his back, the pillar slowly righted itself. It didn't straighten all the way, but it held enough to keep the cavern ceiling from caving in.

"Run!" Thaddeus yelled. Rubble and dust poured down around him. A fissure opened over his head, running outward from where the pillar's support had momentarily given way.

Og came over to help, looking to throw his weight into the pillar as well. But it wasn't wide enough for both to stand against it, and tall as he was, he couldn't reach in over Thaddeus' head.

"Go!" Thaddeus cried. "I can hold it! Get everyone out! I'll follow."

Og hesitated, and Thaddeus glanced back at him, eyes wide and shoulders straining with exertion.

"Go!" he said again.

Og turned and ran, and the others followed. Only Gobius and Silex waited behind, hovering just inside the cavern's mouth.

"Now!" Silex screamed. "Thaddeus, get out of there!"

Thaddeus heard him. He gave a great shove as if he might right the stone once and for all and put it back in place. But it was no use. He turned and started to run, but the moment his support was removed, the pillar snapped like a twig. The fissure in the ceiling widened to a huge crack in a matter of moments, and large chunks of stone broke free, slamming into the floor of the tunnel. Thaddeus ran with speed unbecoming of a man his size. He dodged first one and then another of the stones, and for the span of those few seconds it looked as if he might escape. Then, as Silex and Gobius watched in horror, hands outstretched, a huge, triangular piece broke free and fell in the direction that Thaddeus was headed.

"Look out!" Gobius cried. "Thaddeus!"

The stone crashed down on him, and it was so heavy that it drove him into the ground. More rocks and rubble followed, burying Thaddeus and sealing the tunnel completely in a matter of seconds.

"Get away from the entrance!" Silex cried.

Gobius paused at first, but when he realized that Thaddeus was gone, all he could do was save himself from the oncoming avalanche. As he and Silex ran, the mountain seemed to deflate, almost like a waterskin being emptied too quickly. There was a muffled BOOM, and soon they were rolling forward from the impact.

Gobius pitched headlong over the far side of the road, rapidly tumbling downhill. Then, in a display of unbelievable strength, he managed to catch hold of the trunk of a scrubby tree and halt his slide. Before he'd even regained his balance, he was climbing back up, coughing and gasping for air as the dust from the crumbling mountain filled his lungs and clouded his vision.

He made it back to the road but could go no farther. The area directly in front of where the entrance had been was piled high with stones and debris. He could barely see his hand in front of his face.

"Silex!" he called. "Og, Ferox, where are you?"

There were coughs and muffled cries from all around him. The others slowly appeared, stumbling up as he had. Pugius helped Minstro along, and Sceptrus assisted Cantos. Silex realized that Ferox was missing, and just as he was about to run off in search of him, they heard him call from a short distance away.

"I'm with the horses," Ferox said. "The noise spooked them. They are where we left them, and they still have food and water. But they have to be calmed or we'll find ourselves walking down the mountain."

Gobius' thoughts cleared somewhat, but then the loss hit him hard, and he nearly doubled over. So many weeks, so many miles, through so many obstacles as a single unit… thirteen parts of one whole now cut to ten in the span of a few hours. He turned back to the mountain. The unicorn stepped up beside him, head lowered, as he stared at what had been the entrance to the Labyrinth of Secrets but was now just a huge dustblown tomb, sealed by a barrage of boulders.

"Thaddeus," Og said. "Where is he?"

Gobius and Silex then realized that they alone knew what had happened. They looked each other in the eye, knowing that one of them had to break the news to the others. After a brief pause, Gobius turned and began to speak.

"He's gone," Gobius said. "He sacrificed himself so that we could escape."

"No!" Cedrus said. "Not another one…"

"I'm afraid so," Silex replied.

They all began to lower their heads and reflect upon the

fact that Thaddeus had just given his life for them. Some wept; most stood still with somber looks on their faces. Finally, Gobius broke the silence.

"It is a huge loss for us," he said. "First Nomis and Alphaeus, and now Thaddeus. I know it's difficult to accept, but we have to move on."

"Why?" Cedrus asked. "Why did this have to happen?"

"Unfortunately," Gobius responded, "the trials and tribulations life presents us often require sacrifices, some greater than others. In this case, three men made the ultimate sacrifice, giving up their very lives for what they believed to be the greater good. Nomis and Alphaeus gave their lives to save Thaddeus, and he gave his to save each and every one of us. It's almost as if he felt obligated to return the favor. But rarely is anything monumental accomplished without sacrifice, and though our hearts may be overwhelmed with sorrow at the loss of our companions, we can only mourn their deaths, honor their memory, and move on. It is what they would have wanted. If we don't return the Medallion to Mavinor, then their sacrifices will have been in vain."

No one said a word. Gobius guided them toward the entrance of the Labyrinth, and there he led them in a short prayer. After another moment of silent reflection, they began to walk over to their horses one by one until only Gobius and Cedrus were left. Gobius placed his hand on the young man's shoulder, and soon they too went to join the others.

Despite being completely exhausted, none slept well that night. They couldn't stop thinking about the day's events and the toll it had taken on them—not just physically but also mentally, emotionally, and spiritually. As dawn broke, they heard the sounds of Ferox preparing breakfast. He had managed to catch a small hind during his morning hunt, and he was just finishing butchering the animal so they could roast it over the fire.

They dined in silence, still grieving the loss of their companions. The deaths of Nomis, Alphaeus, and Thaddeus had made their successful discovery of the Medallion bittersweet and thus impossible to celebrate in any manner. When they finished breakfast, they quickly packed their supplies, mounted, and with heavy hearts began riding down through the Northern Mountains. Gobius led them, Silex having tacitly deferred his authority to the man who bore the Medallion…the man who would one day be King of Mavinor.

Just as it had on their arrival, the return trip took several days, and eventually they reached Mortuus Valley. This time they were prepared for the journey through the wasteland, filling their waterskins to the brim and watching closely for any sign of danger. They recalled their battle with the Cyporsks and dreaded the thought of meeting one of those ghastly creatures yet again. But their passing was uneventful, and soon they found themselves staring up at the waterfall from which Gobius had rescued them. They made their way back up the steep slope, and some of them noted how much more difficult it was than their original trip down into the valley. This time they followed the river bank. It was Cantos who recalled that doing so would enable them to cross the road and arrive at their original route through the forest.

At one point Pugius looked across the river and saw what he believed to be the same spot where they had set camp after their dramatic exit from the rapids.

"Anyone care for another crossing?" he said, trying to lighten the mood and eliciting a chuckle from the others.

"Never," said Og. "I don't know that I can ever be near water again after that experience."

"Let's find a spot to set camp soon," Gobius said. "The horses need rest, given the arduous climb up the slope."

"Never mind the horses," Cedrus said. "I could use some rest myself."

"Really?" said Tonitrus. "Perhaps then it will be a good time to train."

"What are you talking about?" Cedrus asked.

"It will be a formidable test of your endurance," Tonitrus said.

"Has my endurance not been tested enough on this journey?" asked Cedrus.

"One can never be tested enough," Tonitrus answered.

Cedrus was less than thrilled at Tonitrus' words, but he knew that refusing the call to drill would make him appear weak in the eyes of his brother and maybe even the others. Therefore he accepted the challenge.

They found a place to camp, and as they unpacked their supplies, Ferox thought he heard something rustling in the trees. His senses, having been trained to perceive even the slightest stimuli during countless hunting excursions, were sharper than those of his companions He turned very suddenly, in a way that almost startled the others. They looked in the direction he was staring but saw nothing.

"What is it?" Sceptrus asked.

"I don't know," Ferox answered. "But I may well go and find out."

"You're not going alone," Silex said.

"Not the Strya again," Cidivus lamented.

"I'd like to think there are none left after what we did to them," said Og.

"One can only hope," Cantos said.

The unicorn also sensed it. It snorted and stamped its feet, which only gave rise to further anxiety among them. Silex and Ferox again volunteered to investigate it, whatever it was, and Gobius consented. But he was quick to tell them that if they did not return within the hour, he would lead the others into the woods to search for them. They assured him that it would not be necessary; they gathered their weapons and disappeared into the forest.

Tonitrus went off to the side and drew his sword. "Are you ready, brother?" he asked.

Cedrus sighed and rose to his feet. "I suppose," he said.

"Then let's go," Tonitrus said.

As Cedrus retrieved his weapon and went to join his brother, Tonitrus called for Og. He took the big man by surprise, and as Og walked over to them, he wondered what Tonitrus had in mind. As it turned out, Tonitrus had no intentions of drilling. Rather, he forced his brother into an impromptu sparring match, with Og officiating.

They walked a short distance down the path to a space that was a little more open. Tonitrus stood on one side of the path with his back to the trees, and Cedrus stood across from him. Og stepped between them, but just as he was about to give the signal to begin, Cedrus stepped back. This frustrated Tonitrus, who glared at his brother with a perplexed look.

"What are you doing?" he asked.

"I saw something off in the distance in that direction," Cedrus responded. He didn't know what it was, but he could have sworn that something darker than the surrounding shadows had flashed by. As he tried to follow it with his gaze, it seemingly disappeared as if it had never even been there.

"It's nothing," Og said. "Let's get started."

They were completely unaware of the danger around them. From the blackness of the trees the pale eyes of a lurid beast were watching, waiting for an opportune time to strike. The creature crept and crawled among the branches, stalking its prey, inching ever closer to the point from which it intended to pounce. It moved on all fours, and its fur was as dark as the depths of the Black Hollow. Its claws were sharp, its teeth sharper. In the moment that Og had given the signal to begin and the brothers had squared off, the beast let out a roar and struck.

There was no time for any of them to react. The huge panther flew through the air and landed on Tonitrus, who stared up in horror. Only a desperate swing of his sword saved him. Even though he missed his mark, the sharp tip of the blade forced the creature to back off of him. Og watched helplessly, his battle axe lying on the ground by his supplies back at the camp. The creature advanced on Tonitrus again, and as he lunged with his sword, it swiped at him with its paw, knocking the weapon from his hands and off into the bushes. Now defenseless against the beast, he retreated off the path and called to Og and Cedrus, urging them to save themselves by running back to camp.

But Cedrus neither listened nor hesitated. From the second he saw that Tonitrus was in trouble, he started making his way over to him, sword at the ready. There was no time to think, yet he was somehow able to remember the many hours of training under his brother, the countless lessons he learned, and the number of times he failed to live up to Tonitrus' lofty expectations. He recalled how his brother had saved him from the Cyporsks and from the Strya. Now the tables were turned. The chance for redemption had presented itself, and there was no room for error if he was to prevent Tonitrus from being torn apart by the savage beast.

Cedrus ran toward the panther and distracted it. As it turned, the big cat pounced, but Cedrus ducked and rolled out of the way. He seamlessly transitioned to his feet, just as his brother had taught him to do, and faced the creature once again. This time it flashed its razor-sharp teeth and roared, but Cedrus showed no fear. He boldly lunged forward and hacked at it with his sword, but it was too fast. The panther leaped to the side, watching the sword drive past. It almost seemed impressed with the speed of Cedrus' swipe, standing back and eyeing him cautiously. Now Cedrus sensed its vulnerability, and he lurched toward it again, staying low to the ground and raising his sword with an uppercut swing.

This time the thing ducked, and as it did, it sensed an opening. As Cedrus' sword shot past, the beast jumped, hoping to get its claws on Cedrus' chest and knock him to the ground. But the young warrior reacted with even greater speed, dropping and eluding the creature as it flew over him. He turned, and as he watched it land just behind him, he brought his sword back in a wide arc and slashed the beast on its hind leg. The panther let out a roar as it skid back, almost falling to the ground on its side.

Now it was angry. After glancing at the gash on its limb, it turned toward Cedrus and attacked. It was acting on pure emotion, sheer rage…and that worked against it. Refusing to stand back on his heels, Cedrus advanced as well. He anticipated what it was going to do, and this time he had a plan. But he had to time it just right.

Just as he expected it would, the panther once again leaped toward his chest. As he saw its front legs leave the ground, he brought his right arm across his chest, gripping his sword as tightly as possible. Then he shot toward the ground with his right shoulder and rolled. As he turned over, he cocked his arm back and swung his sword mightily through the air, putting everything he had into the strike. He saw the beast looming over him, and the tip of his blade made contact with its underbelly, slicing it from one side to the other.

At this point Cedrus was crouched, his left palm on the ground and his sword held outward toward the beast. The huge laceration across its body began dripping blood, and it was evident that it was badly injured. The creature roared again, and as it did, Silex and Ferox leaped from the shadows of the forest. Ferox immediately drew his bow and fired, but the wounded panther was still quick enough to evade the shot. The arrow buried itself in the tree trunk directly behind where the beast had stood. Seeing that it was outnumbered and overmatched, it retreated into the woods before anyone else could mount an attack against it.

"Well, it's about time," Cedrus quipped.

"We were tracking it," Ferox said. "But it was not easy. I don't know that I've ever hunted anything quite like that. If not for your clash with it, I doubt we ever could have caught up with it."

Tonitrus walked toward Cedrus, looked into his eyes, and placed a hand on his shoulder. "You saved me, brother," he said.

"I think it's safe to say that I owed you," Cedrus said. "Everything I know I learned from you. All those grueling hours we spent drilling, all the barking you did when I slipped up or let my guard down…it was all worth it. I can see that now. Thank you, Tonitrus."

"No, Cedrus," Tonitrus said, as he embraced him. "Thank you."

They walked down the path together toward the camp, watching the shadows carefully for another glimpse of the huge cat. When they informed the others about what had happened, Cantos told them about a creature called the Caurio. According to at least one ancient story, it prowled around like a roaring lion, waiting for someone to devour. Only it wasn't a lion. It was something more ferocious, more cunning, and more deadly.

As the moon rose high in the sky, they set a watch with three on guard at any time. They weren't taking any chances with the Caurio still lurking in the forest. But the night passed without incident, and Cedrus slept soundly knowing that he had won the respect of the more seasoned warriors. He felt as if he had finally arrived, and somehow he knew that from this point on his relationship with his brother was going to be far different than what it had been all these years.

Chapter Twenty-Three

The next morning they were back on the road early and less than a day's ride from Mizar; all of them were looking forward to finally arriving at a familiar place where they could rest easy. While Minstro knew he'd be happy to see his old friends again, he nervously anticipated how the elders were going to receive him. What type of punishment would they prescribe for his actions? How severe would it be? The closer they got to Mizar, the more he thought about it. Then he finally told himself not to worry because in his heart he knew that he would not be staying there. It was time to move on, and though he had not yet said anything to Pugius, he had every intention of riding back to Mavinor with the others.

As they approached the moat, the guards on the other side caught sight of them. At first they didn't recognize them. But as Pugius made his way to the front, with Minstro sitting up toward the neck of his horse, the Mizarian guards realized who it was. They ran back into the hills, and when they returned, there were several others with them. By the time they had maneuvered the swing bridge in place, enabling Minstro and the others to cross over, a wagon was already racing down from the hill above the moat. As it came to a stop, two guards stepped up and helped Orn down. The other elders followed close behind.

Minstro dismounted immediately after crossing the bridge. He stood still and silent as a statue, watching as Orn approached. He was prepared for anything. A tongue-lashing, a death sentence—who knew what Orn had in mind? But as he walked up to the young man, Orn's eyes began to tear, and while he was holding a cane, he used his free arm to embrace Minstro, and he started sobbing. Minstro was completely caught off guard and almost didn't know how to react.

"You're safe," Orn said. "It's a miracle."

"I'm sorry," Minstro said. "I know that I have disobeyed the elders through my actions. But I had to go. I just had to."

"I know," Orn said. "I suppose it's time for you to spread your wings now, isn't it? Well, you can only do what you must do. But tonight," he turned to the crowd that had gathered, "there will be a feast in Minstro's honor! Kill the fatted calf, and begin the preparations. For Minstro has returned safely to Mizar!"

The crowd cheered wildly. The other elders welcomed Minstro back as well, and soon they were all riding up the path back to the village. Gobius and the others returned to the building where they had stayed during their last visit, and they wasted no time in tending to the horses. Some of them rested before the feast that evening, and as the sun was about to set, Minstro came to escort them. But before leading them to the center of town, he asked Pugius to speak with him privately while the others were finishing up with their horses.

"What is it, my friend?" Pugius asked.

"I have made a decision, but it can be carried out only if you agree to it," Minstro said.

"What decision might that be?" asked Pugius.

"I want to come back to Mavinor with you," Minstro said. "I cannot stay here, Pugius. I'm no longer meant to be in Mizar."

Pugius paused for a moment, surprised by Minstro's statement. "Are you sure?" Pugius asked. "But your people are so happy to have you back. Look at the response you received upon crossing the bridge. You had barely stepped foot on Mizarian soil when they cheered your return. You're a hero to them now, Minstro."

"I know," he said. "But I am sure this is what is meant for me. Before you came to Mizar, I knew nothing of The Author. However, as we journeyed together, I felt His presence, more and more with each passing day. When you were all caught in the spider's web and I was alone, I bowed my head and prayed for help from Him. I had nowhere else to turn. After that, the unicorn led me to all of you, and so it was only by The Author's grace that you were freed from Lilith's clutches."

"And now you believe you are destined to return with us to Mavinor?" Pugius said.

"I do, Pugius," Minstro said. "But only if you'll agree to take me as your apprentice. I want to become as proficient a warrior as you, and I know that it will take time, but I am willing to do what needs to be done. However, it cannot happen without your consent."

Pugius wasted no time in responding. "I'd be honored," he said. "I've actually been searching for an apprentice for some time now. Hurling daggers is becoming more of a lost art among the warriors of Mavinor, and I won't be around forever. Someone else will one day have to carry the torch. Maybe that someone could be you."

Minstro smiled wider than he ever had in his entire life. He thanked Pugius profusely, and as the others came over to them, Minstro announced his intentions. They made their way to the feast, where Minstro knew he had yet another audience to address. He didn't know how they would take the news, but with the others aiming to leave Mizar early the next morning, he had no choice but to reveal his plans.

The celebration was loud and raucous, far exceeding the last one they had attended. There was music, dancing, and plenty of eating and drinking. They shared stories of their quest, and Pugius had the honor of telling the Mizarians the tale of how Minstro rescued them from Lilith. The hill people beamed with pride when they heard the story, and Minstro was surrounded throughout the night by throngs of Mizar's citizens congratulating him on his achievement. Before it was over, he received permission from Orn to address the crowd, deciding that it was the appropriate time for the announcement he wanted to make.

"My fellow Mizarians," he said, "I humbly thank you for welcoming me back with open arms. But before the night is over, I wanted you to know that I will not be staying in Mizar. I believe now more than ever that my destiny lies beyond these hills. I can't quite explain it, but there is something calling to me. This Author that these men speak of...I have come to believe that He exists. I felt His presence on our journey, and I sensed that He Himself was leading me...

guiding me in my actions. I believe He has a plan for me, a plan that requires me to leave my homeland for a place that He has prepared for me.

"Tomorrow I will accompany these men on their journey back to Mavinor, where Pugius has agreed to take me on as his apprentice. I promise you that I will return to visit, and I will always remember you, each and every one. Please remember me as well and know that I will always call Mizar my home, regardless of how far away I might be."

Though they were sad to hear that Minstro was leaving, the Mizarians applauded his speech and wished him well in his new endeavor. How could they not be happy for such a loyal son of Mizar, one who had done so much to make them proud? Even Minstro's companions during the quest were touched by his words, and none more than Sceptrus, who reflected on what Minstro said in the context of his own personal struggle to overcome his doubt.

As the night came to a close and Minstro was still saying his good-byes, Gobius led his men back to the building. They arranged themselves just as they had the last time they slept there, and immediately they noticed the spaces where Nomis, Alphaeus, and Thaddeus would have been. As they looked around the room at each other, Gobius led them in prayer, again recalling the sacrifice those three had made for each of them. It filled them with emotion, and as they lay on their beds of straw, they recalled with fondness the memories of their fallen comrades before finally drifting off to sleep.

Gobius woke up early as always, and he saw that Cedrus was not lying on his pallet. After stepping outside, he caught the young man standing a few yards away with his back to the building. He quietly walked over and placed a hand gently on his arm.

"Good morning," he said.

Cedrus was startled. He quickly turned and placed his hand behind his back. "Good morning," he said.

"Congratulations again on defeating the Caurio," Gobius said.

"I'm not sure you can say I defeated it," Cedrus responded. "After all, I didn't slay the beast."

"No," Gobius said, "but you wounded it and sent it dashing back into the forest. More important, though, you saved the life of your brother, and perhaps Og's life as well."

"Well…thank you," said Cedrus.

"Yet that's not what you're thinking about, is it?" Gobius asked.

Cedrus stared at Gobius in utter amazement. "How do you do that?" he asked.

Gobius laughed. He looked down at Cedrus' right arm, the one that Cedrus still held behind his back. As Gobius craned his neck, playfully attempting to see what Cedrus was holding in his hand, Cedrus smiled and showed him. It was Magdala's scarf.

"You are right, as always," Cedrus said.

"I sense that you are fearful of something. What is it?" Gobius asked.

Cedrus turned away from him again. "I had a dream," he said. "A while back on our journey, I dreamed that I lost Magdala…forever."

"I see," said Gobius.

"I can't tell you how hard it's been for me," Cedrus said. "If I didn't know any better, I would say that I am the only one in this group who has fallen madly in love with someone. Silex, Ferox, my brother, and pretty much all the others…they have given their lives to Mavinor's army. A man cannot have two spouses, and so they have chosen to devote themselves to the military. As for Cantos, his eyes have been buried in books for so long that I don't know if he's ever caught a glimpse of a beautiful woman."

Gobius laughed. "That may well be true," he said.

"What about you, Gobius?" Cedrus asked. "Have you ever been in love?"

"No," Gobius replied. "My days were always long, sailing out into the sea each morning and not returning to shore until we caught enough fish to earn our keep. After my parents became ill and I had to look after them, there was simply no time for anything but work and serving as their caregiver."

"I'm sorry you had such a hard life," Cedrus said.

"Not nearly as hard as so many others," said Gobius. "We must always remember that somewhere in this world there will always be someone fighting a more-pressing battle than we are." When he finished his statement, they heard the others up and moving about. As he prepared to go back, Gobius said one last thing to Cedrus.

"She'll be waiting for you."

Soon they were all joined by Minstro and had a hearty breakfast before setting out. Orn, the rest of the elders, and what seemed like all of Mizar accompanied them on their ride to the bridge on the south end. As two members of the Mizarian guard began operating the bridge to get it into place, the hill people said their final farewell, and Orn in particular was very emotional as he wished Minstro all the best in the next phase of his life. Gobius led them as they crossed

the moat, with Pugius bringing up the rear. When the expert
knife-thrower crossed, he turned his mount so that Minstro
could wave to his homeland one last time before they left
Mizar behind. The others waited until Pugius turned back
and rode over to join them as they advanced toward the great
tree and one step closer to Mavinor.

***

The moment that the tree came into sight, the group knew
that something was wrong. It stretched just as far into the
sky as ever, but instead of lush foliage, bare branches pointed
skyward, stark and barren. While their initial visit to the tree
had given the impression of girth and life, what they now
saw emphasized the tree's incredible height...and conveyed
its death.

Gobius drew the unicorn up gently, and the others halted
their mounts as well. They stared at the barren branches, eyes
wide and in total disbelief.

"What happened?" Silex asked softly. "By The Author,
what could have caused such...ruin?"

No one answered. The unicorn raised its head and joined
their collective gaze. Gobius felt the creature shake and shiver
beneath him. He recalled their first visit to the tree and how
it was also their first sighting of the unicorn. He remembered
how the unicorn grazed peacefully alongside the tree's monstrous roots. It could not be a coincidence. She sensed it too,
and soon her head dropped down as if in sadness.

The tree drew all their attention as they approached it.
The closer they got to the barren trunk, the more surreal it
became. They hadn't been gone long enough for something
so large and so vital to have just withered. Something was

very wrong, and the fact that they had no idea what it was made them anxious.

"Unbelievable," Cantos said. "How something that's been here since the beginning of time, since life first sprang forth, could die so suddenly is unfathomable."

"We may never figure it out," Og said. "We probably shouldn't even try. Besides, we've got much bigger things to worry about, like how we're going to get across the Black Hollow."

"I know," Silex said. "I've been thinking about that as well. In fact, I've been thinking about it since you all pulled me and Tonitrus up to safety and I stared back across the dark expanse at Cerastes."

"We're going to have to do what I originally suggested," Tonitrus said. "Ride down into the Black Hollow and up the other side. It's clear now that Cerastes was lying to us so we would cross the bridge. There is no 'beast' sleeping down there."

"Strange as it may seem," said Cantos, "I don't believe he was lying. As I said once before, there are ancient writings that mention a great evil residing in that hollow. I would warn against doing what Tonitrus suggests."

"Then what?" said Sceptrus. "What options do we have?"

"Cantos," said Pugius, "is it possible that another bridge exists? Perhaps farther down in either direction?"

"None that I know of," Cantos answered. "The Scrolls don't speak of any other way across."

"We could wander forever looking for one and never find it," Cedrus said.

They were silent a moment, and then Og turned and stared up at the great tree, stretching up into the clouds overhead.

"How far do you think we are from the Black Hollow?" he asked. "Half a mile?"

"Why?" Gobius asked, curious.

"I'm thinking," Og said, "that this tree is wider than any bridge I've ever seen at its base, and it continues that way for a very, very long distance. I don't even know how far, because the clouds are so low it disappears."

"What is your point?" Cidivus asked, impatient. "You want to climb the tree to the clouds?"

"No," Og said simply. "I want to knock it down. I think… if it fell in the right direction it might just cross that hollow. I think that if it did…it would be a bridge."

"But why would you knock it down?" Minstro asked. "It's the great tree…"

"Look at it, though," replied Og. "It's dead. There isn't a sign of life to be found anywhere in its boughs. At least if we can use it as a bridge, it will still serve a purpose."

"No!" Minstro said.

"I agree with Og," said Tonitrus. "Truth be told, the great tree is now little more than a very sad sight. Just look at the dead leaves piled all around it, the barren branches…it's more depressing than anything else."

"Exactly," said Og. "That's why I'm going to chop it down."

"It's impossible," Silex said. "Look at it, Og. It's as big around as a house. What would we use to cut it? How do you fell a tree that has roots reaching to the very core of the earth?"

Og hefted his axe and dismounted. He stepped away from the group and headed for the tree.

"Og, wait," Silex called.

Gobius put a hand on Silex's shoulder.

"Let him go," he said.

"Surely you don't think he can chop down that tree?" said Silex. "No one can do that. It would take *years* of work—maybe a *lifetime*."

"Let's watch him try," Ferox said. "At the very least it will be entertaining."

Og picked up speed as he crossed the clearing. By the time he reached the base of the huge tree, he was almost running. He whirled, gave a great roar, drew the axe back and drove it forward into the huge trunk. There was a loud, solid *thunk,* and a wedge of wood whirled off through the air and away. Og drew back for another swing.

Then there was a swirl of motion above and behind him, and suddenly Apteris, Volara, and Chaelim appeared. Apteris grabbed Og's axe and yanked it back and away, out of his hands. Og spun, arms spread, and he glared angrily at Apteris.

"Give me my axe!" he yelled. "You have taken it one time too many."

"And you, giant," Apteris said, "have been warned one time too many. You have been given ample opportunities to learn your lesson, yet again you raise your weapon against nature. Enough is enough."

The Legans turned their attention to the tree, astonished by the sight of it.

"What happened?" Apteris asked. "What have you done to it?"

"Nothing," Og said. "We found it this way. That is why I went to chop it down without giving it a second thought."

"Give him the axe," said an authoritative voice.

Orius stood, appearing as suddenly as his followers,

watching from the edge of the clearing. "To have struck this tree the last time they were here—that would have been a crime against nature. But this tree is no longer a living thing. It is already dead, and it is only a matter of time before it falls of its own volition…of entropy. He has done no harm."

"You are defending him?" Apteris cried. "How could you? I will not allow this brute to tear down the tree."

"And yet you must," said Chaelim. "Or have you forgotten who our leader is?'

Apteris met Chaelim's eyes but did not respond. He hovered in the air just above Og, out of the big man's reach, still holding the axe. Apteris looked as if he might defy both Orius and Chaelim, but then Volara flapped her wings and flew over to him.

"Chaelim is right," Volara said. "Keeping his axe will not bring the tree back from the dead. You may as well give it back, Apteris." She held out her right hand and gently placed her left hand on Apteris' shoulder. "Please hand it over."

Grudgingly, Apteris handed her the axe. Then he flew away and disappeared into the sky. Volara handed it back to Og, after which Orius asked her and Chaelim to follow Apteris to make sure he was alright.

Og gripped the hilt of his axe and hefted it. He looked at the small mark he'd made in the trunk of the great tree and stared at it sheepishly. He walked around it as if looking for another spot that might be less dense. It took a long time to make the full circumference, and he eventually came back to stand beside the chip he'd cut free.

"It is too big," he said. His shoulders slumped, and he tilted his head back to stare up the length of the dying tree into the clouds.

"Perhaps," Orius said, stepping closer, "perhaps not."

He leaned in, placed his hand on the rough bark and closed his eyes. The others, still across the clearing from them, stared curiously.

Orius stepped away and turned to Og.

"It is as I suspected," he said. "What has caused this rises from within. It has rotted from its heart outward."

"But how does that help?" Og asked.

"If you strike here," Orius said, gesturing at one of the spots he'd touched on the bark, "and keep at it, I believe you'll find the task is not as daunting as you believed. The tree is dead through and through, and it is very, very heavy. Something this magnificent rests on a precarious balance. It already leans slightly in the direction you wish it to fall...if you let the weight of the tree assist you—work *with* nature instead of against it—I believe you will succeed."

Orius stepped away from the tree again. He turned to the others.

"If I were you," he said, "I would move far away from the tree. When it falls, it is not going to be gentle. They will feel it even on the far side of the Black Hollow."

Gobius and the others moved, slowly at first. Then, as Og's axe rose and fell, biting into the wood and sending chips flying, they moved more quickly, hitting the edge of the clearing and continuing on into the trees, moving as far from the path as they could get while still remaining within sight.

After the first swing, Og felt his blood flowing. He saw the break in the tree's bark and sent the great axe singing into it, deepening and widening it with each crashing stroke. The muscles in his shoulders rippled, and he cried out, driving the blade deeper each time he swung, then whipping it back in a wide arc to wield it again. Wood chips flew, great chunks of bark shot through the air, and little by little, as the others could see even from across the clearing, the tree was starting to buckle.

Suddenly there was a loud grinding sound, a tearing and snapping that started from the edges of his cut and spread rapidly. Og drew back the axe to swing again but held the weapon high over his head, not bringing it down, staring, and listening.

"Run!" Orius cried, as he shot up into the air.

Og turned, saw that the Legan was gone, and did not wait to look for him. He slid the axe handle over his shoulder into its sheath and turned, lunging for the edges of the clearing and the wholly inadequate protection of the woods beyond.

The ground rose beneath his feet, rippling, pouring to the sides as roots were dragged free and broken, pulled from the earth like threads from a spinning wheel. The cracking sound rose to a roar that pounded at his ears. He ran, not looking back, desperately trying to get a safe distance from the falling tree.

"Here!" Gobius cried.

Og thought the words had come from his left, so he turned blindly, sliding down the slope created by a rising root, catching his boots in the soil and skidding, barely able to maintain his balance. He hit level ground and tumbled forward. Strong hands helped lift him to his feet, and as he turned, he saw that it was none other than Gobius. He led Og in the other direction, and they started running until finally, exhausted, they fell in a heap, turned, and watched what seemed almost like the end of the world.

It took a very long time for the tree to fall, but once it buckled to the point of no return, it descended rapidly toward the earth. They still couldn't see the top of it. The tree was so thick that, as it toppled, it also seemed to rise to the height of a house, if not higher. The sound of the trunk snapping deafened them, and as it finally landed on the ground in a thunderous crash, the earth quaked, driving them up into the air. They flailed their arms, blinded by dust and debris, and were thrown back even farther.

The ground settled with a shiver, and both Gobius and Og lay very still. The others, including the unicorn, had succeeded in outrunning the danger that had resulted from the falling tree. They immediately came over to assist their companions, who, though a bit sore and covered with dirt, were otherwise just fine. Gobius stood and helped Og to his feet.

Slowly they moved closer to what had been the clearing and stared. There was a huge, jagged shell that had been the tree's base, and its center was black and rotted, eaten away from the inside. The unicorn stepped forward. It trotted down the tree to the first large branch, glanced over its shoulder once, and then turned and made a short leap. It landed on the branch, scrambled up past another branch, and disappeared over the rim of the tree. Ferox turned to Gobius.

"I'm going up there," he said. "I'll see what it's like and whether we can pass."

Gobius nodded.

"I'm going with you," Og said. "If there is anything in the way, I should be able to clear it."

The two followed where the unicorn had led. The rough bark afforded plenty of hand holds, and once onto the great trunk they might as well have been walking on the forest floor. They disappeared from sight, and then, a little bit later, Ferox appeared again at the top.

"Lead the horses up slowly," he said. "Follow the track the

unicorn took. There is room if we are careful. Og is moving ahead and clearing a path. Once you are all up, we'll join him."

They gathered their things, and gradually they led the horses up the side of the huge, fallen tree. Once they reached the top, the animals calmed quickly. The way ahead was as wide as a road. They moved single file, slowly but steadily. There were a few huge branches that they had to make their way around, but the tree was dead and barren, and for the most part the way was clear.

They moved on into the afternoon, cutting straight across to the far side of the Black Hollow before sunset. The tree continued on even beyond the edge of the hollow, but Ferox was able to locate an easy way down in the crook between two great branches. They followed after him, gently leading the horses down one by one, until they stood safely on the other side of the Black Hollow, the great tree above and behind them.

Quietly they made camp, and after a quick meal they set a watch. Again, they had three on guard at any time. Gobius, Silex, and Ferox assumed the first shift, and the others dropped off to sleep under a canopy of dangling, leafless branches that wrapped around them like a great claw. They were so close to Mavinor that they could taste it, and each and every one of them dreamed of finally arriving home.

Chapter Twenty-Four

They got an early start the next morning, having had a quick and frugal breakfast before getting back on the road. As Gobius led them back into the Tenebrae, they were extremely vigilant. They had known that crossing back over the Black Hollow would be a major challenge, given the fact that the Colubri had destroyed the rope bridge. But reentering that dark forest was the part of the journey that concerned them the most. Would the Colubri try to attack them this time? What about the Surnia? Would there be other obstacles that didn't present themselves the first time around? They didn't know what to expect.

They formed up two abreast, with Gobius and Silex leading the way. Ferox and Og followed right behind, then Cantos and Sceptrus, Tonitrus and Pugius, and Cedrus and Cidivus bringing up the rear. As always, Minstro rode with Pugius. They had their weapons drawn at all times, and they moved as quickly as possible down the path that led through the Tenebrae. There were no signs of life anywhere. No talking serpents, no giant owls…nothing moved. But they remained alert the entire time, knowing that the Colubri or the Surnia or both could emerge from the blackness at any moment.

They made camp almost halfway in, dining on some hares Ferox had captured. The night passed quickly, and they were up and moving first thing in the morning. They almost couldn't believe how uneventful the passing had been, but soon they turned around a bend and caught sight of something off to the left. It was the cavern into which Cedrus, Cidivus, and Nomis had gone during their initial crossing of the Tenebrae. Once again they felt the aura of something ancient and powerful, impossible to put into words. They stopped and stared for a moment, but then Gobius spurned his mount and led them away. They all followed except for Cedrus and Cidivus, who stood still, staring into the dark, open portal. Tonitrus looked back and saw them lingering; he called out to them.

"Ride on," he said. "Don't even think of going back in there."

They both felt the pull of the cavern, and for a moment it looked as if they might not heed Tonitrus' words. But they got their wits about them, as if escaping from a fog, and followed after the others. Still, as Tonitrus turned away and their mounts pranced ahead those first few steps, each man pivoted and took one last, long look at the mysterious doorway.

As they progressed down the path, they all saw the catapults off to the right and fondly remembered the one that Cedrus had armed but had not been permitted to fire.

"We're almost there," Og said. "Just a little farther."

Before he finished his words, a piercing cry rained down

from above. They heard wings flapping, and all of them ducked and held out their weapons. Then, as they heard the rustling of leaves from a tree limb just above them, they looked up and saw that it was a raven.

"See you!" it squawked. "See you all!"

"Not again," cried Og.

Gobius laughed. "Remember," he said, "mocking is not sufficient provocation for an attack." The others chortled as they recalled the exact words that Orius had used to scold Og the last time they encountered the raven.

"I know," Og said with a sigh.

The raven looked down on each of them, turning its head in a slow semicircle. When its eyes met Gobius, it spread its wings but didn't take off. Rather, it paused for a brief moment and then, as if it were a perfectly natural gesture for a bird, it bowed ever so slightly. As its head rose once more, it retracted its wings very slowly and uttered a single word.

"King."

Then it was gone. In the blink of an eye it had taken off and had flown back into the forest, its jet-black feathers making it impossible to spot amidst the dark foliage. Gobius looked at the Medallion around his neck, and when he directed his gaze upward again, he saw that the others were staring at him, dumbstruck.

"Let us go," he said. "As Og pointed out, we're almost home."

As they exited the Tenebrae, the North Gate of Mavinor came into view. The emotions elicited by the sight overcame them. Suddenly the air was charged with energy; they all felt it, and the sensation of now being so close to home hit them heavily. Even the unicorn discerned what was transpiring, and that explained what happened next. It took off as if being launched from a catapult, and Gobius made no effort to slow it down. The other horses followed, and soon they were all headed for the North Gate at breakneck speed, almost as if they were racing to see who would get there first.

When they arrived, the guards were in disbelief. They didn't recognize them at first, perhaps due to the incongruous sight of the unicorn. But once they realized who it was, they opened the gate and let them in. One of the guards offered to escort them to the palace, and soon they were on their way to a much-anticipated reunion with their king.

As they arrived at the front steps of the palace, the royal guard came out to meet them. They called for their captain, Kenrick, and he immediately came to congratulate the ten on their return. He took them upstairs to the corridor leading to the king's quarters and asked them to remain there. Kenrick went to tell Talmik that they had come back to Mavinor, and within minutes the king's loyal aide was rushing down the hall to see them.

"You have returned!" exclaimed Talmik. "Thank The Author!"

"Unfortunately, not all of us have," said Silex. "I'm afraid that we lost three men as we made our way out of the Labyrinth."

"I'm so sorry to hear that," Talmik said. "I hope that they did not die in vain."

"They didn't," said Gobius. "They sacrificed themselves to save us so that we might be able to see the quest through to the end." He then exposed the Medallion for Talmik to see, and the young man stood in complete awe of the sight.

"If it's possible, then we'd like to see the king," Gobius said.

"Your return could not have been timelier," Talmik said. "I'm afraid I must inform you that the king is not well. Shortly after you left Mavinor all those months ago, he suddenly fell ill and has been bedridden ever since. His condition has grown progressively worse, and I fear that he may not have much time left."

"Can we see him?" Gobius asked.

"It might be a bit much for him if all of you came to his bedside," Talmik responded. "Wait here; I'll be right back."

Talmik reentered Onestus' bedroom and came out a minute later.

"The king wishes to see the one who bears the Medallion," Talmik said. "If you'll come with me, Gobius." The others stood back as Gobius followed Talmik down the hallway.

Talmik brought Gobius into the room. Immediately it was evident that the king was not the same man Gobius remembered. He looked tired and defeated…all the vitality that shone through on that day when he first convened the thirteen was long gone. Gobius recalled the salute Onestus gave them from the guard tower when they had left on the quest, and while it was only months before, it seemed more like ages. As the king opened his eyes and looked toward Gobius, he began to open his mouth as if to speak. Anticipating that his voice might be weak, Gobius came over to his bedside and leaned in.

"It is you," Onestus said. "I knew it would be you."

Gobius almost responded, but then he thought better of it. It was evident that Onestus was struggling, but he was determined to convey his words.

"You, Gobius…you were the one I saw in my vision. You were the one who I encountered on that misty shore…the one who held out the basket toward me…the basket that contained a golden medallion at the very bottom. Somehow I always knew that it would be you." As he began to cough, Talmik moved closer to the bed, but Onestus waved him away.

"Let me see it," Onestus said to Gobius.

As Gobius showed him the Medallion, Onestus' eyes opened wider than either Gobius or Talmik would have thought possible. You could see that he felt a great sense of relief, as if a huge burden had been lifted from his shoulders.

"Talmik," Onestus said, "Gobius is to be named my successor. This is the prophecy contained in The Scrolls, that he who bears the Medallion is the one who will be named king. Send word to Pachaias and the rest of the Tribunal. They are to schedule a coronation ceremony immediately."

"Yes, my lord," Talmik replied.

As Onestus looked at Gobius one last time, he crossed his hands over his chest. Gobius placed his hand over those of Onestus, a final gesture of compassion to a dying man.

"Please know," said Gobius, "that I will rule as you have ruled, my dear king. With mercy, with kindness, with justice…and in the name of The Author. Be assured that life in Mavinor will not change. With The Author's grace I will be half the ruler that you were and lead the people of this great kingdom toward their destiny."

Onestus said nothing more, but he smiled as Gobius finished his statement. It was as if he could die in peace now, knowing that he was leaving Mavinor in the hands of a man who was not only capable but also chosen.

Gobius left Onestus' chambers and walked back down the hall. The others were still waiting for him, and he informed them of the impending coronation ceremony.

"When will it take place?" Cedrus asked.

"I don't know yet," Gobius answered. "But when I do, you'll be the first to find out. For now, I think you ought to go and announce your return to your families and friends. I have something I need to do; we'll reconvene at some time tomorrow." Without waiting a moment longer, they left the palace and went their separate ways.

Silex and Ferox dashed down the lane leading to their home, past the well in the center and to the porch where the banners bearing their insignia fluttered in the wind. They dismounted quickly and ran up the stairs leading to the house, barely able to contain their excitement. As they entered, Ferox began to shout.

"Father! Father!" he exclaimed. "Guess who has come back!"

There was no reply. As they walked about the house, it looked almost as if no one had lived in it for several weeks. There was no food stored anywhere, and nothing was out of place.

"Let's check the back," Silex said.

They went into the yard, but no one was there. It was then that they noticed there were no goats in the pen, and that made them quite apprehensive. The brothers went around to the front, where they saw their neighbor, Peritus.

"Peritus," Silex asked, "Where is my father? Have you seen him?"

Peritus immediately looked down at the ground and sighed. There was an uncomfortable moment of silence, but he gathered himself and looked up at Silex and Ferox.

"I'm afraid that your father died a few weeks ago," Peritus said. "One day he seemed fine, strong as ever. The next day he was so ill that he could barely walk. Whatever it was that overcame him happened quickly. Within a couple of days he was gone."

Silex and Ferox stood in stunned silence. Neither wanted to believe Peritus' words, though inside they knew that he was telling them the truth. They didn't look at each other, and they said nothing. In the next moment they turned away, not wanting Peritus to see them overcome with grief.

"I'm sorry," Peritus said. "His body has been placed in a coffin, though it has not yet been consigned to the grave. The final rites, of course, were never bestowed, since it is your place and yours alone to carry them out. When you are ready, I will lead you to where he is lying." He then walked away and left the brothers alone to mourn their loss.

Rather than going home, Tonitrus went straight to the house of Ignatus. Just as he expected, Ignatus was in the middle of a training session with Tonitrus' cousins, Solitus and Arcala. Upon seeing Tonitrus approach, Solitus and Arcala ran out to greet him while Ignatus walked casually behind.

"You have returned!" shouted Solitus.

"We knew that you would," Arcala said. "We never doubted, even for one second. But where is Cedrus?"

"He's fine, and he has returned as well," said Tonitrus. "I think you might be able to guess where he might be."

Solitus and Arcala laughed. "Of course," they said simultaneously.

"Thank you for the many prayers you offered while we were away. It is only by The Author's grace that we were able to succeed in our task," said Tonitrus.

"Then you have recovered it?" Ignatus asked.

"Yes," Tonitrus responded. "The Medallion has returned to Mavinor, and with it a new king."

"Who?" Ignatus asked.

"Gobius," Tonitrus answered, "the fisherman turned soldier." Ignatus suddenly looked startled and confused.

"I know," Tonitrus said. "An unlikely candidate, given his humble background, but he is the one The Author has chosen. We are sure of it."

Ignatus remembered how Gobius had shown an aptitude for weapons and how he had sensed something mystical in the man.

"So be it," he said.

"We are ready, Tonitrus," said Solitus. "Ignatus will tell you. We have come so far, both of us."

"Is that right?" Tonitrus asked.

"It is," said Arcala. "I am ready to show the men of Mavinor's army just what a woman is capable of doing."

"Well, Ignatus," said Tonitrus, "they certainly aren't short on confidence, are they?" Both Tonitrus and Ignatus laughed.

"No, they're not," Ignatus said. "I don't know that I'd go quite so far as to say that they're ready to rush into battle just yet, but make no mistake about it, their progress has been steady, and their goal is now well within reach."

"Good to hear," said Tonitrus. "It is only a matter of time before they don the red and gold and make our family proud."

"We will," Solitus said.

"That you can be sure of, Tonitrus," said Arcala. "We will not disappoint you."

<hr />

Cedrus raced his horse toward the eastern end of Mavinor, riding through the streets and into the town square. As he did, he recalled his dream…how he had envisioned Magdala at the fountain and watched helplessly as she drifted farther and farther away from him. He scoured the market to see if she might be present, stopping for a moment to stare at the crystal clear, cascading waters of the fountain. Just for a moment he thought he saw her reflection staring back at him. But Magdala was nowhere to be found. He saw a vendor selling cloth, and as he rode past, he noticed that there was a piece of bright red material on one of the tables.

As he made his way down a narrow passage, one eerily similar to the path in his dream, he suddenly felt a sickening sensation in his stomach. The pain he had felt in his dream returned with a vengeance, as he recalled that instance when he lost Magdala, believing in his heart that she was gone forever. It made it difficult for him to turn the corner at the end of the pathway, and he stopped for a long moment before continuing. After gathering his courage, he made the turn and pointed his mount toward the direction of the house where Magdala resided with her parents.

As soon as he looked up, Cedrus was suddenly overcome. For there, right before his eyes, just off in the distance, was Magdala. She seemed to be making her way to the market with a basket in her hand, and she was walking straight toward him.

At first she did not see him. Magdala had been looking

down, fumbling in the basket as if searching for something. When she finally glanced up, her eyes met those of Cedrus, and she was clearly overcome with emotion. Magdala dropped the basket to the ground, froze for just a moment, and then ran to him. Cedrus dismounted, and by the time he had barely gotten his second foot on the ground, Magdala had already leaped into his arms. He held her tightly, as tight as he had ever held anyone or anything in his life. She began to cry, and he felt the tears touching his cheek as they rolled down hers. It seemed as if they were in each other's embrace forever before Cedrus finally pushed her back to arm's length and kissed her passionately on the lips. They embraced yet again; only then did they speak.

"This, I believe, is yours," Cedrus said, as he presented her with the scarf she had tied around his arm before he left Mavinor. As she took it from him, the tears continued to flow down her face.

"Thank The Author," Magdala said. "You have no idea how hard I prayed for your safe return. Each day that passed was another day when I wondered if I might ever see you again."

"It was the same for me," Cedrus said. "Despite all the dangers we faced on our quest, my greatest fear was that I might lose you."

"Never," replied Magdala. "You are the only one for me, Cedrus. There can be no other."

"And you are the only one for me," Cedrus said. "Know that I will always be at your side, Magdala, no matter what life brings us."

They kissed again, and those who walked by merely smiled as they watched the young lovers lock lips for prolonged periods of time.

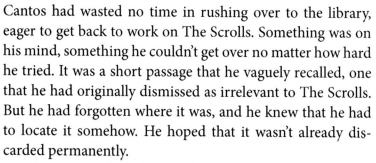

Cantos had wasted no time in rushing over to the library, eager to get back to work on The Scrolls. Something was on his mind, something he couldn't get over no matter how hard he tried. It was a short passage that he vaguely recalled, one that he had originally dismissed as irrelevant to The Scrolls. But he had forgotten where it was, and he knew that he had to locate it somehow. He hoped that it wasn't already discarded permanently.

Cantos searched frantically through the shelves containing countless books, poems, and other literature, the content of which had been categorized as unimportant. But he couldn't find what he was looking for. As he sat in a chair in front of a mountain of ancient scripts and scrolls, Cantos sensed the weight of someone's gaze on his back. When he turned, he saw that it was none other than the man who saved his life during the quest.

"Back to work already?" Sceptrus said.

"I've been eager to return to the library ever since I almost wound up as a meal for giant owls," Cantos replied. Sceptrus laughed.

"I just wanted to tell you something," Sceptrus said. "I want you to know that I have finally arrived at my destination. I have overcome my doubt, and the foundation for my faith has been set. I can no longer reason that man is alone, that no deity exists. Not after what we endured on our quest. How else could we have overcome the obstacles we faced? No man or group of men, no matter how strong or courageous, could have done it alone. I know it now; I see it clearly. How I wish I could have believed without seeing it all firsthand. But I suppose that is no longer important. All that matters is that

I have seen, and I now believe. You told me time and again during the quest that you owed your life to me, but my debt to you is much greater. For I owe you my soul, my friend. Thank you, Cantos, for leading me on this journey. I never could have made it without you."

Cantos was speechless. He rose from his chair, and as he did, Sceptrus moved closer and embraced him. "Good-bye," Sceptrus said. "I'll leave you to your work, but I would hope you'll take time out from it whenever I pass by the library to visit."

"For you," Cantos said, "always."

Sceptrus left, and Cantos turned back to sit in his chair. As he did, he noticed something toward the bottom of the pile of papers he now faced. There was a manuscript that stood out to him, because the bottom portion of the parchment had been charred, as if it had been barely saved from a fire. It jogged his memory, for it was the scroll he had been studying when the king's messenger originally summoned him for the quest. He immediately brushed aside the other scrolls, desperately reaching for the object of his search. When he recovered it he began to read, and it all started to come back to him.

The scroll spoke of a prophecy, a prophecy that foretold the coming of a great king. This king would first be recognized through a vivid dream, which the dreamer would then interpret as a vision. Though coming from a humble background, the future king would show wisdom beyond his years and great prowess in battle despite minimal training. He would succeed in a great quest, returning to Mavinor triumphant, and be named as heir to the throne. Once crowned, he would be a just ruler of and a loyal steward for the citizens of Mavinor. They would one day refer to him as the one who was chosen, the one and only son of The Author.

As Cantos finished reading the text, a chill ran down his spine. He couldn't help but think that the prophecy that he and his fellow scribes had once dismissed was actually a key component of The Scrolls. Something came over him, a force he could not comprehend, that led him to believe it. He put all the pieces of the puzzle together in his mind, analyzed them one by one, and came to realize that it was all true. Though he ultimately kept his speculation to himself, Cantos knew in his heart that not only was the prophecy true but that it was also on the verge of being fulfilled.

Og returned to his home and the pile of logs that lay just outside it. He rubbed his hands together as he anticipated chopping them up for firewood. Without wasting any time, he heaved one of the logs on to his broad shoulders and walked over to the flat stone where he intended to place it.

To say that Cidivus was relieved to arrive back at his estate would be an understatement. He was now at home in his lush gardens, grand courtyard, and spacious mansion. Cidivus was all too glad to exchange the cold, hard earth he had been sleeping on for the past several months for his featherbed, and the first thing he did upon entering his home was lie down in it.

Pugius showed Minstro his new living quarters and got him settled in as they prepared for a long apprenticeship. Minstro knew that he had made the right decision in leaving Mizar behind and sensed that he would fit in quite well in Mavinor. Pugius sent Minstro to retrieve a wooden plank and a drawing of an apple and then led him outside to one of the trees behind the house.

While the others were going about their business, Gobius took it upon himself to comfort the families of those who had been lost. Although Thaddeus had no relatives left, both Nomis and Alphaeus had mothers and fathers who were anxiously awaiting their sons' returns. He first went to the home of Alphaeus, whose parents, while obviously distraught at the news of their son's death, were nonetheless proud that he had followed in his father's footsteps and had given his life in service of his kingdom. Gobius assured them that their son did not die in vain, for the quest was successful and the Medallion had now returned to Mavinor. He said the same to Nomis' parents, who were more disconcerted than those of Alphaeus since they had both opposed their son's decision to join the army. But he told them that they should be proud of the sacrifices their son had made and that he had died doing what he always wanted to do, fulfilling his dream of becoming a soldier.

When he left the home of Nomis' parents, Gobius rode the unicorn to the North Gate. He indicated to the guards that he needed to exit Mavinor for a short moment. They looked puzzled but asked no questions as they opened the gate for him.

After riding a short distance, Gobius dismounted and began to stroke the unicorn. They had experienced an incredible journey together, one during which they had bonded more than any man and horse could ever hope to have bonded. But Gobius knew that he had to let it go. Surely a unicorn belonged in the wild, not in the city. As he peered upon the image of the unicorn on the Medallion, he began to speak to it. It seemed nonsensical, but he truly came to believe that it could understand him. Gobius thanked it for all it had done and said what he thought would be his final farewell to the most magnificent beast in The Author's creation. He cajoled it in the direction of the forests beyond, knowing full well that it could find its way home.

But it refused to go. No matter how hard he tried to coax it, the unicorn insisted on staying behind and even tried to nudge Gobius in the direction of the gate. Soon Gobius realized that his efforts were futile, for what it really wanted was to remain in Mavinor with him. He was incredibly humbled, and he walked the unicorn back to the North Gate. After the guards let them in, he remounted and rode back to the palace.

Chapter Twenty-Five

After receiving word from King Onestus that Gobius was to be crowned as his successor, Pachaias, Chair of the Tribunal, immediately went to see General Sicarius. Tarsus showed him in to where Sicarius was seated, and the general wasted no time in asking him the question that weighed so heavily on his mind.

"Is it true?" Sicarius asked.

"Yes," Pachaias answered. "They have returned, though not all of them. Three never made it back."

"And with the Medallion?"

"I'm afraid so," Pachaias said. "They have recovered the Medallion, or at least what is believed to be the Medallion. How can one possibly know for sure? I suppose that doesn't matter, though. What matters is that Onestus believes it, and he has decreed that the one who bears it is the one who will be our next king. Thus he has already named his successor."

"Who?" Sicarius asked.

"The fisherman," replied Pachaias. "Gobius."

Sicarius scoffed at this. "It cannot be," he said.

"I'm afraid it is," Pachaias said.

Sicarius sighed deeply, with a most incredulous look on his face.

"This cannot happen," Sicarius said. "To think that I will be reporting to a man who had just enlisted among my troops, who has no experience in battle, and no insignia. And a fisherman, no less. It's a travesty the likes of which no one has ever witnessed."

"Do you not think I feel the same?" said Pachaias. "With all my years of service on the Tribunal, rising up through the ranks to lead it, and all the knowledge I have accumulated throughout those years…the thought of me being under this man is unconscionable. To make matters worse, I have to preside at the coronation ceremony."

"I would suggest you not even go through with it," Sicarius said. "It is time for us to make a move. We will seize power through our might. My men are ready."

"No," Pachaias said. "It is not the right time yet. As ridiculous as it may be, the people of Mavinor really believe in what Onestus has preached. They accept the words of The Scrolls as truth, that the Medallion is a real sign, and that the one who bears it is to be our new king. They have fallen for this foolishness, and though we find ourselves on the brink of ruin, we cannot make a move to usurp the throne. If we do, then I'm afraid we'll have a revolt on our hands."

"Then what are we to do?" Sicarius asked.

"Gobius is fairly young, and I suspect that we may be able to mold him into the king we want him to be," said Pachaias. "Maybe we can control him, Sicarius, as if we ourselves were sitting on the throne."

"Maybe," Sicarius said, "but what if we can't?"

"If we can't," Pachaias said, "then the people will soon see what a joke his kingship is. If we are patient and give it time, then they will turn against him. I'm sure of it."

"I will go along with what you propose," Sicarius said, "but not for too long. I am losing my patience, and I refuse to bow to a man who is so clearly unworthy of leading our kingdom."

"Very well," said Pachaias. "Just inform me before you make any drastic moves. Also, know that you will need a new spy at the palace. Valdan is stepping down from the royal guard."

"I was not aware," said Sicarius. "We'll get to work on that immediately."

"Good," Pachaias said. "Let me go now. My fellow magistrates will become suspicious if I am gone for too long."

"Go right ahead," said Sicarius. As Tarsus showed Pachaias out, Sicarius looked through the window at the palace and shook his head. When Tarsus came back, Sicarius stared sternly into his eyes.

"Tarsus," Sicarius said, "we must prepare. When the opportunity arises, I want my men to be ready."

"They will be, General," Tarsus said.

"They had better be," said Sicarius.

Onestus died the day after Gobius had visited him. His death was followed by three days of mourning. A grand funeral ceremony was held in The Author's Temple, the likes of which happen only once in a lifetime. Every priest was present, every leader from Pachaias to his fellow magistrates to General Sicarius, every scribe and scholar, and anyone else who held any position of importance in the kingdom of Mavinor.

All of the ten were in attendance, including Mavinor's future king, along with Minstro. They stood together, shoulder to shoulder, up at the front. That is, except for Minstro, whose shoulder only came up to Pugius' waist as he stood alongside his mentor.

As Kenrick led the royal guard out of the Temple, they carried Onestus' body to the crypt that had been prepared. The people formed a corridor of sorts that allowed the guards to pass through, and each citizen bowed as the coffin went by. It was a solemn moment that no one who was present would ever forget.

Ultimately, the elaborate funeral procession ended at an ornate sarcophagus carved from limestone and laden with precious metals. It was here that Onestus' body was laid, adorned in a royal robe with a magnificent crown on his head and a jeweled scepter resting in his hands. After the priests bestowed the final blessing, the king's body was entombed. The ceremony was over, and the people dispersed. The long, glorious reign of King Onestus had officially come to an end.

Another day was set aside before Gobius' coronation was to take place, partly to give them time to prepare, and partly to allow the citizens one more day to grieve the loss of their king. This ceremony was also held in the Author's Temple, with Pachaias presiding. As it had been with Onestus' funeral, practically the entire kingdom was there, anxious to get a glimpse of their new king. After Gobius was crowned, he was asked by Pachaias to take his insignia. Gobius chose the fish, a sign of his past and a part of him that would always remain. To conclude the ceremony, Gobius was asked to give his first official speech as King of Mavinor.

"My fellow citizens," he said, "I thank you for welcoming

me and accepting me as your ruler. Words cannot describe how humbled I am by this honor, to be chosen by King Onestus, the greatest of monarchs, as his successor, and to be trusted to continue the great work he accomplished throughout his reign. If I am but half the ruler he was I shall be grateful, and only with The Author's grace can I achieve such a feat. I ask for your prayers, knowing that The Author hears us when we call Him and that He listens to our pleas. Know that I will do everything in my power to serve you, to see to it that you have what you need, and to bring our kingdom ever closer to The Author and the path He has chosen for us. May The Author guide me in the role He has given to me and lead me in the task of leading others."

In what could have been interpreted as a sign of things to come, Gobius did something unexpected. He called Cedrus up to stand next to him and presented him as Mavinor's next warrior to receive his insignia. All in the Temple applauded, none louder than Tonitrus, who beamed with pride as his younger brother accepted the honor. Though Magdala stood in the back of the temple, Cedrus managed to meet her eyes as she shed tears of joy for the man she loved so dearly. Later, Cedrus would choose the eagle as his insignia, since it had always been the animal he admired most. Gobius also decreed that a mausoleum would be erected to honor the memory of Thaddeus, Nomis, and Alphaeus, who gave their lives for the kingdom of Mavinor.

The next day, Kenrick came to Gobius and asked permission to step down from the royal guard. He as well as a few others had served King Onestus for many years and were ready to relinquish their roles. It wasn't that they were not fond of their new king. They would have stepped down much sooner, but they felt obligated to remain and serve Onestus as his health grew progressively worse. Now that he was gone, they were ready to move on to the next phase of their lives.

Gobius granted their requests, asking only that they assist their replacements in making the transition to the royal guard. Kenrick accepted, after which Gobius assembled several messengers in the throne room. He dispatched them to summon those men whom he would ask to serve as his new royal guards: Silex, Ferox, Tonitrus, Cedrus, Og, Pugius, Sceptrus, and yes, even Cidivus. Gobius saw the progress that Cidivus had made, especially toward the end of the quest. Though he knew in his heart that it was the Medallion that had saved his life, he never forgot how Cidivus came to his aid, slaying the Strya that had tried to kill him. He wanted Cidivus to at least have the opportunity to accept or refuse his invitation. Gobius was sure that the others would be dubious of his selection, but he extended the offer nonetheless.

One by one they arrived at the palace to accept their new roles. Og was first, followed by Pugius (who brought Minstro along with him), then Sceptrus. As expected, Tonitrus and Cedrus arrived together to thank the king and confirm their commitment to the royal guard.

Then came Cidivus, who was as shocked as the others were that he had even been summoned; he had briefly considered rejecting the offer. Despite the fact that he came to respect Gobius and to finally cooperate with the others as they entered the Labyrinth, he remained somewhat bitter. In his heart he still resented Gobius' kingship, believing himself to be far more deserving of the throne. But he knew that this might be his only opportunity for advancement, at least for the foreseeable future. Thus he grudgingly accepted, using his illusive exterior to conceal his true feelings.

The messenger Nuntius had been sent to summon Silex and Ferox. He had been to their house before, and in fact it was he whom Onestus had originally delegated to summon the brothers for the quest. But when he returned to the palace, he notified King Gobius that they would be unable to respond until the following day. They were preparing the final burial rites for their father and planned to conduct a private ceremony at his grave later that afternoon.

Deep in the heart of the Tenebrae, Cerastes led the Colubri into a large clearing. As they looked overhead, they noticed that the Surnia were also present, perched on branches all around them. This made Cerastes leery, and when he suddenly heard large wings flapping, descending on him from behind, he quickly turned around. In the blink of an eye he shot upward, flared out his hood, and flashed his razor sharp teeth.

"A bit uneasy, are we?" Orius said.

Cerastes hissed in irritation, though he was relieved to see that it wasn't one of the great owls swooping down on him.

"Where are the others?" Cerastes asked. "Apteris, Chaelim, Volara?"

"Not here," replied Orius. "No need to be concerned. I am their eyes and their ears when it comes to entering this world and defending that which we have been called to defend. Thus we can be assured that they will not come."

"Why did you instruct us not to attack the men from Mavinor as they passed back through the Tenebrae?" Cerastes asked.

"I have my reasons," Orius answered.

"And what happened to the Great Tree?" Cerastes said. "How is it that the place from which life sprung is now a mere bridge over the Black Hollow?"

"Let's just say that its demise was not an accident, shall we? You might call it 'collateral damage,'" Orius replied. The response caught Cerastes by surprise, but it also elicited an evil laugh of sorts from the horned serpent.

"What is it you want, and what are they doing here?" asked Cerastes as he looked up toward the Surnia. His forked tongue came into view as he let out a low hiss.

"All of you," Orius said, "will be commissioned. I have tasks for you to complete."

"Commissioned for what?" Cerastes said. "What kind of tasks?"

"I'm afraid I cannot reveal all the details yet," Orius answered. "But I need to know that I can rely on your cooperation when it is needed. You will comply with my request, won't you?"

Cerastes looked up toward the Surnia as if waiting to see how they might respond. He was hesitant to concede to Orius, but at the same time he knew it would be a grave mistake to cross the most powerful among the Legans.

"The Surnia have already agreed," Orius said, sensing what Cerastes was doing. "Now I need only for you to do the same."

Cerastes let out another timid hiss but reluctantly assured

Orius that the Colubri would do whatever it was he needed them to do.

"Good," Orius said, smiling broadly. He turned his back on Cerastes and began walking slowly across the clearing. As he did, he addressed both the Colubri and the Surnia.

"All of you," he said, "will play a major role in the plan. It is not something to be taken lightly, and it may well be dangerous. But in the end you will be handsomely rewarded. You are wise to accept my offer, and in time you will be quite pleased that you did, not to mention eternally grateful to me!" As he turned to Cerastes, his bright, blue sapphire eyes turned jet-black.

———

Silex and Ferox walked toward their father's tomb, gifts in hand, somber as anyone could possibly be. As they looked upon where he lay, they set down the gifts that included one of Silex's swords, an arrow from Ferox's quiver, some gold, and a small teapot. As far back as either one could remember, their father was always drinking tea, often several times a day. In that solemn moment the memories of him boiling the water and calling them to the table for tea buoyed their spirits ever so slightly.

After the gifts had been presented, Silex and Ferox stepped back and stared down at them. They said nothing to each other. In their minds they were having flashbacks of their greatest moments with father, recalling with fondness his blunt manner and the fierce fire that burned within his heart. Though Namon might have appeared gruff or grouchy to some, deep down inside he possessed a tender love for his boys, and both of them knew it. After a few minutes Ferox gently placed his hand on his brother's arm, indicating that it was time. Being the first-born, the onus was on Silex to deliver the lamentation. As he knelt down on the ground, he took a deep breath, and Ferox knelt beside him.

"Having traveled across many lands, Father, we arrive here at your grave so that we might present you with the final gifts in honor of the dead and speak in vain to your silent tomb. Since ill fortune has deprived us of you in the flesh, O poor Father, so cruelly torn from us, now, at least for this one brief moment, hear our laments. Accept our gifts through this solemn ceremony that in the time-honored way of our ancestors was handed down in mournful service to these final rites. Accept them, Father, sodden with the tears of your sons, and for all eternity, hail and farewell."

When Silex finished the lamentation, both he and Ferox wept. They remained kneeling, and each man placed a hand on the other's inner shoulder in a gesture of consolation. They were in that position for what seemed like hours, sobbing and unable to pry themselves away from Namon's grave.

Then each man felt another hand, a hand that came down on their outer shoulders so firmly yet gently that the touch put them incredibly at ease. It soothed them, quieted their fears, and alleviated their sobbing. When they looked up to see who it was, they saw the face of King Gobius, an unequivocal countenance of compassion. Silex and Ferox nodded to him in deference before turning their attention back to their father's grave.

Finally, Ferox rose. He looked Gobius in the eye and then down at Silex. Gobius nodded to Ferox, who then walked away. As Gobius watched him leave, he placed both hands on Silex, who was still kneeling at the foot of the grave.

"I see you have arrived, my friend," King Gobius said.

"You have succeeded in transitioning from the realm of thoughts to that of emotions. I know that it has not been an easy journey for you. Perhaps it has been even more difficult than our journey to the Northern Mountains. But you made it and are to be commended for it."

"I cannot remember the last time I shed tears," Silex said.

"I know," replied Gobius. "But after today you will."

"I didn't even get to say good-bye, my king. I never stopped thinking about him during the quest, and I longed to return home so that he could take pride in his sons' success. I wanted him to feel that joy, the joy of triumph."

"But you have said your good-bye," said Gobius. "I know that you are unable to hear him, but trust me when I say that he hears you. The joy he would have experienced at your return is nothing compared to the joy he feels now. Take comfort in that, Silex, and know that he will always be with you."

Silex rose from his knees, took one last look at his father's grave, and walked away with King Gobius. As they exited the burial grounds, Silex was surprised to see that Ferox and all of their companions were waiting for him. Tonitrus and Cedrus were there, as were the rest of the king's new royal guards: Og, Sceptrus, Pugius, and Cidivus. Minstro was present, and Cantos, upon hearing the news of the ceremony for Namon, came as well. Each of them embraced Silex in turn and expressed their condolences.

When they had finished, King Gobius made the formal request that Silex and Ferox join the others in his royal guard. Moreover, he told them that his captain was retiring and asked if Silex was willing to assume that role. Without hesitation the brothers expressed their willingness to serve their new king. And with that, they all made arrangements to meet at the palace the very next day to begin the process of ushering in a new reign and writing the next chapter in the storied history of the kingdom of Mavinor.

About the Author

Dr. John DeFilippis was born on March 9, 1970 in Bayonne, New Jersey. He grew up in the Greenville section of Jersey City, graduating from Our Lady of Mercy Grammar School in 1984. In 1988 he graduated with high honors from Saint Peter's Prep and went on to study at Rutgers College in New Brunswick, New Jersey. After earning his Bachelor of Science degree, Dr. DeFilippis attended the School of Theology at Seton Hall University for three years, from 1993 to 1996. During this time he earned his master's degree in theology and discerned a call to the Catholic priesthood. After ultimately deciding that he did not have a religious vocation, Dr. DeFilippis transitioned into the field of education. He taught for four years at both the elementary and secondary levels, and earned a second master's degree in educational administration. In 2000 Dr. DeFilippis made yet another transition, this time accepting an offer to become an academic administrator at Saint Peter's College in Jersey City. He would spend the next seven years there, and in 2007 he completed his Ph.D. in educational leadership at Seton Hall University. After finishing his doctoral degree, he accepted an offer to become a director in the Division of Academic Affairs at New Jersey City University.

But through all the years of earning graduate degrees, teaching, and working in educational administration, Dr. DeFilippis never lost sight of his childhood dream. That dream was to become a published author. He loved writing, and he also loved fantasy stories as a child, especially those that contained courageous warriors, arch-villains, and fierce monsters. Inspired by epic stories such as *The Hobbit*, *The Lord of the Rings*, and *The Chronicles of Narnia*, Dr. DeFilippis began to use his free time to formulate ideas for his own series of fantasy novels. Over the course of several years, he developed detailed outlines and finally reached the point where he was ready to start writing. But balancing a full-time administrative position with part-time teaching and doctoral studies made it all but impossible to find the time. That all changed in July of 2010, when Dr. DeFilippis lost his job during the economic recession. Determined to turn a negative into a positive, he used his abundance of free time during his unemployment to focus on his novel. By April of 2011, the first draft of the book was complete. After having it edited for content, Dr. DeFilippis began marketing his novel to literary agents. But soon he discovered how cold, callous, and cut-throat the literary business could be. After enduring over 100 rejections, he refused to give up and started turning his attention toward smaller publishers. Finally David Niall Wilson of Crossroads Press decided to take a chance on *The Quest of the Thirteen*, and in 2012 the dream was finally fulfilled.

Today, Dr. DeFilippis resides in Nutley, New Jersey and works full-time as a school business administrator in the field of public education. He is a devout conservative Catholic, and an avid supporter of religious freedom in an age of growing secularism. In his spare time, Dr. DeFilippis enjoys working out at the gym, watching sports (especially his beloved New York Yankees, New York Giants, and Notre Dame Fighting Irish), fantasy football, taking walks in the park, going to the beach, playing blackjack, annual trips to Las Vegas, and of course, writing. Most of his free time these days is spent planning the sequels for *The Quest of the Thirteen*, the first of which will find Onestus' successor striving to make peace with Mavinor's enemies and bring the citizens of Mavinor closer to The Author and His truth. But as the king struggles to accomplish his goals, the perfect storm begins to brew. For there is a prophecy of a great evil that will be unleashed on the world if certain circumstances occur, an evil that will lead to the entire world being enveloped in the Age of Darkness...

Find the author on Facebook
www.facebook.com/pages/John-DeFilippis/249591448460151

CPSIA information can be obtained at www.ICGtesting.com
Printed in the USA
BVOW03s1317201213

339245BV00005B/10/P